Eight Dogs Flying

Samantha and Dr. Augustin enter the high-stakes, low-life world of greyhound racing—to chase down a clever killer . . .

Copy Cat Crimes

A basket of wet, undernourished kittens turns up at the back door of Dr. Augustin's clinic—on the very same morning that one of his clients turns up dead in a nearby canal . . .

Beware Sleeping Dogs

A series of unexplained illnesses in Dr. Augustin's canine patients has Samantha puzzled. But her discovery of a body in the woods is even more disturbing—and leaves her with plenty of questions to sort out . . .

Praise for the Samantha Holt series by Karen Ann Wilson:

"An interesting setting and entertaining characters that will pique jaded mystery readers' attention."—*Gothic Journal*

MORE MYSTERIES FROM THE BERKLEY PUBLISHING GROUP . . .

CAT CALIBAN MYSTERIES: She was married for thirty-eight years. Raised three kids. Compared to that, tracking down killers is easy...

by D. B. Borton

ONE FOR THE MONEY

THREE IS A CROWD

FIVE ALARM FIRE

TWO POINTS FOR MURDER

FOUR ELEMENTS OF MURDER

SIX FEET UNDER

ELENA JARVIS MYSTERIES: There are some pretty bizarre crimes deep in the heart of Texas—and a pretty gutsy police detective who rounds up the unusual suspects . . .

by Nancy Herndon

ACID BATH

LETHAL STATUES

WIDOWS' WATCH

HUNTING GAME

FREDDIE O'NEAL, P.I., MYSTERIES: You can bet that this appealing Reno private investigator will get her man . . ."A winner."—Linda Grant

by Catherine Dain

LAY IT ON THE LINE

WALK A CROOKED MILE

BET AGAINST THE HOUSE

DEAD MAN'S HAND

SING A SONG OF DEATH

LAMENT FOR A DEAD COWBOY

THE LUCK OF THE DRAW

BENNI HARPER MYSTERIES: Meet Benni Harper—a quilter and folk-art expert with an eye for murderous designs...

by Earlene Fowler

FOOL'S PUZZLE

KANSAS TROUBLES

IRISH CHAIN

GOOSE IN THE POND

HANNAH BARLOW MYSTERIES: For ex-cop and law student Hannah Barlow, justice isn't just a word in a textbook. Sometimes, it's a matter of life and death . . .

by Carroll Lachnit

MURDER IN BRIEF

A BLESSED DEATH

SAMANTA HOLT MYSTERIES: Dogs, cats, and crooks are all part of a day's work for this veterinary technician . . ."Delightful!"—Melissa Cleary

by Karen Ann Wilson

EIGHT DOGS FLYING

CIRCLE OF WOLVES

COPY CAT CRIMES

BEWARE SLEEPING DOGS

CIRCLE OF WOLVES

Karen Ann Wilson

BERKLEY PRIME CRIME, NEW YORK

> If you purchased this book without a cover, you should be aware that this book is stolen property. It was reported as "unsold and destroyed" to the publisher, and neither the author nor the publisher has received any payment for this "stripped book."

CIRCLE OF WOLVES

A Berkley Prime Crime Book / published by arrangement with the author

PRINTING HISTORY
Berkley Prime Crime edition / May 1997

All right reserved.
Copyright 1997 by Karen Ann Wilson.
This book may not be reproduced in whole or in part,
by mimeograph or any other means, without permission.
For information address: The Berkley Publishing Group,
200 Madison Avenue, New York, NY 10016

The Putnam Berkley World Wide Web site address is
http://www.berkley.com

ISBN: 0-425-15780-6

Berkley Prime Crime Books are published
by The Berkley Publishing Group,
200 Madison Avenue, New York, NY 10016.
The name BERKLEY PRIME CRIME and the BERKLEY PRIME CRIME
design are trademarks belonging to Berkley Publishing Corporation.

PRINTED IN THE UNITED STATES OF AMERICA

10   9   8   7   6   5   4   3   2   1

For my parents, Donald F. and Pauline H. Wilson

ACKNOWLEDGMENTS

•

I wish to acknowledge the technical assistance of the following people: Ronald R. Bell, Chief Toxicologist, Pinellas County Medical Examiner's Office, Largo; Opal Schallmo, Urban Horticulturist, Pinellas County Cooperative Extension Service, Largo; John Beckner, The Marie Selby Botanical Gardens, Sarasota; my father, Donald F. Wilson, Bradenton; Alvin Dale, DVM, Lake Seminole Animal Hospital, Seminole; Catherine Koogle, Avian and Animal Hospital of Bardmoor, Largo; Roy Finley, MD, St. Petersburg. Any errors are my own.

I also would like to acknowledge fellow tech and friend, Katie DeCosse, CVT, Minneapolis; my agent, Robin Rue; and my editor, Ginjer Buchanan, for their support. As always, I want to thank my husband, Robert A. Knight, for being there.

PROLOGUE

•

Looks can be deceiving.

"Take the harmless viceroy butterfly," offered my boss, Dr. Louis Augustin, one morning during surgery. That man is a wealth of information, useful and otherwise.

"Makes himself look like the monarch, so that birds who've experienced the monarch's nasty taste won't eat him. And then there's that orchid—*Ophrys* something—that looks just like a female bee, hairs and all. The male bee tries to mate with it and transfers pollen from one flower to another. Ain't nature wonderful?"

As if the butterfly and the orchid planned it that way all along. But Dr. Augustin is right. Deception is as old as life itself. When I was a little girl, my mother continually warned me about strangers offering me candy. What mother hasn't? Candy, toys, cigarettes. Drugs. Children are such easy marks for that sort of thing. Distrust comes with age and experience. Or it should.

Of course, some people never learn. When I found myself waiting at the altar for a creep whose good looks and killer smile (not to mention his Ferrari) had me totally bamboozled, I said, "Never again!" Now I live in Brightwater Beach, Florida, and work for a man who could sell swampland to a Seminole Indian. And she'd thank him for it.

1

2   Karen Ann Wilson

It's a good thing Dr. Augustin is more interested in catching crooked politicians and money-grubbing developers than in selling swampland. So, when he's not giving rabies injections or delivering puppies, he's out helping the cops nab the bad guys. You know what they say about idle hands and mischief. For some strange reason, though, the police tolerate him. To make matters worse, I let him talk me into participating. It's the swampland thing.

Or maybe it's the stethoscope. People trust doctors. I never really knew how much until I came to Florida, the Medicare capital of the world. Here, the state's elderly spend more time at the doctor's office or in the hospital than most children spend in front of the TV. It's a fact of life that as our internal organs begin to fail us, we put our trust in the medical establishment in the hope that they can make us well again. Or lessen our suffering. We trust them, at the very least, to do no harm.

So, when several elderly residents of a pricey retirement center in Brightwater Beach suddenly became psychotic and were committed to the center's psychiatric facility, no one questioned it. Not even Dr. Augustin. It wasn't until a series of accidents befell some of the residents' pets that Dr. Augustin decided to get involved. And when he sent me looking for answers, I found myself, like Aesop's lamb, following a wolf in sheep's clothing. That time, however, I knew that it was going to take more than Dr. Augustin's physical prowess and slick talk to save me.

Some people just never learn.

CHAPTER 1

●

Sunday, November 7

I knew taking Lucky instead of one of Michael's cats was a bad idea. But it also was Dr. Augustin's idea which, of course, made arguing pointless. He wanted the puppy socialized and decided, without consulting me, that my weekly pet therapy visits to the Sunset View Towers nursing floor would be the perfect opportunity.

"Michael *did* suggest I sign up for this program, after all," I countered testily the previous day at the mention of Lucky's name. "Not you."

Dr. Augustin hung his stethoscope around his neck and pried open Mitzi's mouth. The aged little poodle had chronic congestive heart failure, and every breath sounded like her last. Somehow, though, she continued to struggle on.

"How quickly we forget," he said. He idly wiggled one of the dog's two remaining molars. "If you'll recall, back in July I suggested you do a little volunteer work." He sighed dramatically. "Of course, you never listen to me."

He avoided making eye contact, which wasn't like him. His eyes, dark and inscrutable, are his most disarming feature. Well, one of them, anyway.

"You had an ulterior motive for wanting me in that hospital, and you know it. It had nothing whatever to do with community service."

3

Karen Ann Wilson

My courage surprised me. If Dr. Augustin had been looking directly at me, I wouldn't have had the nerve. He wasn't. Just to be safe, I stepped around a rack of cages, as if their stainless steel walls were actually made of kryptonite.

Dr. Augustin transferred the stethoscope to its peg by the door, then went over to the sink and began washing his hands. I picked up the poodle and carried her into Isolation. Behind me, I heard him smack the soap dispenser a couple of times.

"I thought I told Frank yesterday to fill this damn thing. If he plans to continue working here, he'd better get his act together. And I don't mean that band of his, either."

He wasn't about to fire Frank, and we both knew it. But he'd been in a foul mood for almost a week, and it wouldn't have surprised me if Frank up and quit on him. And that would mean Tracey Nevins, the clinic's lab technician, and I would have to clean cages and give baths, in addition to our own jobs.

If he doesn't watch it, I thought, he'll need more than a new kennel manager. I closed the door to the poodle's cage, turned on the oxygen, and went back into the treatment room.

Dr. Augustin pulled a couple of paper towels off the roll over the sink and spun around. This time he looked at me and smiled. It wasn't the warmest smile in the world. In fact, I'd seen patients smile like that just before they chomped on your finger.

"If that pet therapy program appeals to you more than helping out at St. Luke's, so be it. But puppies are far better at cheering up sick people than terrified cats with all of their claws intact. Safer, too. Besides, as I've already mentioned, Lucky needs the exposure. It will do her good."

He leaned against the exam table and let his eyes bore

CIRCLE OF WOLVES

into my brain. The overhead lights made his thick, shoulder-length hair shimmer.

I sprayed the table with disinfectant. "She isn't old enough," I said, hopefully. "She hasn't had all of her shots, yet. They probably won't let me take her." God, I prayed, please help me out here.

Only a few weeks earlier, Lucky had been part of a pack of feral dogs living off garbage and handouts in an upscale development northeast of the clinic. When Animal Control brought the puppy and an adult pack member to Dr. Augustin, they were on death's door. The adult didn't make it, unfortunately. I never dreamed we would end up keeping the puppy. A lot of clinics, us included, have feline mascots—blood donor cats who wander harmlessly around the place, entertaining clients and staff alike. But dogs tend to be less reliable, especially around other dogs, often turning waiting rooms into war zones. And to top it all off, Lucky wasn't entirely housebroken yet. She was undeniably cute, but in need of some serious obedience training. Why Dr. Augustin latched onto her instead of returning her to Animal Control once she was healthy was beyond me. As far as I knew, he didn't have any pets of his own and didn't want any.

"I'll handle the pet therapy people," he said. "You just plan on picking Lucky up tomorrow afternoon." It wasn't a suggestion. "I'll tell Frank to give her a bath."

So now I sat at the red light and listened as the sounds of chewing and gurgling directly behind me conjured up images of torn upholstery and stained carpeting. I was afraid to turn around. In the rearview mirror my back window looked like a shower stall door, thanks to Lucky's tongue. I certainly couldn't see out of it. My car wasn't new by any means, but it wasn't old, either. More importantly, it wasn't paid for.

The light changed. I felt a sudden urge to jackrabbit into

Karen Ann Wilson

the intersection. It would serve the dog right. Then I felt a twinge of guilt. As it turned out, my conscience probably saved Lucky's life as well as my own. As I crept forward, I just missed being plowed into by a dark blue pick-up truck. The driver never saw me. He was bent over the wheel, retching. His face glistened with sweat.

Belatedly, I hit the brakes, heard Lucky slide off the backseat (accompanied by a few more tearing sounds), and watched in awe as the pick-up careened around the corner on two wheels. I could see the words SUNSET VIEW TOWERS— MAINTENANCE DIVISION printed on the door in fancy white letters. A bunch of lawn equipment, including a big weed trimmer and a bright red gas can, suddenly bounced out of the truck bed and smashed onto the pavement, swiping my front bumper in the process. The weed trimmer did a few cartwheels, then broke into several pieces that rolled off in various directions. The gas can, thankfully, remained intact. It landed upright on the sidewalk.

My car was half in, half out of the intersection. The light was red again. A minivan containing two adults and a half dozen Little Leaguers darted around my front end. The driver, a woman, honked at me—a long plaintive screech— then raised her fist. She probably would have given me the finger, if it hadn't been for the children. I smiled as one of her tires ran over part of the weed trimmer. It squirted up under the minivan and clanked noisily.

When the light changed, I proceeded cautiously down the road. Lucky was at the back window again, none the worse for wear, apparently, although I thought I detected an odor of urine coming from somewhere. If I could have gotten the dog into a carrier back at the clinic, I would have. She only weighed twelve pounds, but wrestling an alligator seemed easy after fighting Lucky the Lion. I only hoped I could keep a leash on her.

CIRCLE OF WOLVES

I pulled into the parking lot at Sunset View Towers a little before two. The elderly guard at the gate had me on his list and pointed to the southernmost building.

"Please park in one of the visitor spaces," he said, grinning.

His dentures needed a new brand of adhesive. They clicked lightly with every word and moved up and down a millimeter or so each time the man worked his jaws. I was waiting for them to drop out.

"And remember The Sign," he added, tilting his head toward my backseat.

I assumed he was indicating Lucky and guessed The Sign warned pet owners to clean up after their dogs. It was then that I remembered the roll of paper towels sitting on the table in the kennel.

I nodded at the old man and continued on across a series of speed bumps to the row of visitor spaces outside the Marion R. Hayes Assisted Living Facility, a ten-story, flamingo pink, stuccoed job that looked more like a resort hotel than a nursing home.

There were five other equally radiant buildings scattered about the twenty-acre tract, most of them fifteen or sixteen stories high, and all of them surrounded by exotic palms and bird-of-paradise plants. Each building (with the exception of the Marion R. Hayes) had a long, low carport attached to it. What few cars I could see were on the order of Lincoln Towncars and Cadillacs.

According to Michael, the Sunset View Towers complex was a retirement facility for the very wealthy. Each two-bedroom apartment ran about 2,500 square feet in size and $1,500 a month in rent. When I asked Michael why the units were rental apartments instead of condos, he shrugged and said he had no idea. Logic told me it was because the older residents didn't intend to be there more than a few years. Ei-

8 Karen Ann Wilson

ther that or they didn't have any heirs, so what was the point of owning their homes? Logic also told me that Michael, age fifty and childless, knew this, which was why I refrained from asking him if the name "Sunset View" referred to the sun sinking into the nearby Gulf of Mexico or the residents' presumed outlook on life.

I got out of my car and went around to the right rear passenger door. Lucky was looking up at me from the backseat, her mottled blue and pink tongue lolling happily. There was enough saliva and drool on the vinyl to lubricate a locomotive. I took a couple of deep breaths and, leash in hand, opened the door.

Miraculously, the puppy continued to sit quietly, while I attached the leash to her collar. Then she sort of fell out of the car, waddled over to the grass, and squatted.

"Good girl!" I told her, then thought, *Maybe this won't be so bad, after all.*

At the entrance to the building, I paused, my hand on the door. Then I leaned over and picked the dog up. There wasn't any point in pressing my luck, at least where her potty training was concerned.

The interior of the Marion R. Hayes Assisted Living Facility was just as ostentatious as the exterior. Expensive Oriental runners traversed plush green carpeting. Victorian love seats and matching wing-backed chairs in green and midnight blue and occasional tables with clawed feet made the lobby look like the library at the Biltmore estate. Gainsborough reproductions (although they could have been genuine for all I knew) hung here and there between bookshelves. All that was missing was a Victrola playing a scratchy "Sentimental Journey."

The room was a veritable beehive of activity. Elderly women dressed in watered silk or satin and lace sat side by side like wallflowers on the love seats. Jewelry sparkled

CIRCLE OF WOLVES

from earlobes and throats with the kind of fire that only the real McCoy can produce. Half a dozen equally ancient gentlemen in suits and ties sat by themselves in the wing-backs. Several of the guests were drinking tea or coffee from dainty china cups. A couple of the ladies held sherry glasses by their stems. No one was saying much, which made the lack of background music all the more noticeable.

I felt terribly out of place, dressed in jeans and a knit pullover and carrying a squirming puppy under one arm. Lucky wasn't even a Pekingese or a Pomeranian. Sunset View Towers clearly was more Michael's style. I began to resent the fact that he'd made me agree to do my weekly pet therapy visits there instead of at the little nursing home around the corner from the clinic. And then one of the less wizened men glanced over at me and winked. He looked a little bit like Michael, actually, and I was suddenly reminded of the seventeen-year difference in our ages. How one day, terribly soon I feared, Michael and I might come to reside in a place where a glass of sherry and a nap could pass for an evening out on the town. My palms started to sweat.

"Are you Miss Holt?" asked a female voice to my right.

I turned around. A forty-something woman wearing a stylish pale rose shirtwaist dress and pearls was smiling at me. She reached out to let Lucky sniff her hand. When the dog licked it, I noticed the woman didn't cringe or hold the contaminated hand out in the air like it was a dead rat.

"Yes," I said. "Are you the recreation director? Mrs. Snoden?"

"I am indeed," she said.

We shook hands. Lucky was beginning to get a little antsy, so I shifted her around.

"I hope the nursing floor isn't carpeted," I said. "I told Dr. Augustin she was too young for this, but he thought a puppy might cheer people up more than a cat."

10 Karen Ann Wilson

Mrs. Snoden took my elbow and guided me quickly down the hall to a pair of elevators. "Your Dr. Augustin can be most persuasive," she said. She pushed the "Up" button.

You don't know the half of it, I thought. I wondered if she had actually seen him in the flesh, or if his charm had oozed out over the telephone line.

The elevator door opened, and a young man dressed entirely in white got off. He was pushing an old man in a wheelchair. I stared at the old man. His eyes were open, but he obviously had stopped seeing a very long time before. He was humming to himself and moving his head from side to side. It reminded me of a wolf I'd seen at the zoo, pacing back and forth. Back and forth, not really seeing anything.

Mrs. Snoden gently pushed me into the elevator car and pressed 4. The doors closed.

"Is this your first visit to a nursing facility?" she asked.

I nodded and felt myself blush. Had it been that obvious? "My fiancé read about the program somewhere and suggested it to me," I said. And then I thought, did he want me to see what it was like to care for an aged relative whose faculties had withered away? Was this a prenuptial test of some sort?

"I'm not really sure what to do," I continued. "They give you a few instructions when you sign up, but I went through the screening with a cat." I paused. "I guess it's pretty much the same with a dog, though."

Lucky began to whine.

"A few of our patients live in their own apartments in other buildings," said Mrs. Snoden. "They're on the nursing floor temporarily because of illness or injury: broken bones, the flu, that sort of thing. Several of them have pets of their own."

The elevator stopped, and the doors opened.

"The residents who live in the Hayes Building aren't al-

CIRCLE OF WOLVES   11

lowed to have pets. They're the ones we encourage our volunteers to concentrate on."

We exited the elevator and walked down a long hallway that looked, smelled, and felt like a hospital ward. The floor was vinyl-covered, fortunately. The walls were white and essentially bare, except for an occasional framed picture of New England in the fall or the California coast. Stuff you can buy two for twenty bucks in any discount store. Which surprised me after my trek through the museum downstairs.

At even intervals along the hall were rooms, each identified by a tiny name tag, handwritten on a white card and slid into a holder next to the door. Just like a hospital. And nurses with drug carts and patients in wheelchairs cluttered the hallway like in a hospital. Except here the patients looked like they belonged in the morgue. And it wasn't entirely due to age, either. It was creepy. Like something out of one of those C-grade zombie movies. I tried to concentrate on Mrs. Snoden's voice.

"Why don't we start in the rec room?" she asked. "A lot of the patients congregate there for afternoon tea." She looked at her watch. "We have about thirty minutes before they begin serving." She made it sound like an afternoon social. "Then we can visit each room."

We continued down the hall to a fork. The right branch had a large sign positioned over a set of sturdy-looking double doors. It read *PSYCHIATRIC WING. ALARM-ACTIVATED DOORS. NO UNAUTHORIZED ADMITTANCE.* We took the left branch.

As we neared the end of the hall, a young girl in a nurse's uniform came out of one of the rooms, carrying a small tray. She spotted Lucky, and her eyes grew very wide. Then she smiled and hurried over to us. She was probably nineteen or twenty but looked much younger. She had enormous pale blue eyes and full, naturally red lips. There were several Band-aids on her right arm. The kind with Bert and Ernie on them, which seemed terribly appropriate somehow. Her name tag read, *LONI HERFELD, LPN.*

"What a cute puppy," she said in a childlike voice. She stuck her hand out as if to pet Lucky, then stopped abruptly. "Does he bite?"

"Heavens no," I said.

She proceeded to scratch Lucky's head. Lucky reciprocated by bathing the girl's hand in saliva.

"Loni!" The voice, stern and demanding, came from a room we had just passed. "I need you in here. Now!"

Loni gave the puppy a sad, parting scratch. "Gotta go," she said. Then, hastily wiping her hand on her uniform, she hurried in the direction of the voice.

The rec room was a twenty-by-twenty open area containing an old sofa, a large, circular table, and six straight-backed chairs. The recreation apparently was provided by a bookcase with a fair selection of used paperbacks, a few games, and a television suspended from the ceiling. The TV wasn't on, and there was no obvious way to turn it on.

If the residents seated about the room, most of them in wheelchairs, had been dressed in uniforms with a stripe down the leg, rather than bathrobes, it wouldn't have surprised me. I noticed one or two of them had developed the same repetitive motion the old man on the elevator had, although not all involved the head. One woman kept smoothing out the material of her nightgown. She'd been doing it for some time too, because the patch of nylon was stained and threadbare. I thought again about the wolf in the zoo.

"Ethel," said Mrs. Snoden, softly, "look who's come to visit."

We went over to the woman "ironing" her nightgown. Mrs. Snoden picked up the old woman's hand and put it on Lucky's head. Right on cue, the puppy turned to the side so she could reach the hand with her tongue, and then slob-

CIRCLE OF WOLVES

bered all over it. Ethel suddenly jerked awake, looked down at the puppy, and began to laugh. It was a child laughing.

"See," said Mrs. Snoden, smiling at me. "Nothing to it." She looked at her watch. "I'll be back for you in a few minutes. Have fun." She left.

Fun isn't exactly how I would describe my time in the rec room, but it was gratifying to see the effect Lucky had on the more withdrawn patients. A couple of them even talked to her as if she were a long-lost pet, calling her Patches or Goldie.

When the food cart arrived, I gave a sigh of relief. I was afraid any minute I might start to cry. Not that anyone would have noticed.

"You'll have to leave," said a woman in a hairnet pushing the cart.

Loni was with her. She smiled at me but didn't say anything. Clearly, she'd been cautioned by the voice to mind her p's and q's.

The woman with the hairnet was dressed in a long-sleeved, crisply starched white uniform. Her name tag said, *Wilma Smith, Dietitian*. She weighed about two hundred and fifty pounds, and I questioned the wisdom of putting someone like her in charge of the patients' meals. The terms "sugar-restricted" and "low-fat" didn't appear to be a part of her vocabulary.

"We can't have animals in here with all this food," she continued. She didn't look as if she'd be overjoyed to have Lucky in there even without the food.

I glanced at the tray. It contained three or four kinds of cookies on a round platter, a large teapot, a container of milk, several packets of sugar, a stack of napkins, and a dozen or so unbreakable teacups. The cookies were store-bought. They looked like the ones I'd gotten in the afternoon at summer camp, served up with those little cartons of milk.

Karen Ann Wilson

Long, narrow sandwich cookies. Loni was passing them out. Not too many of the patients seemed interested. I doubted if many of them had enough teeth to chew cookies, anyway.

Mrs. Snoden wasn't back yet, so I decided to tackle the first few rooms alone. My turn in the rec area had given me confidence.

Out in the hall, I looked around for a rest room. My arms ached from holding Lucky still, and I longed to put her on the floor. The fact that she might relieve herself there meant I needed someplace out of the way, preferably with a paper towel dispenser. Unfortunately, the only thing I saw that came close was a supply closet.

I was still pondering the problem when a voice called to me from a nearby room. I turned around. The door was ajar.

"I'd love to see your little dog," the voice said.

I walked across the hall and stuck my head in. A thin, attractive woman with silver hair and a pleasant smile sat propped up in bed. She was wearing a delicately flowered Laura Ashley print nightgown, high at the neck, with slightly puffed cap sleeves, accented in lace. A large flower arrangement sat on the bedside table next to a pitcher and glass. The room smelled of lavender.

"Please," she said. "Do come in. My name is Gretchen. But call me Grey. Everyone does." She patted the edge of the bed with a slim hand. She wore no jewelry.

I pushed the door open a bit farther and went in. "My name is Samantha," I said. "But please call me Sam." I paused. "Everyone does."

She laughed. It was contagious, and I joined her.

"So, little puppy, what's your name?" Grey asked, after I'd gone over to the bed and put Lucky down beside her, praying the dog would behave herself.

"Lucky," I said. I spotted a box of Kleenex lurking behind the flower arrangement and prepared to dive for it if need

CIRCLE OF WOLVES 15

be. "She was a stray," I continued. "The man I work for adopted her. He's a veterinarian, and Lucky was pretty sick when Animal Control brought her to us. So I guess the name is appropriate."

Grey was tickling Lucky's belly, and the dog was chewing lightly on her hand. I started to worry that the woman's fragile skin, turned nearly translucent with age, would tear. And with Lucky's history the little dog would be banished to doggie heaven well before her time, so that slices of her brain could be examined for the deadly rabies virus.

"Be careful," I said, gently, "don't let her scratch you."

"Oh, don't worry," Grey said, "I have a cat at home, and we play like this all the time. A scratch or two won't hurt me, will it, Lucky?"

She withdrew her hand and began stroking Lucky's head. With her other hand, she pointed to the chair next to the bedside table. "Please sit and visit with me, Sam," she said. "I have to remain here for another day or two, and there isn't anyone to talk to, except the staff. And they are usually too . . ." she paused, ". . . preoccupied."

I went over to the chair and sat down. I could tell Grey was lonely and bored. Her tone, particularly when she referred to the staff, suggested mild irritation. She didn't look sick, and she certainly didn't look like she belonged in an assisted care facility.

"Do you have an apartment in one of the other buildings?" I asked.

She nodded. "Yes. In the Morgan building—it's the one closest to the Gulf. I'm on the top floor and have a glorious view of the water." She let her hand rest on Lucky's back and leaned against the pillow propped behind her.

Lucky shoved her whole body up against Grey's hip and slowly sank into the bedspread. Then she put her head down and closed her eyes.

16 Karen Ann Wilson

"I'm here because of the flu," Grey told me. "All I had was a case of the sniffles, but the doctor said I needed to spend a few days on the nursing floor." She frowned. "Of course, they're charging me for this little visit." She looked at me then and screwed up her delicate features. "I'll tell you what, though. Four days is a gracious plenty. They'll have to tie me up to get me here next time. Or shoot me."

She shook her head, as if to clear away the unpleasantness, and smiled. She touched the fabric of her nightgown.

"You don't think this is too young for me, do you?" she asked. "My granddaughter, bless her soul, loves Laura Ashley and sent it to me for my birthday."

"It's lovely," I said. "Just what the doctor ordered."

Lucky woke up suddenly and started to whine. I went to the bed and grabbed her before Grey's pink and mauve nightgown became a bit yellow.

"I think we should be going," I said. "Lucky is still a little young for this."

Grey's smile faded. "I wish you could stay," she said. "You remind me of Kimberly."

"Kimberly?"

"My granddaughter. She's blonde like you and about your age. Maybe a little younger. She's a lawyer up in D.C."

She was obviously very proud of the girl, and I thought, our coloring is about all we have in common, I'm sure.

Grey's pale blue eyes didn't miss much.

"You are doing such a wonderful thing, you know," she said, quickly. "Spending your Sunday afternoons with a bunch of lonely old people. I'm sure a pretty girl like you would rather be at the beach."

"Don't be silly," I said. "I'm enjoying this visit. Besides, all that sun is bad for the skin."

She laughed. "Well . . . you and Lucky take care."

"And you get better," I said.

CIRCLE OF WOLVES

I met Mrs. Snoden in the hall. We visited three more patients, all of whom were permanent residents of the Marion R. Hayes building. They were only marginally aware of our presence, and Lucky's whining grew more insistent as each unyielding hand was placed on her head. I finally told Mrs. Snoden that it was time to take the puppy home.

As we passed the fork in the hall, I saw the woman with the food cart stop in front of the doors to the psychiatric wing. She pressed a red button on the left wall. The doors made a whooshing sound and swung open. The woman pushed her cart through, just as an old man in a long nightshirt tried to exit the wing.

"Help me!" he wailed between the doors. He caught me staring at him. "They're trying to kill me! Please, I beg you! Help me!"

A nurse on the inside grabbed him before he got more than a hand through. As the doors closed, I saw her lead him away, her arm around his shoulders.

Mrs. Snoden shook her head but didn't say anything. We continued down the hall toward the elevator. Lucky's whine had progressed to a growl.

Out in the parking lot, I put the puppy down. She immediately squatted and remained in that position for several seconds. When she was finished, I praised her liberally, then picked her up and carried her to my car.

During my short stay inside the Hayes Building, the milky blue sky had developed a depressing steel grey ruffle to the east. A light breeze carried the odor of wet pavement across the bayou, and I thought I detected a rumble or two off in the distance. *The beach is definitely out now*, I thought.

The guard appeared to be napping inside his little booth. I paused briefly beside the door, in case he was supposed to record the time I left, but his chin never left his chest.

18   Karen Ann Wilson

If he's dead, I thought, *I don't want to be the one who finds him.* So I eased over one final speed bump, silently wondering why they would put speed bumps in a place where everything takes place in slow motion anyway and, after a lengthy wait at the entrance, merged with the traffic on Gulf Drive.

CHAPTER 2

●

Monday, November 8

I am not a vain person, at least I hope I'm not. Because where I come from, vanity is a way of life, something akin to godliness. Back home in Connecticut, the average female thinks the amount of padding on one's derriere should be inversely proportional to one's annual income (which is to say, one's husband's annual income). And most of my friends there had pretty hefty annual incomes. That is one of the reasons I moved to Brightwater Beach, Florida, a place more in tune with Jimmy Buffet than with The Three Tenors. I like beer and nachos too much. And the irony of it is, now that I am on my own and a veterinary technician, rather than the wife of a famous surgeon, the size of my derriere really is inversely proportional to my annual income.

In any case, it is difficult to be vain when your work attire makes you look like a five-foot-ten tangerine Sno-Kone. Dr. Augustin's uniform allowance doesn't provide much flexibility. So, prior to my thirty-third birthday, I didn't spend a lot of time peering in the mirror. Lately, however, I have spotted a few crow's feet starting around my eyes, despite all the sunscreen and moisturizer I invest in. Which is why I noticed how utterly flawless Glynnis Winter's face looked that morning. At forty-six or thereabouts, Mrs. Winter, widow of the late Judge Jameson Winter, looks like she

19

ought to be in an ad for wrinkle cream. Of course, fruit acids can never compete with a good plastic surgeon. I am pretty sure Glynnis can personally attest to this fact.

"I realize this is short notice," Mrs. Winter began, her tone not in the least bit apologetic.

She plunked a large Liz Claiborne bag down on the reception desk. Cynthia Caswell, our receptionist, looked at it suspiciously.

"But poor Frosty simply cannot handle the stress."

She was referring to her Maltese, who stared out at me from beneath the woman's left breast like some sort of prosthesis. He was panting like a miniature steam engine. Tiny pearls of saliva dripped off his long pink tongue onto Glynnis's bronzed arm.

"It will only be for a few days," continued Mrs. Winter. "I can't bear to be without my baby for long, you know."

She kissed Frosty on the head, leaving behind a trace of rum raisin lipstick. She rubbed at the spot with her fingers, then straightened the little black ribbon tied around Frosty's forelock.

Mrs. Winter was wearing a black linen dress with matching short-sleeved jacket and linen pumps. Her jewelry was plain and tasteful: simple gold earrings shaped like sea scallops and her Rolex. She obviously wasn't husband-hunting that day. Her perfume, some delicate fragrance I couldn't identify, did not fill the air like morning fog over a swamp. Still, she could have worn a sheet and looked ravishing. Of course, it would have to be a designer sheet.

"The funeral is tomorrow," she said. "Most everyone will be gone by the weekend."

"Funeral?" asked Cynthia, still eying the bag on her desk as if it had been left there by a terrorist.

"My mother," said Glynnis. "She passed away Saturday."

"Oh, I am so sorry," said Cynthia.

CIRCLE OF WOLVES 21

Mrs. Winter lowered her eyes and smiled faintly. "Thank you." She kissed Frosty again. "But she had been in ill health for some time. And she *was* eighty-three, after all." As if the woman had surpassed some socially acceptable limit for living.

The phone rang, and Cynthia grabbed it. I started to reach for Frosty, then stopped.

"Would you like to speak to Dr. Augustin?" I asked.

Glynnis never hands over her dog willingly to anyone except Dr. Augustin. I always feel like one of those child welfare people whose job it is to snatch babies from the arms of their allegedly undeserving mothers.

Mrs. Winter surprised me. "No, that's all right," she said. She handed Frosty to me, then reached into the shopping bag. "I've prepared enough food to last until Saturday. It needs to be refrigerated, of course." She took out a sheet of notebook paper. "Here are my feeding instructions. Please follow them carefully. Frosty's digestion is easily upset." She smiled thinly. "But, then, you already know that, don't you, Miss Holt?"

I certainly do, I thought, *and your culinary concoctions are not helping the situation one bit.*

Mrs. Winter placed the sheet of paper on the desk next to the bag. "And I've included a few of Frosty's favorite toys," she said.

She put her hand back in the bag and withdrew a small rubber ball shaped like a hedgehog. It had long spines sticking out everywhere and a tiny pointed face. She squeezed gently, and the hedgehog let out a shrill whistle. Frosty wasn't impressed. He was too busy hyperventilating.

Glynnis put the toy back in the bag. She patted Frosty's head and made juicy kissing noises at him.

"You be a good boy for Miss Holt, you hear?" she cooed. "Mommy will be back before you know it."

22   Karen Ann Wilson

Frosty panted and dripped saliva. Mrs. Winter looked at her dog, then at me. Her pupils flashed like a parrot's.

"I have every confidence Frosty is in the best of hands," she said. With that, she turned and walked regally across the room to the door. She hesitated a second or two, then opened the door and stepped outside.

Cynthia hung up the phone and, together, we watched the woman through the plate glass. After Mrs. Winter had gotten in her Mercedes and was backing out of the parking lot, I glanced into the shopping bag.

"I don't believe it!" I said, snickering.

The door to Dr. Augustin's office opened. "What don't you believe?" he asked.

Cynthia and I exchanged a quick glance. There are times when we're convinced the place is bugged.

Dr. Augustin looked around the reception room, then out in the parking lot. Apparently satisfied that the coast was clear, he came over to Cynthia's desk. He was chewing a wad of bubble gum. He blew an enormous purple bubble, then sucked it back into his mouth before it popped. The sound reminded me of a ruptured vacuum line. Frosty jerked in my arms and resumed his panting.

"She left us these little sandwich bags filled with some kind of frozen meat and grease mixture. Probably the remains of one of her dinner parties. Beef stroganoff or something." I held up one of the bags. "Looks like sour cream to me." I wrinkled my nose and dropped the brown and white slab back into the shopping bag. It clattered against its glacial brethren. "What do you want me to do with them?"

Dr. Augustin blew another bubble. He picked up the sheet of paper Glynnis had left on the desk. He smiled as he read it, then wadded it up. "What do you think?" he asked, taking aim at the trash can next to the water cooler. He tossed the paper wad into the air. It soared across the room, missed

CIRCLE OF WOLVES 23

the trash can by several inches, and bounced off the cooler. It landed in one of the reception chairs.

Dr. Augustin frowned and forced his hands into the pockets of his glove-snug jeans. His attire matched his mood. He was wearing a black knit shirt with tiny lightning bolts of white running through the ribbing on the collar and sleeves.

He looked at the clock on the wall over Cynthia's desk. "It's lunchtime," he said in a voice that could squelch even the heartiest of appetites. "We still need to do that dental." He blew another bubble. "I'll be back in half an hour. Have the dog ready." Obviously, he hadn't meant for his staff to partake of lunch.

He went into his office. Then I heard the side door to the clinic slam closed, and pretty soon, Dr. Augustin appeared in the parking lot.

"I sure would like to know what's eating him," I said to Cynthia.

I watched him walk down the street toward McDonald's. Cynthia didn't say anything. I shrugged and picked up the Liz Claiborne bag.

"He has too much time on his hands," I said. "Particularly now that Dr. Wilson is filling in twice a week. I hate to say this, but maybe he needs another murder to solve."

Cynthia cleared her throat and glared at me.

"Well . . ." I said, "what do *you* suggest? Or do you like being snarled at all the time?"

Cynthia took her purse and a stack of magazines out of the bottom drawer of her desk and stood up. "He needs to get married again," she said. "Settle down and start a family."

The notion of Dr. Augustin changing diapers and reading bedtime stories was more than I could handle. I shook my head and turned to go.

"And while we're on the subject," Cynthia continued,

24   **Karen Ann Wilson**

"you promised to go through these and pick out a china pattern."

I turned back around. She was holding up the latest issue of *Modern Bride*. I took a deep breath and tried to control my tongue. I'd been engaged for all of a week, and Cynthia had slipped effortlessly into the role of wedding consultant, as if she'd been practicing for months, which wasn't far from the truth. Cynthia is kind and well-meaning and a sort of surrogate mother to me, but her desire to see me married off (despite her own recent divorce) is beyond annoying.

"Michael and I haven't even set a date yet, Cynthia. Don't you think you're jumping the gun just a little?"

She thrust out her already generous bosom, pursed her lips, and slapped the magazine down on the desk. It wasn't difficult to see I had hurt her feelings. Again.

I put the shopping bag on the floor and shifted Frosty to my left arm. Then I walked over to Cynthia's desk.

"Of course, a little early planning can't hurt, can it?" I asked, holding out my hand.

Cynthia smiled. "I was thinking Valentine's Day might be nice," she said, giving me the magazine. "What do you think?"

I bit my tongue.

I finished polishing the beagle's teeth and was putting the dental instruments in the sink when I heard the back door open. I didn't actually hear the door, but the chorus of barking and whining and rattling of cages in the kennel signaled someone's arrival. Then I heard Frank scream for silence (which he got, almost instantly), and Tracey appeared in the doorway to the surgery. She was grinning.

"Guess what?" she asked me. Her normally rosy complexion was even rosier, making me wonder what she and our kennel manager had been up to on their lunch hour.

CIRCLE OF WOLVES   25

I carried the semiconscious beagle to a recovery cage, made sure he was comfortable, and closed the door. Then I turned around and looked at Tracey.

They are an odd couple, our laboratory technician and our kennel manager. Tracey Nevins is slim but muscular, with beautiful skin and very short-cropped, dark brown hair. She likes nice clothes, and her stepfather, a wealthy physician, is extremely generous. Frank Jennings, on the other hand, is tall, gaunt, and pale, with very long, stringy hair, presumably in keeping with his role as a rock musician. He wears clothes the Salvation Army wouldn't accept. Tracey is moody, often outspoken, and more mature than a twenty-one-year-old ought to be. And she is distrustful of men, particularly the kind who leer. Frank leers a lot (or did before Tracey came along), acts dim-witted half the time, and is more immature than a twenty-four-year-old ought to be. According to Tracey, they are very much in love.

And then I thought, maybe she's going to announce their engagement, incongruous as it might seem. Which would give Cynthia another wedding to plan and take some of the pressure off me.

"What?" I asked, smiling broadly.

"Frank's band is going to cut its first record this weekend," she said.

I felt the smile shrink to nothingness. "Oh," I said. "Isn't that nice."

"Nice!?" she exploded. "It's pretty damned terrific! What's the matter with you, Sam? You should be happy for Frank." She put her hands on her hips and stared at me, her pout pinching dimples in her cheeks as if they were Pillsbury Doughboys.

"I am happy for him, Tracey. It's just that I'm a little preoccupied right now."

She came into the room, picked up the bottle of disinfectant spray, and gave the table a good dousing.

"Of course you are," she said. "I'm sorry." She pulled a handful of paper towels off the roll and began wiping up the foam and dog hair. "So, tell me Sam, where are you registered, and can I afford your china?"

CHAPTER 3

•

Tuesday, November 9

Dr. Augustin was already at the clinic when I pulled into the parking lot at 7:40. He rarely gets to work before nine, unless there's an emergency or we have a full surgical schedule, which was not the case that day. Or, as I feared *was* the case, when something is bothering him. I guess he would rather stew about it at work, where he can upset as many people as possible.

I got out of my car, walked across the pavement to the front door, and stopped. I stood there for several seconds, trying to gather my wits together, like I had a hundred times before. *I shouldn't have to do this,* I told myself rather angrily. *I shouldn't have to muster the courage to go to work every day.* Then I gave a little sigh and went in. *Nothing changes unless you want it to. Remember that.*

The door to Dr. Augustin's office was closed. The top light on Cynthia's phone panel was lit, indicating conversation on his private line, although I couldn't hear anything through the door. I could smell coffee, however, and hurried across the hall to the lab. The pot was only half-full. Since Frank usually doesn't drink coffee, it meant Dr. Augustin had been there awhile.

Oh well, I thought, shoving my purse into the cabinet

over the sink, at least we get a reprieve this afternoon with Dr. Wilson here.

And then I smiled. Lawrence Andrew Wilson is the antithesis of Dr. Augustin. A recent vet school graduate, he is short, not terribly attractive, gets his hair cut regularly, and wears a tie to work. He is also calm, polite, and knows his limitations. He may not be the fastest or most efficient surgeon in the world, but he gets the job done and doesn't scream at anybody or throw things in the process.

Larry mans the local emergency clinic at night and on weekends, and on Tuesday and Thursday afternoons, he fills in for Dr. Augustin at Paradise Cay Animal Hospital. It is a recent arrangement that is supposed to help Larry gain experience working at a regular clinic and give Dr. Augustin time off to pursue other things—like harassing the City Commission.

"Samantha!" It was Dr. Augustin.

The sharp crack of his voice whipped suddenly through the quiet, and coffee sloshed out of my cup onto the floor. I pulled a paper towel off the roll, left it to float over the puddle, and ran through the connecting door into Dr. Augustin's office.

He was at his desk. He had the local section of the *Times* open in his lap. A large cream-colored manila file folder crammed full of papers and clippings lay on the floor next to him. Additional papers and several newspaper clippings were scattered across his desk. I had never seen the folder before. The ones we use at the clinic are red or green.

"Wasn't that pick-up you said nearly hit you Sunday from the Sunset View Towers?" he asked.

"Yes," I said. "A maintenance truck, I think."

"Well, the driver died. Ran into a light pole."

"He didn't look too happy, that's for sure. Maybe he had a heart attack."

CIRCLE OF WOLVES

I was curious why Dr. Augustin had brought the matter up at all. He hates reporters, distrusts newspapers in general, and rarely discusses what he reads in them, unless it has a bearing on one of his cases, as I had begun to think of his extracurricular meddling and snooping into the affairs of the Brightwater Beach citizenry.

"Nope," he said. "The guy was poisoned. With aldicarb, a pesticide, according to this." He pointed to an article on the second page.

I walked over to his desk, stepped around the file folder, and read the headline. LAWN CARE WORKER MISHANDLES DANGEROUS CHEMICAL AND DIES.

"Well," I said, "like you told me last month, people who use toxic chemicals deserve what they get." I couldn't resist saying it. Inwardly, I felt sorry for the dead man and his family.

Dr. Augustin's eyes flashed across my face like strobe lights, and I backed up a couple of steps.

"That's not exactly how I put it," he said. "But in this case, the man probably did reap what he sowed. It says here aldicarb isn't labeled for residential use. He was undoubtedly using the stuff illegally." He folded the paper in half and put it in the trash can beside his desk.

"I may be out of the office a good deal of the time these next few weeks," he said, standing up. "I've asked Larry to fill in for me." He took his exam jacket off the back of the closet door and slipped it on. He wouldn't look at me.

"I wanted you to know. And I want you to help Larry out in whatever way necessary. He'll only be here for weekly afternoon appointments, but I want things to go smoothly. Show him the ropes."

I started to ask him what he was up to, but a little voice inside my head told me it would be unwise. Besides, at that moment, Cynthia arrived, followed by our first spay of the

Karen Ann Wilson

morning. As Dr. Augustin and I left his office for the surgery, I glanced back at the file folder on the floor and resolved to do a little snooping of my own later.

Dr. Augustin left promptly at 1:00. I breathed a giant sigh of relief. He hadn't said much to me during our two spays and a declaw, and our full appointment schedule hadn't allowed for much chitchat the rest of the morning. Even a few of our regular clients noticed his rather bleak mood.

"Is Dr. Augustin feeling all right?" asked Vivian Porter, as we watched Dr. Augustin's Jeep Cherokee zip off down the street.

Dresden, Ms. Porter's Doberman, was busy watching Charlie, one of the clinic's blood donor cats. Charlie, slant-eyed and grinning, sat like an ebony statue on Cynthia's desk, where he frequently dozes when things are quiet. His tail was moving slowly back and forth along the edge of the desk. Charlie knew Dresden was there, and Dresden knew Charlie knew. Except for the pendulum rocking of the cat's tail, neither animal made any overt movement. It was a waiting game.

"Dr. Augustin has something on his mind, that's all," said Cynthia, as she handed Ms. Porter her receipt.

Vivian still looked concerned. Ms. Porter, like a lot of Dr. Augustin's female clients, is a middle-aged woman whose innermost feelings and desires have failed to find satisfaction at home, for whatever reason. They come to gaze upon Dr. Augustin and fantasize, evidently. You'd think we were operating one of those 1-900 telephone services instead of a veterinary clinic, the way they flock to the place.

Vivian tries to hide the effect Dr. Augustin has on her, but the little beads of perspiration that form on her upper lip when he saunters into the room are a dead giveaway.

CIRCLE OF WOLVES   31

"He's fine, really," said Cynthia, when she saw the frown on Vivian's face.

No, he isn't fine, I thought. And then I remembered the file folder.

"You and Dresden have a nice day," I told Ms. Porter, somewhat abruptly. I patted her dog on the head, gave Charlie a quick scratch under his jaw, and went into Dr. Augustin's office.

The file folder was gone. I searched through the papers on his desk, but all I could locate that looked the least bit interesting was a copy of the minutes from one of the meetings of the Brightwater Beach City Commission. I glanced through it. There were the usual service awards and rapid-fire votes on routine or inconsequential business matters like whether or not to add a couple of outdoor showers to the facilities at the public beach, and who should get the contract to sell hot dogs and beer at the local baseball stadium.

I was about to pitch the copy back on Dr. Augustin's desk when I caught the words "aquifer recharge area" and "multi-family residential development." Either topic would have attracted Dr. Augustin's attention, since he apparently sees himself as the local rep for Defenders of the Environment. (Next week it could be Champions of the Downtrodden.)

The project in question was a condominium complex proposed for an undeveloped piece of land northeast of downtown. The topography and soil type apparently were highly conducive to groundwater recharge and, for the exact same reasons, made a pretty terrific site for development.

Dr. Augustin, along with several other people, had given a brief statement opposing the project, which was being presented for a land use variance by Monarch Development Corporation. Dr. Augustin appeared, from what I could gather, to be the opposition's leader.

I flipped through the rather lengthy and heated discussion

Karen Ann Wilson

to the last page and looked for the vote. It was close, but the variance failed to pass, which probably pleased Dr. Augustin no end. I was surprised he hadn't come to work the following day gloating. He usually did. But the meeting had taken place in August, and I hadn't heard a thing about it.

Obviously, there's more to this thing than what's written here, I thought. I picked up the stack of pink phone memos Cynthia clips to the edge of Dr. Augustin's in-box and read through them. Two were from clients. One was from Rachel, Dr. Augustin's ex-wife. She wanted him to come vaccinate three of her dogs and draw blood for their annual heartworm test. Nothing unusual there. The last message was from Dr. Augustin's lawyer. All it said was "Urgent." The call had come in the previous afternoon.

"I'm leaving now," said Cynthia through the open door. She paused. "What are you doing?"

She had her rain bonnet on. I could just hear the faint tap dancing of raindrops on the aluminum storage shed next door.

"I'm trying to find out why Dr. Augustin has asked Larry to show up four afternoons a week instead of two," I said, returning the phone messages to Dr. Augustin's in-box. "I don't suppose you know what he's up to?"

"I certainly don't," she said. "And you have no business going through his desk. I'm sure if he wanted you to know, he would have told you."

She opened her purse and took out her keys. "I'll be back at one-thirty. I'm going to the bank, then to the drugstore."

She turned and left, but not before cocking her left eyebrow and shaking her head. In addition to wedding consultant, Cynthia often serves as my conscience.

"Why don't you ask Dr. Wilson?" she offered from out in the reception room. She didn't wait for me to answer.

CIRCLE OF WOLVES

33

• • •

Larry either didn't know or wasn't saying. "All he told me was he had some personal business to take care of."

He reached into the carrier and pulled out our patient, a scrawny black and white rabbit with badly misaligned and overgrown incisor teeth. "Why hasn't this animal been neutered?" he asked me, looking at the rabbit's opposite end. "I certainly hope he hasn't produced any offspring. Not with those teeth."

The rabbit tried to bite Larry, but his teeth wouldn't co-operate.

"It's a new client," I said. "You can suggest neutering, but I doubt it will do any good. I don't think the client is a big fan of castration. And I guarantee he won't want to spend the extra money."

We were in the surgery.

"Why don't I get any of those lonely female clients Lou is always talking about?" Larry asked.

Larry restrained the rabbit while I held the mask over the animal's nose and mouth. It didn't take long for the anesthetic gas to work. When the rabbit had slumped to the table, I removed the mask.

"Do you really want me to answer that?" I asked.

Dr. Wilson picked up the clippers and quickly whittled the animal's teeth down to an acceptable length, then filed them.

"No, I don't suppose I do. Anyway, I already know the answer."

The rabbit raised its head and started to struggle. I put him back in his carrier, where he lurched around a bit, then stared out at us malevolently. His little pink tongue darted in and out over his front teeth.

"How long did Dr. Augustin say you'd be putting in the

extra hours?" I asked, as Larry made a few notes in the client's file.

He turned around and smiled. "He didn't." Then he handed me the file. "I guess if Flopsy, here, is awake, we can return him to his owner." He stared into the carrier, then opened the door, presumably for a last check of the rabbit's condition.

Flopsy was definitely awake. He lunged forward and nailed Larry on the thumb. Larry cried out, stuck his thumb in his mouth, and closed the carrier door with his good hand.

"I guess he'll be able to eat now, won't he?" I said, grinning.

Dr. Wilson took his thumb out of his mouth and inspected it. "Go tell the owner I'll neuter Flopsy here for free," he said. "Tell him it'll be my pleasure."

CHAPTER 4

•

Wednesday, November 10

I pressed my fingers against the cramp in my side. The light was red. As my neighbor, Jeffrey Gamble, bounced nimbly from one foot to the other waiting for it to change, I silently gave thanks for the chance to catch my breath. And cursed my best friend's athletic prowess.

"Jeffrey," I managed, "do you ever think about growing old?"

He gazed at me with his Aqua Velva eyes and smiled. His teeth are so perfect, they don't look real.

"Every Thanksgiving," he said.

The cramp was subsiding. I straightened up. "Why Thanksgiving?"

"Because that's when my grandparents fly in from Phoenix, and I thank God I'm not old." He giggled.

"Jeffrey," I said, "you can't spend your entire life acting like there's no tomorrow."

"I'm twenty-five years old, Samantha. I refuse to think about Social Security and hemorrhoids now. Or about dying." There was an almost imperceptible catch in his voice. Then he winked at me. "And anyway, I've been told I have a very long life line." He held up his hand, palm facing out.

The light changed, and, as if to emphasize his point, Jef-

36 **Karen Ann Wilson**

frey dashed out into the intersection. A small white import, running the red light, flew around him. The driver honked and swore and stuck his middle finger out at Jeffrey.

"Yeah, you, too, buddy," I heard Jeffrey shout.

Since my life line disappears completely before it really gets going, and the thought of dying does periodically occur to me (especially in the company of Dr. Augustin), I jogged cautiously across the road and took a right down the sidewalk after Jeffrey. We were a block and a half from our apartment building. Ordinarily, the three miles would have taken me a leisurely twenty-nine or thirty minutes, but I knew, without looking at my watch, it had been closer to twenty minutes. Running with Jeffrey Gamble is like being sucked along in a storm sewer during a flash flood.

He was waiting for me on the second-floor landing. "Want a glass of water?" he asked.

"Sure," I said from the bottom of the stairs.

I picked up the towel I had flung over the railing and wiped my face. According to the weather man on the 7:00 A.M. news, the low that morning had been a nippy seventy degrees. A cold front, only the second one to reach us so far that fall, had dumped three inches of rain on the Tampa Bay area the day before. Now, cooler, drier air was scheduled to replace the muggy eighty-degree highs we had been experiencing. For a day or two, at least. It would be a nice change. It would also mean that the annual migration of snowbirds from Canada and Michigan was about to begin.

Jeffrey came down the stairs with two Star Trek collector's glasses. We sat side by side on the grass, sipped our water, and listened to the rustle of palm fronds overhead.

"You're only preoccupied with old age, Sam," said Jeffrey suddenly, "because your birthday was last week. Birthdays will do that to you."

"No," I said, "my birthday has nothing to do with it."

CIRCLE OF WOLVES

"Bull," he said.

"No, really. I just can't help thinking about that old man. The one I told you I saw on the nursing floor. He acted terrified, Jeffrey, like he was stuck in some prison camp, and they were torturing him. I mean, he *sounded* sane. He *looked* sane."

"He was old, Sam," said Jeffrey, sagely. "Some old people forget where they are or why they can't go home. It's sad, but that's life."

I frowned. "Would you want your mother or father to be stuck in a place like that? Where the patients call out to complete strangers for help?"

Jeffrey shook his head. "They only *think* they need help. Besides, not everyone gets Alzheimer's. My parents probably won't. I mean, my grandparents are in their seventies, and they act pretty normal." He laughed. "Well, as normal as anyone who wears polyester can act."

"This isn't a joking matter," I said. "And your parents aren't immune, either."

Jeffrey stared at me. I saw a glimmer of fear mar his otherwise youthful expression. Then it was gone. He hopped to his feet.

"I've got to get cleaned up," he said. "Tom and I are going to Orlando."

"I thought you were off on Friday, not Wednesday," I said, handing him my glass.

"I switched. One of the girls is getting married this weekend and wanted Friday off."

He dumped the remains of our ice water on the lawn and started up the stairs. He stopped midway and looked down at me.

"Why don't you come with us, Sam, since you're off? We're going to do the tourist thing. You know, visit Univer-

38 Karen Ann Wilson

sal Studios. It shouldn't be too bad. Most of the snowbirds don't get here until the week after Thanksgiving."

I smiled. "Thanks, Jeffrey, but Michael and I have plans. Besides, Tom might not appreciate me tagging along."

"Okay. But try not to get too depressed. Thirty-three isn't really old. You still have a few good years left in you." He giggled, then dashed up the rest of the stairs and into his apartment before I could find something lethal to throw at him.

Despite what I told Jeffrey, Michael and I did not have plans. When he called Monday night, he said he was leaving for Tallahassee early the next morning and probably wouldn't be back until late. He didn't say anything about Wednesday. So I fell into my normal routine of laundry and house chores and generally being grateful for having twenty-four hours off from Dr. Augustin's rotten moods.

At 2:30, the phone rang. It was Michael.

"So, what are you up to?" he asked after his normal salutary "I sure have missed you, Samantha, darling." He'd added the "darling" part only since proposing.

"Laundry," I said.

"Good. You'll probably be ready for a break later. I need your opinion on something."

"Like what?"

"You'll see. I'll pick you up at five-thirty. We can eat at that little Italian place you like. Salvatore's." He paused. "Just a minute, Samantha."

I heard him say something to someone about the copy editor being an idiot. Then he was back.

"I've got to go. I'll see you tonight." He hung up.

I sat on my bed, still cradling the receiver, and wondered why saying no to Michael always seemed so difficult. Not that I wanted to decline his offer of dinner that particular

CIRCLE OF WOLVES 39

night, but he didn't even wait for me to say yes. Like I didn't have a choice. Like I didn't have a life outside of being with him. For that matter, telling Dr. Augustin no when he wanted me to play private detective with him wasn't a piece of cake, either. "Why can't you be more assertive?" I asked myself.

Miss Priss appeared in the doorway to the bedroom and waddled her fat body over to the bed. She rubbed her jaw against my leg and purred loudly. I feed my cats their dinner at five, but Priss obviously feels there is no harm in trying to move the schedule up just a bit. It was her third attempt that day.

"I love you dearly, Priss, but the answer is still *no*!

Priss stopped purring. She uttered a few tiny chattering noises at me, which, roughly translated, was her version of giving me the finger, and huffed off toward the kitchen, where she would spend the next few minutes pushing her empty food dish around. My younger, smaller cat, Tina, never budged from her perch on the windowsill.

"Now, why can't I say that to the men in my life?" I asked her.

Tina blinked at me and yawned.

Michael held the car door open, and I got in. I love the way his BMW smells. It is a combination of leather, Armorall, and Azzaro cologne. And I love the way the passenger seat cradles and supports my body. I fear there is some validity to the notion that women choose their men according to the cars they drive. I do know that my first fiancé's red Ferrari played a rather significant role in his becoming my ex-fiancé. Lola with the big tits just loved that damned car.

Michael turned on the CD player, and we listened to classical guitar as he drove across the causeway to the mainland.

40 Karen Ann Wilson

"This thing you need my opinion on," I said, after we'd turned north onto Main Street. "Is it animal, vegetable, or mineral?" I hoped whatever it was wouldn't take long. Sal's clam sauce was calling me.

Michael laughed. "It's a combination of the three," he said. "Trust me, you're going to like it."

Yeah, right, I thought. Where had I heard that before? "Trust me," the boy said, as they climbed into the backseat of his Dodge.

"Why can't you tell me what it is?" I was growing mildly irritated. I hate surprises, particularly from men. And I'd had more than my share from them.

"Patience, patience."

He propped his left elbow against the window and leaned back. The leather creaked softly. He seemed unusually pleased with himself. Michael is not driven the way Dr. Augustin is, not headed for the cardiac care unit at St. Luke's. But ever since the *Times* had promoted him to editor of the City and State section, he'd been—well, "sad" is the only way to describe it. Of course, there was always that personal problem involving his late wife's son. He'd made a couple of trips to New York to deal with the child, but I feared the problem hadn't been resolved. Not entirely. It would still be there when Michael and I got married. And then it would be my problem, too, wouldn't it?

I closed my eyes and imagined I was at Carnegie Hall watching Segovia play.

"Here we are," Michael said.

I opened my eyes. He was pulling into the parking lot at Franklin's Fine Furniture and Interiors. I relaxed. Michael wanted my opinion on a piece of furniture. How dangerous could that be?

We went in. The giant showroom smelled of Old English Oil and fabric preserver. A sort of formaldehyde and

CIRCLE OF WOLVES 41

lemon potpourri. Chrome and glass accessories sparkled like the diamond earrings on the elderly women back at Sunset View Towers. And, like diamonds in a jewelry display case, the price tags on each chair and sofa were turned over to avoid scaring off potential buyers.

We made it as far as the Natuzzi leather before two obviously bored salesmen shot out from opposite ends of the room. They reminded me of the little lizards that hang around the shrubbery at my apartment building, waiting for unsuspecting bugs to light on the sidewalk.

The taller one had the longer legs and got to us first, his mouth stretched into a smile that would have made Martha Raye proud. The runner-up slowed down, then stopped. His smile, not yet at its full potential, quickly faded.

"How may I help you this lovely evening?" the winner said through his stretched lips. He was eyeing Michael's superbly tailored Brooks Brothers blazer, his Florsheims, even my emerald engagement ring. I could almost hear the calculator in his head, mentally tabulating Michael's possible net worth, comparing it to the paltry commission he got, working his lip muscles to the ligaments, as it were.

Michael took careful note. "We are simply looking around at this point," he said. "If we need your assistance, we'll find you."

Michael does not like overly attentive waiters or pushy salesmen. Especially the ones who drool. And this guy was practically foaming at the mouth.

The man loosened his lips a bit and took a card out of his jacket pocket. He handed it to Michael. "You let me know, then," he said.

We continued on to the rear of the showroom, past the little alcoves containing tasteful arrangements of sofas and love seats and coffee tables, through the make-believe dining rooms, the rows of recliners and mile-long entertain-

42 Karen Ann Wilson

ment centers and bookcases complete with copies of *Moby-Dick* and *Little Women*. All the way back to the bedroom furniture.

It was obvious Michael had scoped the place out prior to our visit, because he guided me directly to an elegant contemporary suite composed of a king-sized bed, two bedside tables, a chest of drawers, and an enormous dresser. The wood was solid, gorgeous, glistening cherry. Not a veneer strip anywhere.

"Well," Michael said, "what do you think?"

"It's beautiful," I said, trying not to get too close to the bed, as if Michael might suddenly ask me to try out the mattress.

I noticed our salesman lurking near the children's furniture. He had an arm slung casually over the top of a set of bunk beds, but he was anything but casual. In fact, he looked downright predatory. The wallpaper behind him only added to the illusion. It was a repeating pattern of ivy crawling up (or down) a fence post or column, certainly not appropriate for a bedroom. I could almost see the lizards lying in wait. And then our salesman flicked his tongue out over his lips, and I decided he wasn't a lizard at all, but a snake. A serpent, here in the Garden of Eden.

"I know you'll probably want to change the rest of the furniture, as well," Michael was saying, "but I thought it prudent to begin with the bedroom things." He took a deep breath. "Since they were Mary's selection. Her tastes and yours are so different."

His wife had been dead for over two years, but her ghost lived on, particularly in the delicate floral fabric of her dressing table, the antique white, four-poster bed, the armoire. She floated around the living room, cast her shadow over the dining table, looked out at me from the mirror in the bathroom. I couldn't visit Michael's condominium

CIRCLE OF WOLVES 43

without feeling her eyes on me. She'd never actually been there, but she was there all the same. He'd brought her with him from New York. Her memory, anyway. And her bedroom furniture. And now he was finally cleaning house. At least I hoped he was.

"It's perfect, Michael," I said, softly, risking a closer inspection of the bed.

"I knew you'd like it, Samantha." He looked at the card the salesman had given him. "Shall we try to locate Mr. Duffy?"

"That shouldn't be too difficult," I said, as the serpent glided our way.

"Ah, yes," said Michael. "And I hope Mr. Duffy is as quick with the paperwork as he was to capture our attention. We have a seven o'clock reservation at Salvatore's."

Mr. Duffy was already filling out the invoice.

I sat on my bed, arms wrapped around my legs, chin on my knees. Priss was curled up beside me. It was 10:30 P.M. I stared at the phone. Then I reached over and picked up the receiver, listened to the drone of the dial tone for a few seconds, and hung up. It was my third try at calling my mother.

"It's too late," I said aloud, as if hearing myself say it would make it more believable. "She's probably already asleep." It didn't matter what time I started this little game, it was always too late. Or she wouldn't be there. Or she'd have company or be eating. Like my mother wouldn't want to hear from her only daughter who never calls and who ran away to Florida against her advice. Like she wouldn't want to hear about the engagement. She who believes it is a mother's fault when her daughter is over thirty and still single.

44 Karen Ann Wilson

Priss started to purr. Purring solves everything, she seemed to say. I scratched her ears.

"I'll call her tomorrow," I told the cat. But I knew I wouldn't.

CHAPTER 5

•

Thursday, November 11

I was relieved to find the parking lot empty when I arrived at 7:40 A.M. But Dr. Augustin had apparently already come and gone by then. The light was on in his office, the copy machine in pieces on the floor. His desk was strewn with papers. It looked like he had suffered an attack, a seizure of some kind, and I was glad I hadn't been there to witness it.

I went into the lab, put my purse and lunch away, and started turning on instruments and arranging test kits on the counter. Since Tracey had taken up with Frank (or vice versa), I couldn't count on either of them to make an appearance much before eight. The dogs in the back were their usual insistent selves, their full bladders and empty stomachs complaining about the lack of timely maid service. I poured myself a cup of coffee from the half-full pot (courtesy of Dr. Augustin, presumably), and headed for the kennel. I stopped. The manila folder I had seen Tuesday, the one I felt certain accounted for Dr. Augustin's current mental state, was lying on his desk, its contents ripe for the picking.

I hesitated, then hurried back to his office. Ordinarily, I wouldn't have cared two hoots about what or who had ticked him off. It happened so frequently. But this time, he wasn't just angry because the Brightwater Beach City Com-

45

mission had approved a project he didn't like or because some fat cat was treading all over one of his favorite underdogs. This time I got the feeling Dr. Augustin was scared. Well, maybe not exactly scared. More like helpless. It was as if he'd gotten caught in a trap and couldn't get out, no matter how much thrashing around or barking he did.

I put my coffee cup on the bookshelf and began shuffling through the papers on his desk. Most of what I saw were photocopies of letters to and from the Brightwater Beach planning and engineering departments. They involved Monarch Development Corporation, the outfit in Tampa that Dr. Augustin had crossed paths with in August. The most recent letters were signed by or addressed to a lawyer in the firm of McGowan, Barber, Sly, and Moen, PA. The subject of all the correspondence was a proposed development called The Crossroads, the very same project the City Commission had, at the insistence of Dr. Augustin and company, denied during its meeting in August. The drift of the correspondence was that Monarch Development felt by denying them reasonable use of their land, the city was, in effect, taking the land from them, for which they wanted due compensation to the tune of fourteen million bucks. The city, understandably, was resisting.

I still wasn't sure why Dr. Augustin was so upset. If the City was forced to buy the land, it would mean the groundwater recharge area would be protected. Even if the city refused, Monarch Development couldn't turn the land into a concrete jungle. So what was the problem? Why was Dr. Augustin acting like his very life depended on the outcome of this thing?

I looked in the trash can. It was filled to the top with balled up sheets of paper—evidence that the copier had thrown a tantrum. I reached in and took out a couple of the wads and was about to sit in Dr. Augustin's chair to read

CIRCLE OF WOLVES 47

them when I heard the front door open and Cynthia talking to someone. I stuffed the discarded papers back in the trash and ran into the lab.

Dr. Augustin picked up the scissors and began dissecting out the marble-sized tumor firmly entrenched on the underside of the Doberman's tongue. I held the tongue forward over the dog's endotracheal tube and periodically dabbed at it with a gauze sponge. It was a belated effort, however. Dr. Augustin's scrub top was tattooed with a fine tracing of red, and narrow strands of clotted blood mixed with saliva hung from the dog's muzzle.

The conversation that morning had been restricted to necessary surgical direction and updates on the patient's condition. No fun stuff like "How is good old Michael, that lowlife reporter you are marrying?" I had increased the volume on the heart monitor simply to provide some background noise. I was glad we were almost done. It was 9:40, and I could hear our ten o'clock out in the waiting room.

Suddenly, Dr. Augustin threw the scissors across the room into the sink. They bounced up and out, landing on the floor.

"Whoever autoclaved this pack," snarled Dr. Augustin, "cooked the hell out of these instruments." He looked briefly at me, and my face started to burn. "Those scissors are as dull as a butter knife."

Well, I thought, *they certainly are now, aren't they*? I stared down at the scissors lying awkwardly on the linoleum and realized I often felt that way. Dull and awkward. *Now just exactly whose fault is that?* I asked myself.

Dr. Augustin took a second pair of scissors off the tray and finished removing the tumor and a sizable chunk of the surrounding tissues. He dropped the mass on the instrument tray.

48 **Karen Ann Wilson**

"Package that up as soon as we're through, and call the courier," he said. "But save a small piece of the main tumor and one or two of the margin. Have Tracey prepare a couple of slides for me to examine over lunch. And tell her to look at them and give me her best guess."

I didn't say anything. If Tracey had to guess, she was in trouble.

After a couple of minutes, Dr. Augustin looked up from his suturing. "You left your coffee cup in my office," he said calmly. He went back to work, pulling the gap in the Doberman's tongue together, detaching hemostats as he went, and dropping them on the table.

I felt the color rise in my face again and quickly dabbed at the dog's tongue, as if her blood and mine had the same source.

"I might as well tell you," said Dr. Augustin. He motioned for me to release my grip on the tongue. "I'm being sued. Big time."

So that was it. "By whom?"

He pulled out another length of suture material. "Monarch Development Corporation. I convinced the city to deny them a land use variance for a project they're calling The Crossroads. They claim I cost them something over a million dollars in wasted man hours. Time they say was spent in project design and site surveys. I understand they're thinking about suing the city for the cost of the land. Fourteen million."

"They can't be serious," I said. "I mean, you can't sue a private citizen for verbally opposing a development, can you? Whatever happened to freedom of speech?"

He tossed the needle and remaining suture material onto the instrument tray and pulled off his gloves. "You'd be surprised. Matt says they could have a case." He went over to the sink, carefully avoiding the dead scissors.

CIRCLE OF WOLVES 49

Matthew Kemp was Dr. Augustin's lawyer, and a good one. If he said Monarch Development might have a case, I'd be concerned, too. "You weren't the only one fighting that project, were you?" I asked. "What about the others? And anyway, how can they accuse you of single-handedly influencing the way the commissioners vote? They *never* listen to you."

Too late, I realized what I'd said and quickly closed my mouth. I waited for him to recite a list of his past political accomplishments, but all he did was snort.

"I mean, hardly ever," I continued blindly. "Well— you've got to admit, the Commission doesn't jump up and down for joy when they see you in the audience." I was rapidly digging my grave.

Dr. Augustin tore a paper towel off the roll and began drying his hands. He turned around. "Matt says Monarch's lawyer claims I provided erroneous information to the commissioners. That without it, they would have voted in favor of the variance."

He pulled his scrub top off over his head and tossed it in the sink. He wasn't wearing a shirt. Every major muscle group in his chest and upper abdomen was perfectly defined. He walked past me to the door, took his T-shirt off the hook, and pulled it on. He smelled like bath soap.

"Anyway, the data I quoted came from the U.S. Geological Survey," said Dr. Augustin.

"Data?" I had lost track of the conversation.

"The soils data, Samantha. If Monarch's lawyers want to pick a fight with the feds, let 'em have at it. But I can't see that they have anything substantive against me. Of course, lawyers have a peculiar knack for twisting the truth."

I removed the Doberman's endotracheal tube. Then, with me supporting the dog's head, Dr. Augustin lifted her from the table and carried her to a mat on the floor. She was already trying to get up.

"What is this Crossroads thing?" I asked.

Dr. Augustin opened the door to one of the recovery cages and examined its occupant.

"It was billed as the area's largest self-contained retirement community," he said. Ten multistory buildings, a medical arts complex, shopping center. All that was missing was a damned golf course." He closed the cage door. "My guess is they ran out of land." Then he chuckled. "Guess they ran out of luck, too."

Look who's talking, I thought.

"Have Frank come in here and clean up this mess," said Dr. Augustin. "Tell him to move Maddie to a run in the kennel, as soon as she can walk. And tell him not to feed her tonight. Just water." He hesitated. "Samantha—I'd rather you didn't discuss this suit business with anyone, especially . . ."

"You mean Michael, don't you?"

His eyes locked onto mine, and he nodded. There was something odd about his expression.

"Don't worry," I said, frowning. I leaned over and picked up the scissors, noting that the very tip of one blade was bent. "Michael and I never discuss work."

But only Maddie and the cat in the recovery cage could hear me. Dr. Augustin was gone.

It was an audition. Nothing so grand as the tryouts for *Hamlet* I remembered from high school, where all the guys in my homeroom went around the week before, reciting Shakespeare and straining their postpubescent vocal cords. It was, however, a difficult role—subbing for Dr. Augustin—and Larry Wilson wanted the part desperately.

"You look very nice today, Cynthia," he said, straighten-

CIRCLE OF WOLVES 51

ing his paisley tie. His grin was as lecherous as the pope's. Assuming the pope grins, that is. "If I were just a few years older, I'd insist on taking you out to dinner tonight."

Cynthia patted her hair (resisting the temptation, I felt sure, to pat Larry on the head), batted her eyelashes, and smiled at the lie. "It would take more than a few years, I'm afraid," she said, "but thank you just the same."

We were in the reception room, waiting for our 3:15 to show. We'd had all of two clients so far that afternoon, both men. If things didn't pick up, I was afraid I might fall asleep.

Dr. Wilson sat down and began thumbing through the latest copy of *Bird Talk*. I needed a cup of coffee and was about to leave for the lab, when Glynnis Winter drove up, parked, and got out of her car.

With her mother dutifully ensconced in the local cemetery, Mrs. Winter had shed her mourning dress for something a bit less somber. That day she wore black stirrup pants under a silk tunic the color of cayenne pepper. Her hair was pulled up at the sides and secured with large silver combs. Her lipstick and nail enamel matched the tunic perfectly.

Dr. Wilson's back was to the glass wall that fronts the clinic, so he didn't see her approaching and only looked up when she came through the door. His reaction was swift and predictable. His mouth fell open, his throat constricted, making him wheeze, and he jumped to his feet. The *Bird Talk* fluttered helplessly to the floor.

Mrs. Winter seemed unconcerned about Dr. Wilson's sudden attack of apoplexy. She did a quick survey of his physical features (not the least of which was his age) and dismissed him like he was a bag boy at the grocery store. She walked over to Cynthia's desk.

"I'm here to pick up Frosty," she said. "I know I told you Friday afternoon, but I miss him terribly and cannot go another night without his warm little body on the pillow next to mine.

Larry, looking less and less like His Holiness, acted as if he would be more than happy to warm up the pillow next to Glynnis's. He cleared his throat, then approached the reception desk, his hand stuck out in front of him like a phallus.

"I'm Dr. Wilson," he said. "Larry. I'll be filling in for Dr. Augustin. For the next few weeks, anyway. In the afternoons." He sounded like a VCR that wasn't tracking very well.

Mrs. Winter shook his hand, holding it like one might a dirty pair of socks. "I'm so happy to meet you," she said, her tone clearly not happy. "But I wish Dr. Augustin would let his regular clients know about any change in routine. Particularly when my life is anything but routine just now." She drew a peppery nail over one freshly waxed eyebrow. Obviously the upset in her routine did not include skipping the beauty parlor.

Dr. Wilson could see defeat looming on the horizon. He backed away from the reception desk. "Let me get Frosty for you," he said.

Mrs. Winter looked at him with no expression whatever on her face. Like Dr. Wilson didn't deserve any. "Don't forget his toys," she said, flicking a tiny piece of lint from her tunic in much the same manner as she had flicked Larry away.

Larry's eyes shifted from Mrs. Winter to me. *What a witch,* they seemed to say. *Dr. Augustin can have her with my blessing.* Then he smiled at Mrs. Winter. "Wouldn't think of it," he said and left for the kennel.

Glynnis ignored him, like I imagined she ignored most everyone she felt was beneath her. She opened her purse and took out her pen and checkbook.

"Do you have those charges?" she asked Cynthia. "I re-

CIRCLE OF WOLVES 53

ally must be going. They've given me until tomorrow to clean out my mother's room. Can you imagine? Mother hasn't even been gone for a week, and already they've got her room rented."

She stared at the Humane Society poster on the wall over the water cooler. It was a picture of a little girl holding a puppy. And for a moment, I thought I detected a faint trace of sadness on her normally haughty features. Then it was gone.

"She was never happy there," she continued. "Complained constantly about the food and the staff. Old people are like that, aren't they? Always complaining?"

The question wasn't really directed at me or Cynthia, more at the child in the poster, and I knew she didn't expect a response. She needed to unload a little of the guilt she was undoubtedly feeling and, in the absence of her dog, Cynthia and I would have to do.

Cynthia pulled the itemized statement out of the printer and placed it on the desk. Mrs. Winter continued to stare at the poster.

"Where was your mother living?" I asked, in an effort to distract her.

Glynnis closed her eyes briefly, then turned away from the child holding the puppy. She picked up the statement, read it, and began writing her check.

"Sunset View Towers," she said, her tone implying where else would someone of her station put their mother? "I had to transfer her to the Assisted Living Facility last year. That's when she started complaining in earnest." She tore the check out of the book and handed it to Cynthia. "She wouldn't eat. The doctor said she only weighed seventy pounds when she passed away."

Mrs. Winter put her pen and checkbook back in her purse and snapped it shut with a decided finality. Then she looked

54 **Karen Ann Wilson**

at me, all traces of remorse gone from her face. "I'm sure it was an attempt to get me to move her back to her own apartment. She even told me she thought they were trying to kill her." She shook her head. "Can you imagine?"

CHAPTER 6

•

Sunday, November 14

The lobby was empty, the wing-backs and love seats lonely reminders of a better time. I walked across the Oriental runner carrying Lucky under my arm. A faint musty odor followed us like a ghost. It was a little before one.

They'll be opening the champagne right about now, I thought, a little wistfully. But the weekly ritual of Sunday brunch at the Sea Breeze had grown tiresome, not to mention bad for my waistline. So I told Michael I had to be at Sunset View Towers just after noon. It wasn't really a lie. Any later and I risked running into the Queen of Hearts and her tray of cookies. Besides, I wanted to see Gretchen. Make sure she was all right. I felt certain the old man on the psychiatric wing and Mrs. Winter's mother were imagining things, and no one really wanted them dead, but I couldn't shake the feeling that Grey was in some kind of danger. Thanks to Dr. Augustin, I was forever checking the closets and looking under the beds.

Mrs. Snoden wasn't in evidence, so I got on the elevator without her and punched 4. As the doors were closing, the young man in white I'd seen the previous Sunday darted in.

"Hi," he said, reaching out to push 5. "You were here last week."

I nodded and smiled. "I'm a volunteer—we are, that is,"

56 Karen Ann Wilson

I said, looking down at Lucky, who was wagging her tail and making little whining noises. "Where is everyone? The lobby was full last week."

"Dinner," The young man said. "In the congregate dining room. There's one in every building. I'm surprised you couldn't smell it." He scrunched up his face. "Supposed to be trout almandine and new potatoes. More likely it's scrod or something equally nasty."

"Sounds like the menu at college."

He laughed. His eyes were blue grey, his hair sandy and very short. He had a small ruby in his left ear.

"Do you work here full time?" I asked, as the elevator stopped and the doors opened. I put a hand out to keep them open.

"No," he said. "I work for Gulf Home Health Care. A lot of families hire private nurses to take care of their parents or spouses. Mostly we sit with them, take them for walks. Make sure they eat. The staff here doesn't have time. 'Assisted living' means you get your room cleaned and your laundry done and your meals prepared. Maybe help with your bath. If you need anything else on a regular basis, they put you on the nursing floor. Means more money and you have to give up most of your personal stuff. And they give you a roommate, whether you want one or not."

The elevator doors started bouncing back and forth against my hand, so I stepped out.

"See you around," the man said.

I hadn't gotten his name.

The hallway was a traffic jam of wheelchairs, most of their unresponsive occupants strapped in like toddlers in a car seat. But there were also several more or less alert patients that day, unlike the previous Sunday. The ones in wheelchairs were propelling themselves down the hall, as if racing against unseen opponents or trying to escape imag-

CIRCLE OF WOLVES 57

ined foes. I had to dodge around them to keep from being run over. One elderly man stopped abruptly and looked up at me with a scowl on his face.

"Watch where you're going," he snapped. Then he raced off, his feet scuffing along on the floor, his arms pushing the wheels forward.

The little name tag outside Gretchen's room was missing. I opened the door anyway and looked inside. She wasn't there. Her flowers were gone, her bed stripped.

I dodged a few more wheelchairs as I headed for the nurse's station to see when Grey had been discharged, but halfway there I heard her voice. It was coming from Room 411. The door was cracked, so I stuck my head in.

Grey and another much younger woman, both in street clothes, were sitting on either side of a bed on which a man about Grey's age lay propped up. He was wearing a plaid bathrobe, and he clutched it together over his chest as if from modesty or the cold, even though it was stifling in the room.

Grey looked up. She smiled briefly, then motioned for me to come in.

"William," she said gently, "this is my friend Samantha. And she's brought her little puppy."

I walked over to the bed and put Lucky down on the blanket. The younger woman—I guessed she was about Mrs. Winter's age—looked at the puppy as though she'd never seen one before and didn't quite know what to make of it. She had plain, unremarkable features, the kind you wouldn't remember an hour after she left the room. The kind of face criminals would kill for, because witnesses can only describe them in terms like "average" and "ordinary."

She looked terribly uncomfortable, almost fearful. She sat bunched together on the chair, her hands strangling a taupe handbag. It looked expensive, although the rest of her attire appeared to be off the rack.

William hadn't seen the puppy yet, and it would have taken the "jaws of life"—those giant pliers firemen use to cut people out of wrecked cars—to pry his hands apart. So I picked the dog up and put her in his lap. She immediately stretched her neck forward and licked one of his hands.

William shifted his gaze from a spot on the far wall to the puppy. But instead of smiling and laughing like a little kid, he began to scream, then drew his hands up to his face and covered his eyes.

Lucky went into full reverse, little hind legs pumping, propelling her as far away from the shrieking voice as possible. I grabbed her as she slid off the end of the bed.

The woman with the purse jumped up and backed away from the man. Her expression was a mixture of grief and terror. Tears welled up in her eyes and began to cascade down both cheeks.

Grey, too, stood up, but instead of retreating, she went over to the man and touched his arm.

"William, it's Grey," she said, her voice nearly drowned out by the man's bellowing. "Everything will be all right. William, do you hear me?" She pulled one of his hands off his face—how, I don't know—and squeezed it.

William opened the uncovered eye and peered up at her. Gradually, his shrieks became whimpers and, finally, he shut up altogether.

The woman with the purse edged closer to the bed. She had tiny vertical lines of mascara on her cheeks.

Quite a crowd apparently had gathered outside the room, because I could hear a babble of voices. Then someone pushed the door all the way open, until it caught, exposing several wheelchairs clustered together like a pack of wolves,

CIRCLE OF WOLVES 59

along with three or four bathrobe-clad, but no less hungry, pedestrians.

At the front of the pack were two people, a man and a woman, dressed like nurses. They hurried into the room. The man, who weighed almost as much as the dietitian but stood at least six foot two, was pushing a drug cart. He left it at the foot of the bed and took William by the shoulders, as if to restrain him, although the crisis had obviously passed. The woman picked a syringe up off the cart, along with a cotton ball, and she rather unceremoniously pulled William's bathrobe up, shoved him over, and dragged his pajama bottoms down. Then she rubbed a spot on his left buttock with the cotton ball. She uncapped the needle and stuck it in.

The injection was probably unnecessary, because William evidently had retreated into some happier place. He dropped his arms to his sides and began to stare out into space.

One-handedly, the nurse pulled William's pants back up and arranged his robe around his legs. Then she carried the syringe to the drug cart and snapped the needle off in the red sharps bucket. She looked up at the bouncer, pointed to the cart, and made little fluttering, walking motions with the fingers of her right hand. They were like a couple of mimes, and I was beginning to wonder if the bouncer was a deaf mute or something.

Wordlessly, the bouncer nodded, relinquished his hold on William's shoulders, and, shoving the drug cart in front of him, muscled his way out of the room, moving like his undershorts had a grasp on his privates. He closed the door.

I could almost hear a collective moan of disappointment coming from the spectators in the hall, now that the excitement was over. It occurred to me that televised championship boxing or pro wrestling might be an appropriate diversion for the residents of the Hayes Building. That maybe the bouncer could be talked into performing for them.

"Mrs. Dickerson," the nurse said to the mouse with the purse, "I really feel you should consider moving your father to the psychiatric wing, where he can be monitored and supervised twenty-four hours a day. I don't know what caused this latest episode . . ."

She glanced over her shoulder at me, then frowned at Lucky. She was a small woman, with short, grey hair and pointed features. Her voice, rather than appropriate to her size, was deep and throaty, like she smoked a lot. *A nurse should know better,* I thought.

". . . But, like Dr. Aaron told you Friday," the nurse was saying, "William is having difficulty separating fantasy from reality. He sees things that aren't there and forgets where he is. Even who we are."

Mrs. Dickerson started to cry again. She wiped her face with the back of her hand and sniffed. The mascara was now a broad band across each cheek. She looked like a football player.

The nurse whipped a tissue out of the Kleenex box by the bed and handed it to her. "I know this is hard for you to accept," she said. She sounded about as sympathetic as Ebenezer Scrooge. "But your father will be much happier on the psychiatric wing, where we can deal with his "condition." She made it sound like he was an unwed mother. "You need to convince him of that or have a judge give you power of attorney. It's for his own good."

Grey made some sort of choking sound. "He was fine last week," she said. She took William's hand. "Sharp as a tack, in fact. Then he got that flu bug. *I* think it's the cold medicine Dr. Aaron prescribed—William is allergic to it. Or maybe it's too strong, considering everything else he's taking."

CIRCLE OF WOLVES 61

Mrs. Dickerson looked over at Grey like she had the only life preserver on the boat, and the boat was rapidly taking on water. "What if Mrs. Milner is right?" she asked the nurse. "About the medication? What if Dad recovers? Will he get his apartment back?" She started sniffing again. "I wish Mother were still alive. She would know what to do." Another flood of tears opened a channel up in the mascara.

The nurse headed for the door. She obviously did not take kindly to a lay person making medical diagnoses.

"*I* certainly can't make that kind of determination. *I'm* not a doctor." She left this observation hanging in the air like a pair of soiled undershorts.

Grey wasn't having any. "It doesn't take a doctor to see that something is radically wrong with William," she said. "And it isn't senility." It also didn't take a genius to see that Grey's interest in William was more than just neighborly.

The nurse pulled open the door and stood by it, mentally tapping her foot. She stared at me with blue eyes so cold they could freeze Lake Michigan. *Guilt by association,* I thought, since I hadn't opened my mouth. Or maybe it was the dog.

"We should leave Mrs. Dickerson alone with her father now, don't you think?" she asked.

She looked first at me, then at Grey. But Grey continued to sit next to William, her hand holding his, her arm curled across his belly like an umbilical cord. And under the circumstances, he was probably lucky to have her, a sort of lifeline to reality. Obviously, his daughter was useless in that regard.

I smiled sympathetically at Grey. "Why don't you tag along with me and Lucky," I said. "I could use the company."

Grey hesitated a moment, then carefully disengaged her hand from William's. She stood up. "I'll be back, William. Later. I promise."

62   Karen Ann Wilson

William immediately drew his hands back up to his chest and resumed his bathrobe clutching.

Grey and I left the room, she pausing only long enough to frown at the nurse, and me to notice the woman's name tag. "Elaine Herfeld, RN, Director of Nursing." Herfeld had been the young LPN's name. Loni Herfeld. Were they mother and daughter?

"That woman has no compassion whatever," whispered Grey, as we walked down the hall toward the rec room. "It's like she's running a cell block at Starke."

I smiled at her description. "You said William was fine last week."

We went into the rec room. It was empty. Grey sat on the sofa. She looked tired, her recent bout with the flu still evident in the dark circles under her eyes. Either that or William's current condition was weighing her down.

"He was as lucid as I am," she said. "And I think I'm pretty sharp, all things considered." She shook her head. "It's no wonder he's confused. The medical profession seems to think we elderly are incapable of understanding English or making decisions for ourselves. Granted, there are those who suffer from legitimate memory loss, but that doesn't give Dr. Aaron and his staff the right to treat all of us like children."

She balled up a delicate fist, then released it. The blood in her veins, clearly visible through her papery skin, ebbed and flowed like a deep blue sea.

"They refuse to discuss our medical condition with us and get angry if we ask," she continued. "I don't know about you, Sam, but I like to know what I'm putting in my body."

I let Lucky go and sat down next to Grey. "I don't blame you," I said. "Not one bit."

Grey and I watched the puppy as she wandered over to

CIRCLE OF WOLVES 63

the table in the center of the room and began licking the floor.

"What medication is William taking?" I asked.

Grey shrugged. "Who knows? Blood pressure medicine, of course. I'm not sure what brand. And something for his arrhythmia. Oh, and Glucotrol for his diabetes. Then whatever Dr. Aaron gave me for the flu. William is taking that. The nurses bring it to you in those little paper cups. No bottles with labels. So who knows what it is." She gave a little mirthless chuckle. "With all those chemicals in our bodies, you'd expect us to last forever, wouldn't you? Where would the drug companies be without us old folks?"

"Surely Dr. Aaron would check for drug interactions. Wouldn't he?"

Grey looked down her nose at me. "You're assuming he bothered to read William's file."

A young woman in white, pushing an elderly gentleman in a wheelchair, entered the room. The woman parked her patient next to the table and left. Then a couple of the ambulatory patients I'd seen earlier joined the party, and my conversation with Grey was cut short. I looked at my watch. It was 1:50. In just over an hour, Ms. Smith would be there with her tea and cookies, and Lucky would have to leave. I smiled at the thought of her reaction if she knew Lucky had been polishing the floor with her tongue.

"I'm going back to William," said Grey, as I scooped Lucky up before she was run over by a wheelchair. "It would be wonderful if you could stop by my apartment sometime for a visit, Sam." She stood up and smoothed the wrinkles out of her pink knit dress.

"I'd like that," I said. "What's your phone number?"

She took an old grocery receipt and a pen out of her purse and jotted down the number. Then she handed me the receipt.

64   Karen Ann Wilson

"You would be welcome anytime," she said. "Except Friday. William and I play bridge Fridays at the senior center up the road." She paused. "At least, we used to . . ." Her voice trailed off.

"He'll be fine," I told her, although I wasn't so sure, myself. "Just as soon as he's over the flu."

"Not if his daughter gets him declared incompetent," she said bitterly, "and moves him to the psychiatric wing."

"William's daughter didn't look terribly competent herself."

"She's having trouble with her marriage," Grey said. "Her husband is abusive, according to William, and there are teenaged children, a boy and a girl. She isn't able to make decisions about her father's or her own care, which is why I fear for William. Dr. Aaron seems to think the cause of every elderly person's problems is mental, and the solution is the psychiatric wing. I'm surprised they have any beds left in there." Her pale cheeks began to darken.

The room was filling up, and Lucky was attracting a lot of attention. Several of the patients I had seen earlier in the hallway, their expressions bordering on vacuous, were now smiling and talking and pointing at the puppy. It was as if their brains, mothballed by society, had suddenly come out into the sunshine to air.

"Please give me a call, Sam," Grey said from the doorway. "Promise you will."

I folded the grocery receipt and put it in my purse. "I promise."

I spent about forty minutes in the rec room. Either the shock of seeing what age could do to a person had worn off, or the residents of the nursing floor had taken a dose of ginseng that morning, because I actually enjoyed myself. And, needless to say, Lucky was a hit.

I passed Mama Cass, aka Wilma Smith, and Loni in the

CIRCLE OF WOLVES 65

hallway on my way out. That day the cookies were Oreo impersonators. The teapot and the plastic cups were the same ones they'd had the week before, but Wilma's uniform was different. She was wearing a white, short-sleeved, polyester dress that was at least two sizes too small. It zipped up the front, fortunately, or the cleaning people would have been sweeping buttons up off the floor. Her arms, like the rest of her, were enormous, great wads of fat and skin hanging beneath them like Spanish moss. She gave Lucky a look that most people reserve for vagrants and panhandlers, then she and Loni continued on into the rec room. Loni looked over her shoulder and grinned.

At the nurse's station, Mrs. Dickerson, William's daughter, was talking to a very tall, attractive man in his fifties. He was wearing a stylish brown suit and one of those environmental ties like the Nature Company sells. It had lots of green and brown on it and several colorful tree frogs (poison dart frogs among them) staring out from the tie's center. The guy was handing Mrs. Dickerson his card, and curiosity got the better of me, so I stopped nearby and pretended to adjust Lucky's collar and leash.

"Please let me know," the man was saying, "if I can be of any assistance. The Baker Act was intended to protect elderly patients such as your father but, as we know, widespread abuse of the system has occurred, despite revisions to the law. I am here to help you deal with any unfair treatment Mr. Florin might be receiving."

William's daughter stared at the card, her hand shaking slightly. Then she looked over at the two women sitting at the nurse's station, presumably for some kind of guidance. But the nurses were eyeballing the man like he was a pedophile, which only served to increase Mrs. Dickerson's nervousness. Still holding the guy's card, she backed up and vigorously shook her head.

66 Karen Ann Wilson

"Thank you, no," she managed. "That won't be necessary. I already have a lawyer."

She dropped the card in the ash can by the elevator and ran over to the exit marked STAIRS. Unfortunately, she failed to see the ALARM-ACTIVATED DOOR sign posted on the wall. When she pulled the door open, bells started clanging. I expected her to faint dead away or, at least, fall to her knees in abject submission, but she didn't even hesitate. She ran into the stairwell and quickly disappeared down the steps.

The man wearing the poison dart frogs watched her go, then walked over to the ash can and nonchalantly retrieved his card. He looked my way, smiled, and ambled off in search of another victim.

CHAPTER 7

•

Monday, November 15

Cynthia was late. When she finally arrived at 8:30, she looked like she had been up half the night crying. Her eyes were bloodshot, the lids red and swollen, and no amount of Under Eye Smoother could disguise the dark circles that threatened to swallow up her cheekbones.

"Are you all right?" I asked, after she'd slammed a couple of desk drawers and knocked over the pet ID display.

Variously colored metal tags that read "My ticket home" and "My owner loves me," each with space for a phone number, jingled across the linoleum. Charlie hopped off Cynthia's desk and chased after a red one.

"Of course I'm all right," she snapped. "Just perfect, in fact."

She made a show of sitting down at the computer and calling up the day's appointment schedule. She was still wearing her raincoat.

I didn't say anything. I didn't know what to say. Cynthia's feelings are easily bruised. I had done the bruising myself on numerous occasions, unintentionally, of course. But she usually just sulks for a couple of hours, puckers up her mouth, arches her eyebrows as high above her eyes as possible, until she looks like she's had a face-lift, and avoids talking

67

68 Karen Ann Wilson

to whomever she is mad at. I had never seen her so upset that she cried, however.

Our last surgery of the morning—a Shih Tzu by the name of Mei Mei—pulled into the parking lot. Her owner got out, and Mei Mei jumped from the front seat into the man's arms.

"Mr. Rosenberg is here," I told Cynthia. When she didn't respond, I went over to her desk and flipped through the day's appointment files. The Rosenberg record was on the bottom. I pulled it out. "Get a grip, Cynthia," I said quietly. "Dr. Augustin is not the most sympathetic person in the world, even under the best of circumstances. You know that."

"Mac called me last night," Cynthia announced, matter-of-factly.

My mouth fell open. MacAlistair Caswell was Cynthia's ex. Their divorce had taken place a year before I started at Paradise Cay. According to Cynthia, it had been messy and entirely Mac's doing. His lawyer was one of the area's best. Hers wasn't. After nearly forty years doing volunteer work and keeping house, Cynthia had to go out and find a "real" job, as she put it. Which was tough, considering her secretarial skills were as outdated as the manual typewriter. Computers terrified her. So she went from a three-bedroom house with a pool to a one-bedroom apartment without even a birdbath.

My mouth was still hanging open when Mr. Rosenberg and his dog came through the door.

"I'm sorry we're late," the man said.

He put Mei Mei on the floor, and she shook. Well-groomed Shih Tzus look like multitiered champagne fountains. To say Mei Mei was well-groomed would be an understatement.

"But I had to drop my wife off at the doctor's office." He

CIRCLE OF WOLVES 69

looked a little embarrassed. "Rose and Mei Mei seem to be having some of the same problems."

The Rosenberg dog was a routine spay, more or less. She'd had ten litters of puppies, produced three grand champions, and endured two cases of pyometra. Dr. Augustin finally convinced the Rosenbergs that the next time the dog's uterus became infected, she might not make it, and waiting until she got sick again to spay her was hardly a wise move.

Cynthia stood up, took off her coat, and went into the closet behind her desk to hang it up. Then she smoothed out her skirt, fluffed her hair, and came back to her desk.

"Dr. Augustin is a little late himself, Mr. Rosenberg," she said, her voice calm, her mouth turned into a faint smile. "You don't need to apologize." She took Mei Mei's record from me and opened it. Without looking at either of us, she said, "I guess there are some things in life we just don't have any control over."

"He called to tell me Lynda is pregnant." Cynthia shut the file drawer and sat down at her desk. "He didn't need to do that, you know. I think he wanted to rub it in. I couldn't have children, so he found someone who could." She shook her head. "Honestly, the man is sixty-five years old. It's disgraceful. He'll be dead before that poor child graduates from high school."

"Maybe not," I said. "People are living longer these days. Eating better, you know." Then it occurred to me that Cynthia might not relish the idea that Mac could conceivably outlive her. "Of course, he smokes."

"You know what he told me?" Cynthia asked. "He told me he worries there won't be anyone to visit him in the nursing home. Now, isn't that a dandy reason to have children?"

Yeah, I thought, *just dandy.*

Dr. Augustin inserted the spay hook into Mei Mei's abdomen and pulled out her uterus. It was mildly enlarged and

70 Karen Ann Wilson

obviously thickened. She wasn't going to have any more puppies, anyway.

"Why do you want to know about Glucotrol?" he asked me.

I checked the color of Mei Mei's gums. They were nice and pink. "One of the patients on the nursing floor at Sunset View Towers is having some sort of psychological problems. He's confused and appears to be hallucinating, although I can't be certain about that. Before the symptoms started, he'd had the flu. I thought maybe the cold medicine was interacting with his heart or diabetes medication . . ."

I shut up, as Dr. Augustin's hands came to a halt directly above the uterus, like he was trying to levitate the organ right off the table, and he looked at me over his mask.

"How old is this guy?"

"I don't know. Eighty, maybe."

Dr. Augustin went back to work. "The man is probably in the early stages of dementia," he said. "The flu might have triggered an attack or made his condition more noticeable to those around him." He removed the uterus and ovaries and dropped them in the little red bucket hanging at the end of the table. "It's sad, I know, but unfortunately, there's nothing you can do about it."

"But it *could* be from a drug overdose or interaction, couldn't it?"

Dr. Augustin poked the remains of Mei Mei's reproductive system back into her abdomen. "I suppose." He looked at me again. "Why are you so concerned about this guy, Samantha? You're not supposed to get involved. You're just there to cheer them up."

"Because the man's friend—his girlfriend, I think—says he was perfectly normal last week. She told me he takes so much medication, it's not surprising he's confused. That all the doctors seem interested in, is keeping elderly people like

CIRCLE OF WOLVES

71

William alive. They don't care what sort of life old people have as long as they *have* one."

I turned the anesthesia machine down a notch and went over to the sink. "You, at least, seem to care about the happiness of your patients. About their quality of life." I was becoming maudlin, and I knew it.

"Give it a rest, Samantha," said Dr. Augustin. "Or else quit going to that nursing home. I've got enough problems these days without you getting involved in geriatric management philosophy."

I looked over my shoulder at him and frowned. *If it was your friend in trouble,* I thought, *you'd get involved and expect me to be right there with you. Better yet, if it was some corrupt public official doing the hurting, you'd have the whole clinic helping you put the guy away.*

Dr. Augustin snipped off the ends of a knot. "Why are you so interested in senior citizens all of a sudden?" he asked without looking up. "You used to bitch about them right along with the rest of us. Particularly when that old guy ran into your car in the Publix parking lot." He paused. "It wouldn't have anything to do with your upcoming marriage would it? I mean, Mr. Halsey does qualify for Silver Service Checking down at Union Bank."

I rattled around the dirty instruments in the sink. Then I went over to the anesthesia machine, turned off the gas, adjusted Mei Mei's IV, and scowled at Dr. Augustin.

"You have to be fifty-five," I said, "and Michael is not fifty-five. And anyway, my wedding plans are my business." I took a deep breath. "Not yours."

Dr. Augustin stripped off his gloves and pulled down his mask. He looked at me with his coal black eyes and, for the first time in over a week, smiled.

CHAPTER 8

•

Wednesday, November 17

My morning run with Jeffrey was cut short by an angry cloud that pelted us with a few BB-sized hailstones, just to get our attention, then turned the faucet on full throttle. By the time we'd gotten back to our apartment building, we were drenched. But we were alive.

There are more lightning strikes in Florida than in any other state, and I have seen pine trees that were split down the middle, their charred half trunks looking like giant arms beseeching the heavens for mercy. I was out in a boat once with friends when a channel marker was struck not thirty feet away. The hair on my arms stood up, and I could smell the ozone. Some deep-seated and ancient instinct makes you want to hide under the bed. It seems to work for dogs and cats.

I dripped my way across the carpet to the bathroom, pausing long enough to switch on the TV. I wanted to catch the weather, to see if that cloud meant another cold front was moving our way. In just over a week, while Cynthia was decking the halls at the clinic, I would be dreaming of a white Christmas. My life in Connecticut may have been fraught with problems, but snow wasn't one of them. Which is why I always take my annual vacation in December and visit my mother for two weeks. I can deal with the ever-pre-

CIRCLE OF WOLVES 73

sent (and often painful) reminders of my childhood, as long as I can watch snow fall and listen to the crackle of real wood logs in the fireplace.

I was in the bedroom toweling myself off when I heard a faintly familiar voice. I hurried into the living room. The man I had seen Sunday talking to William's daughter was smiling at me from the television screen. His tie was another woodsy number. This one appeared to have large parrots on it. He was saying something about the rights of nursing home residents in a voice so soft and soothing it reminded me of a cat purring.

"Is someone you love receiving less than adequate nursing care? Have you tried to work within the system to improve that care but without success? Has a loved one been confined to a mental facility unnecessarily?"

He walked gracefully and with obvious rehearsed precision over to an enormous, highly polished mahogany desk and sat down on the edge. It had one of those little green lamps you see in libraries (and on rich lawyers' desks) and several law books arranged so the television audience could see their titles.

"We can help," he continued. "Just call the number you see on your screen and a qualified representative will assist you." He smiled again and picked up a file folder, like he was right in the middle of helping someone and just took a few minutes out to chat with us. "Operators are available twenty-four hours a day."

He stood up. "Don't let your spouse or parent suffer unnecessarily. Let us give you the peace of mind you deserve."

The man's name, printed in large letters beneath a 1-800 number, was Tyler Brock, Attorney at Law. "Specializing in the rights of nursing home residents." There wasn't any firm name given, and I wondered if the "we" he kept referring to was, in fact, Mr. Tyler Brock and an answering machine.

74 Karen Ann Wilson

I remembered the way Mrs. Dickerson had looked at him and the way he had dug his card out of the ash can. He was, by his very presence on the nursing floor (unsolicited and clearly unwanted), an ambulance chaser. But his physical appearance, his attire, and the way he spoke made him seem more respectable than that.

I thought about William and Grey and the sumo wrestler with the ponytail. Could it be that William actually needed Tyler Brock, Esq.? How about the man in the nightshirt on the psychiatric wing? Who was looking after his welfare? Some relative a thousand miles away?

After the weather forecast, I took a shower and ate a bowl of cereal and silently wondered why I was so depressed. It would be easy to blame my mood on Dr. Augustin. The atmosphere at Paradise Cay Animal Hospital was nothing if not combustible. But I had survived more than one storm there without feeling like the end of the world was imminent. So, I thought, it must be that nursing floor—all those miserable people waiting to die. Like Grey, I would rather be shot dead than end up in a place like that.

"Okay," I said aloud, "I can quit going, which would make Dr. Augustin happy, I'm sure, since it was Michael's idea, or I can concentrate on cheering those old people up. And maybe feel better about myself in the process."

Priss rubbed against my leg. "Right?" I asked her. But Priss was more interested in milk than in moral support. So I put my bowl on the floor and went into the bedroom. I hunted around in my purse for the grocery receipt Grey had given me, finally found it, and dialed her number. She picked up on the second ring.

"Grey," I said, "it's Samantha Holt." Silence. "Sam, for short."

"Oh, yes, Sam. How are you?"

"Just fine. I thought I'd take you up on your offer of a

CIRCLE OF WOLVES 75

visit. How about this afternoon? Say, four?" Then I remembered William and added, "You don't have any plans, do you?"

"No, a visit would be lovely, Sam. I'll tell the guard you're coming."

The man with the loose dentures was off that day, or maybe he really had died. In his place was a middle-aged, slightly overweight gentleman with his own teeth (as far as I could tell) and a pleasant smile. When I drove up, he was eating a hamburger all the way, lettuce and tomato wet with mayonnaise and ketchup hanging out of the bun, and quickly put it down on his little desk and grabbed a napkin. He had a small spot of ketchup in the middle of his nice white uniform shirt.

"Sorry," He said, wiping mayo from the corners of his mouth. "Late lunch." He picked up his clipboard.

I told him my name and destination, and he gave me directions to Grey's building.

As I pulled away, I glanced in my rearview mirror. The man was dabbing at the ketchup with his napkin, smearing it out until it looked like a gunshot wound to the chest. I shuddered and lurched over the speed bump.

Gretchen Milner lived on the tenth floor, according to the guard, apartment 1015. I parked in one of the visitor spaces, walked into the lobby, and headed for the elevator.

The walls of the ground floor were tinted glass. Huge terra-cotta planters containing rubber trees and parlor palms and dumbcane stood guard in the corners, while patio furniture filled the spaces in between. Here and there, baskets of immaculately kept fern hung from the ceiling. The temperature was a humid eighty degrees or so. I could almost hear the plants photosynthesizing, breathing in the carbon diox-

76   **Karen Ann Wilson**

ide, exhaling the oxygen. And then I realized they were artificial—expensive plastic and silk replicas, realistic down to the identical dead fronds near the base of each palm. That was what had given them away. I was disappointed. Even Disney used live plants for their topiary animals.

The floor was off-white marble. Clean as a whistle, despite the rain puddles and associated mud outside. Either no one had visited Grey's building that day, or a little maintenance man with a mop would instantly appear to scrub up the footprints, should anyone be so uncouth as to leave them. I considered going back outside and purposely sloshing through the standing water in the parking lot just to test my theory, but didn't have the energy. Or the nerve.

The tenth floor hallway was carpeted a rich burgundy. The walls were pale rose. I found Grey's apartment easily and rang the bell. A dog barked down the hall somewhere, a muted, high-pitched ankle-nipper voice calling out a warning from behind a well-insulated door. The kind of dog burglars fear, not because they do any real physical harm, but because they can be heard for miles. Like an air raid siren. And I heard a dead bolt thrown somewhere behind me and the creak of a door opening. When I turned around, the door slammed shut.

I rang Grey's doorbell again. The door had a peephole in it, and I knew she was probably peering at me, so I smiled stupidly at it. I felt like I had the time my best friend, Jane, and I had gone into the little self-serve photo booth at the mall. At least this time I didn't cross my eyes or stick out my tongue.

The door opened.

"Hello, Sam," said Grey. "Please come in."

She was wearing a beautiful teal velour hostess gown and matching sandals. A hint of lavender drifted my way. She'd had her hair done recently, probably that morning.

CIRCLE OF WOLVES

The foyer was light parquet with grass cloth-covered walls. We went into the living room, which was huge, with high ceilings and lots of light. There the parquet was covered in the center with a thick lemon and green dhurrie rug. The contemporary sofa and matching armchairs were white with green piping. She had several throw pillows tossed just so across the length of the sofa—lemon, green, and one with the face of a cat done in needlepoint. The cat was black with yellow eyes crafted from silk or satin thread that seemed to glow as if struck by a car's headlights. It was weird. The animal's gaze followed you around.

The walls, three of them anyway, were stark white, like the fabric of the sofa, and covered with pictures: pastels and watercolors, a few oils. Scenics, mostly. They had all been done by the same hand. Waves rolling across a beach at sunset (or sunrise, depending on the artist's perspective), an English garden, a clearing in the forest. Incredibly peaceful places, but very much alive.

"Wait until you see the view," Grey said. She pulled open a set of very sheer floor-to-ceiling drapes. Behind the drapes was a four-section sliding glass door that opened onto a narrow balcony.

The heavily overcast sky, reflected in a rolling, gunmetal grey Gulf was cold and brooding. I tried to picture it on a sunny day, the sky blue and the Gulf dotted with tiny, colorful sailboats.

"You were right," I said. "It's quite the view."

Grey pointed to the sofa. "Please sit down, Sam. I've fixed us some cocoa. Dreary days like this were made for hot cocoa, don't you think?" She smiled, then walked across the living room, through a large dining area, and into what I assumed was the kitchen.

I went back to the paintings, preferring their warm tranquillity to the turbulence outside. I scanned a few of the larger pieces. Tucked into the lower left corner of each one were the initials GEL. Gretchen? I asked myself. Her last name is Milner, but she could have used her maiden name when she did them. They certainly looked like the kind of work I'd expect Grey to produce: softly feminine but energetic. Definitely optimistic.

"Do you like them?"

I turned around. Grey was holding two ceramic mugs. She handed me one. A large, fluffy, white pillow floated on the top of the cocoa, and the aroma of rich chocolate and toasted marshmallows conjured up an image of Girl Scout campfires. I looked back at the forest glen.

"I love them," I said. "I can almost imagine myself sitting on the grass in this patch of sun. Who painted them? They look like you, something you'd do."

Grey's eyes traveled slowly over the paintings. She grinned and poked at her marshmallow with an index finger. Then she licked it, the way a child would.

"Yes," she said. "I was an art major in college. A million years ago."

"You don't look like a dinosaur," I laughed.

Grey pointed, once again, to the sofa, and we made our way over to it and sat down at opposite ends. She picked up the cat pillow.

"My daughter-in-law made this for me," she said. Then she turned her head toward the hall. "Riley! Stop being such a snob and come in here."

We waited, and a few seconds later, the pillow's inspiration poked his head around the corner.

"Come on, Riley, honey." Grey patted the arm of the sofa.

The cat was slender, with glossy black hair and enormous brass eyes set in a round face. It moved slowly around the corner of the wall, undulating toward us like a snake, its eyes glowing, never leaving my face.

CIRCLE OF WOLVES   79

"Riley isn't shy," said Grey. "He just likes to make a grand entrance. In keeping with his pedigree, I imagine." She patted the sofa again.

"He's a Bombay, isn't he?"

Grey nodded. "Milner's Life of Riley. My husband's cat."

It was the first time she had mentioned her husband, and I waited for her to elaborate on their life together, but she didn't.

"When Gerald died four years ago, Riley almost joined him. He isn't a good eater to begin with, and I had to feed him smelly gourmet cat food just to keep weight on him."

Riley must have decided I was worthy of his attention, because he gave up the wall and walked across the area rug to the sofa. He hesitated briefly, then vaulted onto the sofa arm, where he resumed his undulations, this time against Grey's shoulder. I wanted to pet him—Bombays have such wonderfully soft hair—but decided to let curiosity drive him my way.

"How is William doing?" I asked.

Grey put her mug on the coffee table, then picked Riley up and settled him into her lap. He began to knead her gown. His claws were obviously intact, because Grey had to disengage one from the velour fabric.

"Much improved, I'm happy to report. I just wish they would let him go back to his apartment."

"Well," I said, "at least now his daughter won't have him moved into the psychiatric wing."

Grey looked at me, her brows knitted together over her nose. "That psychiatric wing is like a great cancer, growing and swelling, sucking up everyone who gets too close."

"What do you mean by that?"

"I've lived here ten years, Sam. When they added that wing two years ago, friends of mine and friends of friends were suddenly found to be incompetent. Their families—at

Karen Ann Wilson

Dr. Aaron's insistence, I am certain—had them moved to the new facility. I never see them anymore. Several have died, I am told. If I do run across them on the nursing floor, they act like they don't know me. Perfectly healthy people, Sam, who just got old. They don't deserve to be locked up like prisoners."

I watched Grey stroke the cat, her blue eyes focused on the rain clouds outside.

"Maybe it was for their own good," I said softly. "You read about Alzheimer's patients leaving their homes and turning up drowned in a lake or dead from exposure. One old man last year drove his wife all the way to Georgia because he forgot where the grocery store was."

Grey shook her head. "You sound just like Dr. Aaron. The people I'm talking about weren't crazy or demented. I've known women your age who were more forgetful than Tade White. She went to the nursing floor with a broken ankle, and a week later, she was on the psychiatric wing. I haven't seen her since."

"Surely the children of these people would object to having their parents treated improperly."

"You'd be surprised," said Grey. "Look at William's daughter. She would just as soon not have the burden of dealing with her father's problems. And a lot of the people I'm talking about don't have any relatives, at least not close ones."

Riley evidently had picked up Gretchen's sudden change of mood, because he jumped off her lap and headed my way.

"Besides," Grey continued, "how do you explain all the dead animals?"

"Excuse me?" I managed through my marshmallow. I put the mug on the coffee table and quickly swallowed.

"Two cats and a dog that I know of. The dog died the same day his owner did. Robert Penlaw. One of William's

CIRCLE OF WOLVES 81

friends. He suffered a minor stroke last year but recovered. He'd been out of the hospital six months. They found him and his dog dead on the bathroom floor."

I reached over and let Riley sniff my fingers.

"One of the cats fell off the balcony," Grey said. "A neighbor down the hall said she found her sliding glass door open when she got home from the grocery store. She knew she'd closed it, because we were expecting rain, and her carpeting was new. Now the woman is on the psychiatric wing, and her apartment is for rent." Grey brushed cat hair from her robe. "In any case, cats don't usually jump off balconies, do they? Not voluntarily."

"You're saying someone broke into her apartment and threw her cat out the window?" I asked, my voice clearly doubtful. "Isn't it possible your friend really *did* forget to close it?"

"Yes," she said. "And no."

"Have you told anyone else?" I asked. "I mean your concerns about the disappearance of your friends and the dead pets?"

"No. Just William. Now you. I didn't want to look like a crazy old woman and end up on the psychiatric wing, myself, although my children would never let that happen, I can assure you. It's just that William's little problem scared me."

She fingered the sleeve of her gown. When she looked at me, I could see tears in her eyes.

"William is more than a friend, Sam. I've . . . I've grown quite fond of him. And him of me."

"I'll talk to my boss about this," I said. "He's pretty good at puzzle-solving."

I wasn't altogether convinced that Grey's suspicions were justified. The fact that she wasn't in any way senile did not mean her friends and neighbors weren't a bit addled, even suicidal. The woman with the cat did end up on the psychi-

82 Karen Ann Wilson

atric wing. Maybe she only thought she'd closed the sliding glass door. Still, I had never heard of a single cat voluntarily flinging itself off a balcony like a lemming off a cliff. Grey had something there.

"I only tell you this," Grey said, "because I have no one else to confide in, save William. My daughter and Kimberly are busy with their law practices, and my son is running for a seat on the state legislature, so he doesn't have a moment of free time these days." She picked up her mug, looked at the now-cold cocoa, and put it back on the table.

"Let's talk about you, Sam," she said, brightly.

Her quick smile did not hide the fear she obviously felt watching her friends fall all around her like comrades on a battlefield. But she was clearly determined to carry on.

"Where do you work and what led you to choose veterinary medicine as a career?"

I smiled broadly. What a terrific lady. Not a single mention of who I was dating and why wasn't I married yet?

I left Grey's apartment at 5:30 with the promise that I would come back soon. Even Riley looked like he wanted me to stay. Before leaving, I gave Grey my business card and told her to call any time, even if she just wanted to chat.

At the elevator, I joined a little old man dressed in a suit and tie, his white hair neatly combed and plastered down with gooey hair dressing. He smelled like he'd taken a bath in British Sterling. He glanced up at me and smiled, but didn't say anything. We got on the elevator, and I punched 1, figuring that's where he was going, but he leaned over and hit 2.

The elevator stopped several times after that and, each time, two or three people got on. They were all over the age of seventy, as far as I could tell, and a couple of them had walkers, which took up a lot of room, not to mention time. I

CIRCLE OF WOLVES 83

had to hold the doors open for quite awhile as each semi-ambulatory resident shuffled onto the elevator.

They were all dressed in their Sunday best. Most of the women wore lots of jewelry and false eyelashes and face powder the color of old flour. Their clothes smelled like mothballs and cat pee. One woman wore a fox stole. I couldn't take my eyes off the poor creature's wizened face, its little jaws clamped securely around its tail, as if in a perpetual game of tag with itself.

By the time we reached the second floor, the car was full. I was three inches taller than the next tallest person, a man, and felt like a giant. The One-a-Day vitamin company could have used me in an ad. I also felt like an intruder, because only one person had the courtesy to say hello to me. Of course, not too many of them spoke at all.

The doors opened, and I stuck out my hand to keep them open, then stood to one side as the little flock began to disembark. I could hear the clatter of china and silverware well before I caught a glimpse of the twenty-odd tables arranged around the dining room. An odor of chicken and boiled potatoes, not terribly appetizing, assailed my nostrils, overpowering even the British Sterling and Tabu that had filled the elevator car.

The last diner, a woman with osteoporosis so severe she looked like she belonged in a bell tower, crept past me, her hand reaching out for support on the edge of the elevator. I took her hand and helped her over the narrow gap between floor and car. She smiled.

"You're a dear," she said. "I don't know why I come here to eat. The food is terrible. And all these old people talk about is what's ailing them." She let go of my hand. "Oh well, beats eating alone, I suppose."

The woman shuffled off. I noticed that she wasn't wearing any jewelry and only minimal makeup. Despite the hump, she walked with an air of authority, and I wondered who she was.

I let go of the elevator door. As it began to close, I saw Wilma Smith and a younger but no less rotund woman pushing two food carts across the room. They were laden with several dozen parfait glasses filled with some sort of pasty white custard that resembled phlegm. I grimaced and quickly punched 1.

CHAPTER 9

•

Thursday, November 18

Dr. Augustin's mood had leveled off. He wasn't wagging his tail, but he wasn't baring his teeth either.

"I assume you're going home for Christmas," he said, pulling on a glove.

I ran a Betadine-soaked sponge over the Labrador's belly. "Yes. Hopefully, I'll get in some skiing." I tossed the sponge in the garbage.

"Don't break anything. I can't afford to have you laid up while I'm fighting this Cronin asshole. Tracey won't do double duty forever."

"Cronin?"

He arranged a sterile drape over the dog's abdomen and secured it with a couple of towel clamps. "Kelsey Cronin, president and CEO of Monarch Development Corporation. Personally, I think the guy is suing me to cover his own debts, not those of Monarch. According to Matt, Cronin's ex-wife got the house, the boat, their golf condo, and the kids. Now she wants to send the eldest boy to some fancy prep school."

"How can he benefit from Monarch's suit against you?" I asked.

Dr. Augustin finished his incision and reached for the spay hook. "He's a major stockholder. Monarch loses, he

86   Karen Ann Wilson

loses. Monarch wins, he wins. Besides, as president and
CEO, I'm confident Cronin has more than peripheral control
of Monarch's purse strings."

I checked the dog's reflexes and adjusted the gas flow,
then went over to the sink. It had been a busy morning. Two
neuters, a spay/declaw, and now the Labrador. There were a
ton of dirty instruments to wash and sterilize. We had less
than thirty minutes before our first morning appointment arrived.

"You remember that old guy I told you about?" I asked,
my back to Dr. Augustin. "The one with the flu who I
thought was hallucinating?"

I heard Dr. Augustin grunt, then fling an instrument onto
the stainless steel table.

I continued, undaunted. Some people go out of their way
to avoid conflict. Not me, evidently. "Well, he's better, according to my friend, Gretchen. So it must have been a drug
interaction. Or a case of over-medicating."

Another grunt.

"However, now she tells me William isn't the only one to
start acting a little odd there at Sunset View Towers. She
says several otherwise normal friends of hers either died or
got stuck on the psychiatric wing for no apparent reason."

Dr. Augustin didn't say anything for several minutes. I
finished cleaning the instruments and dried my hands. Then
I went around to check on the dog. "And . . ." I said, ". . . a
bunch of pets has mysteriously died there, too." Three was
a bunch, wasn't it?

That got him. He looked up. "Define 'mysteriously,' " he
said.

"A dog was found dead in the bathroom with his owner,
who was also dead. And a cat apparently fell off its owner's
balcony."

"That's a 'bunch,' all right," he said.

CIRCLE OF WOLVES   87

He picked up a gauze sponge, wiped around the row of neat little knots, then tossed it toward the garbage. It landed on the floor with half a dozen other, equally misdirected sponges. It is fortunate Dr. Augustin's ability with a scalpel is better than his aim.

"I was just giving you a couple of examples," I snapped.

He stripped off his gloves and pulled his mask down. "Listen, Samantha," he said, "I'm sorry about your friend's friend, or whatever. And it is possible someone over there doesn't like animals and is bumping them off. Maybe a few of the neighbors are feuding. I wish I had the time to help you check it out, but I don't." He took off his gown and threw it across the instrument tray. Then he went over to the sink. "If I lose this suit, I could conceivably lose the clinic. As it is, I've had to dip pretty deep into my savings to pay Matt."

"I thought you were his friend."

Suddenly, Cynthia's voice crackled over the intercom. "Your ten o'clock is here," she said.

Dr. Augustin finished washing up and walked over to the Labrador, who was just beginning to chew on her endotracheal tube.

"We'll be up shortly," I told the speaker on the wall. I turned back around. "Doesn't he give you a break?"

"Matt? Of course he does. But he has to pay that private investigator of his, and the guy isn't cheap. If I could, I'd do the digging myself. But Matt assures me it's better if I don't get caught poking around. And, as I'm sure you're aware, it's driving me nuts."

We transferred the dog to a pad on the floor. I took out her endotracheal tube.

"What are you getting for your money?" I asked.

Dr. Augustin pulled on his exam jacket and zipped it up. "Not a hell of a lot. What I need is to find out if Monarch

88 Karen Ann Wilson

Development paid off a city inspector. Or violated some building code and then covered it up. Particularly if some elderly resident got hurt because of it, no matter how cold that might seem."

I whirled around. "Wouldn't it be great if someone found a rare and endangered plant on that Crossroads site?"

He shook his head. "No. What would be great would be to find that Kelsey Cronin had sprayed it with Roundup."

Our first client of the morning was Ken Williston, a man about my age or a little older, with a yellow Labrador mix puppy named Sunny. Ken was single, fairly cute (very tall), and had shown more than a passing interest in me, although he'd never asked me out. I wouldn't have gone if he had. Of course, Dr. Augustin didn't know this and, following Ken's three previous visits to get his dog vaccinated and spayed, my boss had made numerous unwarranted cracks about him. His aftershave smelled like the inside of a whorehouse (how Dr. Augustin knew this wasn't clear), only sissies wore Birkenstocks (Dr. Augustin owns a pair of Tevas, which, with regard to style, amounts to the same thing), and Williston obviously knew nothing about canine behavior when he asked us why Sunny chewed up all his Rainbird sprinkler heads. Obviously I knew nothing about canine behavior, either, because I couldn't explain it. And, judging from Dr. Augustin's explanation, he was equally clueless.

That day Sunny was at the clinic because her left ear flap looked like a small water balloon.

"I noticed it late last night," Ken said, as Dr. Augustin carefully examined the dog's ear, "and called first thing this morning. I'm sure it wasn't there when I got home from work. In fact, I'd swear it wasn't."

Sunny was her usual chipper self, panting happily and licking everything (and everybody) in sight. The ear flap,

CIRCLE OF WOLVES 89

engorged with blood, stuck out from her head like the proverbial cauliflower.

"It's what we call an ear hematoma," said Dr. Augustin, pleasantly. "They're frequently caused by aggressive head shaking or when a dog digs at its ears because they itch."

He went on to describe the surgical procedure needed to repair the ear flap. I scratched Sunny's back. Her right rear leg started to kick out into the air, and I felt her claws on my arm. The dog reeked of flea dip.

"If she keeps scratching, won't this happen again?" asked Ken. "Maybe to the other ear? I bathe her at least once a week and dip her for fleas, but she still scratches."

Dr. Augustin ran his hand backward along her spine, checking her skin for redness or flaking. There didn't appear to be any. Or any fleas, although it would take a miracle for any to survive the chemical warfare Mr. Williston was obviously waging. The dog's convulsive scratching increased. Then Dr. Augustin checked her belly, which was slightly pink, more from too much bathing and dipping than from fleas, I figured. Otherwise, it looked pretty normal.

Dr. Augustin had just begun his dissertation on the causes and treatment of itchy skin, when a loud crash in the reception room, followed by Cynthia's voice over the intercom asking for Frank's help, caused me to release my hold on Sunny. The dog jumped down and immediately started digging at her ear.

"Go see what the problem is up there," Dr. Augustin told me, grabbing Sunny's collar. He hoisted the dog back onto the table, while Ken stood by looking rather inadequate.

I ran up front and was greeted by a flood of magazines and splintered pieces of the magazine rack, underneath which a six-month-old golden retriever puppy lay, panting and wagging her tail excitedly, as if she'd been given free

90   Karen Ann Wilson

rein of the local landfill. The dog's owner was busy wiping spilled coffee off her pale cream skirt.

"Mrs. Wallace came in to see if we could recommend a good dog obedience class for her puppy," said Cynthia, grinning.

The woman looked up at me and frowned. "You wouldn't know of one that offers express service, would you? Better yet, how about a nice boarding school. At this point, money is no object." I started to ask her what she had done with her human children when they were in their terrible twos but thought better of it.

By the time I was through collecting up the magazines and disposing of the magazine rack (and giving Mrs. Wallace the number for Responsible Pet Ownership, Inc.), Ken Williston had left. I met Dr. Augustin on his way back from the kennel.

"Ken Williston is an okay guy," he said, his hand on the door to Room 2. "What is he, about your age?" He winked. "Nice looking, don't you think?"

I stared at him. I couldn't have been more shocked had he just informed me his mother was an alien.

"I didn't think you liked him," I said.

"Hey, I was wrong, okay?" He opened the door. "Well, shall we?"

All I could do was nod and follow along behind him.

Larry Wilson phoned at 10:45 to say he'd been up all night with a full moon, his way of telling us the emergency clinic had really been hopping. Ask any cop or emergency services employee, and they'll tell you things get a little crazy when the moon is full. I don't think there is any scientific data to back this up, but two years of watching Dr. Augustin in action has made a believer out of me.

"Don't worry about it, Larry," Dr. Augustin told him.

CIRCLE OF WOLVES 91

"I'm not going anywhere, anyway. See you tomorrow." He hung up the hall extension.

Terrific, I thought morosely. With only three appointments scheduled for the afternoon, Dr. Augustin will have plenty of time to bitch and moan.

I glanced at Tracey, who was doing a heartworm test. All she did was shrug. Of course, she didn't have to deal with him directly. Just wait until Christmas, I thought wickedly, pulling the aspirin bottle down off the pharmacy shelf.

At one o'clock, Michael called. I was eating an apple at Cynthia's desk. Everyone else was out to lunch.

"How about dinner tomorrow?" he asked. "I'll pick you up at seven-thirty."

"Okay," I said. I twirled his engagement ring around on my finger. It already needed cleaning. "Michael, are you familiar with the Baker Act?"

"Somewhat. Why do you ask?" Then he laughed. "Are you and Cynthia trying to have Dr. Augustin committed?"

I watched a shiny new black Lexus drive up and park in front of the clinic. Its windows were heavily tinted. I thought about ducking under Cynthia's desk, just in case Dr. Augustin was mixed up in some Sicilian-style family squabble.

"Samantha?"

"I'm still here, Michael," I said, as Matthew Kemp got out of the Lexus.

He'd obviously moved up in the world, since his previous car had been a Mercury Grand Marquis. White. I hoped it wasn't Dr. Augustin's money that had paid for the Lexus.

"Somebody just drove up," I told Michael. "I have to go now. See you tomorrow. Oh, how should I dress?"

"We're going to the Wine Cellar," he said. "Whatever strikes your fancy."

92   **Karen Ann Wilson**

I told him good-bye and hung up. Then I pitched my half-eaten apple in the trash can under Cynthia's desk, as Matt walked through the door.

Mohammed had obviously come to the mountain. I glanced at my watch. It was 1:10. Dr. Augustin wasn't due back for at least forty-five minutes, possibly longer, since we had no two o'clock appointment scheduled. I knew the lawyer code of ethics was a lot like the medical one, with lawyer-client conversations and so forth privileged. But there didn't seem to be any harm in trying.

"Afternoon, Mr. Kemp," I said. I stuck out my chest and tossed my hair around. I am not averse to using a little of what God gave me to obtain information. I did not bat my eyelashes, however. A girl has to draw the line somewhere. Besides, they are almost white and so thin, he wouldn't have noticed anyway.

"Greetings, Samantha," he said. He came over to the desk and leaned against it.

Mathew Kemp, aged forty-five, is short, stocky, and nearly bald. What hair he does have is arranged in a bushy, prematurely grey wreath around his head. Except for the expensive clothes he wears, Matt could pass for a monk. His cheeks are rosy, and he has developed a rather pronounced paunch. Too many client dinners, I would imagine.

"Is Lou in?"

I shook my head. "He stepped out for a sandwich, but I expect him back any minute. Why don't you have a seat. You can keep me company. It gets pretty slow at lunchtime." I was smiling so broadly, my face hurt.

"I'd be happy to keep you company, Samantha," he said. "For a few minutes, at least." He put his briefcase on the floor next to Cynthia's desk, unbuttoned his jacket, and sat down in a nearby chair.

"What's up?" I asked. "We haven't had the pleasure of

CIRCLE OF WOLVES 93

your company for months. Must be that Crossroads thing. Poor Dr. Augustin is a wreck." *And his staff isn't much better,* I thought.

Matt crossed a leg at the ankle. "Yes. The infamous Crossroads. I came by to fill Lou in on a few things my people are looking into on his behalf." He pulled on an earlobe, and I thought briefly about Sunny.

"Dr. Augustin told me you have a real private investigator working for you," I said, wide-eyed. My airhead routine was making me a little dizzy.

Matt smiled. "*Real* private investigators spend most of their time sitting in cars eating fast food and drinking coffee, I'm afraid," he said. "And I've never met a single one who carried a handgun. Not routinely, anyway. It's disappointing, I know." He uncrossed his leg, leaned over, and picked up his briefcase.

"I've got to be in court in forty minutes," he said. "I'm going to leave something for Lou. Tell him I'm sorry I missed him and I'll call him at home tonight."

He opened the briefcase and withdrew a manila envelope. Then he took a pen out of his jacket, scratched through the name already typed on the front of the envelope, and scribbled Dr. Augustin's name under it. He put the pen away, closed the briefcase, and stood up. He slid the envelope across the desk.

"You'll see that he gets this, won't you, Samantha?"

"You bet," I said, admiring the envelope like it was a slice of chocolate Kahlua cheesecake. I could feel my conscience gearing itself up for a fight.

Matt nodded. "It was nice to see you, again, Samantha. Oh, and congratulations on your engagement."

"Thanks," I said, surprised that he knew. Dr. Augustin must have mentioned it to him. But why would he?

Matt said good-bye and left. I kept one eye on the Lexus

94 Karen Ann Wilson

and one eye on the manila envelope. After the car rounded the corner, I picked up the envelope. It was taped closed, but the tape wasn't stuck down very well. I could pull it up without tearing the envelope.

I looked at the writing on the front. The original addressee was Matthew Kemp, Attorney at Law. The return address was a suite in the Union Bank building downtown. "Murphy and Walls, Private Investigations."

I glanced out at the empty parking lot, then over at Dr. Augustin's office. The door was closed. I got up and opened it. If Dr. Augustin came in the side entrance, at least I would be able to hear him in time to hide the evidence.

I sat down again, drew in a deep breath and let it out all at once, then peeled the tape loose. It stuck a little on one corner, ripping a tiny bit of envelope, but I didn't think Dr. Augustin would notice. Matt's secretary had used a letter opener to open the thing originally and who knows, maybe she'd gotten sloppy. And anyway, if Dr. Augustin did notice, I could always say Charlie had been up on his desk again and had chewed on it.

The envelope contained a single sheet of paper. It was a letter to Matt from Richard Walls on Murphy and Walls letterhead. Four paragraphs neatly typed. The subject was "Keith Stone, President, Quetzal Bay Properties, a subsidiary of Monarch Development Corporation."

According to Mr. Walls, Keith Stone managed several of Monarch's properties and, like Cronin, was a big Monarch Development shareholder. He was also a less than honest fellow, having been implicated in a couple of shady business transactions involving Quetzal Bay money. Apparently, Mr. Stone needed some extra cash for a few personal investments and helped himself to Quetzal Bay's bank account. He was lucky. The investments did well, and he paid Quetzal Bay back in short order. But someone in Monarch De-

CIRCLE OF WOLVES 95

velopment found out, and Mr. Stone got his hand smacked. He didn't get fired, however. Mr. Walls surmised that the mucka-mucks in charge of Monarch Development (like Cronin maybe?) probably considered Stone's financial cunning too much of an asset. Sort of like having a really good pickpocket working for you. Useful, as long as it isn't your pocket that gets picked.

I was halfway through the closing paragraph, in which Mr. Walls was suggesting an investigation of Quetzal Bay's various accounts, when the phone rang. I jumped, nearly falling off of Cynthia's computer chair, and sent papers sailing across the floor, among them the empty manila envelope. I reached for the phone, then bent over to retrieve the envelope. The exposed tape had come in contact with one of Cynthia's pink memo slips and was stuck tight.

"Hello?" I said, clearly irritated. "Paradise Cay Animal Hospital. How may I help you?"

"Sam? It's Gretchen."

Her voice stopped me dead. The cheerful optimism was gone. And the little girl who had licked cocoa from her finger Wednesday was gone as well, replaced by a sad, tired old woman.

"Sam," she continued, "William had a heart attack. He's dead."

CHAPTER 10

•

Friday, November 19

The Wine Cellar is a study in contrasts. It is located on a slender strip of sun-drenched land between the Gulf of Mexico and the intracoastal waterway, close enough to the water in fact, that the smell of suntan lotion and the sound of outboards greets patrons as they climb out of their cars.

The interior of the Wine Cellar, however, is cramped and, for the most part, dark. Although cellars in Florida are as rare as those elusive hen's teeth, the main hallway rambles and dips downward as you go, giving the impression of being underground. It is noisy and crowded, but the food is wonderful, an interesting blend of Old and New Worlds, with exquisite sauces and lots of fresh vegetables. The waiters are experienced and do not hover, which pleases Michael, of course, as do the prices, which are quite reasonable.

After the owner, himself, had escorted us to our table, saying how nice it was to see Mr. Halsey again, and our waiter had taken the drink order, I opened my menu. Michael, who never seems to need one, watched me, his expression vague.

I'd eaten fat-free cottage cheese for lunch, in anticipation of another of Chef Karl's culinary masterpieces. Which was

CIRCLE OF WOLVES 97

undoubtedly a mistake—a little like grocery shopping on an empty stomach.

"I suppose you're going to have the beef Wellington," I said to Michael.

"No, I thought I'd have the grouper. How about you?"

"The red snapper. It says here, it comes garnished with shrimp, scallops, mussels, crabmeat, and fresh dill."

Michael raised an eyebrow. "No lunch today?"

"You can't bring me to these places, then expect me to eat like a bird, surely."

"No," he said. "But you're always accusing me of trying to fatten you up. I just want to make it clear that I'm not responsible. Not this time." His voice lacked the teasing quality it usually had, and I didn't say anything.

He picked up the wine list. "Now that we've gotten that out of the way," he said, "what shall we drink with the appetizer?"

I should have skipped the cottage cheese, I thought.

We were halfway through our Key West snapper chowder, or, rather, I was, when Michael reached into his jacket and took out his little spiral notebook. He opened it and flipped over a couple of pages.

"You wanted to know about the Baker Act," he said, reading his notes. No hand holding, no romantic conversation. Like this was purely a business meeting.

"Yes," I said. "In a nutshell, how might an elderly person be committed to a psychiatric hospital or ward against his or her wishes? What exactly constitutes 'crazy,' and who makes that determination, I guess is my question."

"Those are two separate questions, Samantha. One medical, the other legal. I can only tell you what the law permits."

"Okay," I said. "So tell me." I continued eating.

98 Karen Ann Wilson

He cleared his throat and frowned. *This took a lot of time and effort on my part,* his expression seemed to say. *I hope you appreciate it.*

And I feared I was starting to act just like Dr. Augustin: expecting things from the people closest to me, without appearing the least bit grateful.

I smiled apologetically and put down my spoon.

"The Baker Act—passed in 1971—originally was intended to deal with young people, I believe," said Michael. "Kids on drugs or those who were threatening suicide. Anyway, to protect them from themselves, they could be committed against their will (or their parents' will) to a psychiatric facility for observation." He used his swizzle stick as a pointer and aimed it at me.

"I assume your question about the elderly," he continued, "stems from your visit to the nursing floor at Sunset View Towers."

"Yes," I said. "They have a psychiatric wing. I was curious to know how someone gets put there, instead of in the main part of the nursing facility. Or, better yet, how someone might get moved from the assisted-care part of the building to the psych wing. Are people suffering from Alzheimer's considered candidates for psychiatric treatment? That'd be a lot of the old people in the Hayes Building, I'll bet."

"Unfortunately," Michael said, "Alzheimer's disease prompted the medical community here in Florida and, presumably, elsewhere, to treat the dementia these people suffer from as if it were a psychiatric condition requiring emergency intervention.

"It's difficult to say how many Alzheimer's patients were committed under the Baker Act solely to generate funds for the psychiatric facility or because the attending physician believed mind-altering drugs were absolutely required in

CIRCLE OF WOLVES 99

such cases, even though they probably weren't. And, naturally, those drugs could only be administered in a controlled environment."

"You mean, like in a psychiatric hospital or ward?" I asked. "Or wing, in the case of Sunset View Towers."

"Exactly." He took a sip of his drink. "There's no question whatever that more than one psychiatric facility—and I mean those whose entire revenue comes from the treatment of mentally ill individuals—have abused the Baker Act. Regular hospitals with psychiatric wings receive only a small fraction of their income from Baker Act commitments and are less likely to take advantage of loopholes in the law."

"Who actually does the committing?"

"The courts," he said. "A judge is convinced by the attending psychiatrist that a certain patient who has shown violent or suicidal tendencies or in some other way has been deemed a threat to himself or others, must be 'stabilized'—their word, 'stabilized'—with medication. The judge, who certainly isn't an expert, usually accepts the doctor's recommendation. Often, the police are then sent to pick the person up and take him or her to an appropriate facility. Without first contacting the family, unfortunately. The patient can be held for up to seventy-two hours for 'observation.' Many times, the individual winds up staying for weeks or months."

Michael stopped talking while our waiter—Dennis, I overheard him called by another waiter—cleared the table of our soup bowls and the little dish of toast squares. Dennis served the salad, and Michael ordered another drink, which wasn't like him at all.

"Not every community deals with its senile dementia cases by committing them to a psychiatric facility, however," Michael continued. "Some believe medication can be administered and monitored satisfactorily in the patient's regular nursing home, assuming such medication is needed in the first place. And there have been enough complaints over the last couple of years from relatives and concerned legislators to bring about revisions to the law."

He put his notebook away. "Your Dr. Augustin may not think very highly of the press, Samantha, but we have played an integral part in that review and revision process."

Something was bothering Michael, of that I was certain. But what? Had I done something to upset him? Had he finally grown tired of trying to make me love him the way he loved me?

He ignored his salad, concentrating, instead, on his Scotch. I, too, was quickly losing my appetite. No matter how hard I tried to push William's death and its effect on Grey out of my mind, it kept sneaking back in.

"Most of the abuses of the Baker Act," Michael said, "took place in psychiatric facilities collecting from Medicare. You see, they get considerably more for treating a patient in a mental hospital than they would for treating him or her in a nursing home. Even if the care the person receives is essentially the same. Now, thanks to the revisions to the law, it's a little harder to commit people against their will without just cause. Of course, if they can convince the patient to enter the facility voluntarily or get a relative to commit them, they can collect the additional funds without having to explain themselves to a judge, although a specialist not financially tied to the psychiatric facility must first assert that the individual is competent enough to agree to the commitment. Now, I ask you, how difficult can it be to get a friend and fellow psychiatrist to do the job for a little under-the-table money? Where there's a will . . ."

He chuckled at the pun, then picked up his fork and shoved a piece of bibb lettuce around. "Why are you so cu-

CIRCLE OF WOLVES 101

rious about this, anyway? Did someone say something to you about Sunset View Towers? Or is this another one of Dr. Augustin's little crusades?"

So far, the evening hadn't gone particularly well. A cloud hung over the table. I decided telling Michael about Grey's friends would only darken it, possibly bringing lightning and thunder.

"I just wondered," I said, carefully. "I overheard someone mention the Baker Act and I was curious. Thanks for looking it up and filling me in." I took another bite of my salad. "This house dressing is delicious," I said, making dainty little smacking noises with my lips. I looked over at Michael and smiled.

Michael seemed lost in his drink glass, his eyes watching the ice cubes float about in the amber liquid like tiny ballerinas. So I gave up.

Our waiter came by. Although Michael had barely touched his salad, he instructed Dennis to clear away the dishes and serve the entrée, which the man did. Mine was beautifully presented, the snapper piled high with shrimp, scallops, and crab in a fragrant sauce. Two mussels, still in their shells, were artfully arranged on either side of the fish. Green beans and sliced carrots added color. Despite my decaying mood, I felt my salivary glands spring into action.

"This looks fabulous," I said with sincerity.

Dennis seemed pleased, refilled our wineglasses, and left.

Michael poked around on his plate. "I must admit, the food more than compensates for whatever this place lacks in atmosphere." He put a forkful of grouper in his mouth.

We ate in silence for several minutes. I thought about the last time I'd eaten seafood before running away to Florida. David and I had gone to a little hole-in-the-wall place on the water in Boston. We were still speaking to each other then, still planning the wedding. Still "in love." I'd ordered some

102 Karen Ann Wilson

kind of local fish. Tasteless by comparison to what the Gulf of Mexico had to offer. *Everything in Florida seems to taste better,* I thought. *It's like the heat slows things down, gives them time to develop character and flavor. Is that why writers and artists come here?* I wondered.

"Samantha," Michael said.

I looked up. He was toying with his wineglass and watching me eat. I put my fork down and reached for my napkin. "What? Have I been messy?"

"Do you ever miss living up North?" Michael asked.

This is leading somewhere, I thought, hiding behind my napkin. *But where?*

"Sure," I said. "I miss the seasons, and the scenery— everything is so flat here. Water is nice, but I'd like a few mountains occasionally. And I miss the snow. Especially at Christmas. And my family, of course. Why?"

"Have you ever thought about moving back up there?"

"No," I said, simply. "I haven't."

He watched a party of six at a nearby table get up and file out of the room. They were snowbirds. I could tell from the fact that one of the women had asked their waiter if the Dover sole was fresh. Mostly, though, I could tell from the way they were dressed. No Florida native, especially one under the age of sixty-five, would wear a coral golf shirt under a teal V-neck, with matching plaid pants. And another of the men in the party was wearing a lemon sport coat. I glanced back at their table to make sure they hadn't left any golf clubs behind.

"Things aren't working out with Mary's son," said Michael. "The boy ran away again. And he set fire to the laundry room in his dormitory last week. They want him out of there."

Kevin was Michael's late wife's son by a previous marriage. When Mary died, Kevin went to live with Mary's sis-

CIRCLE OF WOLVES 103

ter. But she had problems of her own and couldn't control him, so she begged Michael for help. He put the boy in military school, hoping the structured lifestyle would straighten him out. Evidently, it hadn't.

"I'm sorry," I said.

Michael reached across the table and touched my hand. I looked at him.

"I'm thinking about moving back to New York, Samantha." He locked eyes with me and waited. The unasked question, *Would you be willing to move with me?* hung in the air between us, growing and expanding like water freezing inside a hollow rock, threatening to crack it in half.

"You could bring him down here," I said, finally.

"I could," he said. "But I won't do that to you."

"How is moving to New York to deal with Kevin different from dealing with him down here?"

"I have property up there, Samantha. A house. Investments. There's less involved in moving up there. Where would he live down here? My condo doesn't allow children."

Less involved in you *moving, maybe,* I thought.

"Just think about it, will you, Samantha? Then if you still want to stay here, we will."

Michael picked up the little dessert menu propped between the salt and pepper shakers. "So, what decadent chocolate goodie are you having tonight?" he asked me, as if chocolate could drive away that pesky black cloud over the table.

But even my sweet tooth had run for cover, because now guilt was falling out of that cloud like rain.

"I'm not," I said.

CHAPTER 11

•

Sunday, November 21

It was difficult to ignore the feeling of impending doom that lately seemed to follow me everywhere I went. As if Dr. Augustin's financial situation and Cynthia's ex weren't bad enough, now I had William's death and Michael's revelation about wanting to move on my mind.

I attempted a smile as the guard motioned me on to the Marion R. Hayes Building. It was the old geezer with the wobbly dentures, alive and well, which should have cheered me up, but it didn't. I was having trouble concentrating and had driven very slowly, spending more time than I should at stop signs and green lights. A couple of motorists offered to help me "get it in gear," but I doubted their sincerity. Even Lucky knew something was wrong. She kept whining and sticking her head between the front seats in an effort to crawl in my lap.

It was 1:15 when I finally arrived. The lobby/sitting room of the Hayes Building was filled with tea and sherry drinkers. I recognized several of them from Gretchen's building. *They must hop around from dining room to dining room,* I thought. *Maybe the menu is different in different buildings. Or maybe they come here after dinner for a little nip.*

I got on the elevator with a small group of obvious visi-

104

CIRCLE OF WOLVES 105

tors—middle-aged women holding an assortment of gifts. One of the women, dressed in a beautiful green sweater set, had a cake box from Publix. I couldn't see what was written on the cake, but through the cellophane opening, I spotted a pink rose made of frosting. Lucky spotted the cake, too, or, more likely, smelled it and leaned forward. Her shiny, wet nose lurched and danced at the end of her muzzle like an inquisitive bug, causing the woman with the cake to back up and glare at me. She held the box like it was a donor heart en route to surgery.

On the nursing floor, the little group of partygoers hurried off, while I stopped at the nurse's station to admire a large orchid sitting on the counter. The plant was enormous and had six fragrant purple blooms on it. I thought about my own orchid—a birthday gift from one of Dr. Augustin's more unusual clients. Two lovely white, lemony-scented blossoms had graced my dining table for over two weeks. And then I remembered what the gift-giver had told me that day. "When the question is posed, follow your heart." Had I followed my heart when Michael asked me to marry him? And now would I have to follow him back to the cold and callous Northeast, when I swore I would never live up there again?

"Pretty awesome, aren't they?" a female voice behind me asked.

I turned around. It was Loni Herfeld. She reached out to pet Lucky.

"Yes," I said, "they are."

"Bruce gave it to my mom for her birthday." She lowered her voice. "You wouldn't think someone who looks like Conan the Barbarian would be so sweet, would you?"

"Bruce?"

She inclined her head down the hall. "The aide with the ponytail. Has arms like tree trunks."

106   **Karen Ann Wilson**

"Oh, yes. I remember him."

Loni laughed suddenly at Lucky, who was washing the girl's face with her tongue.

"Loni, honey, don't you think you'd better get to work?" asked a woman in white seated behind the counter. "Your mother is going to be on your case again, if you're not careful."

Loni shrugged. She started down the hall, then turned and smiled at me. "See ya," she said and dashed off, her shoulder-length auburn hair whipping out from the sides of her head like the ears on a springer spaniel.

I watched her go and wondered how much she knew about William's death. Probably very little. *In any case,* I told myself, *she might blab if I question her about any of the patients on the floor.*

I glanced at the nurse behind the counter. She was eating a chocolate chip cookie and reading a paperback novel. A romance, by the look of it. On the cover, a scantily clad woman and a bare-chested man were embracing on a beach, the sky behind them dark and stormy.

I probably can't trust her, either, I thought. *I doubt I can trust any of the staff to say anything the least bit critical about patient care at this place. I need to find a resident who still has his or her marbles. Someone who is stuck on the nursing floor permanently because of a physical disability. Someone bored enough to enjoy local gossip.*

Lucky and I started walking in the general direction of the rec room, pausing to glance through each open door. Most of the patients I saw were asleep or babbling to themselves—poor candidates for undercover work in either case.

As we passed the fork in the corridor, I noticed the party-goers from the elevator. They were standing by the doors to the psychiatric wing. Suddenly, the doors swung open. A

CIRCLE OF WOLVES

107

nurse on the other side smiled at the little group and stood aside so they could enter.

It was pretty obvious one did not get onto the wing without an invitation. Pressing the button on the wall next to the doors probably alerted the medical gestapo. It was also pretty obvious I might never get another chance to check the place out, so I ambled across the hall and waited until the visitors were inside and the nurse had her back to me. Then I squeezed through the doors just as they came together with an audible click. I dashed into the first room I came to and pressed myself against the wall, half expecting to hear alarms go off. Lucky panted excitedly and wagged her tail. Dogs are game for most anything.

"Sandy?"

I looked at the figure in the bed across from me. It was an elderly man with very short grey hair and a face like weathered cypress. He sat up and put his legs over the edge of the bed. They were so skinny and white, they reminded me of bleached bones. The man was wearing a nightshirt, and I realized he was the man I had seen during my first visit, the one who had called out to me for help.

"Sandy," he repeated, "is that you?"

I went over to him. "No, my name is Samantha," I said, gently.

He wasn't looking at me. He was looking at Lucky. "I've missed you, Sandy."

He put out his hand, and Lucky obliged with a big wet one. The man laughed, then stopped abruptly. He stared at me. His eyes were very black and he squinted.

"Who are you?" he asked, "and what are you doing with my dog?"

He wasn't acting irrationally but was, in fact, quite calm. Under any other circumstances, I might have considered him sane.

108 Karen Ann Wilson

"Her name is Lucky," I said. "She must look like your dog. Is Sandy a chow?"

The man seemed confused. He pulled his hand back and started to cry.

Great! I thought. *I should have humored him. Remember how William screamed and screamed until half the floor was outside his room?*

He stopped crying as suddenly as he had started. "Sandy died years ago. I keep forgetting. I'm sorry." He lifted up his nightshirt and wiped his eyes. He wasn't wearing any undershorts.

I put my hand on his shoulder. "That's okay," I said. Then I backed up. "Lucky and I have to go now. Maybe we'll come back and visit you later, when we have more time."

The man waved. "Oh, I won't be here," he said, smiling. "They'll have killed me. Just like they killed Sandy."

In my haste to get out of that room, I failed to check the hallway for prison guards. Luckily, the coast was clear. I started walking, reading the little name tags beside each door as I went. Gretchen's friend, the one with the broken ankle who had disappeared so suddenly, had been Tade somebody. Unfortunately, the name tags only gave an initial and a last name. I tried to remember. It had been a common name, hadn't it? Tade what? Smith? Jones? White! Tade White. I picked up the pace. Lucky was starting to squirm. Besides, with her under my arm, I was going to have a tough time blending in. Eventually, I would get caught.

A couple of presumed residents squinted at me suspiciously as I passed them in the hall. They looked ordinary enough, dressed in street clothes, with their hair neatly combed. But one of them, a man, was talking to himself (or to someone I couldn't see). The other, a woman, kept touching some invisible object directly in front of her, as if watch-

CIRCLE OF WOLVES 109

ing a 3-D movie through a pair of those funky glasses they give you at the door.

I hurried on. When I got to the end of the hall, I stopped. The name tag to my left read "S. Edwards; T. White." The door was open, and I could hear conversation sprinkled with quiet laughter. I took a deep breath and went in.

The party was in full swing. A little old woman dressed in a flannel nightgown was propped up in one of the room's two beds, a napkin tucked under her chin. The woman in green mohair was feeding her small forkfuls of cake, cupping her free hand under the woman's chin to catch any crumbs, while another read a birthday card aloud. Wrapping paper and ribbon littered the bedside table.

All three visitors stopped what they were doing and looked over at me. The birthday girl continued to stare straight ahead, her jaws still working on a morsel of cake.

"I'm sorry for interrupting your party," I said. "I'm here to see Tade." I prayed Ms. White was not the party girl.

"Over here," said a voice in the corner.

I turned and walked quickly across the room. The owner of the voice was sitting in an overstuffed chair eating a piece of cake. She was about seventy and quite plump, with rosy cheeks and hair the color of pewter, gathered into a bun on top of her head. She was wearing a flowered housecoat and worn slippers. Her ankles were horribly swollen, the left one particularly so. She had it propped up on a black naugahyde ottoman.

"I'm not supposed to have sugar," she said merrily. She stuffed a large hunk of cake into her mouth, leaving a mustache of frosting across her upper lip. "Or salt, or fat. Doesn't leave much, does it?" She chewed and swallowed, delicately smacking her lips in appreciation. "If they could keep us alive without feeding us at all, I'm sure they would. All that rot about cholesterol. My daddy ate two eggs every day of his life and he lived to be ninety-three."

She looked up, apparently seeing Lucky for the first time. "Would your little dog like some cake? Maybe you'd like some." She turned toward the party. "I'm sure Susie's friends wouldn't mind sharing another piece. Susie certainly won't know the difference, bless her soul."

"No, but thanks, anyway," I said. I looked around for a place to sit, but the party guests had commandeered the room's two remaining chairs.

"Gretchen Milner asked me to drop by and see how you're doing," I said. "She's worried about you."

I sat down on the edge of the ottoman and scratched Lucky's head in an effort to distract her. To my knowledge, she'd never been offered junk food of any kind, but she was begging for cake like a pro. I thought briefly about digging into my purse for her leash.

"Gretchen?" asked Tade. She let the hand holding the fork drop slowly into her lap.

I was getting used to the expression of vague unease and confusion that marked the faces of the people on the nursing floor. So I tried again.

"How's your ankle?" I asked, gently touching the woman's leg. The purplish, cracked skin felt like waxed parchment.

"Much better, thank you." She cocked her head to one side. "What did you say your name was?"

"Samantha. I'm a friend of Grey Milner."

"Grey is such a lovely woman, don't you agree?" she asked, smiling. It was as if she had a tiny epileptic seizure and wasn't aware of it.

She used her fork to push all the remaining cake crumbs into a little pile on her plate, then mashed them through the tines of the fork.

CIRCLE OF WOLVES 111

I nodded. "And she's so talented," I said. "Very artistic. Her paintings are just wonderful."

Tade ate the cake crumbs. Then she put the plate and fork on the floor next to her chair. She was still wearing her frosting mustache. It looked like a coating of Nair. I wanted to lean over and wipe it off.

"Grey hasn't heard from you since . . . for awhile," I said. "She wonders when you'll be coming home."

Tade folded her hands in her lap. "I live here now," she said sadly. "I won't be going back. Dr. Aaron told me if I move back into my apartment, I could hurt myself again. They tell me I tried to climb over my balcony." She chewed on the inside of her lip. "That I slipped and broke my ankle. Dr. Aaron says next time I could forget to turn off my stove or leave my door unlocked. Or worse."

"You don't sound convinced," I said. "Did you really climb over your balcony?"

She shook her head slowly. "I don't think so. I just don't remember."

Suddenly, she leaned forward and grabbed my arm. It caused me to let go of Lucky's collar. The puppy dropped to the floor and headed for the cake plate.

"I'm afraid," said Tade. "Afraid if I go back to my apartment, the voices will follow me."

I frowned. *And just when the woman had me convinced there was nothing wrong with her,* I thought.

"Voices? What voices?"

"The people Dr. Aaron says are only in my head. They aren't real. But I tell you, I hear them talking. Whispering. Not all the time. When I have trouble remembering, that's when the voices start."

She was digging her nails into my arm. I took hold of her hand and pried it loose.

112 Karen Ann Wilson

"I'll tell Gretchen you're okay," I said quickly. She'll be relieved."

I stood up. Tade watched me. Her expression said more than any words could, and I felt like I was abandoning an injured animal on the side of the road. But I didn't know what else to do. CPR and first aid weren't about to help Tade or the old man in the nightshirt, and that's all I had to offer them.

I looked around for Lucky. The empty cake plate obviously hadn't held her attention, and no one on the other side of the room was complaining about yucky dog germs.

I was headed out the door, when Nurse Herfeld and her buddy Bruce the Barbarian appeared. Bruce was holding Lucky.

"You'll have to leave," said Mrs. Herfeld. "Now. It's against the rules for anyone to be on the psychiatric wing without prior permission. Some of the patients can get quite violent. It's for your own protection."

Lucky was slobbering all over Bruce's face, and Bruce was grinning happily. Mrs. Herfeld, on the other hand, did not look like she'd been happy a day in her life, particularly that day.

"I'm sorry," I said, fishing through my purse for Lucky's leash. "I didn't know. I just thought the residents here might like to play with the puppy for a little while."

Mrs. Herfeld did not say anything. She didn't have to. I reached out for Lucky, and Bruce handed her to me. I snapped her leash to her collar. Then Mrs. Herfeld escorted me down the hall to the double doors. I felt like I'd committed some unpardonable sin and now was being banished from the village. Cast out on the street with my baby and just the clothes on my back.

"In the future," said Mrs. Herfeld, taking what appeared to be a beeper out of her pocket, "I suggest you have Mrs.

CIRCLE OF WOLVES 113

Snoden accompany you on your nursing floor visits." She aimed the device at a small panel on the wall and pressed it. The doors began to open.

"I'll do that," I answered. "And thank you for being so patient with me." I smiled at her when I said it, but her face was a slab of granite.

I left the psychiatric wing and continued on to the rec room. When I got there, Ms. Smith and Loni were serving tea. I didn't even wait for Wilma to tell me dogs and cookies don't mix. I turned around and headed back to the nurse's station. Halfway there, I ran into Mrs. Snoden.

"So how are your visits going, Miss Holt?" she asked, smiling.

She was wearing a wool knit suit and matching silk blouse. Cranberry. Very expensive.

"I'm afraid I was a bad girl," I said. "Nurse Herfeld caught me on the psychiatric wing. I'm surprised she didn't have me thrown in jail."

Mrs. Snoden laughed. Then she put her hand under my elbow, and we continued walking. "Let's go down to my office," she said. "I'll fill you in on some of the management policies for the nursing floor. I'm sorry we didn't go over them on your first visit." She lowered her voice. "I should have warned you about Elaine Herfeld. She's a real stickler for adhering to the rules. I don't know how poor Loni manages. That girl only went into nursing so she could marry a rich doctor—you know the type, I'm sure—although I must say, she is everything her mother is not: sweet, caring, compassionate."

I knew the kind, all right. My father had left my mother for one just like Loni. Noelle something. Twenty-two, going on ten.

We got on the elevator, and Mrs. Snowden punched 1.

"Elaine has been here for ten years," she said. "Almost as

long as Sunset View Towers itself. Her husband died when Loni was a baby, and Elaine had to earn a living. She put herself through nursing school by waiting tables."

The elevator stopped on the second floor, and a young couple got on. The girl had been crying. Neither of them said anything. They were holding hands, and she was leaning against him as if for support.

"Elaine is a strong, resourceful woman," Mrs. Snoden continued. "But I think all those years of just getting by hardened her. She's a fine nurse, but sometimes lacks compassion, which is unfortunate, especially here." She paused. "I can't remember the last time I saw her smile. Except when Bruce gave her that orchid plant."

The elevator came to a halt on the first floor, and the doors opened. The young couple got off. I followed them, nearly bumping into the ambulance chaser who, along with a small group of visitors, was waiting to get on. It occurred to me that he must come on weekends in the hopes of finding concerned relatives to prey upon.

We exchanged smiles, but his was brief. He caught sight of Mrs. Snoden directly behind me, hesitated a couple of seconds, then turned around and hurried across the lobby after the young couple.

I looked over at Mrs. Snoden. She was watching him, her face unchanged except for two very pronounced spots of color on her cheeks.

"My office is this way," she said, pointing to our left. Her voice was firm and calm.

CHAPTER 12

•

Mrs. Snoden (Beatrice, according to the name plate on the door) had a small office—really nothing more than a cubicle—on the first floor next to the administrative director, Nelson Aveneau. I couldn't see how large his was, but Mrs. Snoden could barely turn around in hers. Even so, it was neat and tastefully decorated, with artwork depicting children and seniors interacting, and a silk flower arrangement tucked away in the corner on top of a three-drawer metal file cabinet, probably because there wasn't anyplace else to put it. The floor was imitation parquet, the walls pale mint.

I took off Lucky's leash and let the puppy go, then sat down in what appeared to be a genuine antique Queen Anne. It had a worn needlepoint seat cushion and an assortment of dings and scratches, some of which looked like toddler tooth marks.

Beatrice sat behind the desk. She reached over and picked up a small hinged picture frame, then turned it toward me. One of the photos clearly had been taken several years earlier, because it was of a younger Mrs. Snoden hugging two children somewhere around five or six years of age. The boy was blond and adorable. The girl had light brown hair, chubby features, and was an obvious Down's syndrome child.

115

116 **Karen Ann Wilson**

The second photograph was more recent. In it, Mrs. Snoden and a very stocky balding man in his fifties were sharing a piece of wedding cake. Beatrice was dressed in a simple linen or silk suit—peach—with a corsage of peach rosebuds and baby's breath pinned to the lapel. The man was wearing a rosebud boutonniere.

"My children," Beatrice said, smiling. Then she pointed to the second photograph. "My husband, Joe, and me. Taken last year." She put the frame back on her desk.

What could I say, except, "You looked lovely. And very happy," which was the truth.

"Joseph is an angel," she said. "Not too many men would take on a family like mine."

I was naturally curious about her first husband, presumably the father of her children. Of course, there is never an easy way to bring up the subject. Without appearing to pry, that is. And it certainly wasn't any of my business.

"Was that Tyler Brock waiting for the elevator?" I asked instead. "I saw him on television the other day. I gather no one upstairs is particularly fond of the guy."

Mrs. Snoden frowned. "Let's just say few who work here would be terribly upset if Mr. Brock suddenly vanished from the face of the earth."

"How about you?" I asked. The way Brock had looked at her had puzzled me.

She picked up a large, black coffee mug with some kind of gold insignia on the front, looked in it, then put it back down. "Would you care for a cup of coffee?" she asked. "Or a soft drink?" End of discussion about Tyler Brock, apparently.

I shook my head. "I really can't stay long," I said, as I watched Lucky investigating Beatrice's file cabinet. Something in or on the bottom drawer had her full attention. If the puppy had been a male and a little older, I'd have worried.

CIRCLE OF WOLVES 117

"This won't take long," said Beatrice. "I just wanted to give you a few pointers to help you survive the fourth floor."

She clasped her hands together and leaned forward. The gesture and the expensive clothes made her look like a corporate executive at a board meeting. I wondered if she had always been an activities director at an old folks' home. It seemed unlikely.

"You know this pet therapy program was my idea," she began. "My daughter is mentally challenged and has really benefited from a program called Horses for the Handicapped. Maybe you've heard of it."

I nodded.

"Anyway," she continued, now running her fingers along the top edge of the picture frame, "I thought some of the elderly in our building, especially the ones on the nursing floor, might be helped by regular visits from a dog or cat. Other nursing and convalescent facilities have been participating in such programs for years. According to the literature, severely withdrawn patients often respond to an animal when they won't to a human, even a family member.

"Unfortunately, my predecessor seemed to think pets would introduce fleas and diseases, I suppose. Personally, I would be more concerned about the illnesses our residents are exposed to from some of the human visitors we get."

"I know what you mean," I said. Except for the very tip of her tail, I couldn't see Lucky. She was under Beatrice's desk, hopefully behaving herself. "Of course, with pets there are always going to be accidents," I said.

"Oh, we have plenty of those now, without the pets," she said, smiling. She cleared her throat and the smile vanished. "There are still a few staff members who don't approve of the program, I'm sorry to say."

"You mean like the food service people," I asked. "What's-her-name Smith, for example?"

118   **Karen Ann Wilson**

"Wilma," said Beatrice. The smile crept back onto her face. "Wilma does take her job seriously. So avoid mealtime, if at all possible. The patients eat lunch from eleven-thirty to twelve-thirty. Most of the dishes are removed and the patients cleaned up by one. Tea and coffee are served at three, in the rec room. There's a similar room on the psychiatric wing, but of course, you don't need to worry about that. Dr. Aaron doesn't want you there at all, which is unfortunate, since those are the people most likely to benefit from the pet therapy program."

"Something about violent behavior," I said. "I think that's what Ms. Herfeld told me. It's for my own protection, according to her."

"Yes, well, Dr. Aaron doesn't want to risk having something happen, no matter how unlikely. He's very publicity-conscious. It probably stems from his fear of being sued again."

"Again?"

"We had a patient wander off last year. How, I don't know. But the man turned up a week later, nearly dead from exposure."

She drew her lips together in a line so thin and straight, it could have been one of Dr. Augustin's incisions. I couldn't be certain, of course, but I would have sworn she was thinking about Tyler Brock, Esquire. He probably had had a field day with that one.

"I guess the lawn care guy who died earlier this month didn't help," I said. "With the publicity, I mean."

"That was awful, wasn't it?" Beatrice said. "Our administrator fussed and fumed." She reached into her in-box and picked up a handful of papers, then waved them at me. "And his office has been generating memo after memo stressing the importance of proper procedure. Which is why I felt we should go over the rules for the nursing floor." She put the

CIRCLE OF WOLVES 119

memos back in her in-box. "I would hate to lose this program because I didn't monitor it properly."

I started to apologize for my earlier blunder, but she interrupted me.

"Please, Ms. Holt, don't feel responsible for what happened today. It wasn't your fault. I failed to warn you about the psychiatric wing."

"I should have asked," I said. "By the way, was that lawn maintenance man an employee here, or did he work for a private landscaping company?"

If Mrs. Snoden was curious about my interest in the matter (which had nothing to do with the pet therapy program), she didn't show it.

"Oh, he was employed by the management company that runs Sunset View Towers," she said. "Most of us are. A few families hire private nurses to take care of their relatives. I'd say half a dozen or so work in this building. But even they have to abide by management's rules."

Suddenly, Lucky squeezed her little body out from under Beatrice's desk. She shook, then wandered over to the door.

"I guess we'd better be going," I said, "before we have one of those 'accidents' we were talking about."

Beatrice and I got up, and I bent over to attach the leash to Lucky's collar. I was about to open the door, then hesitated and looked at Beatrice. "You said 'management company.' You mean Sunset View Towers doesn't operate itself?"

"Gracious no. It's one of several retirement centers around the state operated by Quetzal Bay Properties. They hire and fire everyone and establish most of the rules and regulations."

I pushed open the door. "Oh," I said, smiling.

Lucky stopped immediately outside the building and squatted. When she was through, I praised her, and we con-

120 **Karen Ann Wilson**

tinued down the walk toward the parking area with Lucky trotting along on the sidewalk in front of me like a little trooper. We reached the curb, and I was about to pick her up, when a man dressed in a navy workman's uniform approached me. His shirt had "JACK" and MAINTENANCE DIVISION stitched on the side opposite the pocket.

"Honey," he began, "we have places for dogs to do their business. Sidewalks and lawns ain't one of 'em."

He was about thirty, tall and lean, with deeply tanned skin and hair slicked down like he might have been a throwback from the fifties and those "Happy Days." I could see a pack of Marlboros sticking out of his pocket. If he'd been wearing a T-shirt, the pack would have been rolled up in a sleeve. No question.

The word "Sweetie" was forming on my lips, and I quickly swallowed it. "She's only a puppy," I said. "I'm happy she didn't do her 'business' in the building."

"Well, dogs peeing on the grass kills it. Then I catch hell from the management."

"I'll try to be more careful," I said, not concerned in the least about his catching hell. To make matters worse, Lucky growled at him. As I walked the rest of the way to my car, I could feel the creep's eyes on me.

After I had waved good-bye to the little old man in the guard shack and started down Gulf Drive, I went over what I had uncovered. It wasn't much, but I was intrigued by the fact that Sunset View Towers was managed by Quetzal Bay Properties. If I could dig up something illegal going on there and implicate Mr. Stone, possibly even Mr. Cronin, Dr. Augustin's case would be strengthened. I hated to admit it, but proving William's death was not by natural causes certainly wouldn't hurt. That was a long shot, however.

For starters, I decided to dig a little deeper into the death of the grounds keeper. Maybe the maintenance division rou-

CIRCLE OF WOLVES

tinely broke the law to save money, thus endangering the residents. And maybe, just maybe, they did it with Quetzal Bay's blessings. I could almost see the headlines: ELDERLY MAN AND DOG DIE AFTER WALKING ON GRASS TREATED WITH ILLEGAL PESTICIDE.

A little voice inside my head kept telling me to drop what I knew in Dr. Augustin's lap and let him deal with it. After all, wasn't I the one who always complained that the clinic was not a front for a private detective agency? But for some strange reason, I was having trouble hearing that little voice.

CHAPTER 13

•

Monday, November 22

Cynthia dumped an enormous catalog on her desk. The thud sent Charlie scurrying into the supply closet and caused the preserved dog heart sitting next to the heartworm prevention display to jiggle briefly. A cloud of sediment rose up in the formalin like snow in one of those glass paperweights, the kind with lilliputian Christmas trees and children ice skating.

I leaned against the counter and looked at the catalog's cover. It was a *Simplicity* dress pattern book.

"What fabric store did you swipe this from?" I asked.

"I did not *swipe* it," she said. She put her purse in a bottom drawer, then sat down in front of her computer terminal. "I know the manager over at Weiler's Fabrics. She let me borrow it. They had two. I thought we could look through the bridal section. I thought perhaps you'd let me make your wedding gown for you."

She had her back to me, on purpose I was pretty sure. The fact that her ex-husband would soon be a daddy had evidently given new life to Cynthia's role as mother of the bride. And the fact that I already had a mother who might not take kindly to Cynthia's involvement did not seem to deter her one bit.

"Since you haven't picked a date yet," she said, pecking

122

CIRCLE OF WOLVES 123

away at the computer like a pigeon searching for seeds, "and seem to be dragging your feet, there'll be plenty of time for me to make your dress and, if you like, the maid of honor's dress, too. Have you given any thought as to who that person might be?"

"I've been giving thought to elopement," I said, calmly.

Cynthia's fingers stopped in midair over the keyboard, as if suddenly flash-frozen. She turned in her chair and stared at me.

"You're not serious, I hope," she said.

I continued to browse through the little stack of appointment files on Cynthia's desk. It was 9:30. Surgery that morning had consisted of one cat neuter. Less than ten minutes start to finish. Dr. Augustin was in his office talking to his lawyer. Tracey and Frank were in the kennel doing God knows what.

"Samantha?" Cynthia's voice had a note of desperation in it.

"Who's going to pay for this wedding, anyway?" I asked.

"Why, Mike, of course," she said, as if Michael Halsey's bank account were a bottomless pit.

"Traditionally, the parents of the bride are supposed to pay for the wedding," I said. "All but the rehearsal dinner and the booze at the reception, if I'm not mistaken. Since my mother spent a fortune on my last almost-wedding, I'm not going to ask her to fork over even a nickel this time. And we already know I would rather go to a justice of the peace wearing jeans and a T-shirt than ask my father for money."

"I'm sure Mike would be more than happy to give you whatever you want," Cynthia said.

I couldn't be certain she and Michael hadn't already discussed this matter. Behind my back, of course. They routinely conspired against me, or so it seemed.

"I'm sure he would, too, Cynthia, but that's not the point,

124 Karen Ann Wilson

now, is it?" I could feel my stomach start to convulse. Before this is over, this wedding nonsense, I thought, I'm going to have an ulcer.

Cynthia started to say something, when the phone rang. She picked it up.

"Just a minute," she told the person on the other end, then hit the "hold" button. She looked up at me. "This woman says she's a friend of yours. Gretchen Milner."

I reached for the phone, then leaned over the counter and released the "hold." "Hello, Grey?"

"Sam," she said, "Riley is sick. He has diarrhea. My regular veterinarian is out of town—Dr. Zonick—and I'm not terribly fond of his partner. Is there a chance I could bring Riley to your clinic? Do you have any appointments open? It's probably nothing—just a little upset stomach—but, well . . . with William and everything . . ."

"Of course, Grey," I said quickly, "you bring him right in." I told her how to get to the clinic, then hung up.

Cynthia frowned. "Unless this is an emergency, you should have told her to come this afternoon. We're booked solid this morning. You know that."

"Trust me," I said. "This is an emergency."

Dr. Augustin examined Riley from stem to stern, while Gretchen Milner did what nearly every woman still breathing did in his presence—tried not to drool too much as she admired his jeans, among other things.

"You say he got into some food you were preparing?" asked Dr. Augustin, peering down the cat's throat.

Riley wasn't pleased. I could feel a low rumble start in his chest.

Grey nodded. "It was the remains of a pot roast I cooked Saturday. Sunday afternoon, I chopped up what was left, made barbecue, and froze it. Riley must have gotten into the

CIRCLE OF WOLVES 125

garbage. I found a small piece of meat under the kitchen table when I came home from church Sunday night. And another on the floor next to the refrigerator."

She looked at her cat and smiled. "He's never gotten into the garbage before, but nothing that cat did would surprise me. He knows how to open the kitchen cabinets. And he's pushed more than one ballpoint under the refrigerator. I'm still looking for a pair of emerald earrings he pilfered."

I laughed. "We have a couple of cats here at the clinic who drive Cynthia crazy stealing things off her desk."

Dr. Augustin hung up his stethoscope and went over to the sink. He pumped some soap into his palm.

"He's a little dehydrated," he said, his back to us. "I'd like to get some fluids into him. And stop that diarrhea. We'll draw some blood and run a few tests just to make sure nothing else is going on, but I think old Riley is suffering from a case of what we call 'garbage can gastritis'." He rinsed his hands, then reached for a paper towel. "Dogs are normally the ones who snatch the Thanksgiving turkey right off the table, but we do see a few cats from time to time with upset tummies from eating table food."

"I can take him home, can't I?" asked Grey.

Dr. Augustin came back to the exam table and idly stroked Riley's head. The rumble grew louder. My arm felt like I was embracing a vibrating pillow instead of a cat.

"I'd rather keep him here for a day or two," said Dr. Augustin, wisely removing his hand. "We can administer fluids and monitor his condition. If everything checks out, you can pick Riley up Thursday morning. We're closed Wednesday, or you could come get him then."

He opened the Milner file and wrote something in it. "I'll give you a call tomorrow morning," he said, "with the results of that blood work."

126 Karen Ann Wilson

He took Riley, openly growling by that time, from me and went into the treatment room. I heard him yell for Tracey.

I walked Gretchen up front. Our ten o'clock and 10:15 clients were waiting, their dogs staring malevolently at each other from opposite sides of the room. All they needed was an excuse. They were a bomb waiting for a detonator. I couldn't remember who our 10:30 was. I prayed it was a parakeet.

"I'd be happy to bring Riley by Wednesday afternoon, Grey," I told her at the door. "If you promise to fix us some cocoa."

She promised, and we made a date for Wednesday at 4:30.

I watched her walk slowly to her car and get in. That day, she looked every bit her age. Although she'd made a gallant effort to be upbeat, I could see how depressed she really was. Of course, telling her about Tade White hadn't helped.

I led our ten o'clock into Room 2. The dog, a giant schnauzer, had to be dragged from the reception room by his leash. He continued to stare at the other dog, a chow, until we'd rounded the corner. I closed the exam room door with a sigh of relief and went in search of Dr. Augustin. He was in Isolation making some notes in Riley's record. I noticed a thin line of red running down his left arm.

"You need to put something on that," I said.

He looked at his arm briefly, then went back to the file. "It's only a scratch, Samantha."

"Did Matthew have anything useful to tell you?" I asked, picking up the bottle of surgical scrub and squirting a little of it onto a paper towel. I wanted him to volunteer the information about Keith Stone and Quetzal Bay Properties. Like that would somehow make what I did a less serious offense.

"Not really," he said. He put the Milner file on the counter

CIRCLE OF WOLVES 127

and took the paper towel from me. "There's a chance one of Monarch's employees is stealing from the company. It isn't Cronin, unfortunately. But embezzlement, no matter who's doing it, won't look particularly good to a judge. I only wish I could tie Cronin to it a little more securely. He'll probably claim he knew nothing about it and vigorously condemn the man."

He went to the sink and ran water over his wound. Riley had nailed him a good one. I looked over at the cage nearest the sink. Riley's yellow eyes stared out at us from the darkness. He was still growling.

I started to inform Dr. Augustin about Quetzal Bay's connection to Sunset View Towers, but stopped. I didn't have anything solid to tell him. Just a feeling that was probably unfounded. And anyway, when did I ever need help looking foolish in front of Dr. Augustin?

"Samantha, would it be too much to ask for you to join me in Room 2?" Dr. Augustin said from the doorway. He was frowning.

I shook my head to clear it and hurried after him.

CHAPTER 14

•

The man at the local lawn and garden center suggested I try the urban horticulturist at the county cooperative extension service. I told him I was looking for a lawn company to treat my yard and was checking on what licenses lawn care people needed in order to spray pesticides and so forth. From my end, I sounded pretty convincing. My lying skills were obviously improving. One of the many perks of working for Dr. Augustin, evidently.

Cynthia agreed to cover my hour, from 1:00 to 2:00, at the front desk. She drives a hard bargain. I had to promise to look through the *Simplicity* catalog with her. I refused to tell her where I was going, however. I said I had to run a few errands. Unfortunately, she'd heard me talking to the lawn and garden guy, and her curiosity rivals that of my cats. I was glad when our last appointment of the morning headed out the door. I was right behind her.

The cooperative extension service building is a large, squat, masonry structure surrounded by a Who's Who of the plant kingdom. Several narrow walking paths strewn with wood chips lead visitors through gardens designed to educate the mind as well as please the eye and nose. Each vine, shrub, and tree has a little identification tag, and there are exhibits bearing words like "xeric" and "oasis."

128

CIRCLE OF WOLVES   129

The air smells of flowers and wet cypress mulch and humus. Butterflies dance about, "sniffing" the leaves with their feet, pausing here and there to lay an egg or two. I worried about the larvae's chances, considering all the brochures inside the lobby describing myriad ways to bump off caterpillars and other plant denizens. "Pests" they called them. Nobody considers butterflies pests, but they get killed, anyway, along with the leaf miners and sod web worms who aren't lucky enough to be beautiful. Accidental victims, just like Willie Roan, maintenance man at Sunset View Towers.

The receptionist said Mr. Parker was on the phone, and would I kindly wait. She pointed to a bench by an indoor lily pond, complete with motorized waterfall and a nearby hanging cage containing a pair of lovebirds making sharp, off-key remarks.

I went over to the pond and sat down. The water was exceptionally clear, probably kept that way with potentially toxic chemicals. Two large red and white carp were nosing one of the lily pads around. Carp, I reminded myself, can tolerate almost anything.

"Miss Holt?"

I looked up. A tall man in his thirties smiled down at me. He was wearing tan slacks, a plaid, long-sleeved shirt, and a narrow, maroon knit tie. His shoes were Hush Puppies.

"I'm Steve Parker. The urban horticulturist. Sorry to keep you waiting. Shall we go to my office?"

He led me across the lobby to a large room with a nice view of the gardens. He had a big desk, which was fortunate. In addition to his computer, Mr. Parker had various potted plants and stacks of papers and several framed photographs and other memorabilia crammed onto the desk's surface, along with the obvious remains of his brown bag lunch.

"Have a seat," he said, indicating a roomy armchair posi-

130 Karen Ann Wilson

tioned in front of the desk. He sat in his computer chair behind the desk.

I couldn't help but notice his screen saver program. It was the "Sorcerer's Apprentice" from *Fantasia*. Mickey Mouse, wearing an overly large caftan and tall conical hat, was instructing a group of animated mops to do his chores for him. Except the mops had run amok, and the screen was rapidly filling up with water.

"You wanted some information on lawn maintenance companies?" prodded Mr. Parker.

I yanked my eyes away from the screen right as the sorcerer came home to find his castle flooded. Mickey was in big trouble. I shivered. There was something definitely prophetic about that program.

"Yes," I said. "I'm concerned that the people I hire might use illegal pesticides. You see, I have pets and I don't want them getting sick, or even dying like that poor man over at Sunset View Towers. Aren't there licenses or permits of some kind people like that have to get before they can spray people's yards?"

Parker sighed, then smiled. It suddenly occurred to me that I probably wasn't the first concerned citizen to look him up following Mr. Roan's untimely demise.

"Yes there are, Miss . . . ?"

"Holt," I said. "Samantha Holt." Too late, I remembered that Dr. Augustin always makes up a fictitious name when he plays private investigator. I resolved to give Mr. Parker a fictitious address, should he ask where the lawn needing treatment was located.

"In your case, Miss Holt," he said, "the owner of the landscape company you hire would have what is known as a Commercial Pest Control Operator's license, or PCO. He . . . or she . . . may have several employees working for the company who don't have PCO licenses, but, ultimately,

CIRCLE OF WOLVES 131

the owner or individual holding the license is responsible for whatever is done in your yard."

Parker picked up a can of Coke—decaffeinated, I noticed—and took a swig.

"These days, however, most pesticide applicators are licensed, whether they work for themselves or for someone else. It's good business sense as well as safer all the way around."

"Would I need a license? I mean, if I wanted to spray my yard myself, instead of hiring someone? I can't imagine all the do-it-yourself homeowners getting licenses."

"Private individuals doing not-for-hire work on their own property," said Parker, "don't need licenses. Of course, they are limited in what they can purchase. In the way of chemicals, that is."

"What about the guy on the beach?" I asked. "Willie Roan, I think his name was. If he had a PCO license, shouldn't he have known better than to use such a dangerous chemical?"

Mr. Parker frowned. He put the drink can down on his desk and dug into one of the stacks of paper, nearly spilling the top half onto the floor. I reached out and pushed the pile back from the front edge of the desk.

Parker grinned then. "Thanks," he said, pulling out a wad of papers stapled together. "I really need to sort through that mess and file what I can." He leaned back in his chair.

"First off, lawn maintenance people who work for condominiums or apartment complexes don't have PCO licenses. They have what are referred to as Restricted Lawn and Ornamental licenses. They can purchase the same chemicals PCO license-holders can purchase but are only allowed to use them on the condo property." He read a few paragraphs of page two.

"And, in defense of Mr. Roan, that incident was highly

132   Karen Ann Wilson

atypical. Most restricted license people do a very good job. In fact, Willie had an excellent record. Before going to work at Sunset View Towers, he was employed by the Brightwater Beach Municipal Golf Course. For fifteen years. The only reason he left there to work at a residential complex was he wanted to cut back. He had a bad hip, and the golf course was too strenuous a job."

Parker looked over at me and lowered his voice. "Just so you know, Willie Roan and I had been friends, more or less, for ten years. He was one of the most careful and conscientious . . . and honest . . . pesticide applicators I've ever met."

"So what happened?" I asked. "Could the management have wanted him to save money by using a stronger chemical than he normally used?"

Parker shook his head. "Willie wouldn't have agreed to do something like that. Besides, aldicarb—the chemical that killed Willie—is used for nematodes and other pests on citrus, a few ornamentals, and on crops like cotton, peanuts, and soybeans. They use it on pecans in a few states, sugarcane in Louisiana, and on tobacco in North Carolina and Virginia. It hasn't been used on lawns for years, because of its toxicity. Besides, it's granular and applied that way. Unless it's dissolved in water or is actually ingested, it probably wouldn't kill a human. Dissolved in water, however, it becomes very hazardous. I don't know how Willie Roan came in contact with the stuff. Maybe he ran across an old container and didn't realize what it was. Still, he wouldn't have consumed it. Probably wouldn't have handled it without gloves. I just don't know what happened."

He glanced at his watch, put the papers on top of the stack, and gathered up his lunch debris. He threw the bag in the trash can by the side of his desk. The can needed emptying.

"Did you have any other questions, Miss Holt?" he asked.

CIRCLE OF WOLVES 133

"I'm giving a talk to some lawn care people at two and I really ought to go over my notes one more time."

I stood up. "No, that's about it. You've been very helpful."

We shook hands, and Parker walked me to his door. I turned to face him and saw that Mickey was conjuring up the mops again.

"Nice screen saver program," I said, pointing to Parker's computer.

"Thanks. It's a bit distracting, though. But appropriate. I sometimes feel like the sorcerer's apprentice. Too much work and not enough time to do it in. I'll admit I'm tempted to cut corners. But Mickey keeps me honest." He smiled.

"Well," I said. "Thanks."

"No problem."

He went back to his desk and sat down, and I headed across the lobby. The lovebirds had fallen asleep, but the carp were still nosing the lily pad around. Like the pacing wolf at the zoo, they didn't seem to have any goal or destination in mind.

I walked quickly through the xeriscape display. *If Willie Roan didn't purposely use aldicarb on the lawn at Sunset View Towers*, I thought, as I drove back to the clinic, *then where did the stuff come from*? And how did it end up inside Willie Roan? Had someone else there at the complex purchased the chemical in an effort to kill some particularly nasty worm in the grass? If so, that person would need a PCO or Restricted Lawn and Ornamental license, wouldn't he (or she)? Surely aldicarb wasn't something the average homeowner could purchase.

"If I were Dr. Augustin," I said aloud, "I'd look for something evil in all this. Rather than an inadvertent poisoning, maybe Willie Roan was poisoned on purpose. Maybe he was murdered to cover up something illegal going on at the complex. And, suspecting that, Dr. Augustin would con me into helping him find the person or persons responsible."

But Dr. Augustin wasn't interested in the goings-on at Sunset View Towers. Not unless they had a direct bearing on Cronin's suit against him. And so far, nothing I had discovered seemed relevant. Or did it?

I wonder what killed that old man and his dog, I thought. All joking aside, what if they really did get into something toxic? Like aldicarb or whatever, from walking on the grass in the dog-walk area? And who would have that information? The medical examiner's office?

I turned off the causeway onto the island. *Michael will know who to call,* I told myself.

When I got back to the clinic, it was a few minutes shy of two o'clock. Since Larry was back to working Tuesday and Thursday afternoons (Dr. Augustin said the clinic was losing too much money with him gone every afternoon), I had very little time left for lunch. I ran into the lab and took my brown bag out of the refrigerator. I stared at the leftover chicken leg and thought about Riley's run-in with the leftover pot roast. I dropped the plastic bag containing the leg into the garbage and took out the bran muffin I'd brought with it. The muffin seemed pretty safe, so I took a bite.

Tracey turned around on her stool. "Oh, hi," she said. "Dr. Augustin will be back at two-thirty. Our first appointment is a suture removal, followed by a nail trim on Mad Max. Lucky us, huh?" She turned back around and looked through the microscope.

"Great," I said, remembering the last time Tracey and I had worked on Mad Max without Dr. Augustin's help. "Hey, did Frank ever cut that record?" I took another bite of muffin and chewed. "And what do they mean by 'cutting' a record? I didn't think people played records anymore."

CIRCLE OF WOLVES 135

Tracey laughed. "It's just an expression. From the old days." She looked over her shoulder at me and frowned. "No, the studio bumped him for someone else. A group called the Dills. They told Frank they'd have to reschedule his band for sometime in January. Frank was pretty bummed."

"I guess so," I said. "I'm sorry."

Tracey shrugged, then held up a sample cup containing a cloudy red-orange fluid. "Riley's urine," she said. She put the cup back on the counter and pointed to her microscope. "Lots of red cells and some hemoglobin casts. I haven't seen those in awhile. Anyway, it looks like Mrs. Milner's cat has more than just a case of indigestion, doesn't it?"

"Wonderful," I muttered, then threw the rest of my muffin into the trash with the chicken leg.

CHAPTER 15

•

Tuesday, November 23

I heard the fax machine start to whirr and went into the lab. Dr. Augustin came through the door to his office and stood silently by the machine until the tone indicated the end of the transmission. Then he tore the sheet off and began poring over it like it was Kelsey Cronin's bank statement.

It was only 7:15, but Dr. Augustin's early-morning appearance at the clinic hadn't really surprised me. If there's one thing Dr. Augustin hates more than corrupt politicians and greedy developers, it's not knowing why one of his patients is sick.

"BUN and creatinine are up, naturally," he said. "Phosphorus and potassium . . ." He scowled at the paper for a few more seconds, then looked over at me. "According to Zonick's office, Riley had a geriatric exam in October. His kidneys showed no sign of impairment at that time. He's FeLV and FIV negative. Lymphosarcoma seems unlikely. This thing came on so suddenly. I'm guessing it's some sort of nephrotoxicity. And not a result of his eating leftover pot roast, either." He paused.

"Find out from Mrs. Milner if Riley could have gotten into rat bait or some kind of cleaning agent or other toxic chemical she might have hidden under a sink or in a cabinet. She said Riley is good at opening doors and so forth."

136

CIRCLE OF WOLVES 137

He handed me the fax, then headed back toward his office. At the door, he stopped and turned around. "Also ask her if Riley could have swallowed any pain reliever. Ibuprofen, maybe. His symptoms certainly are consistent with NSAID poisoning. A well-adjusted cat isn't likely to eat something like that voluntarily, but maybe he did have a little intestinal upset from the pot roast, and Mrs. Milner didn't know any better and gave him something."

I followed him into his office. He went to his desk and sat down. His briefcase, no doubt filled with the latest dirt on Monarch development, lay open on the floor next to his chair.

"What about a pesticide like aldicarb?"

Dr. Augustin opened his bottom desk drawer, leaned back in his chair, and propped his left foot up on the drawer. "No," he said, shaking his head. "There wasn't any neurological involvement. And with that acute renal damage . . ." He stared at me, a puzzled expression on his face. "Why do you ask?"

The time had obviously come.

"Remember that maintenance man who died from aldicarb poisoning?"

Dr. Augustin continued to stare.

At least I have his attention, I thought. I leaned against the wall. "According to the urban horticulturist at the county cooperative extension service, Mr. Roan—that's the dead guy—would never have used a pesticide illegally or improperly. He apparently was very reliable and had a good record with the license people."

Dr. Augustin allowed a tiny grin to sneak across his features. "My, my Samantha. I thought you hated detective work. And why exactly did that landscaper's death interest you enough to send you to the cooperative extension service?" He crossed his arms over his chest.

138 Karen Ann Wilson

"I figure someone else at Sunset View Towers got the aldicarb," I said, "and Mr. Roan unknowingly came in contact with it and died. Isn't it possible that man and his dog—the ones found dead together in the man's bathroom—died because they got the aldicarb on their skin from walking in the grass? The designated dog-walk area is sodded. I'm sure they spray it, or whatever, for bugs."

Dr. Augustin was still grinning. "It's possible, I suppose," he said, condescendingly. "But Riley is a housecat. He did not come in contact with any pesticide-tainted grass in the dog-walk area."

"It was just a thought," I said. I turned around and went back to the lab. I couldn't be sure, but I thought I heard Dr. Augustin snicker.

Grey couldn't think of any toxic chemical Riley might have come in contact with and had never used rat or mouse poison in her apartment. She hadn't even taken advantage of the complex's bug man because she didn't approve of prophylactic pest control.

"I don't use anything but aspirin," she told me, when I questioned her about the ibuprofen. "And I would never give Riley any medication without first checking with the vet." She sounded mildly put out.

"I knew that already," I said quickly, "but Dr. Augustin wanted me to ask, anyway. Just to make sure."

"I'm sorry," she said. "Of course, I want Dr. Augustin to investigate all possibilities. You say Riley is better? Does that mean he can still come home tomorrow?"

"He is better. His diarrhea has stopped, and he isn't dehydrated any longer. Dr. Augustin can tell you more, though, when he calls." I looked at my watch. "He should be free in about thirty minutes."

After I hung up, I went back to the surgery. Dr. Augustin

CIRCLE OF WOLVES 139

was examining a bearded collie brought to us Saturday. The dog had been run over by its owner, who hadn't seen her asleep behind his car. The right rear leg had been broken in two places, but otherwise, the dog was fine. And very lucky.

Dr. Augustin looked up. "Help me here, Samantha," he snapped.

The collie was not being terribly cooperative, as Dr. Augustin attempted to remove the adhesive tape and cast padding from the leg. I hurried over to the table and grabbed the dog. Her tail pounded the stainless steel table.

As Dr. Augustin cut through the bandage, I told him what Grey had said.

"Maybe someone got into Grey's apartment while she was away and purposely poisoned Riley," I offered. "Maybe the same person who threw her neighbor's cat off the balcony."

Dr. Augustin laughed. "I never knew you were the paranoid type, Samantha."

"Hey, it was you who suggested the possibility that someone at the apartment complex doesn't like pets. Or some of the residents are feuding, and this is the way they get back at each other."

Dr. Augustin pulled the bandage off and threw it in the trash. The dog's leg was a little puffy, but not bad, considering. The incision, of course, looked marvelous.

"Okay, okay," said Dr. Augustin. "You win. Let's assume someone over there is bumping off selected dogs and cats. We need to find out who has access, on a regular basis, to the apartments. Who has Mrs. Milner given a key to? Also—does she have any enemies? And does anyone in management disapprove of the pets policy? In other words, is there some reason, monetary or otherwise, they might want the pets out of there? Find out if Mrs. Milner had to fork over any kind of security deposit for Riley."

140 Karen Ann Wilson

He slid his arms under the collie, then lifted her off the table. "And see if the people who moved into that dead man's apartment brought a pet with them or if there's a policy in place now that prohibits pets for new residents."

I followed him down the hall to X-ray.

"You still need to call Mrs. Milner about Riley's condition. Why don't you ask her about the pets policy?"

Dr. Augustin put the collie on the table. "Because you need the practice," he said.

"Practice?"

"Sure. How are you ever going to solve cases if you don't practice your interviewing technique?"

He isn't taking this seriously, I told myself. *But he will, once I find a connection between what's happening at Sunset View Towers and Kelsey Cronin. And he'll thank me, too.*

Between morning appointments, I found the time to phone Michael. He'd been in Tallahassee on Monday, so I couldn't ask him about what had killed Robert Penlaw and his dog.

I was in the kennel. The noise that day wasn't too bad. Only a couple of our Thanksgiving boarders had come in, and Frank had on his Walkman, so I wasn't being subjected to the sound of electric guitar and drums that I felt certain was slowly eating away at Frank's hearing.

"I'm glad you called, Samantha," said Michael. "There's been a change of plans for Thanksgiving dinner."

I held my breath. Once again, I hadn't been consulted beforehand. Originally, he said we were going to the Hyatt for Thanksgiving.

The thought of spending what ought to be a warm, family and friends occasion with a roomful of strangers, eating a mass-produced roast turkey and pumpkin pie made by Mrs. Smith, instead of my mother (or Cynthia) was upset-

CIRCLE OF WOLVES 141

ting. I had spent more than one Thanksgiving eating peanut butter and jelly because I couldn't afford (or didn't have the time) to fly home. By not eating anything that even remotely resembled turkey, I could get through that fourth Thursday in November without feeling too depressed. But Michael simply could not pass up another opportunity to stuff me full of calories.

"*I'm* cooking dinner this year," he announced.

I exhaled. "What, no turkey at the Hyatt?" I asked, my voice not altogether unintentionally sarcastic.

"No," he said. "You obviously did not relish the idea, so I've decided to do the cooking myself. Turkey, dressing, cranberry sauce. The works."

"Have you ever cooked a turkey before?" I asked. Michael could whip up the best omelette I had ever eaten, but roast turkey was another thing entirely. All I could think of were the warnings about salmonella and other nifty things you can get from underdone poultry and stuffing.

"Yes, Samantha," he sighed.

"Real stuffing? Not Stove Top?"

"Perish the thought," he said.

"Real pumpkin pie? Or will it be Mrs. Smith's?"

"I promise," he said. "Nothing by Mrs. Smith. Or Sara Lee. Or Pepperidge Farm. Scout's honor."

Michael really was a doll. "Sounds wonderful. Just tell me how I can help. I'll do all the dishes."

We laughed at that one. Michael washes up as he goes, so I was safe offering to do the dishes.

"Well," he said, after a minute. "What's up? Or did you just want me to tell you how much I love you?"

"No," I said. "I mean, yes and no. I need your help on something."

"I'm at your service," Michael said enthusiastically, as always.

142 Karen Ann Wilson

Michael, it seemed, loved a good mystery almost as much as Dr. Augustin. Particularly when he could flex his research and information-gathering muscles. Some men show off their masculine prowess by hunting game with high powered rifles. Michael prefers the Internet.

"I'm trying to find out about a death at Sunset View Towers," I said. "It occurred this year, but I'm not sure when. An elderly man was found dead in his bathroom. His dog was with him, also dead. The guy's name was Robert Penlaw. I want to know what he died from. And what killed the dog."

"I take it Dr. Augustin considers the death suspicious."

"No," I said. "Dr. Augustin is wrapped up in a personal matter right now. I'm looking into Mr. Penlaw's death for Gretchen Milner. That woman I told you I met on the nursing floor. She and I have become friends, sort of. And she wants to know about Penlaw. That's all." I wasn't ready to share my suspicions with him just yet.

"I'll get right on it," he said. "An acquaintance of mine over at the medical examiner's office owes me a favor. I'll call you back as soon as I have something. Of course, you realize, if the man's doctor pronounced him dead of natural causes, the medical examiner probably won't have anything."

"Whatever you can get me will be fine," I said.

Michael didn't waste any time. Unfortunately, he phoned while I was at lunch. Cynthia took the call.

"I have no idea what this means," she said, handing me one of her pink memo slips. "What are you and Dr. Augustin up to, anyway?"

"We are not up to anything. I'm checking on something for a friend."

"Meaning it isn't any of my business, is that it?" She got up and took her purse out of the desk. Her lips were a thin red underscore beneath her nose.

CIRCLE OF WOLVES 143

"I never said that, Cynthia."

I quickly read the memo. "I can't tell you what I'm up to," I continued, "because I'm not really sure myself."

Cynthia was silent as she put on her raincoat and plastic rain bonnet. Silent, but certainly not wordless, if body language counts for anything. She had her chin up in the air and her shoulders back in what I had come to recognize as her "ruffled feathers" posture.

"According to this," I began, patiently, "Robert Penlaw, a neighbor of Gretchen Milner, died of a heart attack, which was deemed to be from natural causes. The cops found his dog pinned beneath his body in the bathroom. Apparently, the animal couldn't extricate itself and suffocated. Hmmm . . . I wonder what they did with the dog's body."

Cynthia looked at me then and frowned. "You worry me sometimes, Samantha. Why on earth would you want that poor animal's body?"

"To see if it really suffocated. Dr. Augustin and I think someone may be intentionally killing off people's pets over there at Sunset View Towers. I'm trying to find out if that's true and why."

"Oh," she said, apparently mollified. "How dreadful."

"So where are you off to?" I asked, as she headed for the front door. "And don't forget, Larry will be here this afternoon."

"I'll be back before he gets here. I have some grocery shopping to do." She smiled broadly. "Mike has invited me to his house for Thanksgiving dinner. I hope you don't mind." She blushed suddenly. "I hope I'm not intruding."

"Of course I don't mind," I said. "What are you bringing." My mouth was already watering at the thought of homemade goodies direct from the kitchen of Cynthia Caswell.

"I'm making the pies."

"Pies, plural?" I asked.

"Yes. Mince, pumpkin, and apple. I figure three, maybe four, should be enough. After all, not everyone will want dessert after filling up on turkey and dressing and mashed potatoes."

"You mean, Michael is having more than just you and me to dinner?" So much for the warm, family-and-friends occasion.

"Why, yes," she said. "I believe Mike said there will be nine of us altogether." She cocked her head quizzically. "I'm surprised Mike hasn't told you."

I'm not, I thought, angrily.

CHAPTER 16

•

Wednesday, November 24

Riley continued to improve. Dr. Augustin didn't think the renal damage was permanent. Whatever the cat had gotten into wasn't very concentrated, or Riley hadn't consumed very much of it. He was a long way from being well enough to go home, however.

I decided to keep my date with Grey, anyway. I enjoyed her company. Her vitality and enthusiasm, particularly in light of her age, were refreshing, to say the least. And after everything that had happened recently, I figured she could use a little support. With her family miles away and busy with their own lives, William dead, and Riley in the hospital, she seemed so alone, so terribly vulnerable. Which was the other reason for my visit.

The maintenance man with the greasy kid stuff on his hair was pruning the shrubbery outside Grey's building when I arrived. I had Lucky with me, and the man stopped his pruning and watched me with his beady little eyes, as if waiting for me to let the dog relieve herself on *his* lawn. He held his pruning shears out like a saber, and I wondered if he intended to spear Lucky with them. Fortunately, the puppy had "done her business" right before we left the clinic. She did manage to growl as we went inside the apartment build-

145

146 Karen Ann Wilson

ing. I probably imagined it, but I thought I saw the man's lips curl back from his teeth in response.

Grey was wearing a turquoise warm-up suit and white Reeboks.

"Oh, I'm so glad you brought your little dog," she said, as she opened the door.

Lucky began to wag her tail and whine.

"I hope she doesn't get into trouble here," I said.

I put her down on the parquet, and she stood by my foot, sniffing the air. Cat smells, the aroma of freshly baked cookies, and strange human odors were a veritable cornucopia to her canine nose.

"I'm not worried in the least," said Grey. She went over to the sofa and sat down.

I stood in front of her sliding glass doors and looked out at the fluffy, white clouds racing across the sky like commuters hurrying to start the long holiday weekend. It was a beautiful fall afternoon, with the air refreshingly clean and crisp following Tuesday's rain.

I joined Grey on the sofa. There was no point in beating around the bush. "Dr. Augustin thinks Riley was poisoned," I said.

Grey nodded. "Yes, that's what you told me yesterday. But I've checked everywhere and can't find anything he might have gotten into."

"No," I said. "I mean *poisoned*. As in, not by accident. Who else has a key to your apartment?"

Grey started to say something, then stopped and made a little rasping sound in her throat. She put her hand to her mouth, and her expression quickly changed from casual concern to marked fear, as the meaning of my question settled in.

"Oh my," she said softly. "That cat that fell off the bal-

CIRCLE OF WOLVES 147

cony, and that poor dog. You're saying someone intentionally killed them? Why would anyone do such a thing?"

"We don't know for sure yet that anyone has. It's just that Dr. Augustin is as puzzled as you are about the deaths. And now, with Riley sick . . ."

She put her hand back in her lap and frowned, anger replacing the fear.

"The maintenance people have a key. They have keys to all the apartments. My husband had the dead bolt changed when we moved in, as a precaution. But Mr. Bradshaw—he was the head of maintenance back then . . . I'm not sure who is in charge now. Mr. Bradshaw was fired several years ago. Drinking on the job, I believe."

She had wandered off the path. Deep furrows formed suddenly over her nose, as she attempted to mentally find her way back. It was the first time I had noticed any sign of old age in the woman.

"The maintenance people," she said finally, "have to get into our apartments when something needs repairing. I would rather hire my own plumber or electrician, but the management here says because the property belongs to them, they have a right to do the repairs themselves."

Lucky suddenly bounded across the floor, apparently failed to see the glass doors in time, and crashed head-on into them. She fell backward, got up, shook her head violently, and ran over to the sofa. I picked her up.

"Nothing broken," I said, checking her nose and front teeth. I scratched the dog's head, gave her a hug, then put her back on the floor. She stood motionless next to my leg and stared at the glass door as if it were really a big mean dog who'd just bitten her.

"Poor little thing," said Grey. "I used to have a couple of those paste-on flowers stuck to the glass. So people would know when the doors were closed. I put one about eight

148 **Karen Ann Wilson**

inches up from the floor for Riley's benefit. I guess they must have finally come off."

"To your knowledge, then," I said, pulling her back to the issue at hand, "only the maintenance people have a key to your apartment?"

Grey nodded. "Yes. And my son has a key. And Lily, of course. My neighbor across the hall."

"Lily?"

"In case something happens while I'm away. Lily is to catch Riley and keep him in her apartment."

I thought about this for a few seconds. "Lily is a good friend, is she?"

"You needn't worry about Lily," said Grey. End of subject.

"How does the management feel about the pets?" I asked. "Are new tenants allowed to have them, or is that privilege restricted to people who've been here awhile?"

Grey picked up the cat pillow, smoothed out a few of the black satin threads as if it was Riley, himself, curled up in her lap.

"Quetzal Bay Properties—they're the people who run the complex—brought in a new director last year," she said. "No, it was two years ago. And a new set of rules and policies, some of which I don't care for in the least. But who am I to complain?"

She put the pillow back on the sofa and brushed off her warm-up suit. I had to look again at the needlepoint to make sure it wasn't purring.

"Those of us who came here before the change can keep our pets. When they die, we can't replace them. And new tenants aren't allowed to have pets at all. I'm 'grandfathered in,' you might say."

Till death do us part, I thought grimly.

"Is it really possible," Grey asked, "that someone work-

CIRCLE OF WOLVES 149

ing for Quetzal Bay Properties is killing our dogs and cats, knowing we can't bring in new ones?"

Lucky had settled across my left foot. I moved it gently, hoping she would get up, but she was like the sand bags we use in X-ray to position animals.

"I suppose," I said. "But why did the management say they wanted to end the pets policy? Or did they give you a reason?"

"Mr. Aveneau said it was costing the company too much money for pest control, and dogs were doing their business all over the lawn. He said he was having trouble renting the apartments because the animal smell had permeated the drapes and carpeting. Of course, I find that difficult to believe. There's a waiting list a mile long for apartments here. And in any case, the security deposit they require is more than sufficient to clean and sanitize an apartment three times the size of this one."

She stood up. "Let's not talk about this anymore," she said. "At least not now. I've made cookies to go with our cocoa. It's such a beautiful day. Why don't we go out on the balcony and enjoy the view?"

She headed for the kitchen. I felt Lucky move, and suddenly the dog was trotting along behind Grey, as if she had understood her and was ready for a cookie or two herself.

"May I use your bathroom?" I asked. "I'd like to wash my hands."

Grey stopped in the dining room and pointed. "First door on your right."

When I had finished drying my hands on one of Grey's dainty little hand towels, I opened the bathroom door and stopped. At the end of the hall, where the master bedroom should have been, was a room swimming in light, the white walls and vinyl floor reflecting the sunshine like a parabolic mirror. Even on a cloudy day, I felt certain one would need sunglasses in that room. Curiosity got the better of me, and I tiptoed down the hall to the doorway and looked in.

It was Grey's studio. The room was large, about fifteen by eighteen, with a bathroom at one end and windows on the west and south walls. Blank canvasses of various dimensions and pads of drawing paper were propped up against the east wall and, next to them stood an oversized hutch containing what I imagined were paint supplies. A long, flat chart-and-map–style table with four drawers seemed especially suited for storing watercolors and sketches.

The floor was ivory with a faint texture, and spilled paint, obviously mopped up time and time again, had left traces of color in the crevices and wrinkles. It reminded me of the "antiqued" furniture in my first apartment.

Four tall, narrow paintings, all of green, rolling hills dotted with grazing sheep, were mounted on the longest wall, positioned about four inches apart, so that they made one continuous mural. It was as if you were looking through a set of French doors at an English countryside.

An easel stood all alone in the center of the room. The canvas was facing the south window. I couldn't see what was on it from where I stood and couldn't bring myself to get any closer. I was trespassing. The stark whiteness of the room and the bright afternoon sun blazing through the west window made me think of the light one supposedly sees at the moment of death. It seemed almost sacrilegious for me to be there at all.

"I hope you like raisin oatmeal."

I whirled around and felt my face start to burn. Grey was standing at the opposite end of the hall, holding a tray containing two mugs and a small plate of cookies. Lucky was right beside her, panting happily. I could almost smell her cookie breath.

"I . . . was just . . ." *Just what? Sneaking around where I*

CIRCLE OF WOLVES 151

didn't belong? Stealing some of your privacy, as if enough people hadn't done that already?

"It's okay, Sam," Grey said gently. "I don't mind. I generally don't take people into the studio because there isn't much to see, really. Tubes of paint, brushes, now and then a painting in progress. What I have to show people is hanging in the living room and at a few small galleries here on the beach."

I followed her out onto the balcony. We shut the sliding doors, leaving Lucky to stare mournfully at us through the glass.

"That room was originally the master bedroom," Grey said.

She put the tray down on a tiny white wicker table, and we sat on either side of it in matching wicker chairs with forest green seat cushions. I picked up my mug and wrapped my hands around it. The balcony was sheltered from all but a west wind, and the sun was warm, but I felt chilly anyway, in my T-shirt.

"After Gerald died, I moved my studio there from one of the guest rooms. The light is better, anyway, and I couldn't sleep in that room. Not with him gone."

She took a sip of cocoa and squinted out at the horizon. The sun, a giant orange disk in the evening sky, looked like something out of one of Grey's paintings. Then I looked over at her. I could see the network of wrinkles and folds in her face and neck more clearly in the natural light. Incandescent light has a way of softening everything, masking tiny imperfections. Like the peppering of brown spots on the backs of her hands. "Liver spots" my mother calls them. I've never asked her why. She makes it sound like some horrible affliction. Like growing old is a dread disease to be avoided at all costs. Grey, on the other hand, seemed to revel in it.

152   **Karen Ann Wilson**

"Tell me something, Sam," she said, suddenly. She turned to look at me. "Do you believe in ghosts? Because I would swear Gerald is still here with me. In that room. I feel him watching over my shoulder while I paint. It's ridiculous, I know. And you'll probably say it's because I'm old and lonely. Or crazy. But I just can't shake the feeling."

She poked the remnants of her marshmallow with her finger, then licked it—a child masquerading in an old woman's body. Suddenly, I felt very sad.

"No, Grey," I said. "I don't think you're crazy at all."

I left Grey's apartment at a quarter to six. Dinner on the second floor was in full swing, so Lucky and I had the elevator to ourselves.

When I got outside, I looked around for what's-his-name, but he was gone. On dog patrol, no doubt. I put Lucky down, and she did her thing like a good girl. And the idea that in a couple of days there would be a big yellow spot in the grass cheered me right up.

We started across the lawn toward the parking lot and ran into Beatrice Snoden. She was carrying a clipboard. A tall, decent-looking, albeit overweight, man in a poorly fitting suit was with her. The man's jacket pulled through the chest and across his protruding abdomen.

"Miss Holt!" Mrs. Snoden exclaimed, smiling. "This is a surprise. Hello, Lucky." She held out her hand, and the puppy licked it. "What brings you here today?"

"Lucky and I are visiting Gretchen Milner. I met her on the nursing floor my first day there, and we've gotten to be good friends."

Beatrice turned, as if only just remembering her companion. "Samantha, this is Nelson Aveneau, our administrative director. Nelson, this is Samantha Holt, the pet therapy volunteer I told you about."

CIRCLE OF WOLVES 153

I got the distinct feeling that Ms. Snoden and Mr. Aveneau were not on the best of terms. Beatrice acted nervous and fidgety. She talked too fast and, even in the fading light, I could tell her face had too much color in it.

"How do you do," I said, holding out my hand.

Mr. Aveneau shook it. His hand was rough and weathered, like Michael's hands, and I wondered if he, like Michael, was a sailor. He didn't look the part. And he didn't look overly pleased to see me, either. I got the impression he was studying me, as though the meeting were an interview, and I wasn't doing very well. I felt myself straighten up.

"I'm sure Mrs. Milner appreciates your interest," he said, smiling. His voice was deep and throaty. "Unfortunately, occasional visits from friends and volunteers such as you frequently aren't enough. Many of our elderly residents find they cannot adequately care for themselves without daily assistance." His words came out sounding like the introduction to a speech. Practiced, though certainly not polished.

"Gretchen doesn't seem to be having any difficulty," I said, with more directness than I'd intended.

"Perhaps," he said, his teeth showing through his smile. "I certainly hope you're right."

"We'd better go," Beatrice said, looking at her watch. "Or we'll be late for our meeting."

"It was a pleasure," said Mr. Aveneau, nodding at me.

They headed for Gretchen's building. I watched them go. I didn't like Aveneau. For some reason, he reminded me of a slum lord, although Sunset View Towers was hardly a slum.

"Maybe he used to work for the IRS," I said aloud.

Lucky barked her agreement.

CHAPTER 17

•

Thursday, November 25

When I was a kid, Thanksgiving day meant waking up to the sound of pots and pans clattering in the kitchen downstairs and the smell of celery and onion sautéing in real butter. My mother always began cooking well before dawn, starting with the pies. Pumpkin and mince. The turkey went into the oven at nine, and for the next five hours, my salivary glands worked overtime.

At noon, my grandparents arrived, along with my aunt and uncle (on my mother's side) and my three cousins, only one of whom—the girl—I liked. The other two, being boys, were gross and disgusting, usually on purpose.

Sometimes my father joined the party. Frequently, however, he was off saving lives. He ate his Thanksgiving dinner in the hospital cafeteria with the scrub nurse *du jour* at his side. We always set a place for him, though. Like he was missing in action somewhere.

When I was eighteen, my aunt and uncle moved to Florida, and my grandfather died. Then, as if our family get-togethers hadn't suffered enough already, my father finally left my mother for good. Missing in action would have been preferable.

After that, we still had turkey and dressing and pumpkin

154

CIRCLE OF WOLVES 155

pie, but Mom got four extra hours of sleep on Thanksgiving day and a lot less mess to clean up.

My cats woke me at the usual time, even though it was a holiday, and Dr. Augustin had volunteered to do treatments. It is difficult, if not impossible, to sleep with a cat kneading the side of your face, while her "sister" pretends your foot is a mouse. So I made coffee and drank it and tried to decide what to wear. Michael told me to come over to his place around one. He did mention he had invited a few friends to join us, which was damned decent of him, although I should have been pleased. To my knowledge, he hadn't told anyone at the *Times* about our engagement and had only introduced me to one fellow journalist, a man by the name of Chip Reason, who grinned at me like I was some twenty-year-old chorus girl Michael had fallen for. Elopement was looking better and better.

I decided against wearing a dress, only because I knew that's what Michael expected me to wear, and I was feeling rebellious. I plugged in my iron and lightly pressed a pair of grey wool trousers. Then I took out the sweater my grandmother had given me for Christmas a couple of years before. She never could get used to the fact that I wasn't a teeny-bopper anymore. The sweater is peach and white, with little grey and black kittens chasing balls of yarn around the lower edge. It has a wide white lace collar that makes me look about sixteen. Chip would love it.

I arrived at one o'clock on the nose and was pleased to find I was the first one there. It gave me a faint advantage. At least I wouldn't feel too much like a filly being led into the show ring, while everyone on the rail evaluated my conformation.

Michael, dressed in a burgundy pinstripe shirt, maroon tie, and grey slacks, opened the door. His apron said, "A waist is a terrible thing to mind." He had a glass of white wine in one hand. We kissed, and he offered me the wine.

"Australian," he said. "Quite good, actually."

I could smell roast turkey, butter, rosemary, and sage. And Parmesan cheese. My mouth began to water, and I took the wine glass from him.

"It smells wonderful in here," I said. "When do we eat?"

Michael put his hand on my shoulder and ushered me into the kitchen. "Have a seat," he said. "The appetizers are almost ready." He looked at the clock on the wall. "I wonder where Cynthia is. She said she'd be here at twelve-thirty."

"Primping, I suspect. You know Cynthia."

I sat down at Michael's kitchen table and sipped my wine. I hadn't eaten anything since 7:30, except a glass of milk. The last thing I wanted to do was guzzle alcohol. On the other hand . . .

The doorbell rang, but before I could get up to answer it (like a good little hostess), Cynthia walked in.

"Hellooo," she sang out from the foyer. "Where is everybody?"

"In the kitchen, Cynthia," I said.

A moment later, she bustled in, carrying a large and apparently heavy picnic basket, which she wrestled onto the table with a grunt.

She looked like a Christmas tree. Her long-sleeved blouse was forest green polyester, with shiny gold balls for buttons. The skirt was dark green wool. She had red bell earrings hanging from her earlobes, and every time she moved or talked, they tinkled. She sounded like a musical Christmas card, and all that was missing was a necklace made from a set of battery-operated lights. "Oh Tannenbaum" meets "Jingle Bells."

"Hello, Cynthia," Michael said, giving her a peck on the cheek. "Don't you look festive."

CIRCLE OF WOLVES   157

Cynthia beamed. "I just love Christmas, don't you?"

"This is Thanksgiving, Cynthia," I said, sitting back down with my wine. I took a nice big gulp.

"It's the start of the Christmas season, Samantha," she said. "After all, the Macy's Thanksgiving Day parade always ends with Santa on his sleigh, now, doesn't it?"

I could hear the Pilgrims turning over in their graves.

Michael took a pan out of the toaster oven. The odor of cheese and sage intensified.

"These are sausage puffs," he said, sliding pinwheel-shaped cookie things onto a serving platter. He placed the platter on the table directly in front of me. "Please, help yourself."

Thanks to Michael, I often feel like a goose whose liver is bound for pâté. But I picked up a napkin anyway and took one of the puffs off the platter, leaving behind a little puddle of grease. I stared at the pinwheel and tried to mentally tabulate its fat grams. Sausage, Parmesan cheese, puff pastry. I could feel my arteries hardening. I took a bite carefully. I didn't want to add a third-degree mouth burn to the bargain.

Cynthia opened her picnic basket and began lifting out the pies, each in its own little Tupperware container. She arranged them on the table, then put the basket on the floor.

"I hope you have whipped cream," she said to Michael. "For the pumpkin pies. I forgot to get any."

The doorbell rang, and Cynthia hurried out to answer it. She was obviously in her element. I didn't want to spoil it for her.

"Where did you learn to cook, Michael?" I asked, chewing. The grease puffs were delicious.

Michael began slicing another roll of sausage pastry into quarter inch-thick circles. "Here and there," he said. "Mary and I took some cooking courses together."

I thought I saw him pause briefly, then continue slicing. I

158　　Karen Ann Wilson

was afraid to move for fear it might distract him. Michael is a tightwad when it comes to divulging information about himself, particularly if it involves his past.

"While I was in college, before I decided on a journalism degree, I fancied myself a chef. In those days, running a little bistro on some back alley in Georgetown seemed so romantic. Good food, good wine, good music. Jazz, of course. But it wasn't very realistic, considering I was having to work nights just to pay my tuition." He arranged the slices on the pan, then slid the pan into the toaster oven.

The Christmas tree appeared suddenly in the doorway. "Your guests are here, Mike," she jingled. "I've put them in the living room. They're helping themselves to the bar."

"Perfect," said Michael, picking up the hors d'oeuvre plate. "We were just headed in that direction."

Reluctantly, I got up and followed him and the sausage puffs into the living room.

It was a scene out of *Clue*. Next to the bar stood Colonel Mustard, an elderly gentleman with a fabulous, snow-white moustache, wearing a rust turtleneck and tweed jacket, circa 1945. He had watery blue eyes and a bulbous nose I felt certain would begin to glow before the afternoon was over. He was pouring himself a generous double Scotch on the rocks.

Miss Scarlet, apparently the colonel's date, was a girl of twenty (maybe) wearing a beaded tunic over black crepe pants. Her hair was jet black, certainly not natural, and cut in a very short pageboy. She had pronounced facial bones over cheeks so hollow you could almost see her molars through them, eyes burned in with a pound or so of eyeliner, and pouty, bee-stung lips, devoid of pigment, like the rest of her face. She looked like a black and white photograph. Except for her nails, which she'd gnawed on so severely her fingers resembled the toes on a tree frog. What nail was left was dripping with enamel the color of clotted blood.

CIRCLE OF WOLVES 159

Mr. Green and Ms. Peacock were sitting on the sofa. I had met them before on one of my cat-sitting visits to Michael's condo. They lived a couple of floors below him. Mr. and Mrs. Tilley: Harry and Jane. Harry was close to eighty but in great shape, nicely tanned and with all his glands functioning, if his roving eye was any indication. Jane was in her late sixties or early seventies, still relatively attractive, but clearly an iceberg when it came to sex. She sat primly on the sofa next to Harry and scowled at Miss Scarlet. When we'd met in October, she had given *me* the evil eye. I should have been offended that she'd switched allegiance, but I was actually relieved.

The remaining couple was also from Michael's building. George and Sophie Lasko. They were the same age as the Tilleys, but the similarity ended there. George was devoted to Sophie, and she to him.

"Clint," said Michael, happily, to Colonel Mustard. "Glad you could make it." He put the plate on the coffee table and went over to the bar, dragging me with him. "Samantha, I want you to meet Clint Ridgeway, editorials editor. Clint, my fiancée, Samantha Holt."

Clint and I shook hands. I half-expected him to kiss mine or, at least, bow slightly and click his heels together. He needed a riding crop and a spaniel at his feet. Actually, Miss Scarlet was doing a pretty fair puppy imitation. She sidled up to him and slid her emaciated arm through his. She wasn't slobbering on him or carrying his slippers in her mouth, though. Not yet, at any rate.

"I'm so pleased to finally meet you, Samantha," said Mr. Ridgeway. "Mike's told me so much about you." He laughed suddenly. "All of it good, of course."

His voice was surprisingly thin and reedy. I'd expected something a bit more robust from the colonel.

"Clint . . ." began Miss Scarlet.

160 Karen Ann Wilson

"And this is Angela," said Mr. Ridgeway, as if only just remembering her name. And only her first name, at that.

Angela extended a paw. "Hi," she said. "Glad to meet you." She had a slight Southern drawl. "Love your sweater."

"Oh," I said. "Thanks. Love your nail polish." Sometimes I can't help myself.

"And these are some of my neighbors," said Michael, turning his attention to the sofa. "Harry and Jane and George and Sophie. I think you all met a couple of months back, didn't you, Samantha?"

"Hello, again, Miss Holt," said George. Sophie smiled warmly.

"Well," said Jane through icy lips, "you didn't tell us you and Miss Holt were *engaged.*"

"Yes, he did," said her husband. "As usual, you weren't listening."

Michael, ever the diplomat, smiled and said, "I'm sure Jane would have remembered if I'd told her." He pointed to the sausage puffs. "Please, do try these. And everyone fill your glasses. We eat dinner in twenty minutes."

Harry shook the ice cubes around in his otherwise empty glass and started to get up. Jane grabbed his arm.

"You don't need another drink, Harold," she said.

"Oh yes, I most certainly do," he said, winking at Miss Scarlet. He jerked his arm free and got up.

"All right," said Jane, "go ahead and make a fool of yourself. I don't care."

Harold walked over to the bar. "I'm so glad I have your permission, dear."

He reached for the bottle of gin. I noticed he extended his arm just far enough out of the way to brush against Angela's tunic. Of course, Jane noticed, too. The look she gave poor Angela would have dropped an elk at fifty yards.

Cynthia had been standing on the opposite side of the

CIRCLE OF WOLVES 161

room, next to the entertainment center, checking out Michael's CD collection, presumably hunting for Christmas music. She turned around.

"What does everyone want to hear?" she asked, smiling. She eyed Jane nervously, obviously concerned that the woman was rapidly turning Michael's little party into an ice hockey game. "The Mormon Tabernacle Choir or the Boston Pops?"

The food fight was progressing nicely. While Michael sliced and served the turkey and Cynthia kept everyone's wineglasses full, Jane talked about how much better everything was up North. The food, the theater, the scenery, the temperature . . .

"The snow," said Harry, grinning at Angela, who was seated directly across from him. "And sleet. Don't forget the sleet."

"I like snow," said Angela innocently. "It's so pretty. Everything all clean and new."

She used her fork to fluff up her mashed potatoes into a little snowdrift. While the rest of us ate, Angela sculpted, which probably accounted for her waifish figure.

Jane started to say something, then closed her mouth. Clearly, Angela's unexpected support regarding the snow had confused her.

"A toast," said Michael, picking up his wineglass. "May all your holidays be filled with joy and the company of friends."

We lifted our glasses and said, "Hear, hear," even Jane.

"And another toast to George and Sophie," Michael continued, "who just celebrated fifty years of marriage."

"Oh, wow!" said Angela, admiring the Laskos as if they were newly unearthed from an archaeological dig. "You guys sure don't look that old."

162   **Karen Ann Wilson**

"Angela . . ." began Mr. Ridgeway reedily.

"Sorry. But, hey, I think it's pretty terrific. You sticking together that long. Really. Hardly anyone stays married for long these days. My folks sure didn't."

She rolled a couple of brussels sprouts over to the base of the snowdrift. I decided they were little acacia trees, and the snowdrift was Mt. Kilimanjaro. And if I concentrated, I could almost see Hemingway's ailing narrator on his little cot, his leg rotting away.

Angela put her fork down and took a sip of wine. Then she pushed a lock of hair out of her face with a bloody stump and looked at me.

"So, when is the wedding?" she asked. Then she held up her hand. "No, don't tell me." She stared off across the room as if consulting some invisible calendar. "Let me guess."

"I was a June bride," Cynthia offered. "It's such a lovely time of year for a wedding, don't you think?"

"Michael and I haven't set a date yet," I said quickly. Michael, I noticed, was helping himself to the brussels sprouts. He grinned but didn't look up.

"Jane was a December bride," said Harry. "I recall the day we got married was so cold the church felt like a meat locker. Damn near froze to death." He chuckled. "Seems kind of fitting, now that I think about it."

No one said anything, as knives and forks sliced and diced to the strains of Handel's *Messiah*. But I saw Jane's back arch, then straighten out, and I feared by the end of the meal, there would surely be a dead body in Michael's condo. And my vote for the guilty party was Mrs. Peacock. In the dining room. With the knife.

CHAPTER 18

•

Friday, November 26

Dr. Augustin put Riley back in his cage and closed the door. "It sure is beginning to look like the management at that place is slowly eliminating their 'pet problem', doesn't it?" he asked, picking up Riley's file.

He made a few notes, then put the file back in the basket on the counter. We were in Isolation. It was 8:40.

"And if they're killing off the pets," I said, "isn't it possible they're accidently doing in a few of the owners at the same time? And maybe that landscape guy knew about it and threatened to say something."

Dr. Augustin rinsed his hands off, dried them, then opened the cage containing the poodle with heartworms. He took her out, and she coughed spasmodically a couple of times. Her breath smelled like stale shrimp scampi.

"Could be," said Dr. Augustin, putting his stethoscope to the dog's chest.

I held the animal's mouth closed briefly, while he listened to her heart and lungs. Then I put her back in her cage.

"It could also be that the landscaper's death *was* an accident. And those old people are dying of natural causes."

He went back to the sink and began washing his hands for the umpteenth time that morning. It was almost as if he was trying to wash his hands of more than doggie germs. His at-

163

164 Karen Ann Wilson

titude was really starting to tick me off. I picked up the bottle of disinfectant spray and coated the exam table. When Dr. Augustin turned around, I gave him my best attempt at a scowl.

He stopped and stared at me. "What?"

"I don't understand you," I snapped. "Someone is up to no good over there at Sunset View Towers, and you don't seem the least bit interested. I mean, even if those dead people weren't poisoned—well, except for Willie Roan, of course—dogs and cats are. So why aren't you out trying to find the guilty party?"

I went behind him, grabbed a couple of paper towels off the roll, then went back to the table. I knew my face was red, and my voice had that nasty, high-pitched whine it got when I was mad. Dr. Augustin continued to stand motionless and stare at me.

"And another thing," I said, as if I hadn't said enough already, "it seems to me that you'd want to find out what was going on over there, if only to help your case against Mr. Cronin. Quetzal Bay Properties manages Sunset View Towers. Maybe Keith Stone directed someone there to start killing off the remaining pets. Or maybe, just maybe Cronin himself told Stone to do it. That would certainly help you, wouldn't it? I mean, to know that?"

It didn't take me very long to realize my mistake. It didn't take Dr. Augustin very long, either. He came over to the table and grabbed hold of my arm. He wasn't hurting me or anything, but the implication of it sent a wave of fear through me like a jolt of electricity, and I felt my heart speed up.

"How do you know about Keith Stone?" he asked, his voice very low and quiet.

I am not a good liar, although I must say, I have shown considerable improvement over the last couple of years. But

CIRCLE OF WOLVES 165

under extreme pressure, my brain shuts down, and I start to babble, which is exactly what happened.

"I can't remember, exactly. Someone must have mentioned his name to me. Mr. Kemp, maybe." That was stupid, I told myself. Matthew Kemp would never tell me something like that. "No, it wasn't Matt, so it must have been Beatrice Snoden, the activities director there at Sunset View Towers. She and I were talking about the management's attitude toward the pet therapy program."

I stopped in order to breathe. Dr. Augustin let go of my arm.

"Are you through?" he asked.

I nodded vigorously.

"I know all about Quetzal Bay Properties," he said. "I also know that Sunset View Towers is not reaping the great financial rewards it should be, considering the net worth of its residents. It doesn't surprise me that Stone and company are attempting to cut corners wherever they can."

"So why aren't you trying to find out who's doing in the dogs and cats? I would think you'd be sharpening your lock picks and bolt cutters and telling me to wear my cat burglar outfit."

He started for the door, then looked back at me. "I told you Matt instructed me to keep out of it. That I should leave the snooping to his PI. I can't afford to get involved. It doesn't mean I don't want to, trust me." He pushed the hall door open. "And I want you to stay out of it, too," he said, his back to me. "And stop going through my mail. I appreciate your concern, but this isn't your problem." He left.

Riley stuck a paw through the bars on his cage door and made a tiny mewing sound, a sort of question mark. He was looking right at me.

"You're right," I said aloud. "It most certainly is my problem."

166   Karen Ann Wilson

·   ·   ·

The Christmas decorations were spread out across Cynthia's desk and on all but one of the chairs in the reception room. Our first client of the morning, an elderly woman with a beautiful Russian blue, was helping unpack the decorations box, her cat safely napping in its carrier atop the only empty chair.

Cynthia held up the hand-painted wooden Christmas tree she always puts on our front door.

"What do you think?" she asked. "Should we put the little cat ornaments on this or save them for in here?" She pointed to the artificial fir tree lying in pieces on the floor next to the water cooler.

"Whatever you put on the door," I said, "shouldn't be something you value. Remember what happened to the Halloween decoration."

Cynthia blanched, then frowned. "Thank you so much for reminding me," she said.

The client looked questioningly at me, but I just shrugged and went back to the lab. *Cynthia can tell her about the pentacle drawn in chicken blood*, I thought.

Our 11:30 was Glynnis Winter. Frosty had diarrhea again. It was pointless to suggest to Glynnis that her habit of feeding him people food was the cause of the problem. It was even more pointless to suggest she feed him one of the bland, low-fat, high-fiber foods designed for dogs with chronic digestive problems. The idea of giving her precious puppy anything except stroganoff or chicken and dumplings apparently turned her (and his) stomach.

"I've had to temporarily store my mother's things in his room," she said, "and it's upsetting him, isn't it sweetie?" She made kissing noises at him.

Frosty panted from the crook of Mrs. Winter's arm. His

CIRCLE OF WOLVES 167

eyes darted this way and that, like tiny bats chasing mosquitoes. I had to agree with Glynnis. He certainly looked upset, but it probably wasn't because his Gulf-view bedroom (complete with satin-lined doggie bed and autographed Rin Tin Tin poster, no doubt) was doubling as a storage room. Frosty, unlike most dogs, did not enjoy riding in a car or visiting new places. He'd make a lousy pet therapy dog, I told myself. And then I thought about Beatrice Snoden and her boss.

"By the way, Mrs. Winter," I said, as I showed her to an exam room. "Did you ever meet any of the management at Sunset View Towers? I mean, anyone other than the nursing staff?"

Mrs. Winter carefully examined the chair in the corner of the room like it was a toilet seat in a public rest room, then sat down on it.

"Of course," she said. "I had to sign my life away before they would take my mother in that so-called Assisted Living Facility of theirs. And that idiot doctor who convinced me to move her in the first place! At twice the price, I might add."

I would have sworn moving her mother had been Glynnis's idea, rather than the doctor's, an effort to rid herself of a problem. "What about the administrative director, Mr. Aveneau?" I asked. "Did you ever meet him?"

"I just told you, Miss Holt. When I moved my mother to the Hayes Building." She tightened the ribbon on Frosty's little topknot, then smoothed out the hair around his mouth. "And I went to school with their activities director, Bea Snoden. Of course, it was Peters back then. Followed by Brock. Why she left Tyler for that portly civil servant, Joseph Snoden, is beyond me."

"Mrs. Snoden was married to Tyler Brock, the attorney?"

Mrs. Winter nodded. "She worked for him as a legal secretary. Before he started that advocacy group for nursing

168   **Karen Ann Wilson**

home residents. You mark my words, Tyler Brock is Talla-hassee bound. All Joe Snoden can hope for is some measly government pension."

Dr. Augustin came into the room just then, and I decided to drop the matter. Besides, I no longer had Glynnis's full attention. None of it, actually. Dr. Augustin's stone-washed denim jeans had seen to that.

Michael came by at 5:30. He was sitting in the reception room supervising Cynthia's tree-trimming when I brought the last of the updated accounts receivable files to her.

"It's beginning to look a lot like Christmas, wouldn't you agree?" Michael asked me.

"Its unbelievable, actually," I said.

The phone rang. While Cynthia answered it, I surveyed the room. Despite our crowded appointment schedule and the usual Friday baths, Cynthia had found the time to transform our typical veterinary office decor into an ad for Robert's Christmas Wonderland.

Tinsel garlands (the kind you aren't supposed to hang where dogs and cats can reach them) were draped across the front of the reception desk and around all three tiers of the pet product display shelves. At regular intervals along the silver strands, colored balls dangled like floats on a fishing line. I wondered if Cynthia was trying to lure a few of our patients to partake of the garlands in order to drum up business, not that we needed it. In fact, Charlie, who was sitting on Cynthia's desk, front paws and head hanging over the near edge, tail counterbalanced over the far edge, stared intently down at one of the balls. His face was reflected in the shiny metallic surface.

The Christmas tree blinked and shimmered like a faraway city at night. And from inside the supply closet behind Cynthia's desk, the Mormon Tabernacle Choir was harking the

CIRCLE OF WOLVES 169

herald angels. I almost expected to see them in their choir robes perched on top of the bags of dog food.

"What have you got in here?" I asked Cynthia, peeking into the supply closet. "A radio?"

Cynthia went back to the tree and hung another ornament. There were tiny angel kittens with huge gossamer wings and puppies wearing holly collars and carousel horses spinning around candy cane poles. Most of the ornaments were animals, collected over the years by staff or given to us by clients and vendors.

"Michael lent us his portable CD player and some CDs," Cynthia said. "Wasn't that sweet of him?"

I went over to Michael and sat down in the chair next to him. "It was, indeed," I said, putting my hand on his arm. "Are you here to ask me out? Because if you are, I accept. All I have in my refrigerator is some leftover macaroni and cheese."

Michael shook his head. "Sadly, no. I'm here to ask a favor."

I waited.

"I'm going to Miami for a couple of days," he said. "Four, to be exact. Business, or I'd invite you to come along. Anyway, I need you to take care of the kittens. Would you do that for me?"

He slid his hand over to my knee. Like Dr. Augustin, he keeps his nails short and immaculate. But his fingers are blunt and rough. And the backs of his hands are covered with large freckles, brought on by too much exposure to the sun. And age.

"I'd be happy to," I said. "On one condition."

Michael grinned. "Okay. I promise we'll have dinner at Tuttles the moment I get back."

"I didn't mean that."

I looked over at Cynthia, who was trying to decide where

to put an enormous parrot ornament, complete with gaudy feathers and obviously fake claw-laden feet. Taiwan's idea of realism.

"I need some information," I said, my voice low. The choir was beckoning the faithful to come.

"I won't be back in the office until Tuesday," he said.

"Tuesday is fine. I'd like you to find out all you can about a Dr. Aaron. He works at Sunset View Towers. The nursing floor. And then, see what you can dig up on Tyler Brock, that lawyer who advertises on TV."

"Is Dr. Augustin involved in this, or are you poking around on your own?"

The phone rang again, and Cynthia grabbed it.

"I'm still freelancing," I said. "I think old people are being confined against their will on the psych wing. You remember I asked you about the Baker Act? Well, it seems Sunset View Towers is having some financial difficulties. One of our clients mentioned that the cost of keeping her mother in the assisted-living facility there was twice as much as when she had her own apartment in one of the other buildings. I'm sure being on the psych wing is even more expensive. And Gretchen Milner—my friend Grey—said a number of people she knows have ended up on the psych wing, and she's positive they don't belong there.

"I'm suspicious the management at that place is using the Baker Act to force people to move to the higher-rent part of the building."

"Unfortunately, that's a common practice," said Michael, "although, like I told you, the patients generally get 'Baker-Acted', as it's called, because they threaten to commit suicide or act irrationally, or show hostility toward someone. A doctor usually deems them a threat to themselves or others. Then, once confined, they have trouble getting out."

"That's why I need to know about Dr. Aaron. Maybe he's

CIRCLE OF WOLVES 171

getting a cut from each patient he 'Baker Acts.' Or maybe the management is forcing him to commit patients who don't need to be committed or risk losing his job."

Cynthia hung up the phone and switched on the answering machine. It was nearly six o'clock. She looked over at us but, getting no response, went back to the tree.

"Why do you want to know about Tyler Brock?" asked Michael.

"I'm not sure. But I don't trust him."

"Because he hawks his wares on TV?"

"No," I said, "because I saw him hawking his wares on the nursing floor. He makes his living suing doctors and hospitals for abusing the Baker Act, or whatever. Gets relatives all worked up by insinuating that their loved ones aren't getting the proper care, etc., etc. Maybe he somehow gets the patients committed, then makes a fortune suing to get them uncommitted. I don't know."

Michael looked at me like I needed commitment, but was kind enough not to say so. Then he stood up.

"I'll see what I can find out," he said. "In the meantime, you stay out of trouble. I hope this doesn't have anything to do with Robert Penlaw, the man who died of a heart attack and then fell on his poor dog."

"I hope not," I said.

CHAPTER 19

•

Saturday, November 27

Dr. Augustin wanted no part of my theories regarding Dr. Aaron and the Baker Act. He wasn't even terribly interested in discussing the pet situation at Grey's complex, although he agreed there did seem to be something felonious going on.

"I take it Matt's PI hasn't dug up anything new on Mr. Cronin or Monarch Development," I said.

We were in the lab. I was having to do Tracey's job as well as my own, since Dr. Augustin had seen fit to give Tracey Friday and Saturday off. Fortunately, Frank hadn't skipped out with her. I probably would have slit my wrists if he had. As it was, Dr. Augustin complained bitterly every chance he got. About the lab work not being done on time, about treatments being late, about the cat who scratched him because I wasn't around to hold it (in addition to everything else, I was supposed to be omniscient, evidently). So why was I inviting him to bite my head off? *Because I need help here,* I thought. *That's why. And I'll take it from wherever I can get it, even Matt's PI.*

I'd briefly considered calling Mr. Walls and telling him about the dead pets, in the hope he would be so grateful for the information he would fill me in on Quetzal Bay Properties and company. But only briefly. I could almost hear the guy laughing at me all the way across town.

172

CIRCLE OF WOLVES 173

"Not a thing," said Dr. Augustin. "Not one damned thing."

I looked at the heartworm ELISA test on the countertop. It was negative. I made a notation in the log, then reached for the little brown lunch bag containing Trixie's stool sample.

"Is Riley well enough to go home?" I asked. "I could run him by Gretchen's apartment tonight after work."

Dr. Augustin typed out a prescription label and hit the "Print" button. The printer coughed briefly, then advanced the label. Dr. Augustin peeled it off and attached it to a vial.

"If you think she can keep him out of trouble," he said.

"Grey was not responsible for Riley's illness," I snapped.

"I'm not saying she was. What I am saying is Riley might be better off here. For awhile."

"You mean until Matt's PI discovers who *was* responsible? That could take months at the rate he's going. I don't think Grey is willing to wait that long."

Dr. Augustin took a bottle off the pharmacy shelf and opened it. He poured some tablets into the prescription vial. "Maybe she won't have to," he said softly.

But he didn't give any indication he was finally going to lend a hand. And I didn't have enough energy left to press him on it.

I called Grey to tell her I was coming over for a visit but got no answer. So I drove to Michael's condo to feed his cats.

Katie and Randy were waiting at the door for me. Katie had a spot of dried blood on her left ear, and there were wads of hair (hers, mostly) scattered around the foyer.

"Randy, you should be ashamed of yourself," I told the kitten.

Randy blinked at me and started to purr. Katie crouched in the corner of the kitchen until I had filled their food dishes. Then she slowly crept over to hers and began to eat, her ears

174 Karen Ann Wilson

flat against her head, presumably in case Randy should decide to attack.

I watched the cats and thought about Michael's neighbors, the Tilleys and the Laskos. Harry and Jane clearly got on each other's nerves and spent a good deal of time snapping at each other, while George and Sophie still acted like newlyweds. But both couples had endured a half century of marriage, more or less, and, barring illness, would probably endure at least another decade. Obviously, it was better than eating alone, as the old woman on the elevator in Grey's building had observed.

"If being single is so great," I said aloud, "then why is nearly every single person I know over the age of thirty trying to get unsingle?"

The cats kept eating.

I followed the trail of fur into Michael's bedroom. His new furniture (*our* new furniture?) looked beautiful. All traces of Mary were gone. Even the bedspread was new. I looked around the room and tried to imagine my clothes hanging in the closet, my underwear neatly folded in the solid cherry dresser. My toothbrush parked next to Michael's in the bathroom. But I couldn't. Clearly, being single was a lot easier if you'd never been married.

I scooped the litter pan and refilled the cats' water dish, then left. It was 7:20, still early enough to see if Grey had any cookies left. And any words of wisdom for a single girl about to take the plunge, whether she wanted to or not.

By the time I reached Sunset View Towers, it was nearly eight o'clock. Traffic along the beach was bumper to bumper. According to the news, southbound I-75, like some giant coronary artery clogged with cholesterol, was backed up all the way to Ocala, as snowbirds flocked to their winter feeding grounds. It is 1,000 miles from the Michigan border to

CIRCLE OF WOLVES 175

Tampa, and I suspected a lot of the people on Gulf Drive that evening had left home before their Thanksgiving dinner was digested.

The guard was a man about my age. I gave him my name and destination, and he waved me through. In the semidarkness of his little guard shack, I caught the glow of a miniature TV screen. It looked like a football game was in progress.

That evening, the speed bumps were especially unnecessary. If I hadn't known better, I'd have sworn the cops had evacuated the entire complex. That some toxic gas—chlorine or ammonia—had escaped, or there'd been a bomb threat. Absolutely no one was visible outside, and I detected no movement and few lights on in the buildings I could see from the main road. Only the nursing floor in the Hayes Building was fully illuminated.

I parked in the visitor lot next to Grey's building and got out. I was so used to having Lucky with me at the complex, I paused on the lawn and checked around for the guy with the hedge trimmers. Then, smiling sheepishly, I hurried into the lobby and got on the elevator.

Like the rest of the place, the tenth floor hallway was deserted. The dog with the big mouth barked once, just to let me know he, at least, was still alive. There was a TV on in the apartment next to Grey's, the program a sitcom by the sound of it.

I knocked on Grey's door. I did this a couple of times, but got no response. From Grey, that is. The local busybody three apartments down slid his or her deadbolt and opened the door briefly, then closed it.

"Grey, it's Samantha," I said, not too loudly for fear the busybody might call out the militia.

Still no response. I knocked once more, that time vigorously. Suddenly, a door directly across the hall opened an inch or so. All I could see through the crack was a single eye and part of a mouth. They were only chest-high and, at first, I thought they belonged to a child.

"She's not home," said a mildly emphysemic voice. "What do you want?"

"I'm a friend of Grey's," I said. "Samantha Holt. I work at the veterinary clinic where her cat is staying. Is she all right?"

The door closed, and I heard the chain rattle. Then the door opened about a foot, and I was greeted by a female face so heavily wrinkled it reminded me of a balled-up piece of paper after you smooth it out. The woman's snow-white hair was pulled back in a ponytail. She wore a flowered housecoat and terrycloth mules.

"They took her to the hospital," she said.

She regarded me with surprisingly clear hazel eyes. She could have been anywhere from sixty to ninety, probably a smoker, which would have accounted for her voice and the condition of her skin.

"Hospital?" I asked. "You mean the nursing floor? What's wrong with her? Has she got the flu again?" A tiny alarm went off somewhere in my head.

The woman opened her door another foot and stepped back. "Why don't you come inside," she said.

I hesitated, then went in. The woman closed the door behind me and secured the chain. She turned around and held out her hand.

"I'm Lily Dumser," she said. "Grey has mentioned you to me."

We shook. It was like grabbing onto an ice sculpture. She led me into her kitchen.

"I was just having a cup of coffee. Decaf, of course." She said this with some amusement. "Won't you join me?"

"Please."

CIRCLE OF WOLVES 177

Lily was so thin, the housecoat hung from her shoulders like it might from a wire clothes hanger. She had no breasts whatever and almost no calf muscles. Some progressive disease was eating away at her from the inside. I figured it might be emphysema, although she was breathing without a great deal of difficulty and without supplemental oxygen. Was it cancer?

I sat down at the kitchen table and marveled at the vast pharmacy arranged around the salt and pepper shakers. I couldn't read any of the vials without being obvious. Lily had used a marking pen to print a large black letter on the cap of each prescription vial, to help differentiate them, presumably. The marker was lying on the table, along with a small black notebook.

"Grey is at St. Luke's," said Lily. She got two coffee cups out of the cabinet over the stove. "Came down with some sort of intestinal bug, they told me. When I found her, she was lying on the bathroom floor. I'm so glad I keep a key to her apartment."

She poured coffee into the mugs and carried them over to the table. "Cream?"

I shook my head. They'd found Robert Penlaw on the floor in his bathroom. Dead, of course. And then I remembered Riley.

"Intestinal bug. You mean diarrhea?"

"Something fierce," said Lily. "Vomiting, too." She sat down across from me and began spooning sugar into her coffee. "She was badly dehydrated, according to the paramedics, and wouldn't have lasted the night."

She stirred her coffee, took a sip, then ladled another spoonful of sugar into it. The black liquid resembled crude oil.

"What made you go over there?" I asked.

178 Karen Ann Wilson

Lily got up and went to the sink. She rinsed off her spoon and put it in the drainer.

"Grey had rented a movie," she said. *"Fried Green Tomatoes.* We were going to watch it last night. She said she'd be over about seven-thirty."

Lily came back to the table and sat down. "I don't get out much these days. Grey is kind enough to do my shopping for me. And we frequently watch a movie together. When she didn't show up, I tried calling her. Then I got worried and let myself into her apartment. I dialed 911 as soon as I found her."

"She's very lucky to have a friend like you," I said.

I watched her play with the marking pen, idly rolling it between her fingers, an action not unlike that of a smoker with a cigarette. Her short nails had a faint yellow cast to them. I couldn't smell any cigarette smoke in the apartment or see any ashtrays or packs of cigarettes lying around. At least there weren't any in the kitchen. If she quit, I told myself sadly, it was probably too late, by the looks of her. "Do you know what she had for dinner?" I asked.

Lily shook her head. "No. You think it was food poisoning?"

"Maybe."

We locked eyes briefly. I wasn't sure how much I should tell her, a frail, elderly woman, alone. She obviously relied on others for her day-to-day existence, which made her a perfect target for the unscrupulous. If I told her what I suspected, would it frighten her to death?

"Grey told me about Riley," she said suddenly, as if reading my mind. "And about the other pets who've died. Dear Lord, you don't think Grey got sick from eating something intended for Riley, do you?"

"I hope not," I said.

CIRCLE OF WOLVES 179

And then it struck me. What if Riley had gotten sick from something intended for Grey? But why Grey?

"Could we go over to her apartment and look around?" I asked.

She nodded. "Grey said you reminded her of Kimberly. Her granddaughter." Her smile was fleeting. "I guess I can trust you."

She got the key out of a drawer next to the refrigerator and, together, we went across the hall.

"I meant to come over here and clean up," said Lily. "I just haven't had the energy."

"I'm glad you didn't. Clean up, I mean."

The kitchen was just as Grey left it, fortunately. Her dinner had consisted of a sloppy Joe with coleslaw. Most of the sandwich was still on her plate in the sink. A Tupperware freezer container and saucepan lay next to that. The dishwasher contained a juice glass, a cereal bowl, two coffee cups, and some silverware.

I picked up the lid to the Tupperware container. It had a little paper label stuck to it on which Grey had written "Beef Barbecue" and "11/21." I studied the lid.

"Grey told Dr. Augustin she made barbecue a week or so ago out of some leftover pot roast and then froze it," I said. "She thought Riley might have eaten some of the pot roast, and that's what made him sick."

I put the lid back in the sink and picked up the plate with the remains of Grey's dinner on it.

"I'm pretty sure this is the barbecue," I said.

Lily joined me at the sink and stared at the sloppy Joe as if it had a bit more of "Joe" in it than just his name.

"Shouldn't we get that tested?" she asked.

"You mean for poison?"

Lily nodded slowly and, from her expression, I gathered Grey's kitchen might never get cleaned up.

180   **Karen Ann Wilson**

"Does Grey have any plastic storage bags?" I asked. "The kind you put sandwiches in?"

"I don't know."

We searched through Grey's cabinets and drawers. I finally located a box of gallon-sized zippered storage bags. I dumped the sandwich carcass into one of them and closed it. Then, for good measure, I put the Tupperware in another bag.

I opened the refrigerator. A container of coleslaw provided a third sample.

"I'll have someone analyze these," I said, unsure who I meant, but determined to get it done by *someone,* possibly Dr. Augustin's toxicology friend up in Gainesville.

Lily looked like she could use a cigarette, so I quickly escorted her back across the hall to the relative safety of her apartment. She immediately got a brown grocery bag out of the pantry and handed it to me.

"For your samples," she said with obvious distaste.

After I'd deposited the specimens in the grocery bag, where they were hidden from view, Lily seemed to relax a little.

"If they let me talk to Grey," she said, as I gathered up my purse and took a last swig of coffee, "should I tell her about the barbecue? I don't want to upset her any further."

"Let's not tell anyone about it just yet. If there really is someone out there trying to kill . . . whomever . . . we don't want to let on that we know. Because we don't have any proof yet but, mostly, because we don't know who it is. Just tell Grey I hope she feels better. Oh, and tell her Riley is eating well and should be able to come home soon. That should cheer her up."

I said good-bye to Lily and stood in the hall until I heard the chain clank. Then I headed for home.

CHAPTER 20

•

Sunday, November 28

It was raining, a nice steady, drenching downpour. The kind that rids the air of exhaust fumes and makes waterfront property out of most of the land. I decided to forgo Lucky's potty stop outside the Marion R. Hayes Building. I could just hear Nurse Herfeld complaining about muddy paw prints all over her "guests'" bedsheets.

The male LPN with the earring was waiting for the elevator. I joined him. He was wearing an ID badge that day. It gave his name as Chris something.

"Lovely weather we're having, isn't it?" I asked, trying to fold up my umbrella while clamping down on Lucky, who was wagging her tail so rapidly, it felt like she was about to become airborne.

Chris smiled. "Hey, it could be worse. The wind could be blowing."

The elevator arrived. A woman with a small boy in tow got off, and we got on. Chris pushed 4.

"True," I said.

"So how are you and the mutt doing with the inmates?"

"You make it sound like a prison up there," I said.

"Well?"

I didn't say anything. The elevator stopped on the second

181

182 **Karen Ann Wilson**

floor, and the doors opened. No one was waiting. The doors closed again.

"Once they stick you on the psych wing," he continued, "you're there until your bank account dries up or you croak, whichever comes first."

On the fourth floor, Chris waited for me to get off, then followed. Lucky's head swiveled backward toward him. Her tail stepped up a gear.

"So where are you headed?" I asked, after we'd passed the nurse's station.

There was another orchid on the desk, this one a spray type, with lots of delicate white flowers, each bearing a tiny spot of purple in the throat. They looked like a flock of birds flying in formation.

"Sid's room. You know, the old geezer I look after? They finally got the family to commit him, which is ridiculous." He lowered his voice. "Hell, the guy can't even walk or take a leak without help. How can he be a 'threat to himself or others'?" Chris mimicked Nurse Herfeld.

"At least you're still keeping an eye on him," I said.

We passed a couple of the nursing floor residents. They were slumped down in their wheelchairs, staring at the wall.

"Dr. Aaron must have some way to determine who belongs on the psych wing and who doesn't," I said, pointing to a woman who was humming to herself and gesturing with her left hand.

She looked like she belonged on the psych wing, and I thought about Grey's friend, Tade, who seemed a lot more rational, despite the 'whispering.'

Chris made a choking sound. "Surely you jest. Dr. Aaron wouldn't know a schizophrenic if the voices they heard were actually audible. No, you get stuck on the psych wing if management can talk a relative or guardian into committing you. Better yet, if you don't have any relatives, they can get

CIRCLE OF WOLVES 183

the court to commit you. It's not as easy as it used to be, but, hey, where there's a will . . ." He chuckled at the pun, and I thought about Michael.

"Maybe you're a little forgetful," he continued, "or you don't hear so good, so you yell at people. Or you're depressed. Hell, I'd be depressed, too, if I had to wear a diaper and eat baby food three times a day. Besides, all that damned medication doctors prescribe for old people these days is bound to do a number on a person's mental state. Sometimes I think Dr. Kevorkian had the right idea."

We reached the fork in the corridor, and Chris pushed the button on the wall next to the automatic doors.

"I'll introduce you and the mutt to Sidney. Every once in awhile, the old guy finds his way to the present."

"I'm not allowed on the psych wing," I said. "Ms. Herfeld told me it was for my own good."

Chris made a face. "See what I mean? No, they're afraid you'll start asking a lot of pointed questions. Like, why are these people here?"

"They're not afraid you will?"

Chris looked a little embarrassed. He shrugged. "I can't afford to lose my license. And they could do that to me if they wanted to."

I smiled. "So you tell me, in the hopes *I* will. Is that it?"

Before he could answer, the doors opened. We were greeted by the charming Ms. Herfeld and her bouncer buddy.

"Good afternoon Mr. Cortland," she said, to Chris.

She stepped aside so Chris could pass. He turned back and winked at me, then continued on. Lucky whined softly.

"I believe Mrs. Snoden would like to have a word with you, Miss Holt," Nurse Herfeld said.

She looked down at Lucky with obvious disapproval. Lucky, on the other hand, had apparently transferred her af-

184 **Karen Ann Wilson**

fections from Chris to the bouncer and was pounding my rib cage with her tail and squirming violently. My arm screamed in protest. However, putting the dog on the floor did not seem like an option just then.

"Where is she?" I asked. "In her office?"

"I believe so," said Ms. Herfeld. She and the bouncer stepped back, and the doors began to close.

"Should I visit the patients first?" I shouted through the rapidly narrowing gap in the doors. "Or is Mrs. Snoden waiting for me?"

"Mrs. Snoden is waiting for you. I suggest you hurry." Her voice trailed off like a train rushing past me.

The doors whooshed closed, and I heard the locking mechanism click into place.

"She's not a very nice person, is she?" I asked Lucky, as we made our way back down the hall. The puppy licked at my face and whaled on my ribs.

I stopped briefly at the nurse's station to admire the orchid, then took the elevator back down to the first floor. Beatrice was standing in front of the doors when they opened. She smiled at me, but there didn't seem to be much happiness in her expression.

"I've got some bad news," she said. She continued to stand by the elevator, rather than invite me into her office. When I didn't say anything, she continued. "They've canceled the pet therapy program. Aveneau told me it was too disruptive. And they've had complaints from some of the visitors, apparently. People who are allergic to dogs. Or just plain don't care for them."

"I'm really sorry, Mrs. Snoden," I said. "It's my fault entirely. I let Lucky get away from me last week. And on the psych wing no less, where I wasn't even supposed to be."

"No, Miss Holt—Samantha—it isn't. Nelson Aveneau has been waiting for an excuse to do away with the activi-

CIRCLE OF WOLVES 185

ties director. To save money. If I don't have anything to do except run my little A.M. exercise class and organize card parties—things the nursing staff can manage without me—then he feels justified in laying me off." She frowned, and her carefully sculpted eyebrows formed little V's over her eyes. "After all, the management at this place is under the gun to cut costs, and corporate downsizing is in vogue right now."

"Again, I'm sorry," I said. "Really."

"So am I, Miss Holt. So am I."

We shook hands, and I watched her go around the corner toward her office. Her shoulders, usually straight and square, drooped like a wilting rose.

CHAPTER 21

●

I put Lucky in her cage, did afternoon treatments, then headed for St. Luke's Hospital. Visiting hours were from two o'clock until eight, the operator told me, except for maternity, whose hours took feeding time into account, and the intensive care units, where only family members were allowed, and then only for a limited time twice each day. The operator's disembodied voice had a bored, mechanical quality that reminded me of the computer on the starship *Enterprise*. I told her "thank you," and, before I could ask for Grey's room number, she severed the connection like a surgeon slicing through some vital nerve.

St. Luke's Hospital looks like a student architectural project done by committee, where none of the members was allowed to see his or her classmates' renderings. Every addition (and they are too numerous to count) is joined to the original building by a subterranean tunnel or aboveground passageway that pitches and rolls like an ocean liner in a typhoon. The whole monstrosity wanders over many acres, not including the parking lot. It, alone, covers at least eight city blocks.

I parked my car next to a light pole, hoping that would make it easier to find. The lot is marked in a grid pattern with the names of Florida counties and numbers from 1 to

CIRCLE OF WOLVES 187

100 painted on the blacktop at regular intervals. Unfortunately, it is tough to differentiate "Hardee" from "Manatee" in the dark.

I went in the main door and sought out the nearest information desk. It was manned by a sixty-something volunteer in a white shirt and tannish tie. He was working the *Times* crossword puzzle. With a pen. I cleared my throat, and the guy looked up.

"May I help you?" he asked, shoving the paper aside and smiling distractedly.

If I'd had the answer to sixteen across, I'm sure he would have been happier to see me. His nameplate read "Samuel Morgenstern, Volunteer."

"I'd like the room number for Gretchen Milner. She was admitted late Friday night."

Mr. Morgenstern swiveled around in his chair, punched a few keys on his little computer terminal, waited, then turned back to me.

"She's on C wing, Room 602. Intensive Care." He looked at his watch. "Visiting hours for immediate family are from three to four. It's just three now." He pointed down the hall to his right. "Take the elevator at the end of the hall up to six, then follow the signs to C wing. The nursing station is on your right."

I suppressed a surge of panic at the words "Intensive Care," thanked Mr. Morgenstern, and headed for the elevator. It's probably just because of her age, I told myself. They've got her in intensive care as a precaution. She's going to be fine. And then I realized I was undoubtedly wasting my time going to see her, because they wouldn't let me in.

I reached the elevator after a hike more suited to a mall walker, got on, and punched 6. I looked down at my jeans and sweater. They were still clean, even after hauling Lucky

188   **Karen Ann Wilson**

around and doing treatments. And I didn't detect any doggie odor. The last time Dr. Augustin had sent me on a fact-finding mission to the intensive care unit at St. Luke's, I had masqueraded as a physical therapy student. Obviously, that was not going to work this time, and I was still trying to decide what to do, when the elevator stopped on 5, and a young doctor carrying a short stack of charts got on. I felt my face grow hot as the man gave me the once over. It was like I had the word "Imposter" tattooed on my forehead. It didn't help one bit that the guy looked like Dr. Kildare. I practically fell out of the elevator when it finally (after what seemed like a millennium) reached the sixth floor. The doctor winked knowingly at me.

I rolled my way across the deck of the ocean liner to the C wing then, midway down the hall, stopped and stared at the LIMITED ACCESS: ALL VISITORS MUST REGISTER AT THE NURSES' STATION sign, as if willing the words to rearrange themselves and read, instead, UNLIMITED ACCESS: FEEL FREE TO VISIT WITH ABANDON.

If I had hoped for a busy day with lots of confusion to mask my presence, I was out of luck. The four nurses behind the desk at the nurses' station were calmly attending to paperwork or adjusting the various monitors positioned around the station. I didn't see the woman who'd been on duty in July, when I had done my brief stint as a PT student. With my luck, she would have recognized me instantly and called security.

I took a deep breath and walked up to the desk. Almost immediately, the nurse closest to me turned around.

"Yes?" she asked. She obviously hadn't spotted the "Imposter" tattoo, because she was smiling.

"I'm here to see Gretchen Milner, Room 602," I said, not looking directly at her. I feigned interest in one of the monitors behind the woman. "I'm her granddaughter, Kimberly

CIRCLE OF WOLVES 189

Milner." If Grey was the girl's maternal grandmother, or if Kimberly was married, I was in trouble.

The nurse leaned to one side, picked up a clipboard, and held it and a pen out to me. "Please sign in," she said. "You may stay for fifteen minutes." Her smile broadened. "I'm so glad Mrs. Milner changed her mind and called her family. She didn't want to worry anyone, but I know she'll be thrilled to see you. You're a lawyer, aren't you?"

I grabbed the clipboard like it was a flotation device. Clearly I was drowning and in need of a life preserver.

"That's right," I said.

I started to sign my own name, then changed the S to a K. My hand was shaking so violently, when I was finished, the signature looked like a doctor had written it, instead of a lawyer. Which was probably a blessing.

An alarm went off somewhere, and all four nurses turned their attention to the monitors. I put the clipboard and pen on the desk and hurried down the hall.

Grey was awake and propped up in bed, her various tubes and electrodes dangling from beneath the sheet like fringe on an afghan. She turned her head toward the door when I came in and, after a couple of seconds, smiled faintly. She was very pale, and her hair, usually clean and carefully brushed, was matted down on the back of her head. She was wearing a plain, pale blue hospital-issue gown. I thought about the Laura Ashley gown Kimberly had given her and made a mental note to bring it with me on my next visit, assuming I could pull off the granddaughter impersonation.

"Sam," she said, her voice so low, I could barely hear it, "this is such a treat." Then, a tiny grin, a remnant of the Grey I remembered, crept over her lips, and her eyes widened. "How did you get in here?"

I went over to the bed. "I told them I was your granddaughter, Kimberly. Her name is Milner, isn't it?"

190   **Karen Ann Wilson**

"No, but if the matter comes up, I'll say it was her maiden name, which is the truth."

She pointed to the chair next to her bedside table, and I pulled it over and sat down.

"How are you feeling?" I asked.

"Very weak, but I'll live, they tell me. How is Riley?"

"He's doing much better," I said. "I think he misses that gourmet cat food you feed him."

We chatted briefly about nothing in particular. Then I said, "I guess Lily told you about my visit to your apartment."

Grey shook her head. "I don't have a telephone. If I need to call someone, they bring me a portable phone. And, until now, I just haven't had the energy to talk much." She smiled at me.

"What have the doctors said?" I asked. "About your illness."

Grey drew up her face in disgust. "You really don't expect them to tell an old lady anything, do you?" It was a rhetorical question, of course.

"All I've been able to find out," she continued, "is I had food poisoning, and that put a strain on my heart and kidneys."

She closed her eyes briefly and shook her head, as if the whole experience threatened more than just her physical health.

"One of the nurses here is almost as tactless as Mrs. Herfeld," she said. "The woman told me I probably forgot to refrigerate the pot roast or didn't wash up properly when I handled it."

Grey made a little hurrumphing sound. "I may be old and wrinkled, but I am not senile. Not yet. Not by a long shot. Someone should remind these medical types that, God willing, they, too, will be old someday."

CIRCLE OF WOLVES 191

She seemed better after her little tirade. Her voice was stronger, and her eyes sparkled.

I ventured a comment. "What do *you* think caused the illness?"

"I have to say the barbecue did not taste right. It was almost bitter. Made my throat sore, in fact. I had just opened a new container of Mexican style chili powder. Usually I prefer a milder flavor, but the store was out of my brand. I thought perhaps that was the cause of my intestinal difficulty. And with the burning in my throat and stomach— well, it just seemed that maybe the chili powder was too spicy for me."

When I didn't say anything, she gave me a quizzical look. In addition to not being senile, she was also not stupid.

"You mentioned a visit to my apartment. You have a theory about this, don't you?"

I nodded. "You said Riley ate some of the pot roast you used in the barbecue. And he had some of the same symptoms as you, without the chili powder. I'm guessing there was something in the meat, itself. But something that wasn't there when you cooked it initially. And I don't mean bacteria, either."

Grey waited.

"I think someone poisoned that leftover pot roast," I said, my voice low.

The various instruments and oscilloscopes on the wall behind Grey's bed blinked at me, and I wondered if the nurses could monitor more than a person's cardiovascular system with them.

"I don't know who or why, and I don't have any proof. At least not yet. But I've saved some of the barbecue, and I'll send it off for analysis tomorrow."

"Then this isn't just about dogs and cats, is that what you're saying?" Grey asked.

192 Karen Ann Wilson

"I don't know. Possibly."

Grey's heart rate and blood pressure hadn't risen significantly, according to the monitors, which was a relief. If Dr. Augustin had been there, questioning her, putting stress on her already compromised condition, I would have been furious. But Grey was a strong woman, and I needed her help.

"Can you think of anyone there at Sunset View Towers who might want you out of the way?" I asked, then quickly added, "Someone who might prefer that you live elsewhere?"

Grey thought for a moment. "Not anymore," she said.

I stared at her. I really had expected her to answer "No," without any hesitation.

"What do you mean by that?"

"William's daughter didn't like me very much, I'm afraid. Not toward the end, that is. If I hadn't been there to muddy things up, she would have taken control of William's estate and had him put on the psychiatric wing. She needed access to his money and, well, William was one more burden for her to bear."

"But she wouldn't have tried to *hurt* you, would she?"

"Gracious no. But you asked me who might want me to move. She would have. Of course . . . now that William is dead . . ."

"There isn't anyone else, then?"

Grey shook her head, then looked over my shoulder. I heard the door open.

"I'm afraid time is up, Miss Milner. Your grandmother needs to rest now." It was the nurse who had spoken to me earlier.

I got up and went to Grey's bed, then bent down, as if to give her a kiss.

"I'll be back," I whispered, "with the results of that

CIRCLE OF WOLVES 193

'exam' I told you about." Louder, I added, "You get better, you hear?"

Grey put her hand over mine and winked. "Stop by and see your old granny again, will you, Kimmy?"

I swear, the idea that someone was out to get her had rejuvenated her.

CHAPTER 22

•

Monday, November 29

Dr. Augustin swiveled his head around and stared, almost cross-eyed, at me from Tracey's stool. I could feel the hairs on the back of my neck stand up.

"You can't be serious," he said. Then he turned back to the microscope and the blood smear Tracey had asked him to take a look at.

"Well," I said, "have you got a better explanation?"

He didn't answer me. I continued to fill prescriptions and listen to the Anderson twins ransack Room 2. It was 10:20, and I had finally gotten a chance to tell him my theory on Grey's illness.

He pulled the slide out and tossed it in the container by the sink. Then he picked up the Anderson file and started writing.

"Well?"

He looked up. "It's too bad you didn't think to keep a sample of that barbecue beef. Without one, we'll never know, will we?"

I went over to the refrigerator, opened it, and took out one of the plastic storage bags, then dangled it tauntingly. Dr. Augustin's eyebrows inched up a hair, but other than that, he kept the surprise out of his expression. He went back to his writing.

CIRCLE OF WOLVES

Angrily, I threw the bag back in the refrigerator and slammed the door. Bottles and jars rattled, and something fell over, but I didn't check to see what it was.

Dr. Augustin got off the stool and headed for the door. He stopped.

"I've obviously underestimated you, Samantha," he said. "Get a cooler and pack that for shipment. I'll call Bob and tell him it's coming. By the way, I don't suppose you know what Mrs. Milner's symptoms were?"

I grinned at him and was rewarded by another inch or so rise in his eyebrows. I was about to rub it in even further, when we were interrupted by a loud splintering crash in Room 2. Dr. Augustin rolled his eyes and went to see what damage had been done, and I went in search of a cooler.

The odor emanating from the cocker spaniel puppy's ear was a mixture of bread rising and something green and hairy from the back of my refrigerator. Dr. Augustin stuck a cotton ball down the dog's ear canal and rotated it. The animal yelped and brought a hind foot up, which I grabbed before she could dig at the ear (or at Dr. Augustin's hand).

It was just after one o'clock. We were in the treatment room. Frank had neglected to tell Dr. Augustin that Chelsea's ears were infected until the dog had been bathed and dried, and Tracey was in the process of combing her out. Now Chelsea would need another bath to clean off the ear wash solution and ear wax running down the animal's head in two smelly, brownish streams that resembled chewing tobacco drool.

Dr. Augustin dropped the blackened cotton ball in the trash and reached for another. "So," he began, "why do you think somebody is after Mrs. Milner?"

"I'm not sure," I said. "But it has to do with that nursing floor or, at least, the assisted-living facility there at Sunset

196   Karen Ann Wilson

View Towers. I think the management is trying to move people out of their regular apartments and into the Hayes Building—that's the assisted-living and nursing building—so they can make more money. You even admitted the Towers was in financial trouble. Wouldn't it stand to reason they'd be trying to increase profits by getting elderly people with medical problems to move to the more expensive part of the complex?"

Dr. Augustin filled Chelsea's left ear with cleaning solution, then massaged the canal with his fingers. I strengthened my hold on the dog.

"So, let me get this straight," he said. "You're telling me they're trying to make Mrs. Milner sick so she'll move to the Hayes Building? Sounds a bit far-fetched, don't you think?"

"No," I said, none too patiently, "I'm saying they want Grey out of the way. Permanently. As in D.E.A.D."

Dr. Augustin reached for Chelsea's right ear, and I rearranged my hold on her. We could have been discussing the merits of lateral ear canal resection.

"For what reason, pray tell."

"Because she's not your typical elderly person," I said. "She isn't content to vegetate on the front porch in her housecoat. And she doesn't like doctors, especially those who treat old people like they're brain dead. Apparently she created quite a stir when they tried to put her friend, William, on the psych wing. And that's not the first time she's questioned the staff's treatment of a friend or neighbor. *I* think she's onto something—the fact that more-or-less competent people are being forced to give up their freedom by relatives convinced it's for their own good. The guy doing the convincing is the doctor there at the Towers, a Dr. Aaron." I wiped Chelsea's neck.

CIRCLE OF WOLVES 197

"I've asked Michael to look into Dr. Aaron's background, but he can't get to it until tomorrow at the earliest."

Dr. Augustin finished treating the dog's ears and began collecting up the soiled cotton balls.

"I do believe I've created a monster, Samantha," he said, throwing them into the trash. He leaned against the table and half-smiled at me, his piercing eyes looking every bit like the eyes of Poe's raven.

"A monster? Why?"

"Because last month, I had to practically bribe you to help me poke around up there at Carriage Hill. Now you're a little eager beaver."

I put Chelsea on the floor and watched her shake her head, sending tiny droplets of drying agent across the room and onto my uniform pants.

"I'm not helping you," I said, before I could catch myself. "I'm helping Mrs. Milner. You don't seem to be the least bit concerned that someone may be trying to kill her."

I continued to watch the dog. Allowing myself to lock eyes with Dr. Augustin would be like sticking my finger in an electrical outlet.

"Of course I'm concerned, Samantha. Why do you think I shipped those samples up to Gainesville? Anyway, let's see what Bob has to say before we go off half-cocked."

He sounded like I'd hurt his feelings, saying I wasn't helping *him*, but I didn't care. I waited until he left for his office, then took Chelsea back to the kennel.

Ken Williston drove up at 1:50. He got out of his car, went around to the trunk, and took out what appeared to be a plastic milk crate with a beach towel tied over the top. He slammed the trunk closed, then carried the crate across the pavement. I held the door open for him.

Inside the crate, a bedraggled-looking calico cat thrashed

198   Karen Ann Wilson

around. As it thrashed, it let out tiny hissing and growling sounds, aimed, it seemed, at its own gyrations.

"She started this about twenty minutes ago," Ken said, after he'd deposited the crate on the reception room floor. "It's a neighbor's cat. The man lets her roam the streets. But she's really pretty nice. Everybody feeds her."

We watched the cat twitch and writhe, while Cynthia quickly filled out an exam form for the animal.

"I thought maybe she was the reason Sunny had fleas," Williston continued. "So when I came home for lunch today and found her on my front porch, I gave her a bath. She wasn't happy, that's for sure."

"What did you use to bathe her?" I asked.

"That shampoo you gave me for Sunny." He paused. "And I had some flea spray left over. I used that, too."

Cynthia glanced over at me and cocked an eyebrow.

"What kind was it?" I asked. "Did you check to see if it was labeled for cats?" I was pretty sure I already knew the answer.

"It was in a brown bottle. That's all I can tell you. I used it in the house and in the yard. I didn't read the label very carefully. And I threw the bottle away a couple of weeks ago. The stuff was mixed up and in my sprayer. It never seemed to bother Sunny, and she got it on her paws." He looked down at the calico and slowly shook his head.

"Unfortunately, a lot of pesticides that are harmless to dogs can be fatal to cats," I told him. "When did you spray her?"

"Noon," he said.

I picked up the milk crate, and the cat flung a glob of saliva across my face. She had strings of it hanging like tinsel from her chin.

"Why don't you have a seat, Mr. Williston," I said, "while

CIRCLE OF WOLVES 199

Dr. Augustin examines her. I'll come and get you when he's finished."

Ken looked at his watch and frowned. It was pretty obvious his lunch hour had come and gone, and he was trying to decide what to do with the remainder of the afternoon. Finally, he went over to a chair and sat down.

Dr. Augustin, who could double as a CIA listening device, met me in the treatment room.

"Good thing that idiot doesn't have any kids," he said, taking the leather gloves out of the cabinet.

"I seem to remember you saying Mr. Williston was an okay guy."

Dr. Augustin snorted, then waited while I unhooked the bungee cord holding the towel in place over the crate. I stood back, and he took the towel off. The cat, sensing freedom, attempted to jump out, but her muscles weren't acting in sync, and she collapsed. Dr. Augustin picked her up by the scruff of her neck and pulled her out of the crate. He put her on the table, where she preceded to twitch and salivate and flick her little pink tongue at us. A strong chemical odor began to fill the room.

"How long has it been since he sprayed her?" asked Dr. Augustin.

He still had the cat pinned down on the table. If I hadn't known better, I'd have sworn her convulsive movements and drooling were due to a healthy case of rabies. Just to be sure, I continued to watch from a safe distance.

"Two hours," I said. "Do you want me to try contacting the owner?"

Dr. Augustin gave this inquiry a good thirty seconds' consideration.

"I'm sure Mr. Williston will take responsibility for the animal. Draw up three-quarters of a cc. of atropine."

• • •

Ken Williston went back to work after agreeing to pay for the cat's treatment, which Dr. Augustin said might extend over a period of a couple of days. Ken also promised to call the neighbor, a chore I was more than happy to relinquish.

Dr. Augustin and I stood side by side in front of the exam table in Isolation and watched the calico through the bars of her cage. She wasn't twitching anymore, and the salivation had stopped. Frank had given her a bath to remove any last traces of the spray and clean off the strings of saliva. Her green eyes were almost fully dilated, a result of the atropine, and resembled small lumps of iridescent coal.

Suddenly, I thought about the people on the psychiatric wing—the old man in the nightshirt who claimed "they'd" killed his dog, Sandy. Their eyes had been very dark, their pupils almost fully dilated. I remembered they had squinted at me in the bright light of the hallway.

"When I was visiting the nursing floor at Sunset View Towers," I said, "before they canceled the program, I noticed several of the patients had dilated pupils, like this cat's. What would cause that, do you suppose?"

Dr. Augustin had his arms folded across his chest. He shrugged. "Any number of things. Medication, some eye disorder . . ."

"I could see one or two maybe. But I ran across half a dozen or more. And they were all acting sort of demented— you know, mumbling and doing strange things with their hands. Why?"

Dr. Augustin turned toward me and frowned. "Do I look like a shrink, Samantha? How the hell should I know? They were old. Old people suffer from all sorts of neurological problems."

He walked over to the cat and stuck a finger through the bars. The cat rubbed the edge of her jaw against it.

CIRCLE OF WOLVES   201

"Let's keep her on the atropine. Half a cc. every three to four hours as needed to alleviate the symptoms."

I was about to leave, when Cynthia poked her head around the corner.

"Bill is on the phone. He wants to know if you're going to the commission meeting tonight. He said to remind you that they're having it tonight, because last Thursday was Thanksgiving."

She waited. I waited. Dr. Augustin never misses a commission meeting if he can help it, politicians being the scourge of the earth in his eyes, and in need of careful monitoring. But lately, he hadn't shown any enthusiasm about fighting City Hall. I was beginning to look at the twice-a-month commission meetings as a sort of gauge of Dr. Augustin's mental health.

He started for the door into the surgery. "Tell him I have a difficult case here," he said over his shoulder, "that'll need my attention probably through the night."

"I can stay and keep tabs on the cat until you get back," I said.

"No, that's okay, Samantha. I have paperwork to do, anyway. Those accounts receivable Cynthia has been after me to deal with."

He didn't look back. He disappeared into the surgery, and then I heard the door to the kennel open and close.

"I wish he would snap out of this mood he's in," Cynthia said.

"Ditto," I said.

CHAPTER 23

●

Wednesday, December 1

Grey was out of intensive care. She called me at home to tell me she was in Room 642, in a transitional area adjacent to the sixth floor ICU.

"According to the doctors, I'll be here for another week, possibly longer," she told me. "Heaven help me is all I can say. If I thought the food back on the nursing floor was bad, I was sadly mistaken."

"I guess they've got you on a pretty restrictive diet," I said.

"This isn't a diet, Sam. This is torture. I think I might commit murder for a piece of chocolate."

"Well, if it's any consolation, Riley is free to eat his regular food now. So, there's hope for you yet." At least Grey had her appetite back.

She laughed, which I took as another good sign, and I promised to visit her as soon as I could.

"Bring Lily with you," she said. "It will do her good to get out."

I thought for a moment. "Maybe Sunday. In any case, now that you have a phone in your room, we can talk."

"True," she said. "And you can tell me all about your investigation and what the test results were on that barbecue."

Rather than being repulsed, as Lily had been, Grey

202

CIRCLE OF WOLVES 203

sounded downright thrilled that someone had poisoned her dinner.

"You're supposed to be taking it easy," I told her.

"Humph," she snorted. "If I was taking it any easier, I'd be dead."

Michael phoned at three to tell me he had the information I'd requested about Dr. Aaron and Tyler Brock. We agreed on dinner that evening. Casual. Of course, casual to Michael meant no tie. So, in lieu of jeans and a T-shirt, I chose a dress. Nothing fancy, but something with a skirt. My little attempt at rebellion Thanksgiving hadn't given me the satisfaction it should have, mostly because Michael hadn't appeared to notice.

He arrived at a quarter to six wearing jeans, a knit pullover, and his deck shoes (with socks).

"You look lovely as usual, Samantha," he said. "Shall we go?" He stood by the door, waiting.

I gawked at him. I couldn't remember ever seeing him in jeans and was, until then, fairly sure he didn't own a pair. Jeans were more Dr. Augustin's style. But I had to admit, Michael looked pretty good in them, even if they weren't molded to his body like a wet suit, like the ones Dr. Augustin wears.

"Is something wrong?" he asked, the corners of his mouth turning up, the catch-light in his eye twinkling.

"No," I said, quickly. "Not a thing. Just let me get my purse."

We ended up at the mall, which was another surprise. I was always under the impression malls and store chains were beneath Michael. I began to wonder if I really knew the man at all. To say we weren't terribly open about our innermost fears and desires would be an understatement. Still,

204   **Karen Ann Wilson**

I thought I had him more or less figured out. Good ol' predictable Michael was turning out to be anything but, it seemed.

"I'd like us to look at rings," he said, as we got out of the car. Then, almost as an afterthought, he added, "If that's all right with you."

I didn't say anything. He put his hand under my elbow and guided me across the parking lot. We dodged a couple of teens on skateboards and a woman with a small child on a retractable dog leash. The woman looked exhausted. The child, on the other hand, reminded me of Lucky, before Tracey started working with her—wide-eyed and happily out of control. The kid had ice cream smeared across his T-shirt, and the seat of his little corduroy overalls looked suspiciously wet. I didn't envy the Santa who got that kid on his lap.

"Samantha?" Michael was staring at me.

I smiled and nodded. "Sure, sounds okay to me."

"And I thought maybe we could look at home furnishings and kitchen ware. Towels and china and such. I've been cleaning out a lot of the things I brought with me from New York. To make room. Cynthia informed me you'll want to register at Dillard's or Burdines. So your friends will know what to get you. I'm certainly not the one to be making those kinds of decisions, am I?"

He was suffering from another one of his thyroid attacks. All I could do was continue to nod and smile, while he dished out what Cynthia had obviously been feeding him over the last several days. *At least now I know why he brought me to the mall*, I thought. *The bridal registry at Dillard's. And when they ask me for the date, what will I say?*

We stopped at Ruby Tuesday's to check on the line. Apparently, Wednesdays are slow there, because they took us right in and seated us at a table next to the window.

CIRCLE OF WOLVES 205

Our server that evening was a Mary Lou Retton lookalike named Jill, who was being assisted by Ted, evidently in more ways than one, because they were having trouble concentrating. They made me feel old, and I hated them for it.

"The specials this evening are a slice of spinach quiche and your choice of soup or salad," said Jill, after carefully consulting her little note pad, "a hot baked potato stuffed all the way"—giggle, giggle—"and Ruby Tuesday's famous vegetable fajitas."

Ted left to get our drinks, and Jill's powers of concentration improved. However, Michael made her repeat our order twice, after she wrote down "soup", instead of "salad" for my quiche order, and "beef" instead of "chicken" for his fajitas.

"What did you find out about Dr. Aaron?" I asked, after Ted delivered our drinks.

Michael picked up his windbreaker and extracted an envelope from the pocket. He took out a couple of sheets of computer paper and scanned them.

"Dr. Julius Aaron has worked for Quetzal Bay Properties for eight years," Michael began, "the whole time as resident physician for Sunset View Towers. Appropriately enough, his specialty is geriatric medicine. Before he joined the staff at the Towers, he worked at the VA hospital in Tampa. I have no further information about his tenure there."

Michael paused, took a drink, stared at his glass, and frowned. "If this is Cutty Sark, them I'm Captain Kirk." He put the glass down and went back to his notes.

"His record is clear, as far as I can determine. No disciplinary action, no malpractice suits."

"How can he oversee the psych wing?" I asked. "Shouldn't they have a psychiatrist do that?"

Michael shrugged. "It's a private nursing facility. Aaron is suitably qualified to treat elderly patients, including those

206 **Karen Ann Wilson**

suffering from depression and other mental conditions elderly people often suffer from."

I drank my beer and fumed. I had expected Michael to uncover something sordid in Dr. Aaron's past, possibly a few unexplained deaths, a temporary suspension of his license. *Something,* anyway.

"What about his personal life?" I asked. "His financial situation. Maybe he gambles or is going broke paying his ex-wife alimony."

Michael grinned. "This crime solving bent you and Dr. Augustin are on has made you terribly suspicious, Samantha. Isn't it possible Dr. Aaron is just what he seems—a fairly competent physician working a little out of his league? Diagnosing and treating mental illness is an inexact science at best. It's not like finding worms in a dog's heart, you know."

He made it sound so easy—diagnosing and treating the ills of dogs and cats. Except I knew that wasn't what he meant. Still, he'd made me mad. Why couldn't he ever take anything seriously?

Our dinner arrived. While Jill and Ted served it and offered glowing commentary about the culinary prowess of the chef back in the kitchen. (He uses three, count them, three cheeses in the quiche, the chicken is marinated in lime juice and then grilled.) Michael ran a finger around the rim of his glass. When Jill asked if there was anything else she could get us, he held up his still-full glass.

"I would like another Scotch and soda. And this time use Cutty Sark, like I ordered the first time." He smiled.

Jill and Ted exchanged glances. Then Ted reached out and took the glass.

"Absolutely," he fawned. "I'm so sorry about that. Our bartender is new, and she probably got the order wrong. I'll see to it personally this time."

CIRCLE OF WOLVES 207

They hurried off. Michael looked at his watch. "I'm guessing two, maybe three minutes. Ted can see his tip going down the drain with my drink." He picked up a flour tortilla and began filling it.

"You have a mean streak in you, Michael," I said. "Did you know that?"

He looked up at me. "No, Samantha, I simply know the value of a dollar."

"So, did you find out anything useful on Tyler Brock?" I asked, not willing to debate the 'value of a dollar' issue with him. Periodically he reminded me of the reason I left Connecticut.

Michael waited while Ted, who was breathing a little rapidly after his race to and from the bar (in under three minutes), put the glass on a cocktail napkin. Then Ted stood at Michael's elbow waiting for the verdict, which Michael obviously had no intention of rendering at that time.

"Thank you," he told the boy. Ted glanced over at me, as if for guidance, then left.

Michael took a bite of his properly layered and very tidy fajita and chewed.

"Tyler Brock, Esquire," he said after a moment, "is an interesting man." He picked up his notes.

I was about to put a forkful of the quiche made with three kinds of cheese in my mouth, but stopped and held my breath.

"Following graduation from Stetson Law School, he went to work for McGowan, Barber, Sly and Moen."

I exhaled suddenly. Kelsey Cronin's lawyer was a partner at McGowan et al.

Michael took another bite and chewed, this time seemingly in slow motion.

"And . . . ?" I said, the quiche still airing on my fork.

"And then he quit and went to work for the Public De-

208 Karen Ann Wilson

fender's Office, then on his own. His practice concentrates on nursing care abuse cases, the Baker Act, and rights of the elderly in general. He started a not-for-profit advocacy group that helps elderly residents of nursing homes maintain control of their assets and so forth, when the courts threaten to assign control to a guardian for one reason or another."

I ate my dinner in silence. The guy sounded like Mother Teresa. Certainly not the type to force little old ladies into psychiatric institutions against their will just so he can be paid to have them released. I was getting nowhere. Instinct told me to drop the matter entirely and rely on the professionals, aka Matthew Kemp and his buddy Richard Walls.

I put my fork down. I'd lost my appetite.

Michael folded up the sheets of paper, put them back in the envelope, and handed it over. "For you," he said. "Sorry I couldn't dig up any dirt this time."

"That's okay," I said. "Thanks for trying."

He picked up another tortilla, then glanced over at my quiche. "Is there something wrong with your dinner, Samantha?" He started looking around for the Bobsey Twins. "I can have them bring you something else."

"No," I said, poking at the remains of my salad. "I'm just not terribly hungry."

"Jewelry always cheers a woman up," he said, his face and eyes doing a pretty fair job, themselves. "At least that has been my experience. What say we leave this mess to Jack and Jill and do a little shopping?"

When we finally left the mall, I'd managed to select a china pattern I didn't like, silverware I didn't need, and bath towels the color of rotting kelp. And when Mrs. Fanello, the woman in the bridal registry department at Dillard's, asked me for the dreaded date, I thought about April the first, since it seemed appropriate, but didn't have the nerve to actually

CIRCLE OF WOLVES

209

say it. Michael came to my rescue and told the woman we were really only looking, because we hadn't selected a date, but spring seemed likely. I looked at him and frowned.

"Well, Cynthia said you'd mentioned how the weather here in Florida is so nice in March," he chirped.

I never told her that, I wanted to scream. *She made it up because she wants to be a mother of the bride so bad she can't stand it.*

Mrs. Fanello stared at us like we had no intention of getting married and were merely wasting her time and the ink required to fill out the registry form. At least she didn't ask Michael if he was the father of the bride.

"When is Easter?" I said suddenly.

Then they *both* stared at me, clearly wondering what that had to do with anything.

"I'm not sure," said Michael. "Why?"

"Because I want to get married the Saturday before Easter," I said. *Now there was darkness over all the land until the ninth hour.*

"Wouldn't the Saturday *after* Easter be better?" Michael asked. "So many people will be otherwise occupied Easter weekend."

"My point exactly," I said. "So, when is Easter?"

CHAPTER 24

•

Thursday, December 2

Cynthia was on her hands and knees peering under the magazine rack when I came up to the reception room to get our first client of the morning.

"What are you doing?" I asked.

Her derriere looked like an archery target. The client, an elderly man with a miniature schnauzer named Sadie, grinned broadly. Our 10:15 client, Mrs. Vaughn, watched Cynthia out of the corner of her eye, as if too embarrassed to actually *look* at her. Mrs. Vaughn was eighty-two, and women in her day didn't wear pants, let alone crawl around on the floor in front of a man.

Cynthia's hand disappeared under the rack, then reappeared holding a Christmas tree ornament. She struggled to her feet and brushed off the knees of her red stretch slacks.

"Every morning," she muttered. "Every morning I have to round up the bottom row of ornaments from the tree. I swear I'm going to kill that cat."

She was obviously talking about Charlie, since Pearl hadn't learned how to get out of her cage. Not yet, anyway.

"You ought to be complaining about this to Frank," I said, picking up the schnauzer's file. "He's the one who forgets all the time to padlock Charlie's cage."

"We had a cat once," said Sadie's owner. "Me and Alice.

210

CIRCLE OF WOLVES
211

That cat was the orneriest creature God ever made. Only purred the day it died. Like it was actually looking forward to it."

Cynthia hung the ornament back on the tree and admired her work. Then she went over to her desk and sat down.

"Sometimes animals are smarter than people," the old man added. He tickled his dog's pointy little ears. "Isn't that right, Sadie?"

The dog licked the man's hand and wagged her stump of a tail.

"We're ready for you, Sadie," I said, standing by the door to the hall.

The old guy put his dog on the floor and, with some difficulty, got up. Then he shuffled across the room. He stopped and looked back at Mrs. Vaughn.

"'Course, that cat didn't have a pretty little girlfriend, either. He probably would've wanted to hang around a bit longer if he had."

He winked at Mrs. Vaughn, then guided Sadie around me and into Room 1. He was humming a little tune I didn't recognize. Mrs. Vaughn blushed through her Eve Arden. Daytime TV simply could not compete with *The Old and the Lonely.*

Cynthia has a way of squeezing information out of people that Dr. Augustin would be wise to take advantage of. She asked me three separate times about my dinner with Michael: "How was your evening, Samantha?" (Cheerful smile, fluttering eyelashes, look of innocence); "Where did you and Mike go last night, Samantha?" (Less innocence, voice half an octave lower); "Did you visit the bridal registry at Dillard's?" (Forced smile, eyebrows knitted together, voice razor-sharp).

Frustration was beginning to set in. I would have let this

212   Karen Ann Wilson

go on until lunch, just to see how desperate Cynthia could become, but every time I went to the reception desk to pick up or deliver a client's file, I sensed a dangerous increase in her blood pressure. So, for the sake of her cerebral vascular system, I finally relented.

"Yes, Cynthia," I said. "Thanks to you, I will soon own china too expensive to ever use."

She fluttered a hand. "That's ridiculous. Of course you'll use it. Thanksgiving, Christmas, Easter. Parties." She smiled. "Romantic little dinners for two." Then she pulled open a drawer and took out one of the many pocket calendars we get free from vendors. "So, when is the big day?"

Bob phoned from Gainesville at 12:30. I was in the lab, helping Tracey recalibrate the blood machine. It occasionally has a mind of its own and requires a good kick in the tires, something Tracey is afraid to do.

Dr. Augustin had taken our lunch orders and was on his way to the Subway down the street, so Cynthia transferred the call to me.

"Hi, Bob," I said into the lab extension. "This is Samantha. Dr. Augustin just left. Can I take a message?"

"Please tell that boss of yours he is going to have to start paying for these tox screens. This latest one cost me a fortune. *And* I had to do some of the analyses in the dark, once I figured out what I was looking for. It's a damned good thing you all gave me the woman's symptoms."

"In the dark?"

"Colchicine," he said. "It's photosensitive. I would have missed it, except Lou said the woman's throat burned. Coupled with her gastrointestinal and kidney problems, I was able to narrow the field down somewhat. But it still cost money, just like the other times, none of which I have received any payment for, I might add."

CIRCLE OF WOLVES   213

He was breathing fire into the phone on his end. I held the receiver away from my ear for fear of being singed.

"I'm sure it's an oversight," I said, lamely.

"Listen, Samantha. I've known Louis Augustin for almost thirty years. It is not an oversight, trust me. He can dupe and connive better than most con men and strongly believes, 'If you can't use your friends, who can you use?' I've spent the night in jail for him—twice, actually—had my learner's permit revoked because of him, and did volunteer work at a soup kitchen one summer instead of going on a class trip to Europe."

"Soup kitchen?"

"In the tenth grade," he said, "Lou talked me into helping him plug up the outfall from a local trailer park's sewage lagoon. The owner of the trailer park threatened to sue. It took some doing, but my parents managed to talk him out of it."

I wanted to ask him what happened to Dr. Augustin that summer. Had he worked at the soup kitchen, too? Probably not, knowing him.

"It doesn't sound like he's changed a whole lot," I admitted. "He can still con with the best of them. Listen, I'll have him call you as soon as he gets back."

"Yeah," said Bob. "You do that." He hung up.

"Who can con with the best of them?" asked Tracey.

"Who do you think?"

I gave Dr. Augustin the message, then stood by the door to his office and listened while he called Bob back. I'd purposely left out the part about Bob wanting to tar and feather him. Let Dr. Augustin find out himself, I thought sadistically.

But evidently Bob didn't have the nerve to yell at one of his best friends or else he'd vented all his anger on me, because the conversation appeared to center on the test results, not on Dr. Augustin's habit of sponging off his friends. Dr.

214 Karen Ann Wilson

Augustin did promise to send Bob a check to help defray the cost of the toxicology screen. Whether he actually did it or not was another matter entirely.

After he'd hung up the phone, I carried my half a turkey sub, minus mayo, and my unsweetened iced tea into his office and sat down on the day bed. Dr. Augustin had gotten himself a foot-long meatball sub and a Coke. The garlic and oregano totally overpowered the cold processed turkey meat, making my sandwich about as tasteless as a latex surgical glove.

I stared at the marinara sauce oozing from the sub roll onto Dr. Augustin's chin and thought about my size ten wedding gown, hermetically sealed in nitrogen gas by the local furrier. My mother refused to sell it, hoping that someday I would get the chance to wear it longer than twenty-two minutes, the time it took David to decide he wasn't ready for marriage. I remember sobbing quietly in the church dressing room, while my bridesmaids undid all the tiny pearl buttons on my sleeves, because my hands were shaking too much to do it myself. And nobody was talking, because, after all, there wasn't much to talk about. So I kept on crying, because there was plenty to cry about.

Now, thanks to Michael, I was a size twelve. And, also thanks to Michael, I had less than four months to shed twelve pounds, if I had a prayer of squeezing into that gown.

I put my sandwich back in its little plastic sleeve and picked up my tea.

"What is colchicine?" I asked.

Dr. Augustin wiped his mouth. "A plant alkaloid used in the treatment of gout, I believe." He got up and pulled a book from one of his shelves and began flipping through it. "Here it is." He read silently for a minute or two, then aloud.

"'Colchicine, found in the flowers of the meadow saffron (*Colchicum autumnale*), is the drug of choice in the treat-

CIRCLE OF WOLVES 215

ment of gouty arthritis. It is a potent inhibitor of cellular mitosis and has been used in the treatment of some forms of cancer. Acute poisoning causes burning of the mouth and throat, nausea, vomiting, bloody diarrhea, fever, hematuria, renal failure, metabolic acidosis, respiratory distress, and cardiovascular collapse.'" He looked over at me. "Nasty stuff, if given as an overdose. But tough to detect, according to Bob. Particularly since, except for the burning sensation in the mouth and the hematuria, symptoms of colchicine poisoning mimic a lot of things, including the flu and food poisoning."

"Arthritis," I said. "A lot of old people have arthritis. Wouldn't they take this colchicine? Maybe one of Grey's neighbors somehow got into her apartment and put some of his or her gout medicine in that pot roast."

"Gout, Samantha, is different from rheumatic or degenerative arthritis. And it isn't restricted to the elderly. It's a result of urate salt deposition in the joints and affects men, primarily. Certain foods trigger it. Red meat, beer." He paused, took a bite of his nice, meaty sandwich and chewed. All he needed was a beer to wash it down.

"Well," I said, "cancer certainly happens to a lot of old people. Maybe someone with cancer poisoned Grey's pot roast."

"I'm more inclined to believe it was some staff person from the nursing floor," said Dr. Augustin. "One of the nurses or that doctor you mentioned. What was his name?"

"Aaron. Dr. Julius Aaron. But now I'm not so sure he had anything to do with it."

"And why is that?"

I started to tell him what Michael had unearthed. Then I stopped. "Does this mean you agree with my theory about transferring people to the Hayes Building and the psychiatric wing to make more money?"

216   Karen Ann Wilson

"Let's just say I agree that someone may be trying to get rid of Mrs. Milner. And there may be merit in your theory, yes."

I smiled. "So. Would colchicine make people act weird and give them dilated pupils?" I tried to remember what William's eyes had looked like.

Dr. Augustin shoved the last of the sub into his mouth, wadded up the wrapper and napkin, and threw them in the trash. I waited for him to swallow.

"Confusion, maybe," he said. "Bob mentioned some photosensitivity, but not mydriasis. You'd expect dilated pupils if some anticholinergic like atropine or scopolamine had been administered. They're used to treat a variety of intestinal problems, specifically diarrhea, and medical personnel would certainly have access to them. They used to be available without a prescription in preparations like Donnagel." He thought for a moment.

"They can produce delirium and hallucinations under certain circumstances. Central nervous system stimulation. In addition to dilated pupils. Of course, there are dozens, possibly hundreds, of drugs and toxic substances that can have anticholinergic activity." He shook his head. "Give it up, Samantha. There's probably a perfectly rational explanation for their behavior."

"Then how do you explain someone trying to kill Gretchen Milner?" I asked.

Dr. Augustin put the book on his desk and stretched. He reminded me of a cat. Dinner, a nice stretch, then a nap. What more could you want out of life?

"I can't."

He ran a slim index finger across his chin and up his jaw. He was staring at the colored spheres in his gumball machine. Suddenly, he opened the top drawer to his desk, fished around until he found a nickel, then put it in the ma-

CIRCLE OF WOLVES 217

chine. He turned the knob, and a green orb rolled out. He popped the ball in his mouth, then picked up another coin. He held it out questioningly.

"No, thanks," I said.

He dropped the coin back in the drawer and closed it.

"So what do we do now?" I asked.

Dr. Augustin leaned back in his chair and chewed slowly, like a cow chewing its cud. And, in a way, he *was* ruminating—working over the facts, breaking them down, digesting the ones he found important, discarding the ones he didn't need. After a few seconds, he looked over at me. But rather than the soft brown of a cow's eyes, his had that dark, piercing quality of a carnivore who has picked up the scent of prey. I had to admit, the excitement was contagious, and I felt my pulse quicken.

"Is there anyone on that nursing floor you can trust?" he asked. "Maybe the activities director, Mrs. Snoden."

"She wouldn't know anything," I said. "But there is an LPN who works for one of those private home care companies. He spends a lot of time on the nursing floor. He even told me he thinks there are people on the psych wing who don't belong there, although I'm not sure he suspects foul play. More a case of Alzheimer's patients being labeled psychotic, when they shouldn't be."

"Well, talk to him, anyway. Try to find out if any of the patients you saw acting demented had any unusual symptoms of drug toxicity. Also, find out if the patients he says don't belong on the psych wing have any relatives, or if they were committed by the courts." He leaned forward. "See if Mr. Halsey can put his finger on the number of beds in that place routinely assigned to Baker Act commitments."

I got up, feeling almost euphoric. Dr. Augustin's sudden reversion to his private detective persona should have filled me with dread, but it didn't.

218 **Karen Ann Wilson**

"Samantha," he called out, as I was leaving his office.

I turned around.

"You realize this is a long shot," he said, "this drug-induced dementia idea of yours. We could be wasting our time."

"But you don't think so, do you?"

"Well," he said, "that colchicine in Mrs. Milner's barbecue didn't get there on its own, now, did it?"

CHAPTER 25

•

Friday, December 3

Thursday evening after work, I called the nursing floor at Sunset View Towers and asked for Chris. Earlier that day, when I called, they hadn't been able to find him. I called back three separate times (Thursday afternoon was predictably slow, with Dr. Wilson at the helm), but to no avail. Finally, at 7:30 I was informed Chris no longer worked there. Sid was receiving twenty-four-hour care on the psychiatric wing and didn't need the services of a private nurse. Or so the woman said. When I asked if Chris had been assigned to anyone else in the Hayes Building, the nurse told me she had no idea (and obviously didn't care) and suggested I call Gulf Home Health Care, Chris's employer. She didn't have the number, which seemed highly unlikely, but I didn't argue with her. She acted like it was beneath her to look it up.

Gulf Home Health Care was a St. Petersburg listing in the yellow pages. When I dialed it, I got their answering service. The woman told me, unless it was an emergency, I would have to call back after eight the following morning. I thanked her and hung up. Then I dialed my mother's number, but got a busy signal. My relief was like finding out you don't have cancer after all.

•   •   •

219

220   **Karen Ann Wilson**

Fridays are always a little crazy at the clinic, but that Friday reminded me of the after-Thanksgiving sales at Macy's. Ten baths, a full surgical schedule, and four walk-ins, on top of an already full house, appointment-wise, meant no lunch break and no time to call Gulf Home Health Care.

"That old geezer with the bulldog is driving me crazy," whispered Cynthia.

It always amuses me when someone over the age of sixty refers to someone only a few years further along as "that old geezer."

"I saw Gannet's name in the appointment book," I said. "What's he in for this time?"

Cynthia and I were in the hall between Room 1 and the lab. She followed me into the exam room and watched, while I cleaned off the table.

"Pudge is 'scooching' again, to use Mr. Gannet's terminology. She wrinkled her nose.

"I assume that means he's dragging his bottom across the carpet."

"Yes," said Cynthia. "And leaving a little trail of 'you know what,' although I don't, not exactly. And I didn't have the nerve to ask him to elaborate."

"Coward." I grinned at her.

"This is not funny, Samantha. What if he asks me out on a date?" Like "date" in this case was a trip to the gas chamber.

She had her left hand balled up into a fist, and her right one clenching the Parker file so tightly, it was buckling. I pointed to it.

"Easy, Cynthia. That file never did anything to you." I put the disinfectant spray back on the shelf, opened a drawer, and took out a 3-cc syringe. "And what if he does? I think he's nice."

CIRCLE OF WOLVES 221

"Samantha, *really!* He's got to be eighty years old. Sixteen years older than I am, for Heaven's sake."

"Hey, Michael is seventeen years older than I am, and you can't wait for us to get married."

"That's different."

"Why?" I asked, taking a vial of rabies vaccine out of the refrigerator next to the sink. "Because Michael is rich and handsome? And Mr. Gannet is just another widowed retiree living on a fixed income?"

Before she could manage a proper reply—something particularly caustic—the door to Room 2 opened, and the client came out. She was blushing, no doubt in response to Dr. Augustin's parting smile and pat on her shoulder. Her dog, on the other hand, acted extremely happy to be leaving.

Without looking at me, Cynthia stuck the Parker file in the door holder and hurried up front to get Mr. Parker. From the expression on her face, I knew I had gotten my point across. *At least maybe now she'll lay off on the wedding plans*, I thought hopefully.

Mr. Gannet and Pudge left without the old guy asking Cynthia out. I felt like slipping him her number but reconsidered when I remembered that Cynthia's phone is unlisted. She would know where Mr. Gannet had gotten it, and my life would be, as they say, "dog shit" for days.

At three o'clock, we had a cancellation. I grabbed my lunch and, between mouthfuls of leftover Tuna Helper, called Gulf Home Health Care.

"Mr. Cortland is working at Buena Vista Manor," the receptionist told me. She gave me the number. "He should be there until five-thirty."

I finished my lunch and called Buena Vista Manor, a nursing and convalescent home just up the street from Paradise Cay. When I asked for Chris, I was put on hold and

222   **Karen Ann Wilson**

spent the next minute or so listening to "Stairway to Heaven" by Led Zeppelin. The radio station was one of those "golden oldies" stations. Unfortunately, it wasn't old enough, by a good half century. Still, the recording seemed appropriate, somehow, all things considered.

"Hello?" Chris sounded out of breath.

"Chris? This is Samantha Holt. The volunteer at Sunset View Towers. The one with the puppy."

He laughed. "Oh, yeah. Sorry to hear you were terminated."

"And I'm sorry to hear about Sid. I understand he doesn't need you anymore, or so they told me."

"It was only a matter of time," he said. "That's the third one I've lost to the psych wing this year. It's sort of like a black hole, isn't it?"

Someone else had referred to the wing in those terms. I couldn't remember who.

"What can I do for you?" Chris asked.

"I was wondering if we could get together and talk. Maybe meet for supper someplace."

He hesitated. "I'm really not . . ."

"I just want to ask you a few questions. About the psych wing and the nursing floor. About the matter we discussed briefly my last day there. You remember that?"

"I remember," he said. Again, he hesitated.

"This isn't a date, Chris. I'm trying to find out what's going on over there. You're the only person I can trust."

"You don't even know me," he said.

"I'm a pretty good judge of character," I said, trying not to gag. That was about as far from the truth as you could get.

This appeared to amuse him, because I heard him chuckle. "Sure," he said, "why not?"

"Great. How about tonight after work? We could meet at the Paper Moon. You know where that is?"

CIRCLE OF WOLVES   223

"Sure. When?"

"Seven. No, better make that seven-thirty. The way this day is going, I'll be lucky if I'm out of here before then."

He agreed. The amusement was still evident in his voice when he told me good-bye. But I didn't care. I wasn't interested in his private life, or in how he viewed me, or what he thought the reason for my interest in the Hayes Building was. He might be robbing his patients of their life savings, or worse, but I knew one thing. I knew I could trust him not to tell the management at Sunset View Towers about our little conversation, and that's all that mattered.

CHAPTER 26

●

The Paper Moon was packed, mostly with runners. The Moon is a popular watering hole for the after-work sand-slogging set. Bill O'Shea, the owner, knows a good thing when he sees it jogging by and quickly installed an outdoor shower on one end of the building. And he gladly provides pitchers of ice water and paper cups free to runners in the hope that later they'll switch to beer. Usually they oblige, most runners being the avid beer-drinkers that they are.

Bill was at his regular spot in the corner, drinking coffee and smoking a cigar. He looked up and smiled when I approached. Then he pulled out the chair next to his and patted it.

"Samantha. What a pleasant surprise. Have a seat." His T-shirt read, "Save a panther. Shoot a developer." It had a cartoon drawing of a fat guy in a suit and hard hat with a big bull's-eye painted on his forehead.

"Can't," I said, when he started to signal the bartender. "Thanks, though. I'm meeting someone."

I had to raise my voice to be heard over the jukebox. Jimmy Buffet and his Coral Reefers were deciding where to go "when the volcano blows." Several of the patrons were singing along and banging their knuckles on the bar.

224

CIRCLE OF WOLVES   225

I looked around. "Where'd all these people come from? Was there a beach race I didn't know about?"

"Practice, I guess," he said. "That Jingle Bell Run is Sunday morning." He paused, grinning. "So, hot date tonight? You finally talk that reporter friend of yours into coming here? I thought the Holiday Inn was more his style."

He knew Michael hated beach bars. "You've got to stop hanging around Dr. Augustin," I said, feigning irritation. "You're starting to sound like him."

I scanned the room again. Finding Chris in the sea of damp nylon running shorts and singlets surging around the bar was going to be difficult.

"No," I said, "this is a business meeting. In a way. I'm doing a little research for Dr. Augustin."

Bill took the cigar out of his mouth and stuck it in the plastic ashtray on the table. The thing looked like a gift from one of my cats. Then he cracked a couple of the knuckles on his right hand. I couldn't hear the snapping, but the action made me grit my teeth anyway.

"Thank God," said Bill. "Lou's been entirely too preoccupied lately with that idiotic civil suit. Or is this research in support of his case?"

"Possibly," I said. And then I caught sight of Chris coming through the front door. "Gotta go."

"Tell Jimmy to give you the reserved table," Bill called after me. "And a couple of beers on the house." When I looked over my shoulder at him, he winked.

"Thanks," I said, nearly colliding with Patsy, one of the Moon's shapely little waitresses.

She expertly maneuvered her tray laden with coffeepot and cream pitcher around me and headed for Bill's table.

Chris acted like he'd never seen me before. I've been told the best way to get people to notice you is to walk your dog

226 Karen Ann Wilson

on a crowded street. Evidently, those same people remember the dog a far sight better than they remember its owner.

"I hardly recognized you without the pooch," he said.

He was wearing faded cutoffs and an REM T-shirt. His solitary earring blinked in the bar light like a turn signal. Or maybe just a signal.

"Thanks a lot," I laughed, then led him to the table in the back marked 'Reserved,' and we sat down.

Jimmy caught sight of us and was heading over, presumably to evict us, when Patsy grabbed him. Then he nodded at me and took a couple of beer glasses down and began filling them from one of the taps.

"Thanks for coming," I said. Even if it wasn't a date (and a first date at that), I felt uneasy. The last guy I'd shared that table with turned out to be every girl's worst nightmare.

"No problem," he said. "So what did you want to talk about?" No need for small talk, either, apparently.

"Remember how you told me that the management at Sunset View Towers tries to commit its elderly residents in the Hayes Building to the psych wing, even if they don't need to be there?"

He fingered his earring and looked around, clearly more interested in the bar's occupants than in our conversation, which ticked me off.

Patsy came over with our beers, and I waited until she was gone. "Chris, you *do* remember our conversation, don't you?"

He looked at me then and nodded. "Yes. Why are you so interested, anyway? I thought they stopped the pet therapy thing. You have a particular person incarcerated there that you're concerned about?" He picked up his beer, made a passing stab at a toast, then took a sip.

"Yes and no," I said. "It's a long story, but I'm beginning to think Dr. Aaron and company are drugging patients on the

CIRCLE OF WOLVES 227

nursing floor. You know, to make them appear crazy, then convincing their relatives, or whatever, to commit them to the psych wing. All in the name of money."

Chris stared at me, his beer glass dangling midway between his lips and the paper coaster on the table.

"You're kidding, right?" He put the glass down. "I do think Aaron is sticking people on the psych wing when they'd do just fine in the general population on the nursing floor. Alzheimer's patients, mainly. But *drugging* them? Come on." He grinned at me. "That Milner lady has been talking to you, hasn't she?"

I felt the breath catch in my throat. How did he know about Grey?

"What do you mean?" I asked, trying not to give myself away.

"Gretchen Milner," he said. "Everyone on the staff knew she was upset when a couple of her friends ended up on the psych wing. She essentially accused Dr. Aaron and Mrs. Herfeld of incompetence. Of inadvertently overdosing her friends on prescription meds and then blaming the side effects on age-related dementia. If you ask me, they were in the early stages of senility, and Aaron, encouraged by that asshole, Aveneau, reclassified them as mental patients. The ones they couldn't get onto the psych wing voluntarily, they Baker Acted."

He shook his head. "But drug-induced dementia? On purpose? I don't think so." He drank his beer and resumed his assessment of the crowd.

"You're telling me you never noticed all the psychiatric patients with dilated pupils and weird hand movements?" I asked. "And most of them were mumbling stuff like 'They're going to kill me.' Couldn't that be from something like atropine, given to them without their knowledge?"

Chris laughed. "You and Mrs. Milner ought to get to-

228 Karen Ann Wilson

gether and open a detective agency." Then he stopped abruptly and frowned. "You're not a reporter, are you? Come to think of it, you never did tell me what you do for a living."

"I work at a veterinary clinic," I said.

He continued to stare at me, as if trying to decide where I was coming from. The frown faded. "A lot of meds can produce anticholinergic-type responses, even with proper dosage. Parkinson's disease is treated with atropine-like drugs," he said. "You know what Parkinson's disease is?"

"Of course I know what Parkinson's disease is," I snapped.

Patsy had come over to our table with a couple of menus and was about to hand them to us, when she evidently decided food was low on our list of priorities just then. She whirled around and went back to the bar. It didn't matter. I had a feeling my dinner was going to be leftover Tuna Helper.

"Those 'weird' hand movements you mentioned," said Chris, "and the uncontrollable shaking and jerking that are characteristic of Parkinson's disease are treated with drugs like Cogentin and Artane. They dry up the drooling just like atropine and dilate the pupils."

He looked at me and smiled condescendingly. "A lot of those patients on the psych wing are being treated for depression and a whole variety of psychoses. Haldol—you've heard of Haldol, haven't you?—is one of the drugs of choice to treat hallucinations and such. Anticholinergic-type drugs are given to counteract the side effects of Haldol."

When I didn't say anything, he continued. "So, you see, lots of things can produce dilated pupils, urinary retention, dry mouth. Some antidepressant drugs, like Elavil. Antihistamines will, too, under the right circumstances.

"And trust me, even without drugs, Alzheimer's patients

CIRCLE OF WOLVES 229

occasionally become convinced that the nursing staff is out to get them. It's sad, but its true. Even the ones who act perfectly sane most of the time talk to themselves." He laughed, but there was very little humor in it. "Sometimes it's because they're the only ones who'll listen."

I ran my finger down the side of my glass, leaving a snail trail through the condensate.

"Listen," Chris said softly, "old age is a socially unacceptable condition in this country. Marketing departments promote youth above all else. Add to that the physical limitations of old age—arthritis, cataracts and other eye disorders, heart disease, incontinence and impotence, deafness, digestive problems—God, the list is endless. And depressing. It's no wonder our elderly are often treated like old photographs. You can't bear to get rid of them, because they remind you of your childhood and all the neat things you did when you were a kid. But there isn't any place to put them in your home, so you tuck them away in the attic for safe keeping. Or in a nursing home.

"Unfortunately, a lot of old photographs end up covered with mildew or eaten by rats. You don't find out about it until the damage is done. Well, old people in nursing homes are often abused, and their families don't know about it until it's too late. But I find it tough to believe the people you're talking about are victims of some scheme or other. They're just victims of time and society."

"How long have you been taking care of elderly people, Chris?" I asked.

He pulled on his earring again. It was like a baseball coach signaling his guy on first base to make a run for it. And it caused me to reach up to my own earlobes to make sure my little gold hoops were still there.

"Too long," said Chris. He let go of the earring. "Fifteen years. I started out working at a day care facility for

230   Karen Ann Wilson

Alzheimer's patients. At least those folks had family members who cared about them. But dealing with Alzheimer's is tough on the caregivers. So, a lot of the people I saw during the day finally ended up in nursing homes, when the stress got to be too much for their families."

Patsy wandered over again and, this time, she handed us the menus. Neither of us needed a refill on our beers, so she said she'd be back.

"Eventually, I went to work for a private nursing outfit on the other coast. Things over there didn't work out."

He paused and stared across the room. I was pretty sure the "things" that didn't work out were personal rather than professional.

"Anyway," he continued, "I came back to St. Pete and joined Gulf Home Health Care. It's a good outfit, and I'm happy with the work they give me. It pays the bills."

"Doesn't seeing all those people slowly lose their faculties depress you?" I asked.

"Doesn't putting animals to sleep depress you?"

Touché, I thought.

Patsy caught my eye and held up her order pad, so I opened my menu. "I guess we should make a decision here," I said. "I'm buying, so please order whatever you want."

Chris didn't bother with his menu. "I don't eat meat," he said. "Or dairy products. Or eggs. Kind of limits what you can get at a beach bar, where everything is fried in animal fat or covered with Cheese Whiz." He made it sound so inviting. "The salad with oil and vinegar is fine by me. Or lemon juice."

I was completely surrounded by people who could pass for Auschwitz internees, and the thought of a tossed salad with lemon juice instead of a grouper sandwich with extra tartar sauce and curly fries brought tears to my eyes. And then I remembered my size ten wedding gown.

CIRCLE OF WOLVES 231

"A salad sounds good," I lied, closing the menu quickly, before I could change my mind. "I notice you drink beer, though."

Chris nodded. "Beer is very nutritious, actually." He winked. "All those yeast by-products, you know."

I wasn't ready to give up my intentional drug-induced dementia theory. I downed the rest of my yeast by-products and took a deep breath.

"Let's assume," I said, "for purposes of discussion, that somebody is giving selected patients on the nursing floor at Sunset View Towers drugs to make them appear mentally unsound, even dangerous. Who do you think would most likely be involved?"

Chris shook his head slowly, as if *I* was the one who was mentally unsound.

"Like I told you before," he said, "I can't believe Dr. Aaron would do something like that. Not knowingly, anyway. He's far from the best doctor in the world, but he doesn't strike me as being unethical. And the nursing staff there at the Towers is extremely competent. Don't get me wrong, Mrs. Herfeld belongs in a prison infirmary. No question, she must have missed the class on compassion and sensitivity in nursing school. But she would never do any harm to anyone."

Patsy brought two more beers over and asked if we'd decided on dinner. When she gave us the choices for salad dressing, most of which contained either egg or dairy products, or lots of nasty preservatives and artificial flavorings, Chris sighed.

"Lemon it is," he said.

I ordered fat-free ranch, against the better judgment of my taste buds, then pressed doggedly onward.

"I'm not talking about competence, Chris. I'm talking about money. Sunset View Towers is in financial trouble. I figure the administrative director is the one pushing to get beds on the psych wing filled. No matter what it takes. By the way, you don't happen to know how many beds on the psych wing are assigned to Baker Act commitments, do you?"

Chris looked at me quizzically, as if he still didn't believe I wasn't moonlighting as a reporter. "No, I don't," he said. "Too many, I'm sure, in spite of the supposed safeguards the state has in place. Sid's new roommate was a Baker Act commitment. They caught him chasing after one of the cleaning girls down on the third floor. He was buck naked and waving his penis at her. Now, there's a dangerous weapon if there ever was one. And the woman had a good fifty pounds and three inches on the old codger. But he was declared a threat and moved upstairs. His family didn't give two hoots."

"What about the food service people?" I asked, trying another angle.

"What about them?"

"Could Wilma What's-Her-Name—Smith—be slipping something to the patients in their food?"

Chris breathed in and out dramatically and pulled on his bejeweled earlobe. It was the bottom of the thirteenth and he desperately needed a run to end the agony and send his team to the showers.

"'For purposes of discussion,'" he mimicked, "where would she get the drugs? You don't find anticholinergics on the shelf next to the paprika, you know."

I was considering yanking out the damned earring when Patsy arrived with our dinner. She put the salad bowls in front of us, along with my container of ranch dressing and Chris's little dish of lemon wedges.

"Would you guys like anything else?" she asked, looking

CIRCLE OF WOLVES   233

down at our meager repast. "Could I bring you some fried cheese sticks or jalapeno poppers?"

I started to say maybe an order of cheese sticks would be nice, but Chris was shaking his head vigorously.

"No, I guess not," I said. "Thanks."

She was about to leave when she stopped and turned around. "Almost forgot your crackers," she said, putting a little red plastic basket filled with packages of saltines on the table between Chris and me.

"You're a doll," I said.

Chris picked up a lemon wedge and squeezed it over his salad. "Besides," he began, once Patsy was out of earshot, "that cow Wilma still hasn't figured out why you don't feed table sugar to a diabetic. How do you expect her to know the dosage of atropine, or whatever, required to produce symptoms of toxicity without causing the recipient to have a heart attack or stroke?"

I stuck my fork in the salad dressing, then into my mouth. I winced, put the fork down, and reached for a package of crackers.

"You do realize an overdose of atropine or Elavil or Phenergan, to name a few, can initiate a heart attack or stroke? While I was working in the Hayes Building, I didn't hear of any sudden increase in the number of myocardial infarctions or strokes. I mean, over and above what you'd expect to see in a bunch of octogenarians."

I thought about Robert Penlaw and his dog. And William.

"No, Samantha, you're barking up the wrong tree." He stuck a forkful of lettuce in his mouth and worked it over like a rabbit. "So why exactly are you so interested in the residents of the Hayes Building? You never told me."

Three strikes and you're out, I thought morosely, and reached for another pack of crackers.

"Just curious," I said.

234 Karen Ann Wilson

•   •   •

I dialed my mother's number and waited for her answering machine to cut in. It was 9:30, and most children my age expect to find their mothers home at that hour, doing motherly things like knitting or watching sitcoms. We certainly don't expect to find them out "gallivanting", as my own mother used to say about my father. But loneliness makes a lousy companion. After a few years of solitude, my mother decided she needed more than a cat to keep her company, so she joined a couple of clubs aimed at mature singles who are still "young at heart." They have card parties, do dinner cruises, pile into buses and visit points of interest around the state (including every McDonald's and Wendy's along the way). Anything to fill the void. Now my mother is out more than she is in. I sent her an answering machine for her birthday. Of course, I never leave a message. She might call me back.

"You've reached the Holt residence," my mother's recording began. "We aren't able to take your call right now. Please leave a message, and one of us will get back to you. Thanks so much and have a nice day."

The royal "we," I thought, intended to fool potential thieves and rapists into thinking there was a *Mr.* Holt.

I waited for the tone, thinking I ought to at least let her know I'd called. Make it something innocuous, like "Hi, Mom. Just thought I'd find out how you were doing. And by the way, I'm getting married."

The little musical scale ended with a plaintive beep, then silence, as the machine started recording. How could I tell her I'd been engaged for over a month? Whatever I said wouldn't come out right. I'd have to lie, and my mother would know. She always knew.

"How's the weather up there?" I said, finally, so she

CIRCLE OF WOLVES 235

wouldn't think my breathing was an obscene caller. "Think we'll have snow for Christmas? Gotta go."

But before I could drop the receiver back into its cradle, I heard my mother's voice.

"Samantha? Is that you? Don't you dare hang up!"

Reluctantly, I lifted the receiver to my ear. "Hi, Mom. Gee, I didn't expect you to be home at this hour."

"Then why did you call?" she asked, her voice typically short and accusatory. "And don't tell me you were intending to leave a message. It was an afterthought is all. You bought me this machine in March and haven't left a single message until today. Not one."

"That's not true," I said, trying to remember if it really was. Surely not.

"It certainly is. I always have to call you. You have no consideration for your lonely old mother. Why is that, Samantha?"

I started coiling the telephone cord around my finger. The tiny tooth marks left by my cats formed an intriguing pattern, like the footprints a bird makes in the sand.

"You are not old, Mother."

"Well, you could have fooled me," she said. "I've got arthritis in my fingers, and now I think I'm getting a cataract in my left eye."

I didn't say anything. Arguing with her was a waste of time.

"Samantha?" Now my mother's voice held a hint of concern. "Are you all right? Is something wrong?"

"No," I said. "Nothing's wrong. I just called to see how you were doing. How is that friend of yours? The one with the daughter in the Army?"

While she filled me in on the daughter's experiences in boot camp, I searched for a way to tell her about Michael and me.

"And how is that friend of yours?" I heard her ask. "The one who works for the newspaper. Michael something."

I couldn't remember how much I had told her. Certainly not enough.

"He's fine," I said.

"I'd love to meet him. He sounds like such a nice man."

How do you know that? I wanted to ask. She was digging. If I didn't tell her something, she'd go on digging, too. All the way to China.

"He *is* nice," I said. *Nice and safe. Every mother's dream.*

"Why not bring him home for Christmas? Does he ski?"

"He's more the boating and fishing type, Mother," I said. "I'm not even sure he likes snow. Besides, he has his own family to visit over Christmas."

She didn't say anything. It wasn't like her to give up so easily.

"But I'll ask him anyway," I relented. I could almost hear her gloating.

"And how is your job?" she asked then. "I hope that boss of yours hasn't gotten you mixed up in any more shenanigans."

"The job is fine. We hired a new laboratory technician. Tracey Nevins. Did I tell you about her?" *After all, it's only been four months*, I thought.

"No, Samantha. You didn't." The accusatory tone again.

"She's really very efficient. Of course, she's only twenty-one and thinks she's in love with Frank. You remember Frank, our kennel manager? The rock musician?"

"Yes," she said. "I remember Frank."

"Anyway, other than that, Tracey and I get along very well."

"You can't fault the girl for being in love, Samantha."

Oh God, I thought, here we go again. "You'd have a fit if

CIRCLE OF WOLVES 237

I fell for a rock musician, and you know it," I said angrily. Why was I so angry?

"Yes, I probably would," she said. "I just . . . worry about you, Samantha. I love you and want you to be happy. To find someone who'll make you happy. That's all."

I felt my hand reach out into the air, as if to touch her. I was thirty-three years old and I wanted to curl up in her lap, like I did when I was a child. She could always make the bad things better back then.

"I know," I said.

She and I were silent for several seconds. I could hear the television in the background.

"Why aren't you out on one of your dinner cruises or whatever?" I asked suddenly.

"I've been fighting off a cold for several days," she said. "I thought I ought to stay home."

"You're okay, aren't you? I mean, it isn't anything serious, is it?"

"No, just a little head cold." *But thank you for your concern,* I imagined her thinking. "Listen," she said, "this is costing you a fortune. Why don't we quit for now? I'll call you next week, and we can talk some more. We'll make Christmas plans. Okay?"

"Okay," I said.

I hung up and sat on my bed, absently fingering the telephone cord. It was just a cold, she'd said. Nothing serious. But I felt panic grab at my stomach anyway. What had Chris said? Something about old photographs in the attic. I should have told her about the engagement, I thought. I should call her back right now and tell her. No. I'll tell her next week when she calls me. Maybe by then I'll know what to say.

CHAPTER 27

•

Sunday, December 5

Saturday came and went with no new developments in the Hayes Building mystery. I didn't even bother to tell Dr. Augustin about my "date" with Chris. What was there to tell, anyway? That the whole thing was my imagination? That all the dementia I thought I observed on the nursing floor had a perfectly rational explanation? That, other than the presumed abuse of the Baker Act, which undoubtedly still went on all over the state, despite the amendments to the law, nothing illegal was taking place at Sunset View Towers?

Except for the attempted murder of Gretchen Milner, of course. Don't forget that. And don't forget Willy Roan, whose death probably wasn't an accident, either.

I chewed on the inside of my cheek as I pulled my hair back and secured it with a rubber band.

"I think we should call Sergeant Robinson and tell him about the colchicine," I said to my reflection in the mirror. "Let *him* investigate the matter. What do you think?"

Tina was in her usual spot on the back of the toilet, watching me, her dainty little face and enormous eyes hanging on my every word.

"*I'm* certainly not getting anywhere, am I?"

Tina blinked. Then, a rap on the front door sent her flying off the toilet, out of the bathroom, and under my bed.

238

CIRCLE OF WOLVES   239

I gave my ponytail a final tug and went to let Jeffrey in.

"Golly," I said, after I'd opened the door, "you're actually on time. Maybe we'll arrive early enough to get a T-shirt."

He glared at me but didn't say anything, not even "Hello." Jeffrey is not a morning person. He brushed past me and headed for the kitchen. I heard him take a mug out of the cabinet over the sink and lift up the coffeepot.

"Good morning to you, too, Jeffrey," I said sweetly.

"Sorry, Sam," he said through the kitchen doorway. "But I didn't get off work until after one o'clock this morning. I'm beat."

I handed him my mug and he poured me a refill. "Yes," I said, "but did you make any money?"

He brightened slightly. "Tips were better than usual last night. One party of three left me thirty bucks on a seventy-dollar tab. Pretty good, huh?"

"Better than pretty good. You must have made quite an impression." I put my cup in the sink and pointed at my watch. "Drink up," I said. "It's time to go."

I got my T-shirt. They had plenty. The turnout for the Jingle Bell Run wasn't all that great. It was a joint-cracking morning with a heavy fog that apparently kept away all but the diehard runners and locals like Jeffrey and me, who lived right up the road and didn't have to drive very far. Most of the people milling around the starting line I recognized from other races or from the Moon. And most of them, as opposed to me, actually looked like runners.

"I'll stay back here with you, Sam," Jeffrey said, as we waited for the start. "I'm too tired to do anything respectable, anyway."

"Gee, thanks a lot," I said.

"Hey, I didn't mean . . ." he began, cheeks blushing like he'd just been slapped.

240 **Karen Ann Wilson**

"Never mind, Jeffrey. I'd appreciate the company. To tell you the truth, I'm only here because I need to lose a few pounds. I'm hoping by coming in last, I'll be shamed into running more than twice a week."

"You're not going to be last," he said. "I won't let you."

Great, I thought. "I'd like to survive this, Jeffrey, if you don't mind."

The gun went off, and we began to move, slowly at first, then more rapidly, as the front runners took off into the fog at a sub-five-minute mile. I noticed Jeffrey was fighting the urge to join them. As it was, I feared we would hit the one-mile mark at under eight minutes, which was an impossible pace for me to maintain for very long. I slowed down.

"Come on, Samantha," Jeffrey said, running in place, until I'd caught up.

"Go ahead, if you want," I panted. "I am not going to risk injury just so you can work up a sweat." I looked over at him. "And don't bring me or the cats any more leftovers from the restaurant, either. I mean it, Jeffrey. I absolutely have to lose fifteen pounds."

Jeffrey switched to a lower gear. "Why fifteen? You don't look *that* bad now, so what makes fifteen so magical?"

"It'll put me into a size ten," I said. The cramp in my side—the one I always seem to get when I run with Jeffrey—was making it difficult to breathe, let alone talk.

"Why a size . . . oh, I get it. The *wedding.*" Like it was the social event of the season.

He jumped in front of me and started jogging backward, something I find extremely humiliating. That and the fact that he can talk so effortlessly. I reached out and pushed him aside. He resumed his position next to me.

"Does this mean you've set a date? How exciting!"

We passed the one mile point. The guy with the stopwatch

CIRCLE OF WOLVES 241

appeared suddenly out of the soup like an apparition and yelled "Eight-fifteen." Immediately, I felt a lot better.

"Jeffrey, do you think Michael and I should elope? I mean, every time I think about getting married in a church, with all those people sitting in the pews and me in my wedding gown, waiting . . . I don't think I can go through with it."

"Michael is not going to be a no-show, Samantha," Jeffrey said. "That was David. That was different. Michael loves you."

"David loved me. At least he said he did." I took the little handkerchief I keep tucked in the waistband of my running shorts out and wiped my face.

"Obviously, he didn't," said Jeffrey. "Not really, or he wouldn't have stood you up in front of all those people."

"I guess."

We ran in silence for another half a mile or so. The fog was beginning to lift a little, and I could see several runners up ahead of us. We were actually gaining on a couple of them.

"How is Dr. Augustin taking this wedding thing, anyway?" asked Jeffrey suddenly.

"I have no idea. He's dealing with some personal problems of his own right now. I doubt he even knows about the engagement."

"Don't bet on it," said Jeffrey. "If he's anything like the nosy bastard you've told me about, he knows."

We ran around a couple of women, an apparent mother-and-daughter combo. The older of the two had peroxide-blonde hair, combed out and sealed with a protective coating of lacquer. The moisture-laden air had deposited perfect little dewdrops on the lacquer, making the hair resemble a sequined turban. When I looked back at her, she smiled and waved, and I realized I knew her. I couldn't remember her name. She'd lost a lot of weight.

242 **Karen Ann Wilson**

"So, is your mother excited about the wedding?" asked Jeffrey.

When I didn't answer, he looked over at me, his eyebrows raised. Don't tell me you haven't told her yet!"

I grinned. "Okay, I won't."

"You should be ashamed of yourself," Jeffrey admonished. "You know you're going to have to tell her sooner or later."

"Later is good," I said. The cramp was back.

"What's the problem? I thought she wanted you to get married. I thought you said she'd love Michael." He paused. "You *have* told her about him, haven't you?"

I made a display of wiping my face again and coughing, but it didn't fool Jeffrey. He laughed.

"I can hear it now," he said. "Hey, Mom, why don't you fly down to Florida this weekend? The weather is great, and I'm having a few friends over Saturday. We'll drink champagne and . . ."

"Jeffrey! Shut up!"

He did. For a full minute. Then, "Sam," he said, "what are you so afraid of?"

And I thought, *I wish to God I knew.*

There was only one Dumser in the phone book, an L. Dumser, no address given. When I dialed the number, Lily's raspy voice answered.

"Hi, Lily, this is Samantha Holt," I said. "Grey's friend. How are you feeling?"

"Oh, yes, hello Miss Holt." She sounded a little tired. "I have my good days and bad days." She wasn't clear which she was having that day.

"I told Grey I'd drop by the hospital for a visit this afternoon," I said. "She made me promise to bring you along. Are you game?"

CIRCLE OF WOLVES 243

"I don't think so. I'm really not feeling very well. Not well enough to go out. But you tell her I'm looking forward to her return." She paused. "Tell her I miss our little evenings together."

"Why don't you tell her yourself, in person? I can come by for you about three, and I promise we won't stay long."

Lily was quiet. Then, "I cleaned up her apartment, you know. And put her garbage out in the hall for the maintenance man to take away. I just couldn't leave that mess to rot in her kitchen."

I could almost see her screwing up her nose in disgust. "That was so sweet of you, Lily," I said. "Grey will be pleased, I'm sure. You are all she has now, with William gone. Here in town, I mean. I know she misses you, too. It's so lonely there in that hospital. And the doctors told her she'll be there another week or two. You know how boring hospital stays can get." I was really pouring it on. Even an idiot could tell that. My mother would be proud, she being such an expert on guilt trips.

Lily coughed lightly, probably to conceal her amusement. "All right, Miss Holt," she said. "I'll go with you."

CHAPTER 28

●

I dropped Lily off at the main entrance and went in search of a parking place. Sunday afternoon at St. Luke's Hospital is worse than Christmas Eve at the mall, and I ended up across Temple Street in an auxiliary lot. I should have skipped the Jingle Bell Run that morning. By the time I met up with Lily ten minutes later, I was sweating lightly, and my breathing was almost as ragged as hers.

"I was afraid you'd gotten mugged," she said nervously.

She was sitting in a pale blue vinyl upholstered reception chair just outside the gift shop. An elderly gentleman, wearing a white straw hat and a pin-striped seersucker suit, sat next to her, staring straight ahead. His shoes were white—the kind with about forty coats of polish on them. He looked like he should have been holding a croquet mallet instead of the cellophane-encased bouquet of carnations he was clutching the life out of.

Lily struggled to her feet. The old man woke up suddenly and started to help her, then saw me sticking my hand out, and sat back down. I smiled at him, but his attack of chivalry was over, and he was staring straight ahead once again.

Lily and I made our way slowly to the elevator, then

244

CIRCLE OF WOLVES 245

rode the car in silence up to the sixth floor. It was painfully obvious Lily had no desire to be at St. Luke's, even as a visitor. I imagined she'd spent more than her share of time in a hospital. Or, possibly, she could see the handwriting on the wall.

With Lily's attention rigidly focused on the floor, we trudged across the connecting corridor to the C wing, and I located Grey's room. I knocked lightly on the door, which was ajar.

"Come in," said Grey.

I pushed the door open, and Lily went in. I followed her and pulled the door closed behind me. I was relieved to see that the adjacent bed was vacant.

Grey was still shrouded in typical hospital garb: a pale rose, open-backed cotton gown that made her look almost skeletal. I felt a twinge of guilt. I'd intended to retrieve the Laura Ashley gown from her apartment but had forgotten.

"Lily! Sam! What a wonderful surprise."

She was propped up in bed and had the Sunday paper spread out across her lap. Her color was good, and her voice had regained some of its marvelous vitality. And with all of her tubes and wires removed, she no longer resembled a limp marionette.

"Sam, could you bring over that chair?" she asked me, pointing to the chair on the far side of the room. Then she made Lily sit in the one next to her bedside table.

I got the second chair and slid it over to the foot of Grey's bed, then sat down.

"I was afraid you wouldn't come," Grey said to Lily.

Lily smiled. "What? And miss the chance to see you at the mercy of the medical profession? Not on your life."

They laughed briefly, then grew silent. Awkwardly so.

"Lily cleaned up your kitchen," I offered.

Grey shook a finger at her. "You shouldn't have done

246   Karen Ann Wilson

that. I certainly don't want you tiring yourself out on my account. You should have called that service. Maids Inc., or whatever they're called. The one Louisa uses."

"Maids Inc.?" I asked suddenly. *Oh great!* I thought. *Another variable in this already confusing mess.*

"Don't worry, Sam," Grey said. "Louisa's fit as a fiddle. So's her dog. Maids Inc. has been around for years. They've got impeccable credentials. The women they use are bonded and insured. The only reason I don't employ them is because I enjoy cleaning. It's therapy for me. Helps me think. Besides, I'm a tightwad. Isn't that right, Lily?"

She gathered up the newspaper and put it on the bedside table. "No, Sam, Maids Inc. wasn't responsible for that poison in my pot roast. But for the life of me, I can't figure out who was."

"The people you told me about," I said, "your friend Tade and the others. The ones Dr. Aaron moved to the psychiatric wing. Did any of them have relatives locally who might have complained about the transfer?"

Grey thought for a minute. She rubbed the first two fingers of her right hand back and forth along the hem of the sheet. The action was so similar to the repetitive motion I had witnessed coming from the vegetables on the nursing floor, it made me shudder. Suddenly, she stopped and looked at me.

"That's an interesting question, Sam," she said. "None of the people I told you about—Tade, Mrs. Willow, Margaret—she's the one with the cat who 'fell'— Robert— has, had . . ." She paused. ". . . family here in Florida. That I know of, anyway. They never came for a visit."

She started the hem thing again and turned her head toward the window. Lily shifted around in her chair. And it dawned on me that it might have been some time since ei-

CIRCLE OF WOLVES 247

ther of them had been visited by family. I didn't even know if Lily had family.

"So, Dr. Aaron could have convinced Tade and the others to commit themselves," I said, thinking out loud. "I do know he told Tade her confusion might cause her to burn her apartment down or whatever."

And then I wondered about Sid, the man Chris had cared for. Where were Sid's relatives? Of course, convincing the family of an Alzheimer's patient that he or she is dangerous would be easier, wouldn't it?

Grey looked back at me. "It's just like I said. They take all that medication for heart trouble or blood pressure or a bad back. Then they fall or catch a cold, probably because they're overmedicated, and end up on the nursing floor, where Dr. Aaron decides they're depressed—that's his favorite word, 'depressed'—and eventually declares them mentally incompetent. Except they're not. Not really. They only seem that way."

Lily hadn't uttered a peep during all of this. She just sat there stonily gazing out the window. Suddenly, she turned toward me and frowned.

"Why are you asking all these questions about Dr. Aaron, Miss Holt? What does this have to do with Grey? You think Dr. Aaron poisoned her?" Her tone was accusatory.

"No," I said. "Well, I really don't know. But somebody sure wants Grey to shut up about this psychiatric wing business."

"Maybe it doesn't have anything to do with the psychiatric wing," said Lily. "Or Dr. Aaron. Maybe that nut Fred Ralston poisoned her."

"And who exactly is Fred Ralston?" I asked, a little angry at Grey for not telling me everything that might be pertinent. If Lily thought the guy was capable of murder,

248   **Karen Ann Wilson**

that certainly made him important enough to mention. I rubbed my temples.

"Pay no attention to her," said Grey. "Mr. Ralston is harmless, Sam." She cocked an eyebrow at Lily. "He's just lonely and crotchety. Like a lot of people our age. Isn't that right, Lily? He needs to get out more."

"No," countered Lily, "he's a spiteful old man who thinks he owns the tenth floor. Probably the whole damned building. Mr. Kiss My Butt." She blushed suddenly.

Grey laughed. "Fred doesn't like Lily because she puts her garbage bags outside her door for the maintenance man to dispose of, which is a no-no, according to our lease. And she has a delivery boy from the market down the street deliver things to her door. Fred doesn't trust strangers and doesn't like anyone who doesn't follow the rules."

"What reason would he have to poison *you*?" I asked her. "Assuming he could get in your apartment, that is."

"He wouldn't."

Lily began fumbling around in her purse. "I need to take my medicine," she said. "I probably shouldn't have come. I had a bad night last night."

She pulled a little zippered cosmetic bag out of her purse and opened it. She rummaged around in that for a few seconds. Prescription vials rattled against one another. She took out one of the vials and unscrewed the cap.

"I'm sorry, Lily," I said, getting up. "Do you have a spare glass, Grey?"

I got her water pitcher off the bedside table. Grey handed me a paper cup, and I poured out some water. Then Grey and I watched as Lily dumped a couple of peach-colored tablets into her hand.

CIRCLE OF WOLVES 249

"I shouldn't have brought the matter up," I said. "This was supposed to be a nice little visit."

Lily swallowed the tablets, then handed me her empty cup. "Forgive me," she said. "This whole thing with Grey and the barbecue . . . And poor Riley. He's just a sweet little cat."

Grey leaned over and patted Lily on the shoulder. "I'm fine, Lily. Riley is fine. And Sam will figure all of this out eventually." She looked at me and smiled. "Won't you, Sam?"

"Absolutely," I said, just to be polite. At that point, I doubted Sherlock Holmes could have figured it out.

Lily closed her purse. "I think we should be going," she said.

She pulled herself up, using the edge of the bed and the table for support. She really did not look at all well, and I jumped up to help her.

"I'll call you this evening, Lily," Grey said, "to make sure you're all right."

At the door, I stopped and looked back at Grey. "By the way," I said, "do those Maids Inc. people have keys to the apartments?"

Grey nodded. "But only their clients' apartments. Not mine."

"How about the lady whose cat fell off the balcony?"

Grey chewed on her lower lip like a small child deep in thought. "No, not hers, either," she said, finally.

"This Fred Ralston," I continued. "He wouldn't be in the apartment three doors down from yours, would he?"

Grey smiled. "Ten-ten. I guess you noticed he's the local snoop. He hasn't given you a bad time, has he? He probably saw Lucky. He dislikes dogs, you know."

"He dislikes everything and everyone," muttered Lily.

250 Karen Ann Wilson

"Well," I said, "he may actually turn out to be of some help this time."

"Humph," said Lily.

After I'd deposited Lily in her apartment and listened for the chain, I headed down the hall toward the elevator. When I got to Fred Ralston's apartment, I stopped. I knew he was probably watching me through the peephole, so I put on my best smile and knocked lightly.

"Go away," said a voice on the other side of the door.

"Mr. Ralston," I said, "I need your help. It has to do with one of your neighbors. I'm told you are sort of in charge around here."

I prayed his ego would overcome his reluctance to talk to strangers. And then my smile broadened when I heard him retract the dead bolt and take off the chain. He opened his door a couple of feet.

He looked like something out of *Wind in the Willows*. The mole, perhaps. He had tiny little eyes and wore reading glasses. They were balanced on the end of his nose, which was quite long and pointed. His salt-and-pepper hair was exceptionally greasy and deliberately plastered down on his very round head. He wore a plaid bathrobe and slippers.

"What do you want?" His breath, as well as the air escaping from the apartment like pent-up hostility, was a combination of stale cigarettes and vinegar.

I knew he would never ask me in and was extremely grateful for that. I could just imagine what evil lurked in the darkness behind him. At the very least it was undoubtedly in need of housekeeping.

"I was wondering if you'd seen anyone going into Gretchen Milner's apartment. Within the last few weeks, that is."

CIRCLE OF WOLVES 251

"Why do you want to know?" he asked. "And who are you, anyway? The cops?" He sounded more like Mr. Toad or Badger than the shy little mole.

"I'm a friend of Mrs. Milner's. She had . . . something stolen out of her apartment."

"She should go to the police, then," he said, starting to close the door.

I grabbed the doorknob to stop it, and he regarded me suspiciously.

"She doesn't really know for sure," I said. "And you can imagine the police wouldn't like her to bother them needlessly. If you could just think back . . ."

"You've been in there. With that dog."

"Yes, I have. And her neighbor, Lily Dumser, has also been in her apartment. But has anyone else? Anyone you might have noticed using a key?"

"One of those maids," he said.

"Maids?" I gripped the doorknob.

"One of those cleaning people."

"How do you know it was a maid?" I asked.

He looked at me over his half-glasses and blinked a couple of times. There were traces of some kind of ointment coating his lashes. And the skin on his nose was flaky.

"She looked like a maid, that's why," he said. "Like the rest of 'em. The ones who come in those shiny white vans."

"And she had a key?"

"I just said she did, didn't I?"

"Well, I guess maybe you did. And when was that?"

"When was what?" he asked.

I drew in a deep breath and regretted it instantly. Kosher dill pickles and nicotine assailed my nostrils.

252   **Karen Ann Wilson**

"When did you see this maid go into Mrs. Milner's apartment?" I let go of the doorknob and stepped back.

"I didn't write it down in my calendar," he snapped and started to close the door.

"Anyone else go into her apartment using a key?" I asked. "That you can remember, I mean."

"Mrs. Milner uses a key," he said, grinning. His teeth were worn down almost to nubs and badly stained.

"Yes, I realize that, but . . ."

Mr. Ralston shut the door and slid the dead bolt. Behind me, a dog barked. One quick, ear-shattering yelp. Then silence. I hurried for the elevator.

CHAPTER 29

•

Monday, December 6

Dr. Augustin was almost an hour late. We had two spays and a neuter to do before ten and only forty minutes to do them in. To make matters worse, he was actually cheerful that morning and seemed disinclined to work. I told Cynthia to call our ten o'clock and 10:15 appointments and try to reschedule them for the afternoon. She frowned, mostly at Dr. Augustin's office door, which was closed, and reached for the phone.

I had just finished swabbing the bulldog's belly with Betadine, when Dr. Augustin graced the surgery with his presence. I glared at him and looked pointedly at the clock.

"Glad to see you've got things under control in here," he said cheerily. He went over to the sink and started to scrub.

I couldn't stand the suspense another minute. "Why are you in such a good mood?" I asked. "Did Cronin drop the suit?"

"No, he said, "unfortunately. But Bob called me at home this morning from Gainesville. Guess what he told me?"

"I couldn't begin to."

"He said he got curious about that colchicine in Mrs. Milner's barbecue. So he did a little research and found that, in addition to gout and cancer, it's used for horticultural pur-

254   Karen Ann Wilson

poses. To increase the chromosome count in plants. You remember I told you colchicine inhibits mitosis?"

He rinsed his hands and reached for the towel in his gown pack.

"Why would anyone want to increase chromosome number in plant cells?"

"To make the plants bigger," he said. "Or the flowers bigger. Bob told me orchid growers and hybridizers commonly use colchicine to produce tetraploid plants. You know, instead of the normal diploid, or two sets of chromosomes, it would double the count, which makes the flowers larger and the plant stronger."

He put on his gown and turned, so I could tie it closed for him. Then he pulled on a glove.

"Orchids, huh?" I said. "One of the nurse's aides at Sunset View Towers is into orchids. At least I think he is."

"It might explain where the pesticide came from," said Dr. Augustin. He walked over to the table and began arranging a drape across the dog's abdomen. "The aldicarb that killed that maintenance man could have come from a plant nursery, I suppose."

I watched him make his incision. "Well, I found out something yesterday," I said.

Dr. Augustin picked up a gauze sponge and dabbed at a couple of bleeders, then reached for a hemostat. "Oh?"

"Yes. One of Mrs. Milner's neighbors said he remembers seeing a maid going into Grey's apartment recently. The maid had a key, evidently."

He looked at me over his mask. "Maid? You didn't tell me Mrs. Milner employs a maid."

"She doesn't. That's the point. According to Grey, one of those housekeeping services—Maids Inc.—cleans for a lot of residents at Sunset View Towers. Grey's neighbor said it was one of the Maids Inc. people he saw going into Grey's

CIRCLE OF WOLVES 255

apartment. Except Grey told me they're extremely reputable. Besides, they only have keys to the apartments they clean. Since she isn't a client, how would the maid get a key to her apartment?"

Dr. Augustin worked in silence for a couple of minutes. I checked the dog's reflexes and adjusted the gas flow, then went over to the sink.

"How did the neighbor know it was one of these Maids Inc. people?"

"I asked him the same question," I said. "He told me because she *looked* like a maid. Whatever that means."

Dr. Augustin dropped a hemostat onto the instrument tray. "I assume that means she was wearing a uniform," he said. "White, probably. So, who else wears clothing that might be construed as a maid's uniform?"

I thought about this for several seconds. "A nurse," I said.

He flung another hemostat at the instrument tray. "Ah, give that girl a Kewpie doll," he said.

"Okay," I said, "how are you planning to tie all this information together? The nurse, the colchicine, the pesticide. You *do* have a plan, don't you?" He always had a plan.

He looked at me, his eyes shining. "You and Mr. Halsey don't have a date tonight or anything, do you?"

CHAPTER 30

•

He was down in the parking lot, waiting, when I looked out my front door. He'd said 7:30. It was 7:10. He couldn't get to the clinic on time, but give him a chance to break and enter, and he was like the early bird.

He told me to wear nondescript, casual clothing, not my black ensemble, because we needed to look like everyone else, not cat burglars. When I asked him where we were going, he'd grinned and said, "To check out the employment opportunities at Sunset View Towers." He'd refused to elaborate and, with the rest of our day running approximately ninety minutes behind schedule, I didn't think about it again until it was time to go home. However, I felt sure "employment opportunities" did not mean what it sounded like, but I had no clue as to what it did mean.

I grabbed my purse, locked my front door, and ran down the stairs. Dinner had been a Lean Cuisine. There was a stack of them in my freezer. It was day two of my diet and, although Michael had fixed fettucine Alfredo and bananas Foster for dinner Saturday night, I could feel the pounds melting away already.

I got in the car and watched Dr. Augustin finish a Whopper and fries.

"How can you eat like that and not weigh three hundred

256

CIRCLE OF WOLVES 257

pounds?" I asked. "Besides, don't you worry about cholesterol?"

He wadded up his napkin and the paper wrappers and
tossed them over the seat to join the rest of the fast-food
container armada on the floor of the Jeep.

"I have better things to worry about right now than my
diet, Samantha. And, anyway, life is too short to sweat the
small stuff."

Yeah, I thought, *and you can bet all that junk food is making it a whole lot shorter.* But he had a point about the small
stuff.

"I'm considering bringing Larry in as a partner sometime
next year," he said.

"You mean, full-time?"

"Yep, full-time. What do you think?"

"I like Larry," I said. "But, let's face it, when all our female clients ask for you, what is he supposed to do, twiddle
his thumbs? Remember, it was you who dropped him back
to two afternoons a week. You said we were losing money."

"I know, I know. But Cynthia claims Larry always looks
so professional. Like I don't. What is it, the tie? Or the
hair?"

"I don't know," I said. "It's a perception thing, I guess.
People see the tie and automatically think professional.
Blame it on social custom. I mean, after all, don't those re-
ligious missionary types—the ones who come to your door
to preach the word and hand out little booklets—don't they
always wear ties? The men, I mean. To make them look
more respectable. It doesn't mean they necessarily are."

He didn't say anything as we turned into the Sunset View
Towers complex. He wasn't prepared for the speed bumps,
and the Jeep lurched over the first one like a drunk.

"In any case, Mr. Halsey seems to have attracted you," he
continued, as if Michael were a strip of flypaper. "I expect

258 Karen Ann Wilson

there are like-minded women out there who will fall for Larry eventually."

I wasn't sure what he meant exactly, and some small part of me took offense at the implication, although I couldn't explain why. Fortunately, our conversation was cut short by the old guy in the guard shack.

"We're here to visit my aunt," Dr. Augustin lied. "She's in the Hayes Building."

"Name?" the guard asked. He had his clipboard and his pen.

Dr. Augustin paused, then said, "Tony Sebastian."

The man bent over and peered suspiciously into the Jeep. He might have been an airport security guard looking for assault weapons.

"Her name is White," I said, quickly. "Tade White." I smiled at him, although it was dark in the Jeep, and he probably couldn't see me. "I'm Samantha Holt. I've been here before. With the puppy. You remember?"

The guy squinted at me, then checked his list. He evidently remembered me or Lucky or both, because he made a notation, then waved us through.

"Thanks," said Dr. Augustin, after we were under way again. "I knew there was a reason to bring you along."

"Now that my name is etched in that guy's mind forever, and you're protected by one of your many aliases, will you kindly tell me where we're going?"

"The administrative director's office. I want to look through his personnel files. The answer to all this has got to be there somewhere."

"Turn here," I said, pointing toward the Hayes Building. "Of course, you brought your lock picks."

"Of course."

•   •   •

CIRCLE OF WOLVES 259

The lobby of the Marion R. Hayes Building was empty, which made me a little nervous, since I was definitely not there on official business. But I tried to appear casual as I led Dr. Augustin down the hall to Nelson Aveneau's office.

"What if he hasn't gone home yet?" I whispered. "Or if the cleaning people are still here?"

"Then we'll wait. Maybe go visit my aunt Tade."

He was grinning. It didn't do a thing for my nerves. Happily, no one was about, and we couldn't hear anything going on in Mr. Aveneau's office. So Dr. Augustin took out his set of lock picks and went to work on the door. I kept glancing up and down the hall, waiting for a guard to come around the corner. But the only thing I found the least bit threatening was an odor of split peas and floor cleaner.

Suddenly, Dr. Augustin straightened up and turned the doorknob. He felt along the wall for the light switch, flipped it on, and ushered me inside.

Surprisingly, Aveneau's office wasn't a whole lot bigger than Mrs. Snoden's. It had one extra desk for the department secretary, apparently. A Nora James, according to the little brass sign on the desk. She had a computer, a weather-beaten dictionary, a coffee mug full of pencils and pens, a stack of purchase requisitions by the look of them, and an in/out-box combo, with the "in" part nearly full. Most importantly, Ms. James had a four-drawer file cabinet.

"You check out Mr. Aveneau's desk," said Dr. Augustin, "while I see what's in here." He pulled on the top drawer and, finding it unlocked, began to thumb through the hanging file folders.

I went over to Mr. Aveneau's desk. His, in contrast to his secretary's, was nearly bare. He had a brand-new blotter, courtesy of a local engineering company, a Rolodex, an in/out-box combo—the "out" part was overflowing—and a stack of unopened mail, most of it third class.

260 **Karen Ann Wilson**

I opened the top drawer of his desk. It held the usual: pens, pencils, nail trimmers, chewing gum, breath mints, a ruler, paper clips, rubber bands. A date book caught my eye, and I lifted it out. He'd made numerous entries in it over the past month: meetings, dental appointments, lunch and dinner engagements. He was pretty stingy with names, so, I didn't learn a great deal, except he liked expensive restaurants and whoever he was wining and dining had prompted him to draw little exclamation points (sometimes two) under the name of the eating establishment.

I gave up on the date book, closed the drawer, and started to pull out the file drawer. It was locked.

"I need your lock picks," I said to Dr. Augustin.

He came across the room, carrying a manila folder. "Take a look at this," he said, handing the folder to me. He pulled his picks out of his back pocket.

The folder contained Willie Roan's personnel file. The top sheet was a letter from Roan to Mr. Aveneau, in which Willie stated he was resigning from Quetzal Bay Properties because of what he felt were "unacceptable practices on the part of management." The letter was dated November 3, just a few days before his untimely demise.

Dr. Augustin popped open the drawer and stood up. He put the lock picks back in his pocket and reached for Willie's file.

"So Willie Roan did uncover something illegal or otherwise unacceptable, as he put it, going on here."

"So it would seem," Dr. Augustin said.

"I can't believe Aveneau left this letter in the file for just anyone to look at. It certainly gives support to the notion Willie was murdered, doesn't it?"

"It would seem to be an unfortunate error on Mr. Aveneau's part, I'll admit. His secretary probably filed it." He pointed to the bottom drawer. "See what other errors might

CIRCLE OF WOLVES   261

be hiding in there. I've still got the nursing staff to check on."

The telephone rang suddenly, and I jumped a good foot off the floor. Even Dr. Augustin was rattled, because after the ringing quit, he took a bright yellow gumball out of his pocket and put it in his mouth, a sure sign he was under stress. Then he went back to the file cabinet trailing an odor of fake lemon-lime.

I was starting to perspire lightly, and my hands were cold. I wanted to get out of there in the worst way, but I sat down in Aveneau's chair and started browsing through the man's personal files. I ran across a copy of his résumé and took it out. After a couple of paragraphs, I realized I had struck pay dirt.

"Listen to this," I said. "Following graduation from high school, Aveneau worked for a pest control company, Dalton and Sons, over in Tampa. Then he quit there and went to work for a local outfit, Jernigan Ornamentals and Landscape Services. In 1980, he went back to school and eventually got a degree in horticulture from the University of Florida." I read the next couple of pages to myself.

"Then he went to work as head groundskeeper at Hidden Cove Condominiums over near Vero Beach," I said aloud. "According to this, it's a Quetzal Bay Properties establishment. He was there until two years ago, when he was hired to run this place. Your classic 'boy makes good' success story." I looked over at Dr. Augustin. He was smiling.

"Well, well. Jernigan Ornamentals," he said. "I'll bet they have an interesting array of chemicals on hand." He put the file he'd been reading back in the file drawer and closed it. "This Aveneau sure was a lucky bastard, going from groundskeeper to administrative director in such a short period of time, don't you agree?"

"You think he was brought here from Vero Beach for

262   Karen Ann Wilson

more than his good looks?" I asked. "You think maybe Cronin saw the potential for an accomplice in Aveneau? Like maybe the guy had done something illegal over at Hidden Cove?"

"I think it's worth investigating further. Unfortunately, these files aren't going to tell us anything."

"Nothing about the nursing staff? No idea who might have gone into Grey's apartment?"

"No. Everyone looks squeaky-clean." He came over to Aveneau's desk and took the résumé. He glanced at it, then handed it back to me.

"According to his date book," I said, "Aveneau has been entertaining somebody on a regular basis. Hits all the best restaurants, too. Maybe it's the 'maid' Grey's neighbor saw going into her apartment."

"Maybe. But short of tailing Aveneau or obtaining photographs of every woman who works at Sunset View Towers, then showing them to Mrs. Milner's neighbor, I don't know how we'll discover the woman's identity. I think our time would be better spent checking out Jernigan Ornamentals, don't you agree? See if they have any colchicine on hand. And find out if somebody at Sunset View Towers is moonlighting as a lab tech in the nursery. A woman, perhaps."

He started for the door. I put the résumé back in the file drawer, then shut it. To make sure it was locked, I gave it a tug. It opened.

"I think you broke the lock," I said. "The drawer won't stay closed."

Dr. Augustin turned around. "Nonsense," he said. He came over to the desk and slammed the drawer. Then he pulled on it. It opened. He shut the drawer again, then opened it.

"Great!" he exclaimed.

CIRCLE OF WOLVES 263

He took out his lock picks and was about to insert one into the lock, when we heard conversation in the hall.

"Get the lights," Dr. Augustin whispered.

I tiptoed across the room and hit the light switch. The room was instantly gobbled up by the darkness, and I froze where I stood.

The voices grew louder, then fainter, as two, possibly three, women walked past the office. They were matter-of-factly discussing their latest sexual encounters. Their descriptions were so explicit, my heart rate would have shot up, had it not already reached its maximum a few moments earlier. I tried to control my breathing, which had become quite labored.

When I thought the coast was clear, I turned on the lights. Dr. Augustin was looking at me, his eyes large and luminous, his lips parted slightly, as if he, too, was having difficulty breathing. And he was perspiring. I hadn't noticed him doing that earlier. The look on his face was clearly unprofessional, in fact, almost feral, a look Larry Wilson would never be able to muster. And, of course, that was why bored or unhappy housewives would never flock to him the way they did to Dr. Augustin. I considered all of this in the time it took for the voices to fade around the corner.

Dr. Augustin leaned over and jiggled the lock on Aveneau's file drawer a couple of times, then shut the drawer. That time, it wouldn't open when he tugged on it. He put the lock picks back in his pocket, and we left.

CHAPTER 31

•

Tuesday, December 7

Cynthia looked up the number for Jernigan Ornamentals and Landscape Services in the telephone book, then gave them a call to find out what their Wednesday hours were. Naturally, she wanted to know why I was interested in a landscape company.

"Orchids," I said, for once being truthful. "Somebody told me they grow orchids, and I thought I might get a friend for the one Katrina gave me."

That part wasn't entirely true, of course. Since I don't lie very well, and Cynthia, although childless, has a mother's instinct for that sort of thing, she frowned at me and raised an eyebrow. I was about to embellish the lie when her face suddenly blossomed.

"The wedding!" she exclaimed. "Of course. Orchids would be perfect." She winked. "You go right ahead and get a 'friend' for that plant Mrs. Treckle gave you. I won't tell."

Then she turned back to her computer terminal and began humming to herself. I couldn't be sure, but it sounded an awful lot like Mendelssohn.

Larry gave the poodle a final scratch and turned to the owner, a middle-aged divorcee with hair the color of a rusty nail. The drink, not the real thing. Actually, it only looked

264

CIRCLE OF WOLVES 265

that way under the fluorescent lights. In daylight, it was more the color of Hawaiian Punch.

"She's right on schedule, Mrs. Lange," he said, picking up the woman's file. "I count four, maybe five puppies. Sometime around Christmas. Wouldn't that be nice?"

Mrs. Lange nodded slowly, ponderingly, as if the idea of a birth at Christmas was a novel idea. She was a nice-looking woman, despite all the makeup she wore, and she kept herself fit at the local health club. "Swimming," she'd said, which no doubt accounted for the color of her hair, since I felt certain no normal person would voluntarily choose to look like a cherry Popsicle. Chlorine and sun can do strange things to hair, dyed or not.

But what was *really* amazing was the fact that Mrs. Lange requested a Tuesday afternoon appointment, knowing that Dr. Augustin wouldn't be there. Larry was pleased, of course, and spent a lot of time examining her dog, even commenting on what good care the scrawny little thing was receiving. He did suggest that Mrs. Lange begin increasing her food intake, since she was "eating for six."

"*I* only gained eight pounds with my first," said Mrs. Lange, rather haughtily. "And only six with my second. So many women think they can eat and eat when they're pregnant." She smoothed back the curls on Muffin's head. "I don't want little Muffin to look like a bowling ball. The groomer suggested I put her on one of those high-fiber foods."

Larry started to say something doubtless on the order of, "No offense, but the groomer probably isn't the best person to be giving out advice on prenatal care," then stopped. He looked over at me. "What would Dr. Augustin say to this woman that wouldn't offend her?" he seemed to be asking.

I smiled sympathetically. How could I tell him it has less to do with *what* Dr. Augustin says than with *how* he says it.

266 **Karen Ann Wilson**

How he looks at the client, how he stands. His faint arrogance that women, in particular, interpret as great wisdom and infallibility.

"Poor little thing," I said quickly. "With five puppies inside her, Muffin is going to look like a bowling ball no matter what she weighs."

"I suppose," said Mrs. Lange.

I stepped behind the woman and caught Larry's eye. Then I crossed my arms over my chest and leaned casually against the wall. Like a child imitating a parent, Larry did the same.

"And when she begins nursing all those puppies," he said, "she'll need the extra nutrients and calories. High-fiber foods are good if the animal's caloric requirement is low, but Muffin's needs are pretty high right now and will get a lot higher."

It was working, evidently. Mrs. Lange listened and nodded. And when Larry was through, she asked him what brand of food would be good and how much Muffin should receive each day and if she should give the dog vitamin tablets.

I winked at Larry and left them to discuss the merits of folic acid. An air of professionalism, complete with tie and haircut, is admirable, I thought, but there's definitely something to be said for swagger.

Dr. Augustin, the king of swagger, stopped by the clinic at 5:30 to check on one of his patients. I ran into him coming out of Isolation.

"Listen, Samantha," he said, his voice low, "I don't want you to do anything stupid tomorrow. Just look the place over, see if they have a lab where they do hybridizing and plant tissue culture. Don't ask any unnecessary questions. You're supposed to be looking for a plant for your mother. A gift. Maybe a poinsettia. Be vague. And if they . . ."

CIRCLE OF WOLVES 267

"Why don't you go? You know what to look for. Besides, you're a lot better at thinking up aliases than I am."

He drew his brows together, took aim at my forehead with his high-intensity stare, and blew a grape-colored bubble. I concentrated on the bubble, willing it to burst across his face, maybe stick in his hair. But he sucked it in right before it popped, chewed for a few seconds, then smiled.

"Because who would think twice about a nice girl buying a plant for her mother?"

"Do I get overtime for this?" I asked, suddenly, the question surprising me almost as much as it did Dr. Augustin.

His smile withered. "A week ago you were PO'd because I refused to get involved in this drug-induced dementia theory of yours. Now you're PO'd because I ask you to do a little reconnoitering."

A little reconnoitering? I said to myself. Breaking into someone's office and going through their stuff is a lot more than that, I should think. But he was right. I should have been grateful for his interest.

"Listen, Samantha," he said, "if you don't want to do this, just say so. Nobody's forcing you to." He continued to stare at me.

Right, I thought. "No, no, I'll do it. I don't know what I was thinking. I mean, you certainly pay me enough already to risk my life, don't you?" I gave him a toothy grin and hurried into the kennel, letting the door swing shut before his blow torch eyes could singe my behind.

CHAPTER 32

●

Wednesday, December 8

Jernigan Ornamentals and Landscape Services was located in the northeast part of the county, just inside the city limits. That was lucky for Jernigan, or whoever owned the place, because it was about the only area of the county with enough vacant land left for new development. So it didn't surprise me to see row upon row of hibiscus, bird-of-paradise, and pygmy date palm thriving in the sun behind a large stockade fence. Nobody who moves to Florida from up north wants plain old pine, oak, or palmetto. Florida is supposed to be a tropical paradise, and native slash pine and live oak just aren't tropical enough for people craving a piece of Tahiti.

I drove through the gate and headed for a complex of greenhouses and outbuildings, one of which had OFFICE AND SHOWROOM printed in large letters over the doorway. Several cars were parked in the gravel lot adjacent to the building, so I pulled between a minivan and a Lexus.

A nicely dressed woman came out of the office, followed by a man in green overalls over a yellow T-shirt carrying a large, flat box stuffed full of bedding plants: marigolds, zinnias, and assorted other brightly colored specimens. He stood quietly, while she opened the rear hatch on the minivan, then slid the box into the car. They exchanged a few

268

CIRCLE OF WOLVES 269

words, then the man went back into the office, and the woman got in her car and started the engine.

I waited until the woman was on her way down the drive, then got out of my car and locked it. I had absolutely no idea where to begin looking for a laboratory and was scanning the property, when a voice behind me made me jump. I turned around.

"Were you interested in anything in particular?" he asked, smiling. "Bedding plants, maybe. Now is the time to put in that winter garden. We've got several varieties of tomatoes."

He was a little older than Dr. Augustin but was dark like him, with jet black hair on the longish side and a Roman nose that made him look raptorial. He was wearing the same green overalls and yellow T-shirt the other guy had been wearing. I was close enough to this man to read JERNIGAN ORNAMENTALS AND LANDSCAPE SERVICES printed in green on the T-shirt. Their logo was, ironically, a huge live oak tree.

"I'm, uh, looking for an orchid," I stammered. "For my mother. It's her birthday."

The man was still smiling, but given his overall appearance, it looked more like a leer.

"We have a nice selection of blooming orchids in our showroom," he said, pointing to the building with the sign. "Go on in and look around. Someone there can help you."

I murmured, "Thanks," and hurried away toward the office.

The showroom was a large, open, high-ceilinged area with long, overhead fluorescent lights. Benches and tables throughout the room were crammed with living examples of Jernigan's expertise. There were several dozen orchid plants, all in full bloom, numerous tea rose bushes, none of which had a single dead or dying flower, lots of ornamental foliage plants—Chinese evergreen, diffenbachia, ponytail palms, ferns—all healthy and devoid of dead leaves.

270 Karen Ann Wilson

Gorgeous photographs on two of the walls depicted various English-style gardens, resplendent with perfectly nurtured and groomed flower beds. Butterflies and small children swooped and fluttered about the blooms. I could almost hear the laughter.

On one side of the room was a long, flat table piled high with cardboard boxes and stacks of old newspapers—packing material, presumably—and next to it, a large desk with a computer terminal. It was manned by a petite brunette dressed in green slacks and yellow Jernigan Ornamentals T-shirt. She looked up at me, smiled, then mouthed the words, "Be right with you," and went back to her call. She and the individual on the other end of the line apparently were discussing a large shipment that had vanished from the face of the earth. The brunette was doing her best to shirk all responsibility for the lost shipment.

I continued my examination of the room. Directly inside the front door was a set of metal shelves containing every legal (I hoped) herbicide and pesticide available in the U.S. to keep those immaculate lawns and gardens bug, fungus, and weed free. Despite the foil lining and shrink-wrap, a strong chemical odor made my nose burn and left a nasty taste in my mouth. I tried to read the active ingredients on a few of the pesticide containers to see if aldicarb was present but was interrupted by the brunette. She had gotten up from her desk and come across the room.

"Sorry about that," she said, evidently referring to the phone call. "How may I help you?"

"I'm looking for a plant," I said, as if people actually came to Jernigan's for some other reason. "A gift. I was interested in an orchid."

Right then, a young couple came through the door, accompanied by the swarthy man in overalls.

"Peggy," the man said to the brunette, "these folks are in-

CIRCLE OF WOLVES 271

terested in our landscape service. Could you buzz Tom and have him come up here?" He nodded at the couple, then left without waiting for Peggy to reply.

Peggy looked first at me, then at the couple, indecision clouding her smooth features.

"Do you have other orchids?" I asked quickly. "That I could look at before making a selection?"

The look of indecision grew more pronounced. "Yes," she said, pointing to her right, in the general direction of the greenhouses I'd seen when I drove up, "but you need someone to accompany you. They're very careful about . . . you know . . ."

I didn't but had no desire or time for an explanation. "Sure. I'll just wait until you're finished with these people." I smiled warmly, and the girl relaxed.

"Right. Thanks." She walked over to her desk and picked up the phone. The young couple followed her.

I immediately went outside and looked around. There were several pairs of green overalls scattered around the place, tending to plants, the sprinkler system, and whatnot. Fortunately, there were also several visitors wandering up and down the rows of trees and shrubs, so I ambled toward the greenhouses as if I, too, were simply admiring the merchandise. No one seemed to notice.

The first greenhouse I looked in contained nothing but poinsettias—hundreds of them—in red, pink, and white, all in top condition. A man wearing a plastic jumpsuit, gloves, goggles, and some type of gas mask was spraying them with a water wand attached to a mile-long hose that traveled along behind him as he made his way down the row. The smell was awful, so I quickly backed out of the house and hurried to the next one.

It contained rose bushes, tea-sized mostly, in various shades of pink and coral. No one was in evidence, so I went

272   **Karen Ann Wilson**

inside. The bushes were so beautiful, the air so fragrant, I couldn't help myself and momentarily forgot why I was there in the first place. Eventually, I came to my senses and exited the house through the rear door.

The last greenhouse in that row was larger than the others. Its north wall was, for the most part, composed of a series of panels constructed out of corrugated cardboard or something similar. Water dripped onto the panels from a long, horizontal PVC pipe peppered with tiny holes. The paper panels were completely soaked and stained unevenly with a green-brown color. Excess water collected beneath the panels in a gutterlike trough. The trough emptied into a tank sunk in the ground. Obviously, a circulating pump returned the water to the PVC pipe, although I couldn't see or hear it.

I went around to the east side of the building and tried to figure out what was growing inside, but the glass was painted with a watery coat of whitewash and was essentially opaque. I looked around but didn't see anyone so, without a whole lot of hesitation, I went through the door. It was tough to open—like breaking a vacuum seal—and rattled noisily, then whapped closed behind me.

If I hadn't known better, I'd have sworn I was lost in some South American rain forest. The humidity in that greenhouse was approaching 100 percent. The air was so thick, I could practically swim in it. I felt sweat pop out on my face and arms. Enormous vent fans on the south end of the building were drawing air through the soaked cardboard panels, and the temperature grew noticeably cooler the closer I got to the panels.

Everywhere orchids smiled at me in the jungle atmosphere, their blossoms thrust upward from the benches toward the sun like owl faces or winged insects seeking the light of a lamp. I was standing inside a rainbow, complete

CIRCLE OF WOLVES 273

with the elusive pot of gold. Every now and then I caught a whiff of something spicy or sweet.

The vacuum seal suddenly broke and, above the din of the exhaust fans, I heard voices. I kneeled down below the level of the benches and duck-walked along the aisle until I reached the end of the row. The voices weren't getting any louder. I could see two pairs of green-clad legs at the far end of the greenhouse, along with someone wearing shorts and tennis shoes—a woman. Apparently she was being given a quick tour, because I caught the words, "This time of year," and "dendrobiums," along with "mail-order business, mostly."

My knees were complaining bitterly, but I managed to hang on until the suck and whap of the door indicated the tour party had vacated the premises. I stood up. There was a door on the opposite side of the greenhouse from where I'd entered, so I trotted up and down several aisles until I reached it.

The door had a glass panel in its top half. I couldn't see any green overalls from where I stood. I held my breath, pushed the door open, and hurried in.

The temperature was noticeably higher in the second greenhouse. The north wall was devoid of cardboard panels, and the vent fans served only to move air through the place. Instead of row after row of waist-high benches containing various sizes of clay pots, long metal rods had been strung up lengthwise along the ceiling from which wooden baskets hung. The baskets and their contents reminded me of Portuguese man-of-wars. The plants—orchids, mostly—had masses of long, coiled, whitish roots that extended almost to the floor. I had difficulty walking down the aisles without these orchid tentacles snagging my hair. I was actually glad to get out of there with all of my body parts intact.

The air outside was refreshing, and goosebumps replaced

274   Karen Ann Wilson

the beads of sweat on my neck and arms. I brushed damp
strands of hair off my face and tried to get my bearings. Another row of greenhouses, these made of screen material
rather than glass, ran parallel to the line of glass houses.
They appeared to contain foliage plants. Beyond them was
an all-white, windowless concrete structure. It looked
promising, so I headed that way.

The number of visitors had increased. I looked at my
watch. It was 12:30. A plant nursery seems like an odd place
to spend one's lunch hour but, from the number of suits and
dresses browsing through the petunias, Jernigan's apparently was a big draw in that part of town. I smiled and nodded at a couple of women checking out the tomato plants,
then continued on.

The door to the block building said NO ADMITTANCE. It
was unlocked, however, so I risked a peek. I didn't see anyone. What I did see made me curious enough to step inside
and allow the door to close in my wake.

Dr. Augustin probably hadn't intended for me to do much
more than locate the lab. Snooping around inside it, in direct
violation of the NO ADMITTANCE. sign was more his style.
But I was already there, I told myself, so what the heck.

The room was air-conditioned, spotlessly clean, and extremely bright. The walls and ceiling were painted white.
Light, oddly cool despite its pinkish cast, was provided by
several dozen fluorescent tubes.

The room resembled a library to a certain extent, but, instead of books, the floor-to-ceiling shelves held hundreds of
clear glass quart milk bottles—the kind the milkman used to
leave by your door in those insulated boxes. The bottles
were turned on their sides and plugged with rubber stoppers.
Each bottle contained some sort of agarlike substance on
which grew clumps of green plant material. Some of the
plants were large enough to resemble orchids. The bottles

CIRCLE OF WOLVES 275

were labeled, but the code, like "ES27D495", meant nothing to me.

There was a second, smaller room off to my left. I went over and looked in. It was the lab Dr. Augustin had been hoping to find. Rows of brown bottles and jars containing various chemicals were neatly stacked on a bench, along with glassware, boxes of rubber stoppers, an autoclave, a propane torch mounted on the edge of the bench, and assorted instruments, even a blender. A sterile hood was positioned on a table in one corner, while a desk with a computer, a telephone, and miscellaneous office stuff sat in the other corner.

On the opposite side of the room was a sink, a drainer filled with milk bottles, a small dishwasher, a refrigerator, and a shelf containing coffee-making supplies. It reminded me of the lab at the clinic—doing double duty as a kitchen. Everything was very tidy and smelled faintly of bleach. The walls were bare, except for a poster from the thirteenth World Orchid Conference in Auckland, New Zealand, and a calendar. The calendar was clean—no nefarious notes like, "Poison Gretchen Milner today."

I looked back at the chemicals and was about to check the labels when I heard a voice say, "I'm sorry, miss, but this building is off . . ."

I turned around. Nelson Aveneau was standing about fifteen feet away. He was dressed in a suit and tie, the tie loosened, the top button on his shirt open wide. Like his mouth. Flies could get in, it was so wide.

"Well, now," he said, "isn't this just peachy."

I stared at him, my tongue temporarily paralyzed. He was sweating, and there were dark areas under the arms of his suit coat. He really would have been more comfortable in overalls and a T-shirt, I thought absurdly.

276 Karen Ann Wilson

"Who sent you, Miss . . . Holt, isn't it?" he asked. "More important, how did you know to come here?"

"I can't imagine what you mean," I said. "I'm shopping for an orchid for my mother. The nurses at Sunset View Towers told me that beautiful orchid on their desk was from here, so I decided to stop by on my day off."

I certainly thought I sounded convincing. I only hoped he bought it. And that he wouldn't say anything incriminating. Because, if he did, he might decide not to let me go.

He shifted from one foot to the other and squinted at me. He seemed caught off guard, unsure about me then, as if I really had just gotten lost.

"What are you doing in here, if orchids are what you're after?" he asked, stepping closer to me.

I caught myself backing up and stopped. Like Aveneau was a junkyard dog who'd found me on the wrong side of the fence. Run and I was lunchmeat. I smiled innocently.

"That girl in the office was busy. She said I could look around."

He shook his head. "Peggy never told you to come in here." He pointed over his shoulder at the door. "You have a habit of breaking into areas marked PRIVATE and OFF LIMITS?"

All the time, I thought. I faked a grin and shrugged. "I was curious. I don't know very much about plants, especially orchids. This place . . ." I spread my arms as if Jernigan's Ornamentals and Landscape Services included the entire universe, ". . . is so incredible. You people grow the most wonderful things here." Then I leaned forward and pretended *I* was the one whose property had been trespassed upon.

"Wait a minute," I said. "You're the administrative director at Sunset View Towers. So what are *you* doing here?" I put my hands on my hips and stepped forward.

CIRCLE OF WOLVES 277

The guy actually backed up a foot and got this "little boy caught in the act" look on his face.

It was a fleeting juxtaposition. "I *own* this place," he growled. "I think that gives me the right to be here. I bought out old man Jernigan last year." He was back to eyeing me suspiciously. "I think you'd better stay right where you are until I can sort this through. Maybe I'll have to contact the authorities."

Please, go right ahead, I thought. *I can even give you their number.* But I just stared at him.

He headed for the door, then stopped and looked over his shoulder at me. "If it's orchids you're interested in, Miss Holt, we have hundreds of thousands of them here." He waved his arm around the room. "Knock yourself out."

Then he left, pulling the door closed behind him. I heard him insert a key in the lock. It was one o'clock.

CHAPTER 33

•

I was hungry. The raisin bran I'd eaten for breakfast was long gone, and I was beginning to suspect lunch was no longer an option. Dinner was looking pretty iffy, as well.

Since Mr. Aveneau hadn't appeared totally convinced that I was a threat to him, his locking me up in the orchid neonatal unit didn't worry me too much. He'd come back sooner or later, apologize, and let me go. At least, that's what I wanted to believe.

For almost an hour, I entertained myself looking at all the bottles of baby plants and browsing through the lab. I located the colchicine and several other equally hazardous (by the look of the warnings on the labels) compounds, as well as some rather innocuous ones, like sodium chloride and isopropyl alcohol.

I checked out the contents of the refrigerator: reagent bottles, boxes of growth media, a Tupperware container with a nice crop of penicillin developing in it, a carton of milk that was so old, it felt like a brick of aged cheddar, a Domino's pizza box with two slices in the process of mummification, and enough bananas to feed every primate at the Lowry Park Zoo. I glanced over my shoulder, which was ridiculous, and helped myself to one. I figured they owed me that much.

278

CIRCLE OF WOLVES   279

The place had a small half-bath, a "powder room," as my mother would say, with a sink and toilet. Reading material on the back of the toilet included a couple of horticultural magazines and an obscure journal, the title of which I had to read several times just to make sure I wasn't seeing things. It was the *Journal of Ethnopharmacology*. One of the articles was, "Hallucinogenic Plants of the Tarahumara." I had no idea what or where the Tarahumara was, but the term "hallucinogenic" certainly grabbed my attention. *Could that be what's making Grey's friends seem demented?* I asked myself. William had certainly acted like he was hallucinating. Would these hallucinogenic plants give them dilated pupils?

I took the magazine out to the lab and put it on the desk next to the computer. I picked up the telephone and was greeted by silence. No dial tone, no voice, no heavy breathing, no static. Nothing. I checked to see if it was plugged in, and it was. Mr. Aveneau apparently was smarter than I'd given him credit for. Either that or Jernigan's Ornamentals and Landscape Services was behind on their phone bill.

I finished the banana, found a relatively clean coffee mug, rinsed it out, and filled it with water. Then I took the mug and went back to the desk.

A box of computer disks next to the computer contained over a dozen poorly labeled (from my standpoint) diskettes. One read "MERIST.95". Two others had only sets of letters and numbers that looked like the IDs for Swiss bank accounts. Another said "POL.96," which could have been in reference to the '96 presidential race for all I knew. Another diskette had "WILDCATT" printed on it, which had possibilities.

I turned on the computer. After a few seconds. I got the menu, saw that someone had loaded a Games section,

280 Karen Ann Wilson

called it up, and got a choice of three. I selected Space Aliens, only because I have never been very good at poker or solitaire.

Initially, I'd kept one ear on the front door in anticipation of Mr. Aveneau's return. Unfortunately, fighting cyborgs was taking most of my powers of concentration.

"What do you think you're doing?"

I jerked my head around. A man, definitely not Mr. Aveneau, was standing in the office doorway. He was short, thin, about fifty, dressed in a suit and tie. The clothes and hair were expensive.

I tried to compose myself. "They locked me in here—with no lunch, I might add—and I got bored. This game . . ." I pointed over my shoulder at the computer, ". . . is pretty neat." I gave him my best blonde look.

Unlike Nelson Aveneau, the new guy did not seem overly taken in by my attempt at innocence.

"Breaking and entering is a felony, Miss Holt," he said, calmly.

I was beginning to think the whole world knew who I was. I tried to remember if we'd met. His demeanor was very different from that of Mr. Aveneau. He was smooth, totally in control. From his clean, perfectly manicured nails and pale skin, his expertise in the landscape business, assuming he had any, was not "hands on."

"I did not *break* anything," I said. "The door was unlocked. At most, I trespassed. Trespassing, I believe, is a misdemeanor." *So much for the blonde act,* I thought.

"And what, exactly, were you looking for?" He came across the room and stood by the desk.

I shrugged nervously. "Nothing, really. I came here to buy an orchid for my mother. The girl in the office was busy, so I decided to look around." I put my hands in my lap.

CIRCLE OF WOLVES 281

"There isn't anything in here to interest you, Miss Holt. Just a lot of little plants. Nothing valuable except to another grower. And then only with the cross names. According to the folks in the office, without the crosses, those little plants are practically worthless."

He glanced down at the computer disks. He seemed to be implying that I was some sort of corporate spy. I almost laughed. Then, out of the corner of my eye, I saw the magazine I'd swiped from the lavatory. It was upside down. Still, the words "hallucinogenic plants" appeared to jump off the page.

Under the guise of getting more comfortable, I shifted around in my chair while easing it along the edge of the table, until I was obstructing the man's view of the magazine. Then I crossed my legs. If I'd been wearing a skirt, I would have hiked it up several inches. But I wasn't.

"Where did you say you worked, Miss Holt?" the man asked.

"You know," I began, "I'd really like a sandwich. I'm not feeling very well."

I touched my stomach and grimaced dramatically. In fact, I really wasn't feeling all that great. It had nothing to do with missing lunch, however. I'd missed lunch more times than not. No, the queasiness in my stomach was due to the look in the guy's eyes. Like he routinely shot people for a lot less than stealing orchids.

"Where do you work, Miss Holt?"

If I'd had any sense at all, I'd have said, "McDonald's." In my haste to assure him that I did not work for some competing orchid company, I said, instead, "Paradise Cay Animal Hospital. I'm a veterinary technician. Now do you believe I only came here to buy an orchid for my mother?"

The man stood there in front of me, his face totally placid. All except the eyes, of course. They were little

282   **Karen Ann Wilson**

chunks of dry ice. Then he smiled, slowly, as if savoring some very expensive cognac.

"Really." He glanced around the lab, perhaps trying to determine how curious I'd actually gotten, then back at me. "How interesting."

He looked at his watch. "I'm afraid you'll have to stay here a while longer, Miss Holt. By your own admission, you were trespassing. For all I know, you were looking for drugs." He sighed. "These days, so many young people are into designer drugs. It's such a pity." He seemed to be having this conversation with himself.

I didn't say anything. He knew very well that wasn't why I was there.

He started for the door. "I'll send in some lunch," he said over his shoulder. Like I was a guest at his estate. Then he was gone.

I heard the door close. There was no reason to check it. I knew it was locked.

At four, after successfully attaining the third level in my quest to stave off the evil Larn and his buddies, I heard a rattle in the plant room. I jumped up and ran through the opening between the rooms in time to see a feminine hand disappear around the edge of the front door. She closed the door and locked it before I could wedge a foot in the crack.

The rattle I'd heard was from a small tray the woman had placed on one of the shelves. The tray contained a ham and cheese sandwich wrapped in plastic—like something you'd get from a vending machine—a bag of chips, an apple, and a pitcher of tea, along with a glass and a couple of napkins.

I lifted the tray and carried it back into the lab. The computer screen had brightly colored tropical fish swimming back and forth over a rocky seabed. I'd missed my chance

CIRCLE OF WOLVES 283

to reach the fourth level. I'd have to start all over. Not that I was going anywhere or had anything to do.

I picked up the sandwich and stared at it. The plastic wrap was sealed and tight, but anybody with an iron could manage that, after first tearing it open and sprinkling the ham with poison. The apple was definitely out. How many times did I hear about parents finding razor blades or needles in the apples their kids got at halloween? I threw the sandwich and apple in the trash.

The bag of chips looked okay—airtight and the original seam unbroken. I pulled the seam apart and sniffed. They smelled okay. I took a tiny bite of one and chewed. It tasted okay. I settled back in my chair and ate the chips, while I worked my way back to the second level. I was finally getting the hang of Space Aliens, when I heard a car drive slowly past the building, its tires crunching over the gravel like boots on new-fallen snow. I ran over to the back door and pounded on it.

"Help! Help!" I screamed.

The car continued down the drive, until I couldn't hear it anymore. I should have screamed "Fire!" I thought sadly. Isn't that what they tell you to holler, even if you're being raped? Not that the car's driver could have heard me through the block walls.

I went back to the desk and sat down.

"This is ridiculous," I said aloud. "This is kidnapping. Kidnapping beats trespassing, doesn't it?" As if the proprietors of Jernigan's Ornamentals and I were playing some sort of scissors, paper, rock game.

I poured myself some tea and sipped it as I went out to the plant room. The hinges on the front door looked pretty tight. The air conditioner was a window unit. I pushed up on it, but it wouldn't budge. I went back to the lab and checked the hinges on the rear door. They were rusted solid. For good measure, I kicked the door. It sounded pretty secure, but the action gave me an idea.

I put my glass down and started looking for something strong and sharp. Like an ax or a machete. Or a chisel. Tools one always finds in an orchid lab, isn't that right, Miss Smarty Pants? If you'd done what you were supposed to, you wouldn't need a chisel.

I finally located a length of metal pipe in the lavatory and carried it out to the plant room. The air conditioner seemed like an appropriate target, since the doors were too substantial for anything short of a bazooka.

The Gro-Lux lights in the plant room were a shock after the relative darkness of the bathroom, and I felt a stab of pain jump from one eye to the other. I squinted, but the pain only grew worse.

"Too much staring at that damned computer," I said.

And I was dizzy to boot. I left the pipe on the floor under the air conditioner and headed back to the lab. My purse was on the desk, and I went through it searching for my little container of aspirin. My brush and keys fell out on the floor, but when I bent over to pick them up, I felt like I was about to faint, so I left them on the floor. I couldn't remember what I was looking for, anyway.

I went to the refrigerator and got out another banana. "All we need now is some butter, brown sugar, and rum," I said, peeling the banana. "For the bananas Foster." I turned to see if Michael had heard me, but he wasn't there. "Of course he isn't," I said angrily.

I took a bite of the banana, but it was tasteless and mealy. I tried another and another. Same result. They were all inedible. Like eating mashed potatoes without salt or butter, I thought. Lumpy potatoes at that. Even I can make better mashed potatoes.

I turned to go, stepped on something squishy, and had to

CIRCLE OF WOLVES 285

grab the edge of the counter to keep from falling. I looked down. A pile of bananas, bruised and flattened, covered the floor in front of the refrigerator.

"God, what a mess," I said. "These people sure are a bunch of slobs, aren't they?" My invisible companion didn't answer.

I was burning up. And thirsty. So thirsty, in fact, that I was having trouble swallowing. My glass was empty, and I couldn't remember where I'd put the coffee mug. The pitcher, however, was sitting on the desk. I took a step, then grabbed the counter again. The room seemed to be breathing—in and out, in and out. Part of the time, the desk was just inches away, part of the time it was so far away I could barely see the fish gliding across the computer screen. I was afraid to let go of the counter, afraid I might be sucked in and exhaled out like a swimmer in a rip tide.

I kept staring at the pitcher. Something about the pitcher bothered me. I watched the pitcher grow and shrink with each breath the room took.

"I need a drink of water," I said, peeling my tongue off the roof of my mouth. "God help me, I need a drink of water."

I waited until the desk surged toward me, held my breath, and let go of the counter.

There were voices coming from the plant room. They were whispering, so I couldn't hear what was being said. They sounded familiar, though. A man and a woman.

"Michael?" I said, my voice like a dry saltine. "Cynthia?" They couldn't hear me. And then they were gone.

Dr. Augustin had his hand on my neck, except the hand was rough and calloused. Not Dr. Augustin's hand. I tried

286 Karen Ann Wilson

to look at him, to see his eyes. He was angry. Who was he so angry at? Was it me?

He picked me up. The room breathed bananas Foster on me, and I closed my eyes against the nausea.

I was being swept out to sea.

CHAPTER 34

•

Thursday, December 9

I couldn't move. Not without excruciating pain, anyway. Every muscle in my body screamed when I tried. My neck, my back, my legs. When I breathed, it felt like somebody had inserted tiny razor blades between my ribs. Even my scalp hurt.

I opened my eyes. At least my eyelid muscles weren't complaining. The eyeballs were another matter, however, and I concentrated on the view directly in front of my face.

For a second, I thought I was still in the plant room, except the tiny green plantlets had grown up and brought forth rose blossoms instead of orchids. I moved my head a fraction of an inch to gain a little perspective. The roses—at least two dozen of them stuffed in a glass vase—sat on a small table a couple of feet from my head. White roses. Something Michael would send.

"How are you feeling, Sam?" asked a voice behind the roses.

It was Grey's voice. And suddenly I felt like crying. Like I had as a child when I was hurt or sick, and my mother would put her cool hand on my forehead.

"Grey?" I asked, choking back the tears. My eyes and throat burned.

Pretty soon, I heard a rustling noise and then a chair scrape

287

288 Karen Ann Wilson

across the floor. Grey, dressed in a plain white terrycloth robe, sat down next to my bed and smiled at me.

"It's nice to have you back, Samantha," she said, gently. "You were delirious most of the night."

"How did I get here?" I asked. "I mean, in your room? This is your room, isn't it? In the hospital?" I tried to sit up, but it hurt too much. "I could use some aspirin."

"Tylenol," said Grey. "That's all you'll get in here, I'm afraid. Should I call the nurse?"

"No, that's okay. What time is it? Or should I ask, what day is it?" There was an IV catheter in my left hand. The tape holding it in place was burning my skin.

"Thursday," said Grey. "Two-thirty. P.M., not A.M. And to answer your first question, that nice boss of yours, Dr. Augustin, convinced the doctor—a friend of his, he said, to put you in here with me. He's a hard man to turn down, it would appear."

"Hmmm," I said, closing my eyes.

Consciousness came and went several more times before I finally woke up for good at just after five o'clock. They'd given me something in the IV for the pain, and I was able to attain a more or less sitting position, with the help of the adjustable bed.

Grey ate her dinner while I tried not to think about food. According to her, Cynthia had called a couple of times earlier in the day, and they'd talked at length, probably about my love life, as well as my health, although Grey didn't say as much. Cynthia apparently was beside herself with worry and wasn't speaking to Dr. Augustin, who she blamed for my condition. Grey assured her I would live.

"Now, tell me all about last night," Grey said with enthusiasm, after she'd finished her tasteless, colorless (according to

CIRCLE OF WOLVES 289

her) meal and had come over to sit in the chair next to my bed. "If you're up to it, of course. If not, please say so."

"How did I get here? The hospital, I mean. Did Dr. Augustin bring me?"

Grey shook her head. "The police called him, I believe. The nurse said the police and the paramedics brought you here. A poisoning of some kind, is all they would tell me. Was it the same poison you found in my pot roast? The symptoms were different, weren't they?"

"Dr. Augustin didn't bring me, then?" I remembered he was there in the plant room and he was angry. Or had I imagined it? The whole thing was a cloudy mess. I remembered going to Jernigan's. And the lab. There'd been a man in a suit. Or was it two men? I tried to clear the cobwebs but couldn't.

"Sam?"

I looked at Grey. "I can't remember," I said. "I just can't remember."

"Maybe I can help," said a male voice from behind the partly drawn curtain.

A hand drew the curtain back, and Grey and I looked up. It was Detective Tom Hummer and another man I didn't recognize. Tom and I had first met in October, during one of Dr. Augustin's crime-solving adventures. I hadn't seen him for several weeks. He was as cute as ever, although his expression indicated this was not a social call.

"How are you feeling, Samantha?" Tom asked gently. He was holding my purse, the one I'd had with me at Jernigan's.

Grey got up and went back to her bed. The two men stood next to mine. Neither seemed inclined to sit in the vacated chair. The second man wasn't looking at me in an overly sympathetic manner.

"I guess I'll live," I said.

I did have the presence of mind to check my gown and sheet to see that I was adequately covered. Then I made a fee-

290 **Karen Ann Wilson**

ble effort at a smile. I don't care what they say about fewer muscles being required to smile than frown. Smiling was definitely more painful.

"You said you might be able to help me remember," I said to Tom.

He put my purse on the bedside table, next to the vase of roses. "I believe this is yours. It has your driver's license in it at any rate. Some of the contents were on the floor near where we found you. A hair brush. Lip gloss. I hope I retrieved everything." He smiled bashfully.

I was staring at his companion, and Tom suddenly turned toward the guy, then back at me, as if, deep down, he had hoped the man might disappear before the introduction.

"I'm sorry," he said, not really sounding sorry, "this is Detective Fanning." He paused. "From our narcotics division."

Detective Fanning did not offer his hand.

"Narcotics?" I asked. "Whatever for?"

Tom grimaced and shrugged lightly, as if to indicate he, too, was uncertain. "Let me start at the beginning," he said. Then he reached behind Detective Fanning and pulled the curtain back around my bed. Like Grey wouldn't be able to hear through the flimsy material.

"At midnight, the department got a call that a white female named Samantha Holt was suffering from a bad trip on some chemical substance. That she'd been caught breaking into the orchid laboratory at Jernigan's Ornamentals nursery. Because of your condition, the responding officer gave drugs as the possible motive for the break-in, although there aren't any in that lab. We checked."

"Who called you?" I asked.

"It was anonymous. I overheard the call and recognized the name. I figured it had to be someone else with your same name but decided to meet the patrol car there, anyway. Things

CIRCLE OF WOLVES 291

were slow up till then. Of course, it turned out to be you, and my evening definitely picked up."

He sat down in the chair next to my bed and ran his fingers through his hair. I wondered how much sleep he'd had, if any. His violet eyes looked a little grey.

"We found you propped up against a concrete building," he continued. "Unconscious. The paramedics brought you here. I phoned Sergeant Robinson, who gave me Dr. Augustin's number. I didn't know who else to call."

Detective Fanning took a step forward. "What were you doing at Jernigan's at midnight, Miss Holt, if I may ask? Your boss told me you were checking something out for him. Exactly what was that, and how did you end up seeing aliens?"

"Well, I certainly wasn't breaking into the lab, looking for drugs. If I was into drugs, I'd get them at my place of employment. Believe me, we have a lot better stuff there than what was in that orchid lab."

"You admit you were inside the lab, alone?" asked Detective Fanning, "breaking and entering" written all over his face.

"Yes, but I didn't break in. The door was unlocked, and the girl in the office said I could look around."

"And you were just looking around? For what?"

"She was helping me, detective," said Grey from the other side of the curtain.

Both officers turned around, and Tom pulled back the curtain. Grey was standing there in her bathrobe, several inches shorter than either man, trying to look dignified. Her expression was very commanding, like her expression the day Mrs. Herfeld had tried to talk William's daughter into moving him to the psych wing. "Don't mess with me, buster," she seemed to be saying.

"I beg your pardon," said Detective Fanning.

"She was trying to find out who poisoned my cat, Riley,

292 **Karen Ann Wilson**

and me. That's why I'm here, you know. Someone put poison in my pot roast."

Detective Fanning studied Grey like maybe *he* was seeing aliens. Then he looked over at me, then at Tom. "Was this poisoning reported to the police?"

"No," I said. "It wasn't. Dr. Augustin wanted to check it out first."

"You're saying Dr. Augustin instructed you to trespass on Jernigan's property?" asked Detective Fanning. "Does he do this a lot? Ask you to break the law?"

Tom cleared his throat, which saved me from having to lie. "Sergeant Robinson can fill you in on Dr. Augustin," he said. "He's sort of an unofficial consultant to our department."

I made a faint choking sound that caused Tom to grin, in spite of his efforts to the contrary.

Fanning just shook his head. "I'll let Robinson pursue the trespassing issue," he said. "I'm only interested in the drug angle. You haven't explained why you were in the lab in the first place, Miss Holt, and what caused your hallucinations."

"Mrs. Milner is one of Dr. Augustin's clients," I said. "She brings her cat to us. Anyway, as it turned out, her pot roast was contaminated with colchicine. Dr. Augustin found out colchicine is used on plants—orchids—and at least one of the people who has access to Mrs. Milner's apartment has ties to Jernigan's nursery. I went there to see what I could find." I winked at Tom. "You know, before Dr. Augustin called the police. I don't remember anything very clearly after Mr. Aveneau locked me in the lab."

Both men stared at me.

"Mr. Aveneau is the man who has access to Mrs. Milner's apartment. He's the administrative director at her apartment complex and he owns Jernigan's Ornamentals. He found me in the lab. He thought I was there to steal the nursery's orchid plant records or something. I guess there's a lot of money at

CIRCLE OF WOLVES 293

stake. You know, like stealing the formula for a new perfume. Anyway, he locked me in there. Then he, or someone—I don't remember—delivered a tray of food and some iced tea. I'm pretty sure the tea was poisoned. I didn't eat the sandwich, but I stupidly drank the tea. I don't remember much after that."

Detective Fanning wrote a few more notes in his little notebook. "I'll be contacting you again, Miss Holt, once the toxicology report comes back."

"Don't worry, detective," I said, "I won't leave town."

He obviously got a chuckle out of that one, because he smiled at me. He was actually very nice looking, particularly when he wasn't playing Joe Friday. I put him somewhere around forty—Dr. Augustin's age—with Dr. Augustin's build, but not his coloring. Detective Fanning was a strawberry blond with green eyes and freckles.

And then I felt my memory lurch into motion. "Tom," I began, as the two men were turning to leave, "you said you had to call Dr. Augustin at home, is that right?"

Tom nodded. "I woke him up, apparently. Why?"

"Because, unless this was another hallucination, a man who looks a lot like Dr. Augustin came into that orchid lab and carried me outside. I remember thinking it was Dr. Augustin, except his hands were very calloused, and Dr. Augustin's hands are anything but."

"Maybe that's the man who called the police," offered Grey. She was still standing behind the detectives, her hands in the pockets of her robe. She winked at me.

"I'll certainly check it out," said Tom. "Thanks."

"One other thing," I said, suddenly. "A neighbor saw a woman in a uniform going into Mrs. Milner's apartment when she wasn't there. This was about the time the pot roast was contaminated. She had a key and, according to Mrs. Milner, no one has a key except the maintenance people—which

294   Karen Ann Wilson

probably means Mr. Aveneau—and a friend. I'm not sure what kind of uniform, but it was probably a maid's or a nurse's."

Tom grinned again and came back over to my bed. He sat down and got out a little spiral pad and a pen. He flipped open the pad.

"You want to tell me all of it, Samantha?" he asked. "From the beginning."

Detective Fanning sighed loudly, looked at his watch, and went for Grey's chair, after first helping her back into bed.

Detectives Hummer and Fanning stayed until a quarter past six. Grey and I recounted everything that had happened, beginning with the unexplained (from Grey's way of thinking) deaths of pets at Sunset View Towers and the subsequent imprisonment or death of their owners. Grey provided the motive for her poisoning in characteristic Milner style. Tom seemed to be trying very hard to take her seriously. However, he did smile just a little at her indignation when Detective Fanning asked her what medication she was taking, as if maybe she, too, was "under the influence."

"Aspirin," she'd snapped. "One a day. Exactly what you ought to be taking, young man." If she'd been any closer, I feel certain she'd have poked him in the stomach with her finger.

Detective Fanning shut up after that.

I did manage to leave out the real reason Dr. Augustin was involved, i.e., Cronin's suit against him. And I conveniently left out our little nighttime excursion to Aveneau's office. Fortunately, Tom didn't want to know how we'd found out that Aveneau was associated with Jernigan's.

"It's good that the police know about this now, isn't it?" ey asked, after we were alone and after the nurse had done

CIRCLE OF WOLVES   295

her evening thing with the thermometer and blood pressure cuff.

"Yes," I said. "I don't think I'd get very far snooping around again at the nursery."

"I'm so sorry you nearly died, Sam, trying to help me."

"First of all," I said sternly, "I did not nearly die. Fortunately, I didn't consume enough of that tea or whatever for that. Second, Dr. Augustin sent me there. He has an interest in this whole mess aside from what happened to you and Riley and the others at Sunset View Towers. It's too complicated to explain. You'll just have to take my word for it."

Suddenly, another snippet from my stay in the orchid lab surfaced. The guy in the nice suit with the subzero eyes. Who was he? For some reason I felt I knew him. But I needed a name.

Just then, Dr. Augustin came through the door. "Hi," he said. He smiled at Grey, then came over to my bed.

I didn't have to see myself in the mirror to know I looked pretty ragged. I needed a shower, my hair was a mess, and the hospital gown I had on did nothing for me, despite the little duckies and chickies parading around on it. I felt like an escapee from the children's ward. I pulled the sheet up as high as it would go and slid down under it. I could feel my face burning and, this time, it wasn't from an elevated temperature.

"Hi," I said.

"I see you got my flowers," he said, pointing to the roses.

"*You* sent those? There wasn't any card. I just assumed . . ."

"What? That Mr. Halsey sent them? Does he even know you're in here?"

"I . . . I guess not. Strange. I wonder why he didn't call the clinic to find out where I was."

"Maybe he hasn't tried to call you yet. Maybe he doesn't know you're missing."

296   **Karen Ann Wilson**

Clearly, Dr. Augustin was taking great pleasure in pointing out the fact that he, rather than Michael, was providing moral—and floral—support in my time of need.

I didn't say anything.

"Instead of sending you flowers," he said, "I should be docking your pay. I told you not to do anything stupid. Why in the world did you go into that lab, anyway? I told you to *locate* it, that's all."

His brief attack of compassion evidently was over.

"So you could go in and browse around, is that it?" I asked, angrily. "And I suppose you wouldn't have drunk any of that spiked tea they gave me after they locked me in there?"

"Tea, was it?" He paused. "No. *I* wouldn't have gotten locked in there in the first place."

"Children, children," said Grey. And then she clucked her tongue and waggled her finger at us.

Dr. Augustin went over to the chair next to my bed and sat down. "Sorry," he said. "But you could have been killed, Samantha. With or without the tea or whatever it was. Did Aveneau catch you in the lab and lock you up?"

"Yes," I said. Then it hit me. "What does this Cronin guy look like?" I asked.

"Short, thin, anemic-looking. Hair is sandy and glued in place. Oh, and his eyes are blue. Why do you ask?"

"Because he was there at the nursery. He came in the lab after Aveneau locked me up. He wanted to know where I worked."

"What did you tell him?"

I felt around in my head for an answer, but came up empty. "I can't remember for sure," I said. I looked away. "I guess Matt isn't going to be pleased, is he? If Cronin's lawyers can connect me with you, they'll use my excursion last night against you in that suit, won't they?"

CIRCLE OF WOLVES 297

Dr. Augustin was silent. When I looked back at him, he was smiling, certainly not the reaction I'd expected.

"What?"

"Who do you think the court will side with," he asked, "our more or less innocent attempt to help this poor woman . . ." he pointed at Grey ". . . or someone who willfully and forcibly detained a young woman, then tried to poison her?"

Grey started to giggle.

"Oh, I see your point. I guess my almost getting killed worked out to your advantage, after all."

As usual, he ignored the sarcasm. "You *can* identify him, can't you?"

At that moment, one of the nurses stuck her head in the door, saw Dr. Augustin, and blushed.

"Visiting hours are just about over," she said, looking at Dr. Augustin through her lashes. "I'm so sorry. If it were up to me, I'd let you stay a bit longer, of course."

Of course, I thought. *If it were up to her, he could stay all night. Preferably in the nurse's lounge.*

Dr. Augustin got up. "You didn't answer me, Samantha. Can you identify Cronin as being there in the lab with you?"

I nodded.

"Thata girl," he said. "Well, get better. I don't expect you to come to work until Monday."

He headed for the door. The little nurse was hanging around outside in the hall, probably waiting to personally help him find the elevator.

After he was gone, Grey coughed politely. "You didn't tell him about those detectives who came by earlier," she said.

I looked across the chasm between our beds. She was smirking.

"You think I have some kind of death wish?" I asked.

She giggled again.

298 Karen Ann Wilson

I phoned Jeffrey to let him know where I was and to ask him to feed my cats. I got his machine, so I left a message. If he didn't bother to listen to it, I could expect to find my kitchen in shambles when I got home. Miss Priss will go to any lengths to locate food, including opening and inspecting every cabinet within reach.

Then I dialed Michael's number.

"Where have you been, Samantha?" he asked, exasperation evident in his voice. He sounded more like a parent than a soon-to-be husband. Or maybe he did sound like a husband. What did I know?

I bristled.

"I called you this morning at seven," he continued, "to tell you I was flying up to Jacksonville for the day and could you please feed the kittens their dinner. You weren't there. When I phoned the clinic, I got Cynthia's recording. I left a message, which, of course, you never got. My ankles can attest to that. Randy was most upset."

"Are you through yelling at me?"

"I was worried, Samantha. When I called you at home this evening, and you still weren't there . . ."

"I'm in the hospital, Michael."

"Hospital! Are you all right? What happened?"

"Obviously, I'm not all right or I wouldn't be here," I snapped.

Grey clucked her tongue.

"But I'm going to be all right," I added quickly, glancing at her. My world was full of mothers, it seemed. "It's a long story. They said I can go home tomorrow. Late morning. Can you pick me up?"

"Of course, Samantha. But please fill me in now. Don't make me fret all night."

I sighed loudly and dramatically, which elicited another cluck from Grey, settled down in my bed, and told him.

CHAPTER 35

•

Friday, December 10

"Grajales," said Michael. "Raymond Grajales."

We were in his car on the way to my apartment. I really wasn't in the mood for conversation. All I wanted was a bowl of tomato soup, a bath, and my own bed. And not necessarily in that order.

"Who?" I asked.

"The man who called the police. The one you said looked like Dr. Augustin."

"Oh."

"The police located him from your description. He's employed at Jernigan's Ornamentals and Landscape Services. Has been for several years, way before Aveneau bought the outfit. He was on his way home Wednesday night after making some emergency repairs to the ventilation system in one of the greenhouses when he noticed a strange noise coming from the air conditioner in the laboratory. Someone had smashed the fan to smithereens."

I thought about the metal pipe I'd found in the lavatory. I couldn't remember actually using it, but obviously I had.

"He was pretty sure Nelson Aveneau was running some sort of scam at Sunset View Towers," Michael continued, "but wasn't aware of the particulars. He wasn't asked by

299

300 Karen Ann Wilson

Aveneau to get involved and wouldn't have, anyway. He doesn't like Mr. Aveneau, apparently. Of course, now that Aveneau is under arrest for locking you in that lab and drugging you and under investigation for fraud at Sunset View Towers, among other things, the future of Jernigan's Ornamentals is in question. Mr. Grajales may be out of a job, unfortunately."

"How did you find all this out?"

He looked over at me and smiled. "I'm a reporter, remember? This whole business—the Baker Act, the financial shenanigans there at Sunset View Towers, your unfortunate brush with death—makes for a great story, believe me. Besides, I like to know where my fiancée spends her free time."

I watched a string of pelicans glide effortlessly along, just above the water. The lead pelican flapped, then the next, and so on, as if each bird took its direction from the bird in front. I thought about how simple my life had been before my engagement. In less than four months I would have to start answering to someone else, in addition to myself. And that thought troubled me more than it should. "What about the woman who delivered the tea I drank? The one who got into Grey's apartment and tried to poison her? Assuming they're one and the same, of course. Did this Grajales person mention her?"

"I'm afraid not," said Michael. "But it's only a matter of time before the police identify her. Aveneau is not an experienced criminal. It won't take much to get him to talk, I shouldn't think. Although my police contact did say that so far he's refusing to mention any woman, girlfriend or otherwise. Very gallant of him, don't you agree?"

"She's still out there, then?" It was ridiculous to think the woman would come after me with an ax, I knew. In any

CIRCLE OF WOLVES 301

case, I told myself, strychnine is more her style. And I wanted to go on a diet, right?

"Samantha," said Michael, "why don't you stay at my condo until this business is over?" He was staring straight ahead, rolling the palm of his right hand over the steering wheel.

"I refuse to let this bother me, Michael. Besides, my cats would never forgive me." I tried to laugh.

Silently, Michael parked the car, then made an attempt at helping me up the stairs.

"I'm fine, Michael," I said, gently disengaging his hand from my arm. "Just a little tired."

But he wouldn't listen, and I was afraid he'd insist on hanging around the rest of the afternoon to make sure I really was okay.

In the end, though, he left. He did say he'd drop by that evening with dinner. "Nothing heavy or rich," he said. "Maybe just a nice pasta salad from that Greek deli down the road."

At the thought of garlic, olive oil, and balsamic vinegar, my stomach began doing push-ups. But I smiled anyway and said that would be nice. When I finally closed the door and headed for my bathtub, I was so tired, I really didn't care about much of anything, Michael included.

The phone woke me from a very sound sleep. I'd been dreaming about snow, its silent whiteness disturbed only by the crackle of a fire. I was sipping a cup of cocoa at my mother's house and staring out the big picture window in her living room. The flakes drifting and twirling downward had a calming effect on me. I was alone, which seemed a little odd.

"Hello?" I said into the receiver. My voice was like a block of ice cracking.

"Samantha," my mother said, "you promised you'd call,

302   Karen Ann Wilson

and here it is Thursday, and I haven't heard a peep out of
you."

"*You* were going to call *me,*" I said, turning on the light
and sitting up. The snowflakes were dissolving, along with
my composure.

"Oh, dear, I did, didn't I?" Her voice dropped a few deci-
bels.

I was silent as I rubbed my eyes.

"I'm sorry, Samantha," she said. "You're home early
tonight, dear. I wasn't sure I'd catch you. You aren't sick, are
you?"

"It's just a headache, mother. My allergies, probably.
Stuff in bloom."

"You'll feel better once you get up here, where all the
trees have the decency to go dormant in the winter.
So . . . have you gotten your ticket yet? You realize the
longer you wait, the harder it will be to get a seat. And you'll
pay top dollar."

She was preaching now, one of her favorite avocations.
And I lacked the strength to stop her. So I listened without
hearing, a defense mechanism I had perfected as a teenager,
inserting a grunt or groan here and there, and occasionally a
"Yes, Mother." I leaned against my pillow and closed my
eyes.

"Samantha?"

I opened my eyes. "Yes?"

"I asked you if Michael was coming. I need to know. Will
he be staying with us? Will he be here for Christmas dinner?"

"I don't know yet. He's coming over tonight. I'll ask him
then. I promise."

"And you'll let me know?"

"Yes, Mother. I'll let you know."

"Tomorrow. Call me tomorrow."

CIRCLE OF WOLVES 303

"I'll call you this weekend," I said firmly. "Sunday. I promise."

As I was hanging up the phone, the doorbell rang. I grabbed my housecoat, took a peek in the mirror (wished I hadn't), and stumbled out into the living room.

Michael had trouble hiding his concern. "If you'd rather I didn't come in . . ."

"It's all right, Michael. I really feel better than I look. I just need to eat something, I think." I was relieved to see he wasn't carrying any garlic-laced take-out bags. "What happened to dinner?"

He came in and I shut the door. "I was running late. I thought I'd check with you first. See if perhaps you'd like to go out. But, obviously . . ."

"Why don't you fix me an omelet, instead. You do them so well. And a tossed salad."

He beamed. "I can do that. What have you got in the way of ingredients?"

We went into the kitchen, where I was quickly informed that one egg and half a green pepper did not constitute an omelet.

"I need to pick up my car, anyway," I said. "Let's go to Jernigan's and get it, then you can continue on to the store."

He agreed, and I did what I could to make myself presentable.

It was dark when we got to the nursery, but the gate was open, and there were two cars parked next to the office: mine and a Saturn with a crumpled front quarter panel. Michael pulled up next to my car, and I dug into my purse for my keys. They weren't there.

"Terrific," I muttered. "My keys are missing."

"Maybe you left them at home. We can go back. Better yet, I can come up here tomorrow with someone from the

304   Karen Ann Wilson

office and get your car. You're not going to work tomorrow,
I hope."

"I want my car, Michael. Someone might decide to take
revenge on it. Besides—you saw what was in my refrigerator. I need to do some grocery shopping first thing in the
morning. I need cat food and . . . some personal items." I
thought for a minute. "My keys might have fallen out of my
purse in the lab. Detective Hummer said he found my purse
on the floor and some of my things were scattered around.
Maybe the keys slid under something, and he missed them."
I pointed up the gravel drive. "Let's go over to the lab building. If I'm lucky, the door won't be locked."

Reluctantly, Michael drove to the lab and stopped. I got
out. A perfumy fragrance—a mixture of citrus and cinna-
mon—greeted me. The night air was heavy with it.

"I won't be long," I said.

The door to the orchid building wasn't locked. And the
light was on. I shivered, not from the cold, but from the feeling of dread that greeted me as I went inside. I tried to ignore it and walked past the bottle babies to the lab. I was met
in the doorway by Loni Herfeld.

She let out a tiny gasp and dropped the box of computer
disks she'd been carrying. She was wearing her nurse's uniform.

"What are you doing here?" she squeaked.

"I might ask you the same question," I said. I was gen-
uinely puzzled for a moment.

"I'm . . . I'm picking something up for Nelly." With one
eye on me, she crouched down and began gathering the
disks together.

"*Nelly?*" I started to laugh. "You mean *Nelly* Aveneau?"
Suddenly, it all fell into place.

Loni stood up. "Yes. What of it?"

CIRCLE OF WOLVES 305

"Nothing. Absolutely nothing. Except I can't see Nelson Aveneau being referred to as Nelly. What a hoot."

She was trying to inch her way around me. I made sure she couldn't pass. I was angry, now, and for once in my life, grateful for being a size twelve instead of a size four.

"By the way," I said, "what did you put in that tea? You nearly killed me. Or was that the plan? To make the cops believe I died from some designer drug overdose?"

"You wouldn't have died," she said, indignantly. "It was just herbal tea. Brewed from some orchid blossom. Nelly said lots of Indians in Mexico or South America or somewhere drink it to get high. You didn't die, did you?"

"No, but William Florin did, and Robert Penlaw. How many others?"

"They had heart attacks," she said, her voice starting to waver, along with her fortitude, apparently, because she balled up her fists and backed away from me. "The tea didn't kill them. Nelly said they had bad hearts and would have died eventually. That I wasn't responsible."

"'Eventually' is the key word here, Loni. William and Gretchen Milner might have had several more years together. Of course, you tried to kill her, too, didn't you?"

"Nelly said she was old and all alone and depressed. We were doing her a favor. It would be quick and painless. She wouldn't suffer."

"And you believed him?"

"Nelly wouldn't lie," she stammered. "Nelly loves me."

"Nelly used you," I said.

She started to cry and went into the lab and sat down in the chair by the computer. I spotted my keys on the floor under the chair.

"I wanted to give her the tea when she was on the nursing floor," Loni said. "But Nelly told me no one would believe she was senile. Her son and daughter—they'd start asking a

306   **Karen Ann Wilson**

lot of questions about the psychiatric wing." She looked up at me. "I swear I didn't want Mrs. Milner to die."

She was blubbering by this time. I grabbed the towel hanging under the sink and handed it to her. She wiped her eyes and nose.

"I suppose you threw that cat off the balcony," I said, "just to be mean."

"No. I only wanted to lock it out there, so the old woman would think she'd done it and forgot. Nelly said, if we could convince the old coots they were crazy, you know, with the tea and these little accidents and stuff, they'd commit themselves voluntarily." She blew her nose. "But the damn cat bit and clawed me. I was trying to pull it off my arm when it fell."

"Was Dr. Aaron in on your little scheme?" I asked. "Of course, he'd have to be, I guess."

"Dr. Aaron did pretty much what Nelly told him," said Loni. "He really seemed happier if he didn't have to make any decisions on his own, anyway."

"What about Wilma?"

Loni shook her head. "Wilma is pretty stupid. Nelly brought her in because he knew she wouldn't catch on. She's not even a real dietitian, did you know that?"

Big surprise, I thought. "What about your mom?"

Loni looked at the towel and threw it on the floor. She didn't say anything.

"Your mom," I prompted. "Did she know? I don't think she's stupid."

Loni sniffed. "My mother doesn't seem to care about much of anything these days. Oh, maybe she thought there was something going on with the patients. I mean, she did know what meds they were taking. But I don't think she cared enough to say anything to anyone. Nelly would have cut her in. The guy from Quetzal Bay told him to pay Dr.

CIRCLE OF WOLVES   307

Aaron a lot to keep him quiet. I guess he'd have said the same thing about my mom. Especially if I asked."

"Either that, or your mother would have met with some kind of accident," I said. That certainly got Loni's attention. Her head jerked up. "Or maybe Nelly could have fed her some of Mrs. Milner's pot roast."

"Nelly would never hurt my mother!" Loni snapped.

I heard a noise behind me and turned my head. Michael was standing just outside the doorway to the lab, listening. He caught me looking at him. He held up his little tape recorder and winked. It was a reporter's dream come true. I could see it in his eyes.

"Shall I call the police, Samantha," he asked, "or would you like to do the honors?"

It was after nine when Michael finally got around to cooking the omelet. It smelled wonderful, but I found I wasn't really hungry, after all. Even the fact that Loni Herfeld and Nelson Aveneau were in custody, and the cops, according to Sergeant Robinson, were already looking for Cronin, since Mr. Aveneau did not intend to take all of the blame himself, didn't do much to improve my appetite.

"I talked to my mother earlier," I said. I was standing in the doorway to my kitchen, watching Michael cook. Tina and Miss Priss were on either side of him, looking up, willing small pieces of ham to fall off the counter and into their mouths. They reminded me of baby birds in the nest.

"How is she?" Michael asked, his back to me.

"Fine. She wants to meet you. She wondered if you'd like to come to Connecticut with me. Spend Christmas at her house."

He lifted one edge of the omelet and tilted the pan, so the uncooked egg mixture could flow under the cooked part.

"I'd love to, Samantha. I just don't know if I'll have time.

308 Karen Ann Wilson

I need to do something about Kevin. And, because I took so much time off earlier this year to deal with the boy, I can only get a couple of days this month. I was kind of hoping you'd come with me for a day or so, then fly on to your mother's for Christmas. I'm afraid I'll have to spend the holidays with the kittens. Unless, of course, you can get back for New Year's Eve. We could welcome in the New Year properly. Go out, drink champagne." He looked at me over his shoulder and winked.

"I should be able to do that," I said. "My mother will understand." *No she won't,* I thought. *Of course she won't. But she'll get over it.*

Michael flipped half of the omelet over and held out the pan. "You sure you don't want any?"

"Actually," I said, "I am a little hungry. Maybe I will have some."

EPILOGUE

●

Monday, December 13

I heard Cynthia make a convulsive, choking sound. I was in the closet behind her desk, doing an inventory of our supplies. Charlie was perched, vulturelike, on the mound of dog food bags, watching me. In unison, he and I turned our heads toward the door. I put my clipboard down and hurried out to the reception room. Cynthia was trying not to laugh and not doing a very good job of it. Her face was quite red.

"What is so amusing?" I asked her.

She mouthed the word, "Look" and pointed toward the parking lot. I turned, saw Dr. Augustin's Jeep and Dr. Augustin. He was bent over the passenger seat, fiddling with a large white box.

"Yeah, what's so fun—?" I began.

Then Dr. Augustin stood up and closed the car door. I felt my eyes widen. He'd cut his hair. And not just a trim, like he got twice a year whether he needed it or not, but an honest-to-God haircut. His ears were actually exposed. And he had on tan slacks, instead of jeans. He looked downright conservative. All that was missing was the tie.

Cynthia took a tissue out of the drawer and blew her nose. "Now why did he go and do that, I wonder?" she said, between honks.

I watched him and the box disappear around the corner

309

310 **Karen Ann Wilson**

toward the back entrance to his office. The box looked like the kind a sheet cake might come in.

"Is it someone's birthday?" I asked. "That looked like a cake box."

Cynthia was over the worst of her convulsions. She dabbed at her eyes with the tissue. "Not that I know of," she said.

I heard the door to Dr. Augustin's office open, and dashed back into the supply closet. I knew sooner or later I'd have to face him. We hadn't spoken since his visit to the hospital, and our first encounter at the clinic would be awkward at best. Now with the hair thing . . ."

"Samantha!" His voice penetrated the wall between the closet and his office. Charlie flattened his ears and swished his tail.

I sighed and went out, past Cynthia's desk and Cynthia, who grinned at me ("Better you than me," her expression said), and on into Dr. Augustin's office. I closed the door.

He was opening the cake box. He turned around and smiled. He looked considerably younger without the hair, and less roguish. Mrs. Winter was going to be disappointed. A lot of women were going to be disappointed.

"What's the occasion?" I asked, purposely avoiding any mention of his new look. *Let him stew,* I thought.

"Cronin dropped the suit," he said. "It's hard to look like a victim when you yourself are about to be indicted for victimizing a bunch of helpless old people. Mr. Aveneau and his girlfriend have been most informative, according to Matt. I am surprised Cronin got directly involved in this one. Apparently, he stayed clean in the past by having subordinates, like Keith Stone, do all the work. If they got caught, Cronin would say he knew nothing, saw nothing, etc. The word of an upstanding citizen against that of a

CIRCLE OF WOLVES

311

known lowlife. That's why he kept Keith Stone around, evidently. To do his dirty work."

"What about the lawn maintenance man?" I asked. "Do the police have any idea who bumped him off?"

He shook his head. "I'm afraid they'll probably never pin that on anybody."

I came a step closer and looked at the cake. It said, "Thank you, Samantha."

"Thank you for what?" I asked.

"For risking your life to help me," he said. He paused. "And Mrs. Milner and company."

Yes, let's not forget them, I thought. "You're welcome. But the cake wasn't necessary."

"Oh, yes it was," he said. He went over to his desk and sat down. "It'll make up for what I'm about to say to you."

I swallowed and waited.

He crossed his arms over his chest, leaned back in his chair, and took aim at my forehead with his eyes. Even without the hair, those eyes were deadly. My feet would not move.

"I don't want to catch you doing something dumb like that again, Samantha," he said. "I may disregard the law occasionally, and maybe we have found ourselves in some tight situations. But at least I've always been there to get us out of them."

"Hey," I said. "Who was it managed to escape and round up the police back in July? Not you, certainly."

He opened the file drawer to his desk and propped his feet up. I noticed he was still wearing his hiking boots. There were limits to the new look.

"Okay, okay," he said. "But it took two of us to pull it off, and you know it. And that's my point. The Lone Ranger you are not. Understand?"

"The same thing can be said for you, you know."

312 Karen Ann Wilson

He inspected the nails on his right hand. "I just don't want you getting hurt on my account."

"So, tell me, why did you cut your hair?" I asked.

He checked out the left hand. "You and Cynthia seem to prefer short hair. More professional, remember?"

"I never said I liked short hair, particularly on you. You just assumed I did."

He raised his eyes and looked at me, his expression unnerving.

"I'll make a deal with you," I said, quickly, mostly to ward off the silence.

"What's that?"

"I promise never to play the Lone Ranger again, if you promise to let your hair grow back."

He smiled. "Deal." He got up. "Now, let's cut this cake. I haven't had any breakfast yet." He opened his desk drawer and took out a knife. "How hungry are you?"

I thought about my size ten wedding dress. Briefly. "I'm starved," I said.